CH00524728

Rachel discovered her passion for writing while living in Grand Teton National Park when on a whim, she decided to write down one of her dreams, and just like that her debut novel, *Awakened*, was born. These days she lives in Australia with her growing family and their dog. Find Rachel on Instagram @RL.Pope and learn more about her upcoming works at www.RLpope.com.

For Kota bear.

R.L. Pope

AWAKENED

AUSTIN MACAULEY PUBLISHERS™

LONDON • CAMBRIDGE • NEW YORK • SHARJAH

A CIP catalogue record for this title is available from the British Library.

ISBN 9781398472518 (Paperback)
ISBN 9781398472525 (Hardback)
ISBN 9781398472532 (ePub e-book)

www.austinmacauley.com

First Published 2022
Austin Macauley Publishers Ltd®
1 Canada Square
Canary Wharf
London
E14 5AA

I know this book would never be where it is today without my incredible support system. I'm lucky to have every single one of you in my life.

A special thanks to my mom. You were the first person I told I had started writing a book—thank you for meeting the crazy idea with so much enthusiasm and asking for more. And thank you for reading every single draft. I promise this time it really is the final one.

Thank you to all my early readers (you know who you are). You're all my favourite cheerleaders.

To my current reader, thank you for your support. I hope you enjoy the first part of Rosalia's story.

Thank you to the team at Austin Macauley for making this book a reality and taking a chance on me as an author.

I know it's weird to thank the Tetons. But also, I don't care. Living among them was life-changing, and I wouldn't have found my calling if I didn't answer theirs.

And last but certainly not least, a huge thank you to my husband, Daniel, and his unwavering love and support for me since day one. Thank you for always entertaining my random ideas as they pop into my head at all hours of the day, even as we're falling asleep.

Table of Contents

Chapter One

A cold dampness settles deep in my bones, but I barely notice. I'm transfixed on small orbs of light gleaming off a long wooden table. I've become a set of unblinking eyes mesmerised by the glow.

A cough breaks my trance. It takes me a second to get my bearings; I'm looking down on some sort of meeting. It takes me another moment to realise there are no strings or wires supporting the lights that have been holding my attention. They're *floating*, their slight movement casting eerie shadows across the faces of those seated around the table, making them look unearthly and monstrous.

One of the creatures whips their head up in my direction. Huge elk-like antlers protrude out of his head, their shadow tripled in size on the rough cavern wall behind him, moving as he moves, making me think of old horror films and the dread of discovery is immediate. My heart quickens, a scream bubbles out of my chest before I can stop it.

Except no sound exits my mouth.

The antlered man swats at something in the air, before returning his attention back to the table before him.

Surprise and relief flood my body at his unexpected indifference. It's like he didn't see me at all. I move a little, keeping my eyes on the gathered. No reaction. I'm a silent, invisible observer.

"I have called this meeting to discuss the Awakening of Rosalia."

I go stiff as my name echoes around the chamber, my eyes going to the woman addressing the others. She's seated on a throne that appears to have been grown, rather than built: huge wooden limbs twist and turn, bending into the shape of what must be a royal seat. The woman is small—

tiny in fact. She's dressed in a lacy gown that's snowy white and exquisite, she wears a sparkling tiara balanced upon her carefully arranged silver hair. And now I notice her more prominent features—delicate wings extruding from her shoulder blades and her ears ending in fine points—and I realise, with not a little amount of excitement, that she's a Fairy. My mouth drops open in awe.

She continues, "The boy has been aware of his alter being for almost two years now. She should have Awakened at sixteen. She turns eighteen in six weeks. I am growing concerned they will not have enough time. The darkness is growing stronger—we need The Stave."

"Perhaps we should send a jolt?" the man with the antlers suggests.

"A jolt could be extremely dangerous," a woman chirps at him from across the table. A fresh wave of horror hits me as I watch her lift a large bowl of steaming liquid to her face, dipping her *beak* into it. She throws her head back in a swift motion to gulp down the liquid. Before she's able to set the bowl back down, three tiny finches swarm to it and start drinking in the same manner.

"We said there were to be no children present today." The antlered man doesn't bother hiding his annoyance.

The Queen throws a warning look in his direction. "Robin is right. The girl learning too much, too fast, could be counterproductive. I will not send a jolt. However, we do need her and the boy to find one another fast. It is our only hope and is why I have asked The Fates to this meeting."

"What of the third?" Robin asks.

"He is believed to be dead, or worse," the Queen responds, her tone icy. "Thank you, Fates, for joining us this morning."

My eyes follow as the creatures turn their attention to an odd trio of identical sisters, seated along the opposite wall. The first is busy knitting a giant blanket that has green mist rising from it, the second is weaving what must be a basket, but so much light is pouring out of it I have to squint and shift my eyes to the third, who's own eyes look wild as she stares off into nothingness.

The Fate who's knitting slows her needles, growing still, the green mist settling, sinking to the floor as her lack of movement stops its production. Her eyes go to the Queen. "Your Majesty, we have been sending her all the normal signs. A FaeDog even found her right before her sixteenth birthday. Her Awakening was on track, but something stopped her course and we aren't able to see what it is. We fear our murky sight could be due to an Underling attaching itself to her." She stares unblinking at the Queen until finally the second sister pokes her in the ribs. Her hands spasm gently in her lap, and resume their vigorous work, the mist exploding back to life around her in an ominous green veil.

"That would be grave indeed. If Herne knows her location, we are out of time," the Queen says.

"Herne knows her name?" The antlered man's voice rises in panic.

"It is safer to assume everyone knows her name, Quill. A Fairling's Awakening is no secret. But I did not expect him to make any headway in learning her whereabouts." The Queen turns back to the Fate. "Try sending signals she won't be able to ignore. We need her to Awaken as soon as possible and to get her somewhere he cannot find her." There's a command in her voice that reverberates around the room, sending a chill through me.

"Yes, Your Majesty, my sister is weaving a destiny dream for her now. I foresee Rosalia waking from it in the morning and being rather shaken." A spine-chilling smile spreads across her face. She looks directly at me and winks. It's almost too fast to notice but I catch it before she returns her attention to those at the table.

I try to swallow the lump that has lodged itself in my throat as the Fate continues, "She'll be where she's meant to be before the end of the month, and fully awake soon after." She bows her head in a deep nod to the Queen.

"Good. This meeting is adjourned. If the girl is still too thick-skulled to receive these signs, I'll let you send a jolt, Quill," the Queen stands and exits the chamber.

Spots blot over my vision, inking out the cavern and its occupants until I'm fully engulfed in blackness.

Solid ground forms beneath my feet. A brilliant light replacing the dark, I raise my hands to shield my eyes from the sudden gleam. I'm standing in a deserted barn. Sun beams are pouring in through an open door across the space.

"ROSALIA!" Someone shouts. Something about his voice stirs recognition deep in my gut, but my mind is foggy and I can't place who it belongs to. Jesse, maybe? But he calls me Lia, he never uses my full name.

"Rosalia! We need to find each other!" The voice has an accent. Definitely not Jesse. I look around, trying to locate the origin of the sound. It must be coming from outside. I take a hesitant step towards the open door, just as a silhouette of a tall man appears in front of the light.

I freeze. He begins to make his way towards me, his features coming into focus as he draws near.

He has brilliant blue eyes, a striking contrast to his dark wavy hair that appears as he takes off a cowboy hat, hanging it on a rusty hook on the barn wall. I'm staring, but can't seem to tear my eyes away from him. He's beautiful. My cheeks are burning by the time he's in front of me. I open my mouth to say something, anything, I can't find words.

A smile tugs at the corners of his mouth as he steps towards me, "There you are." His left hand finds my waist, his right one gentle on my face as he starts to lean towards me. My body goes rigid but my heart goes into overtime, pounding hard enough I worry it will burst out of my chest. His lips find mine, a shock of electricity flows to my core.

My heart calms, and a warmth begins to seep through my body, waking my limbs. I melt into the familiar and safe feel of the stranger's kiss.

He pulls away but keeps a firm grip on my shoulders. I stand frozen, in a daze looking up into his beautiful eyes; a trace of a smile lingers on his rosy lips. Who is he? Why do I want him to kiss me again?

"Listen to me, Rosalia," he whispers. "We don't have much time. You need to know there's someone in your life you shouldn't trust. You need to get away." His voice sounds further away as he continues, "Come find me."

I feel myself being pulled. I fight it, I want to stay. I want to stay with him. I want to stay where it feels safe.

"I'm searching for you, but I need you to look too. Come find me!" His final words barely audible.

Once again I'm swallowed by darkness, but this time it doesn't fade. I can't move. My arms are tied behind my back and my ankles are secured to something solid. Panic bubbles in my chest. I try to wiggle loose, but the bindings don't budge. A set of glowing blood-red eyes appear in front of me lighting up a razor-sharp smile. Just as my scream erupts out of me, I come crashing down onto my mattress.

I barely have time to realise it was just a nightmare before my sister bursts into my room, "What's going on?" Her voice is borderline hysteric. "Are you okay?"

I can't move, still seized by terror. I lay still, trying to catch my breath as beads of sweat roll off my forehead.

My mattress depresses as Jen sits on the edge. She brushes my dampened hair away from my face. "Lia, you're shaking. Bad dream?"

I can only nod.

"Do you want to talk about it?" Her earnest brown eyes shining with concern.

I manage to push myself up right.

"Here, Kodi!" Jen pats the space between us. My dog bounds up, curling into a tight ball, resting her head in my lap, her cool blue eyes gaze up at me as though she wants to hear too. My hand automatically starts stroking her soft black fur and my heart rate begins to slow.

"What happened?"

I surprise myself when I don't hesitate, the need to get them out of me is too strong. I don't leave out a single detail as I relay the dreams to my sister.

Jen stays quiet, nodding her head every once in a while, to show she's listening. When I finish, she doesn't say anything. I rush on, "Now that

I've heard them out loud, they sound pretty stupid." I let out a breath of a laugh, "They just felt so real, you know? Like I was there. And then it felt like I was crashing back to Earth when I woke up…" I trail off with a shrug, trying to play it off like I'm not completely freaked out by what I just witnessed.

"They aren't stupid, Lia." Jen's voice is soft. "In my First Nation history class—"

"Please! Not another history lesson!" I groan sliding back onto my bed pulling the covers over my head.

"Don't be rude!" She scolds, pulling the blankets away. "We spent an entire week on the power of dreams. I really believe that some dreams are more than your brain sorting through the day."

"All right old wise one, what do my dreams mean?"

"Well," she picks at imaginary dust on my comforter as she collects her thoughts. Her voice comes out thoughtful. "In your first one, a crazy lady said she was weaving up destiny dreams that would leave you quite 'shaken'. THEN you had two dreams after it that have left you, well rather shook! It can't be a coincidence, I'd say they're messages pointing you towards your *destiny*."

I roll my eyes, but humour her by asking, "Messages from whom?"

She shrugs. "I don't know. Your spirit guide or your subconscious, which maybe are the same thing." She looks at me pointedly, "Think about it. You graduated yesterday. All your friends already have their futures laid out for themselves, you don't have any plans. Even your summer is unplanned. Maybe you're feeling a little lost, looking for direction. They seem like warnings though, I wonder who in your life you shouldn't trust?" She stands up and places her hands on her narrow hips. "Also, start looking for the hunky guy immediately! He sounds cute and he's definitely part of your *destiny*." She wiggles her eyebrows up and down suggestively, erupting into a fit of giggles.

I prop myself up on an elbow and toss a pillow at her. "I already have a super cute boyfriend in case you forgot."

"Well, I wouldn't tell your *super cute boyfriend* that you're dreaming about other men." She glances at the turquoise watch secured around her wrist. "I have to go, I'm opening the store today." Concern crinkles her face, pushing any lingering laughter away, "Are you ok?"

I nod.

She pats the top of my head and bends over to kiss Kodi, "Good. I'll see you girls later!" She spins towards the door, her long chestnut hair fanning out behind her, settling perfectly straight down her back as she walks out of my room. She was blessed with the perfect hair gene, leaving the unruly blonde waves for me.

I slump back down and stare up at the glow-in-the dark stars that have survived the test of time on my ceiling, and the faded marks left behind from the ones that didn't. Who can't I trust? Everyone I'm close to I've known forever. I *know* them, that's why I *trust* them.

I groan, squeezing my eyes shut. I pull my covers back over my head.

They're just *dreams*. Not divine messages sent from the beyond. *I* don't believe in that stuff.

Chapter Two

"Earth to Lia!"

The box in my hands goes flying, sending screws scattering across the tiled floor.

"Jesus, Jen! Are you trying to give me a heart attack?" I drop to my knees and start sweeping the screws into a pile with my hands.

She laughs, "Why so jumpy? Were you thinking about your dream guy?" She wiggles her eyebrows suggestively, again.

I glare up at her. "The opposite actually, I was thinking about the day I met Jesse."

She bends down and starts helping me collect the screws, lining them neatly in their box. "You met at an end of the year party two years ago, right?"

I nod.

"Am I a horrible sister for never asking for details?"

I nod again, but can't hold back my grin. "I'll forgive you though." I take the box from her hand and place it on the shelf next to the others.

"Is it a good story?" She asks grabbing another box, helping me load the shelf.

"Like a scene straight out of an old movie." I glance at her as I continue stocking. She's listening so I go on. "It actually felt like everything was moving in slow motion. Abby and Bianca somehow got me to do karaoke with them. They constructed a tiny stage in Abby's backyard. I happened to look up just as he came around the corner of the house, our eyes met and I froze. I think my heart may have even skipped a beat," I smile at the memory of seeing Jesse's face for the first time. His sandy blonde hair

18

was messy, like he'd just woken up from a nap. His chocolate brown eyes bore into mine from across the yard with an intensity I'd never experienced, it was thrilling, like we were the only two people at the party. "Bianca had to elbow me to snap me out of my daze. Her and Abby were so mad at me for messing up their performance." I laugh remembering the looks of horror on their faces. "By the time the song finished, he was gone." I finish, bulging my eyes at the word *gone* to add suspense for Jen's sake.

She humours me by chuckling at my theatrics, "That's cute, I'm guessing you found him after you finished the song?"

"Yeah, in the kitchen. I was digging in a cooler looking for a soda and someone bumped into me." My lips tug upwards, "Jesse told me later that he bumped into me on purpose, so he'd have a reason to talk to me." I meet my sister's eyes, "You know the rest, we have basically been inseparable since."

"Yes, I know the rest. My sister was stolen away from me and I'm lucky if I get to spend time with her outside of work."

I snap my head up at her words, her face doesn't show any signs that she's kidding, but she's too focused on the task of stocking. I open my mouth to say something, but no words come to me. So, I close it. Is that why she has never warmed to Jesse? Because she thinks he stole me away from her? I open my mouth again. I want to tell her it's not his fault and she should have said something to me sooner, it wasn't intentional. But my mom's voice over the store's loudspeaker interrupts me. "Rosie, phone call line one." Blood floods to my cheeks at my mother's pet name for me being broadcasted across the entire store. I throw an apologetic glance at Jen.

"Go," she says forcing her mouth into a smile. "I was just joking."

I can tell she wasn't. Still, I offer her a small smile and let my feet carry me towards the front of the store.

My mom meets me in the main aisle, shaking the portable receiver at me, her palm covering the mouthpiece.

"You're sure it's for me?" I crinkle my brow, I can't think of a single person who would be calling me on the hardware store's land line.

"It's your Great Aunt Rose." Her dark eyes widen as her eyebrows shoot up, like that name should mean something to me. She shoves the phone closer.

"Why does she want to talk to me?" I whisper, dreading the awkward small talk that's sure to come if I accept this call.

"Why don't you talk to her and find out?" My mom hisses, shoving the phone into my hands and scurrying up the aisle towards the register before I can object.

I stare at the phone for a second before finally lifting it to my ear, I take a deep breath. "Hello?"

"Rosalia! It's Rosalia, although everyone just calls me Rose." An old woman chuckles through the line. "You probably don't remember me. You were just a baby the last time I saw you."

I walk up the aisle. "Hi Aunt Rose, how are you?" I spin on my heel and walk back to where I had just been standing.

"Oh, I'm all right. I just had a wonderful chat with your mother, it sounds like you have grown into quite a remarkable young woman."

I make my way up the aisle again, settling into a rhythm of nervous pacing. I mull her words over for a second, not sure how to respond. Can I tell her she's wrong, would that be rude? *Sorry Aunt Rose, you're mistaken. I'm not a remarkable young woman. All I've managed to accomplish in life is to graduate from high school and now I have zero plans for my future, zero dreams, zero goals.* I spot a stray screw on the floor that must have rolled out of the aisle when I dropped them, I bend down to pick it up.

"Anyhow," Rose continues when I don't respond. I groan inwardly, she probably thinks I'm inept now. "I was filling your mother in on a recent accident. I slipped and fell on some ice this winter, I'm fine now." She hurries on, not leaving a gap for me to offer my condolences to her injury. "I broke my hip, and though it's healing well, tourist season is about to get into full gear and I could really use some extra help around the flower shop. I'm not getting around very well with this walker."

I smash my head into a shelf as I stand back up too fast. I hold back a whimper, my fingers spring to my skull to check for wetness. What is she suggesting? I decide to side step that part of her statement. "That's terrible that happened to you, I'm really sorry to hear that."

"Oh, that's fine dear, really, I'm okay. It's an unfortunate reality when you get to be as old as I am." She pauses for a moment, "Your mother was saying you don't have much going on this summer, and that you have quite the green thumb. You make herbal medicines?"

Why can't she just hire a local kid? "Uhh, not really," I say, I even sound lame to myself. "I mean, I haven't made much. I have sensitive skin, so I've just made some soaps and lotions for myself." There's a long silence so I add, "and a pimple treatment for my friend Abby…" I throw my head back and stare up at the water stains on the ceiling tiles. Why do I say things?

"That's more than most people." Her voice is thoughtful. "I don't know if you know this, but I own a flower shop in Jackson Hole. We have a natural remedies corner where we offer handmade personal care products to our patrons. Everything is made in house, using all local and organic ingredients. If that's something you're interested in learning more about, I think my business partner, Maggie, would be able to teach you a lot."

My heart does a summersault of excitement. I resume my pacing. Why had it never occurred to me that my side hobby could be a plausible future plan? Is this a job offer? For a job in…Jackson Hole? I'm not even sure where that is. "I would love to learn more," I say.

"That's fantastic! So it's settled! You can come out west for a couple of months. It would be a huge help!" She sounds delighted and my stomach twists into a ball of nerves. Half excitement at the idea of having *some* kind of plan for my future, but also dread at the idea of leaving the only place I've ever called home.

"I don't know." My voice wavers, I come to a stop and stare down at an old price sticker stuck to the shelves. I slip a fingernail under its corner with my free hand, scraping the metal surface as I peel it loose. Am I brave enough to move across the country by myself?

"You don't need to decide right now! I've put you on the spot. Take some time to think about it, the offer stands. And I won't be in your space all the time, so don't let that impact your decision at all. I would set you up in my guest cabin out back, I know how important privacy is for teenagers."

"Okay," I let out a breath. "I'll think about it." I crinkle the sticker and toss it towards the garbage can at the end of the aisle closest to me. I realise I'm smiling, maybe this is something I want to do.

"Lovely! We'll chat soon, buh-bye dear."

The line goes dead before I can say my own good-bye. I stare at the phone in my hand, replaying the conversation in my head. Where had that come from? I weave through the aisles to the register. I hold the phone out to my mom when I reach the counter.

"I think you should go." She says placing the phone back in its cradle.

I raise my eyebrows. "You trying to get rid of me?"

"Of course not. But," she holds up a hand anticipating a smart aleck remark, "Lia, just hear me out. You're not sure what you want to do. I think a change of scenery and fresh mountain air will do you good. Clear your mind, cleanse your soul." She smiles at me, but her eyes are sad as she looks me over. "You would love it out there."

"But I already told Dad I'd help out here this summer…" I know my argument is weak, but I can't say what's actually holding me back because she'd ridicule me for it.

She lets out a soft laugh, "Your father and I will be fine. Don't worry about us, or anyone else." She gives me a pointed look, "You're young, you get to be selfish. You need to try to make this decision by only thinking about yourself. Don't let anyone else factor in." She doesn't say it, but I know she means Jesse. She doesn't want me turning down an opportunity just to stay close to my boyfriend. But how can I not factor him in? She sighs, as though reading my mind, "Just think about it. It's a great opportunity and it's coming at the perfect time."

I nod as I start to walk towards the back of the store to finish stocking. Fresh mountain air does sound nice. Kodi would probably love it out there. I make a mental note to research Jackson Hole when I get home. God knows I could use some direction.

* * *

"Well, I must say you girls have certainly outdone yourselves! This lasagna is incredible." My mother beams at my sister and me from across the dining room table as she digs in for a second bite.

"Yes, it's very good." My father agrees around a mouthful of food.

I offer a weak smile of thanks, but know they're just saying it to be polite. The smell alone is making my stomach churn. We messed this meal up big time. I pick up my fork and cut a tiny corner off my piece, I bring it to my mouth hesitating for a moment before popping it in. I chew a few times before forcing myself to swallow, I grab my glass of water and gulp it down. It doesn't help. I drop my fork, it clatters loudly as it crashes onto my plate. I leap to my feet, the chair scraping against the hardwood as I rush out of the room and down the hall, slamming the bathroom door behind me. I throw myself in front of the toilet without a second to spare.

After a moment, there's a gentle rapping on the door, "Honey? Are you all right?" My mom's gentle voice asks from the other side.

I lift my head off the floor. The cool tiles against my face are the only thing that can soothe the clamminess that has sent my body into a cold sweat. I uncurl myself and slowly sit up. "Yeah, I think so." Gross, my voice is so raspy.

"May I come in?"

"Yeah."

The doorknob turns and my mother hesitates for a moment before she steps into the room. "Oh, my poor baby," she clucks her tongue, her almond eyes welling with sympathy.

"I'm sorry the lasagna was off. Do we have frozen pizza or something we could have instead?"

"Honey, the lasagna is perfect. Everyone is about to help themselves to seconds."

"Oh, something's going on with my stomach then. It tasted like road slush to me."

She smiles at my analogy as she gets down on her knees, leaning back onto her feet. She reaches out placing her cool hand to my forehead. "You don't feel warm, but we could take your temperature. Maybe you have a tinge of a stomach bug?" She suggests.

"That's okay, I'm feeling better now. I'll just steer clear of the lasagna. Garlic bread sounds appetising enough."

"Good idea," my mom rises to her feet and brushes imaginary dust from her jeans before offering me her slender hands.

I accept the help, and the hug she pulls me into. I nuzzle my face into her familiar soft brown curls and breath in her comforting scent of vanilla with a hint of cinnamon.

"Come on, you're missing out on the life advice your father is giving to Jenny." She laughs.

I smile, we like to tease my dad that he's trying to be a wise old man before he's even an old man.

"I think college should be your next move." My father's baritone voice reaches us before we re-enter the dining room. "Pre-law or maybe even pre-med?" He suggests.

Jen just rolls her eyes, as we reclaim our seats. "You know I don't want to be a lawyer or a doctor, Dad."

"We all know its detective school she wants to go to," I quip.

Everyone bursts into laughter at the memory, my dad's deep guttural laugh drowning out everyone else's. When Jen was in kindergarten, her teacher asked her what she wanted to be when she grew up. She answered straight-faced that she wanted her little sister and herself to become the trench coat twins, the best detectives in the whole world. Her Olsen twin fandom was borderline obsessive.

"No! Don't start!" My dad pleads as he continues to laugh raising his bear-like hands to cover his ears in mock horror. "I can't take any more of their songs!"

"Relax Dad! We aren't going to sing." Jen giggles, "I know I'd make a great detective, but I've been thinking I'd like to be a nurse."

"Oh, I love that! You'd make a wonderful nurse!" Mom says. "Have you thought about any schools you want to apply to?"

"I've already applied to the University of Wisconsin and the University of Minnesota."

"That's great!" I haven't seen my mom's smile so big in a while, pride practically oozing out of her.

I smile at my sister, "You'll make a great nurse."

"I'm just happy you know what you want to do with your life." My dad beams before shifting his attention to me, his soft brown eyes suddenly sharp, like someone flipped a switch. He inspects me from behind his square glasses. All traces of laughter scattering from his face. "Lia, have you given much thought to your future? Or are you still adamant about taking a year off?"

"I don't want to start school with my declared major being undecided." I mumble, tearing off a corner of my garlic bread and popping it into my mouth. "I'm not sure what I want to do with my life. I want to find the right path, not just choose one for the sake of having a major."

"That's fine. I took a year off." Jen says, trying to come to my rescue.

"You took a year off because you had a fantastic opportunity to work for Doctor Meyers." My mom points out. "Lia, maybe you don't need to take an entire year off, just take the summer, and then look into applying to colleges in a couple of months."

I shrug, not in the mood for arguing. I avoid eye contact with my parents by letting my eyes flit around the room. My mom had read in some magazine that dining rooms should be red—it increases appetites—so she painted our dining room a deep burgundy. It doesn't make me feel hungrier though, it makes the room feel smaller and too dark. I don't like it, and tonight it's making my stomach feel queasy.

"You're not going to have a free ride while you're on your little break, young lady. It won't be treated like a vacation." My father scolds. "I'll expect you to work full time at the hardware store if you stay here."

"I graduated yesterday. I'm not on a vacation." I sigh, "And I already am working full time at the store." I pull my eyes back to the table and meet my dad's eyes briefly. "May I please be excused? I'm supposed to meet Jesse at the beach." I rise to my feet, not waiting for permission.

"Wait." My mom says throwing me a pointed look. "Sit back down, we have news to share with you both."

"Can you share later? I'm gonna be late." Ignoring her request to sit back down I make my way towards the door.

"It'll only take a second." My mom shoots me a look that tells me I better not move another inch.

I stop in my tracks and wait for one of them to continue.

"We're going on a family vacation!" My dad exclaims, his voice changing tone from scolding to chipper. His cheeks flush with excitement as he looks between my face and Jen's to catch our reactions.

I concentrate on keeping my face neutral. I already know where we're going. Part of me is beyond ecstatic. As soon as Jen and I got the lasagna in the oven earlier this evening, I had situated myself in the backyard with my laptop. I pulled up Pinterest, and before I could even click my cursor on the search bar, my heart stilled. The first meme on my news feed was a beautiful picture of a mountain range, bold letters across the top read *Keep calm come to Jackson Hole.* I sucked in a breath, how *weird* is that? I had to cast my eyes around the back yard, the big maple standing sturdy in the middle of the yard, my old tire swing hanging from its lowest branch, the trampoline with leaves collecting across its surface, and mom's big garden where the peonies are beginning to bud. Everything was how it should be, but that didn't stop the momentous feeling from creeping up my spine. I don't have the Pinterest app on my phone, so it couldn't have been advertisers listening in on my conversation with my mom from my pocket. I'm pretty sure Pinterest's algorithm for suggested pins is based off browsing history. I've never looked at anything even remotely close to Jackson Hole before. I hadn't even heard of it really, not before this morning. *It's fate.* A small voice in the back of my mind had whispered. A small voice that sounded just like my sister. I hovered my cursor over the picture, hesitating for only a second before taking a deep breath and whispering, "here goes nothing." I clicked on it and started scrolling. It's breath-taking. I greedily clicked through picture after picture, each one leaving me more in awe. Wyoming has it all; mountains, lakes, rivers, not to mention the wildflowers and *wildlife.* Grizzly bears, elk, bison, moose, wolves, the most magnificent creatures you can think of, they all live there. A big part of me *wants* to go, it feels like a magnet *pulling* me to those mountains. Then there's the other part of me that feels like my parents are forcing me into something I should be deciding on my own.

"Oh my gosh!" Jen's loud voice pulls me back to the present, "We haven't been on vacation in so long! Where are we going?" Her eyes are bright to match the excitement in her voice.

"Wyoming!" My mom says, a big smile on her face.

Jen's face drops. "Wyoming? What's in Wyoming?" She looks at me and sticks out her tongue in disgust. I laugh, but my heart is filled with butterflies at the thought of Wyoming.

"There's a lot in Wyoming! Your Great Aunt Rose, for starters, not to mention white-water rafting, hiking, and an amazing opportunity for your sister." My dad says.

"What kind of opportunity?" Jen raises her eyebrows at me, as if to say *Why didn't you tell me?*

"I haven't decided anything yet." I glare at my dad for pushing before I could properly consider it.

"She's been offered a job at your aunt's flower shop. She'd get to learn about medicinal plants and herbs. She'd be stupid not to take it." My dad says to my sister, but his eyes stay riveted to my face.

"Hey! I'm not stupid, I said I'd think about it, and I am. But it's far away, and my life is here."

"What life?" My dad challenges.

Ouch, "Well you guys, and my job at the hardware store, and Jesse is here…" My voice trails off.

"You are not passing this up to be closer to your boyfriend young lady. You're too young for that, and if he cares about you at all he'll encourage you to accept this offer."

I cast my eyes down and focus on my shoelaces. I don't even know why I'm arguing with him. I'm already leaning towards saying yes to Rose, I just *hate* that he's pushing me.

I sneak a peek at my sister, she's watching me, her eyes gleaming and that annoying know-it-all-smile of hers is on her lips. "When are we going?"

"We'll start driving Friday after work." My mom says.

My head snaps up. Friday! *That's so soon.*

"Rosalia, you can take the time we're all out there to decide if you want to stay, and of course you can come back with us if you don't want to."

I nod. "Sounds good." I glance around, everyone's eyes are on me, I feel like there's a spotlight shining down on me. I clear my throat, "I really am supposed to meet Jess at the beach though. Can I go?"

My mom sighs, "That's fine. Have fun, hun." She laughs at her rhyme as I leave the room.

* * *

The sun is already sitting low in the sky when I pull into the beach parking lot, painting the sky a beautiful watercolour of purples and pinks and reflecting onto Lake Michigan below. My inner nerd squeals with delight when the only spot available is one next to another Jeep Wrangler.

I grab Kodi's leash and clip it onto her collar before she jumps over my lap to lead the way. We start walking towards the sand where I can see Jesse waiting for us. I pause behind the other jeep, my eyes widen at the sight of the license plate. It's one I've never seen before, a cowboy waving his hat riding atop a bucking horse. The state is Wyoming. I shake my

28

head and start making my way towards the beach again. *I don't believe in signs.*

Still, as I trudge through the sand, I turn the events of the day over in my head one more time. The dream of antlered and winged things, not to mention the weird bird lady and the crazy old woman talking about sending me signs. Aunt Rose's phone call. The keep calm come to Jackson Hole pin. Now this Jeep with Wyoming plates. Have I been hanging out with Jen too much? Are these signs, or can all these things be *just* coincidences?

"It's about time!" Jesse says, pulling me out of my head.

I force a light smile. "I'm sorry, it's mostly my parents' fault." I go up on my tip toes and plant a light kiss on his lips. "Forgive me?"

He smiles and leans down for another kiss. "Of course." He whispers as he pulls away.

The stranger's face from last night flashes in my mind, and guilt rises in my stomach. I push the feeling away as I begin walking. "It's a beautiful night." I say to distract my thoughts from going back to my dream. Back to *him.*

"It's finally starting to feel like summer." Jesse agrees. "You look beautiful, by the way."

I can't help the smile, he's always so sweet. I shove the image of the stranger further from my mind and remind myself that he isn't real and I don't need to feel guilty about anything my subconscious does.

"Were you outside a lot this weekend? You look like you have a fresh glow about you."

"I was, and you know I do feel pretty glowy," I laugh, "if that's a word."

He chuckles, "It's a word now, my glowy little Lia." He grabs a hold of my hand, intertwining our fingers as we make our way down the beach. I love that we don't have to say where we're going anymore. It's like auto pilot at this point, we're both headed for the big log, just past the bend where you can't see the crowd anymore and it feels like a private beach. Our spot.

"How was your day?" I ask, casting my focus out over the water. It always amazes me how much it looks like the ocean. It even *smells* like the ocean, must be the seagulls. For some reason the thought unsettles me tonight, my dreams have gotten in my head. Still, it's unnerving how something can look, and even smell like one thing, but in reality, be something completely different.

"Same old, same old. Helped my dad around the house. Went and picked up my books for class, they start next week already."

"Oh wow, that's fast." I bend down and pick up a stick I know Kodi will like.

"How was your day?" He asks, giving my hand a gentle squeeze.

"Interesting, to say the least."

"How do you mean?" Jesse stops, we've arrived at our log. He plops down and pats the space next to him, inviting me to join him.

I unclip Kodi's leash and whip the stick as far as I can before I sit next to him. "My Great Aunt Rose called. She lives in Wyoming and we're going on spur of the moment family trip to see her at the end of the week."

"That should be fun."

I nod. "I was telling Jen about the day we met, too." I smile. "I can't believe it's two years ago now." I laugh, "I told her I think my heart skipped a beat when I first saw you come around the side of the house." I wrap my arm around his waist and rest my head on his shoulder.

He wraps his arm around me and kisses the top of my head. "You wanna know what I was thinking when I first saw you?"

"I do."

"I was thinking you were the most beautiful person I had ever seen."

I smile, straight out of an old movie. Our very own meet-cute.

I watch as he stretches his arms over his head and lets out a bellowing yawn. I know I need to tell him about the rest of my conversation with Aunt Rose, but I'm afraid. My dad's words stuck in my head, *if he cares about you at all he'll encourage you to accept this offer.* I take a deep breath and let the words pour out fast, before I can lose my nerve. "My aunt, the one who called wants me to stay for the entire summer."

Jesse just laughs at this. "That would be absurd. What does she expect an almost 18-year-old to do in Wyoming for an entire summer?"

"She owns a flower shop." I pause to pick up the stick Kodi dropped at my feet and launch it towards the water. "She wants me to help out, she broke her hip and isn't getting around too well lately. She also makes lotions and stuff and thinks I'd be able to learn a lot."

"What did you say?" His voice has gone hard.

I whip my head up startled by his change of tone, but his face is unreadable. "I told her I'd think about it."

"You're actually considering it?" His eyes bore into mine, I have to look away. I concentrate on the horizon, the sun is almost out of sight now.

I nod. "She's family, and she needs some help. It'd only be for a few months..." my voice trails off and I shrug. "My mom thinks it'd be good for me to get away from here, maybe help me figure out what I wanna do with my life."

Jesse leaps to his feet, blocking my view of the water, forcing me to look at him. "Your mom thinks it'd be good for you to get away? Away from what?" His hands are on his hips and his eyebrows raised, waiting for my response.

I freeze. I wasn't expecting a reaction like this. I stir, uncomfortable. I don't like how he's looming over me. "Milwaukee? I don't know. Life?" Kodi woofs, letting me know it's time to throw her stick again, I scoop it up and lob it as far as I can up the beach. I look into his eyes. They're so dark I can barely see his pupils. "I'm lost. Nothing in my life is feeling right. You know? Like I'm nowhere near the path I'm supposed to be on."

His eyes narrow. "Nothing in your life is feeling right?" He begins pacing back and forth, his feet forming ruts in the sand.

Kodi stops a few yards away from him, her head cocks and eyes gleam. She abandons her stick as she makes an arc around him, settling herself on top of my feet where she continues to watch.

"Please sit down, you're making Kodi nervous." I do a quick scan of the beach around us, but we're alone. My stomach turns, I wish we didn't

31

come to our log. "You're making *me* nervous." My voice comes out a whisper.

He ignores me and continues to pace. "*Nothing* in your life feels right?" He says again coming to a stop directly in front of me.

Kodi lets out a low growl, a warning.

He looks down at her, and takes a small step back. "What about you and me, Lia?" Hurt flashes through his eyes. "Do we not feel right?"

"Of course we feel right." I mumble, stroking Kodi's head, letting her know it's okay. "It's just everything else." I say, tears start to build behind my eyelids. I look away and suck in a lungful of air. I will not cry in public. "I just feel disconnected from myself. My mom said something about soul cleansing this morning, I think she's right, maybe that's what I need right now. A good soul cleanse."

"So you're willing to abandon this," he motions between the two of us, "two years down the drain so you can go *cleanse your soul*?" He asks, mocking my mom's word choice.

"I never said I was going to *abandon* you." I say, my voice gaining its strength back as anger floods through me. "I love making my soaps and lotions. I'd get to learn so much, it's a great opportunity. It'd only be for a couple of months." I stand up, "I'm not sure how I expected you to react, but I never thought in a million years you'd yell at me over something like this." I stare towards the direction of the cars, I can't look at him. All I want to do is curl up under my covers and cry. I can't believe my *perfect* boyfriend is behaving like this. "It's getting dark." I say, "I wanted you to know what was happening in my life, and maybe get some support in making this big decision, but I guess I'm on my own, good night, Jess." I start walking, Kodi close at my heels.

"Lia! Wait. Please don't leave like this." He jogs to catch up to me, grabbing a hold of my arm and forcing me to stop.

A loud bark rips out of Kodi's throat.

Jesse drops my arm and takes a few steps back, his hands raised in surrender. "That dog has some screws loose." He glares at Kodi, her cool blue eyes don't waver from his face. "Look Lia, I don't want you to be mad at me. I'm sorry how I reacted, you just caught me off guard that's all. It is a good offer, but you don't need to go all the way to Wyoming to find a job at a flower shop. Apply for something around here. You can do some local soul cleansing." He draws his gaze away from Kodi and meets my eyes. "I think Wyoming is a terrible idea, stay here with me. This is your home. Wisconsin is where you belong."

I search his eyes for a hint of how he's actually feeling but don't find anything. My dad's voice rings in my ears, *if he cares about you at all he'll encourage you.* I sigh, "I'm not mad. But it is getting dark and I should be going, I have a lot to think about." I reach out and give his fingers a squeeze offering him a weak smile. "I'll call you tomorrow, I think I need to sleep on it."

"I hope you decide to stay." He steps forward, his arms open for a hug.

Kodi plants herself in front of me, her unblinking eyes locked on his face.

I laugh and bend down, "What's gotten into you girl?" I stand back up and shrug, "I guess it's not me you have to worry about being mad at you, but Kodiak."

He forces a laugh, glancing at my dog out of the corner of his eyes as we all begin to make our way back towards the parking lot. She has him uneasy and he keeps a safe distance between us the entire way.

Chapter Three

I toss and turn that night, not finding sleep easy. There's too much weighing on my mind. When at last, it claims me I find myself in another dream. Except this time the setting is familiar.

I smile up at the stars from my cosy nest of blankets. I'm tucked into a hammock outside my family's lake house in northern Wisconsin, feeling happier than ever. It's summer vacation, I have the perfect new boyfriend who I met a month earlier. His name is Jesse and he's so sweet. He planned this weekend with my parents for all of us to come up and celebrate my 16th birthday—a complete surprise for me. Not to mention, he's super cute. He's up by the house now, getting wood from the pile so we can enjoy a campfire, just the two of us while I wait in my hammock nest.

Something cold and wet nudges my hand snapping me out of my daydream. I jerk my arm back and scream. My hammock twists and I fall hard to the ground. I look up into the face of a wolf! I scream again.

The wolf lies down and looks up at me with bright blue eyes and wags its tail.

I breathe out sigh of relief. It's just a dog. One of its ears is flopped to the side as it inspects me, inching closer to get a good sniff. "Hello puppy." I say softly, not wanting to scare it even though it just managed to scare the living daylight out of me. I clamber to my feet, brushing the dirt off my bottom. "Are you lost?"

The dog just stares back at me with its intense blue eyes.

"Let me see…" I reach out and feel for a collar around its neck, but find nothing. "That's not good, but don't worry, I'll help you find your family." I reassure the dog as I scratch its soft ears. "Who's a good," I peek at its underside before finishing with, "girl?"

She wags her tail and leans against my legs, like she's trying to hug me.

I crouch down to hug her back. "Yes, you're such a good girl."

A low rumble emits from her throat.

I pull away, but she's not growling at me. Her eyes are fixed on something in the forest behind me.

I stand up squinting into the dark to get a better look.

The dog repositions herself so she's in front of me. The hair along her back rises.

I let out another breath of relief. "Jesse! You scared us. Look, I found a stray dog."

Jesse doesn't look at me, he doesn't move. His eyes fixed on the dog.

The dog lets out another low rumble, the forest floor crunches under my feet as I take a step back, unsure what to do.

Jesse drops the logs cradled in his arms, they crash through the silence sending an echo over the lake. His face twitches as his eyes light up like burning embers. An inhuman snarl rips from his chest. I take quick steps backwards and fall to the ground startled as the dog continues to growl. I scramble to my feet, preparing to run. I only make it one step before Jesse opens his hands and blows a dark mist towards me. I drop back to the ground, unable to move. The dog, motionless next to me is the last thing I see before everything goes black.

I startle myself awake, breathing heavy. I glance at the clock on my bed side table, its reads three AM. I shiver and pull Kodi, who is snoring in my ear, into a hug. There's no way that happened that night, my mind is twisting my memories around.

I try to pull up the real memory of when I found Kodiak, but it's diluted. Almost as if I've told the story so many times that my actual memory has been simplified down to the one line as well, "I found her in the woods up by the lake house." I scrunch up my nose concentrating on the details of that night, but all I can see are Jesse's glowing red eyes from my nightmare. I push the image from my mind. That's not what happened, I tell myself. It's a stupid dream, my imagination got carried away because of how Kodi was acting at the beach. I pull my comforter around my shoulders and curl up into a tight ball, hoping for sleep to reclaim me.

"It's just a dream." I whisper to myself, but it doesn't ease my nerves. With the way he reacted to my news at the beach and Kodi's behaviour, the perfect image I've been carrying of Jesse is beginning to crack.

I wake up the following morning knowing what I must do. I'm going to spend the summer in Jackson Hole. I need distance to figure out who I am, and that includes distance from Jesse. I have a strong sense my life is about to fall into place, I'm meant to go to Wyoming. Everybody I talk to about my decision, my friends, my parents, and my sister, are all genuinely happy, and excited about my upcoming adventure. Everyone, except for Jess. I called him Tuesday morning to let him know my decision—he hung up on me, and has been dodging my calls since. It's Thursday now. We leave tomorrow afternoon.

I'm sitting in my parked car in front of his house, my hands slick with nervous sweat and I can't seem to loosen the death grip I have on the steering wheel. I've never had to break up with someone before. Tuesday when I woke up, I was sure we'd be able to make the distance thing work for a few months, but how he's been acting since I broke the news to him, I know I have to end things with him. I take a deep breath and release the steering wheel.

His street is quiet, making my door shutting behind me feel too loud. "Like a Band-Aid." I whisper as I walk up his porch steps. It was Jen's parting advice when I left the house, "Just make it quick, like a Band-Aid. It'll hurt less for both of you," she had said.

My stomach is in knots. I stare at the door, there's a post-it informing me that the doorbell is broken. I take another shaky breath and reach my fist out in front of me and knock. A door slams and some cabinets shut as heavy footfalls sound like they're coming closer to the door. But no one opens it. Instead, another inside door slams. Weird. I knock again, this time using more force so it's louder.

The door opens right away revealing Jesse's smiling face. "Lia! I'm so happy to see you. Look, I'm sorry I haven't called, I was just shocked by the news of you going away. But—"

I stop him, "Can I come in? I think we should talk."

"Of course!" He steps aside so I can enter, shutting the door behind me.

I haven't spent much time at Jesse's house, we usually hang out at my place or in our friend's basements. His parents don't like guests. He leads me down a dark hallway to his living room, which is also dark, all the shades are drawn tight. There's a thick layer of dust on the furniture and a shrivelled house plant in the corner, it looks like no one has been living here. "Are your parents out of town?" I ask as I sit down on the worn, brown couch.

"No, they just ran to the store. Why?"

I just shrug, not wanting to be rude commenting on the cleanliness of his home. I think breaking his heart is enough for today.

Jesse sits down next to me, angling his body so we're facing each other, his knee brushing against mine. "So you're going to Wyoming." He says matter-of-factly. "That's fine! It's just a few months, we'll make it work." He forces his face into a look of excitement, "I'll come visit, it could be fun!"

"Jess," I say his name softly. I'm focused on my hands in my lap, but I force my eyes up, to meet his. "I am going to Wyoming, but it's something I'm going to do on my own."

"But I'll still—"

I hold up my finger silencing him. I have to get it out. *Fast like a Band-Aid*, or I'll chicken out. "There's a lot changing in my life right now, and it all feels very sudden. I don't know who I am anymore. I need to be by myself so I can figure that out."

His face contorts in an unnatural way, his eyes flickering red.

I jump to my feet, my heart pounding in my ears. I pinch my arm. This is real, I'm not dreaming. A cold sweat breaks out on my neck, I need to get out of here. My feet won't move. I stare down at his face in horror as

I watch him mould his features back to normal, his eyes returning to deep brown. He seems to be using all his concentration to keep his features under control. His hands begin to twitch, snapping me out of my frozen state. Something isn't right. I start to back away towards the exit.

"I don't expect you to understand, and I'm sorry I hurt you, but this is something I need to do." My words are rushed as I reach the hallway. "Bye Jess," I turn around and walk as fast as I can to the front door, breaking into a full-blown run as soon as I reach his lawn.

I lock my car door as soon as it slams shut and crank the ignition. The stranger's warning from my dream bounces around my head, "Someone isn't *what* you think they are." Is this all real? Is Jesse not human? I push my foot down on the accelerator, wanting to put as much distance between me and my *ex*-boyfriend as possible.

* * *

I don't tell Jen what I think I saw at Jesse's house. I try to convince myself it didn't happen. I know I'm in denial, but I don't know how to process everything that's been happening these past few days, so I'm bottling it all up and sticking it on a mental shelf to deal with later. I know it's not a healthy coping mechanism, but it's the only thing keeping me feeling semi-sane.

I keep my recollection short and sweet. I tell her we broke up, and he was upset but took it pretty well.

"Of course he's going to be upset though." Jen says as she throws clothes from my closet into a suitcase for me. "You're perfect, and he knows it. And you know I'm not his biggest fan, but he's a reasonable guy. He'll realise you didn't do this to break his heart, that you need this summer for personal growth."

"You're always so sure about everything." I start folding the pile of clothes she's thrown at me. "Tell me, how and when did you become so wise?"

"Well, I'm a year older than you, so with that comes the wisdom. As for the when, I'd say somewhere right around the day I was born."

I laugh, "You walk the fine line between wise and stupid very well."

"HEY! You have to be nice to me, we aren't going to be living under the same roof anymore. You should be savouring these moments." But she can't hold her serious face, a broad smile cracks it.

"I'm only going for the summer. You're making it sound like it's forever."

She winks. "We'll see." She throws the rest of my clothes from my closet into a heap on my floor. "Want a Coke? I saw mom got some in the glass bottles, your fav'! Plus, I think some toasts are in order. The end of a sisterly era and to you embarking on a grand adventure!" She doesn't wait for me to answer as she slips out of my room, calling back over her shoulder, "Not to mention the fact that we're just plain awesome!"

An involuntary grin spreads across my face. "Yeah, I'd love one and don't forget the toast for you, college-bound grown up!" I shout in the direction of her retreating back.

I give up folding everything and cram the rest of my clothes into my open suitcase. I have to sit on it to get the zipper to close. My grin broadens, I can't believe this is actually happening. My heart flutters, the terror of what happened at Jesse's house mostly forgotten. This is right. My path starts in Wyoming.

Jen skips back into the room holding two old-fashioned bottles of Coke, each complete with a red and white straw bobbing out of their necks; the proper way to drink the fizzy beverage. "Speaking of college bound, "She hands me a bottle. "I got into Madison!"

"That's amazing!" It's been her dream school since she was seven. My cheeks are beginning to hurt from smiling so much, but I don't care. I'm just so *happy,* and I couldn't be prouder of my big sister. "It won't be the same without you here though."

"No," she smiles shaking her head in her knowing way. "It won't be. With you in Wyoming and me up at school, Mom and Dad are going to be empty nesters."

I laugh, "I'm only going for the summer. I'll be back by the time you leave for school."

"Please. You're not coming back. The track you'd be on if you did would be too ordinary. You're not destined for a normal 'what's expected' kind of life," she plops down on the floor in front of me, "you're going to forge a path that's all your own."

My eyes start to moisten at her words, tears threatening to spill over. I blink them away, "Well, if that's a fact, you better promise you'll visit because I'm gonna need you to be a part of it."

Jen smiles and raises her bottle into the air. "To us and our awesomeness!"

Our bottles clink and I add, "We're going to do great things!" I take a sip. A warm feeling of happiness bursts in my chest and spreads throughout my body warming me up from the core. "So, let's sort through these DVDs. I'm warning you though, you are *not* getting Pride and Prejudice. It's my favourite and it's coming with me." I set my bottle down and look up at my sister, expecting a more vocal protest.

She's frozen in place, her bottle still in the air, her face ashen.

"What?" I ask, "You don't love it nearly as much as I do."

She doesn't say anything.

"What's the matter with you? You look like you've seen a ghost or something."

"Your eyes." My sisters voice cracks.

"What about them?" I ask, panic rising in my chest, drenching out my warm feeling of happiness. Oh God did I really see what I thought I saw this afternoon? Am I the same as Jesse? Do my eyes burn like fire too?

"They're back to normal now…" Jen shakes her head as if to clear the image of whatever she's just seen. She studies my face, looking intently into my eyes.

"You're freaking me out, please tell me what you saw." My voice is shaking.

"Your eyes were *glowing*."

"Red?" I ask, as the horror of what's happening makes my feet go cold.

"What? No, green like normal, but...*Glowing*." She shakes her head again. "Man, I must not be sleeping well. That was we-ir-d," she says, stretching the one-syllable word into three.

"Ha-ha... Uhh yeah, maybe you don't need to be drinking any more sugar." I try to laugh it off, but on the inside I'm pure panic. Something's happening to me, but what?

"So! The DVDs?" Jen asks getting the conversation back to something normal, but I can tell she's still shaken by what she thought she saw.

* * *

I heave the last suitcase into the back of my dad's black suburban and push the button for it to close.

"You follow us, and stay in contact. Call if you get tired, or if someone needs to stop for a restroom break, if you get hungry, anything, and we'll find the closest spot." My dad instructs as he and mom climb into the suburban.

"Aye-aye captain!" Jen confirms as she climbs into the passenger seat of my Jeep.

I load Kodi into the back seat and hop in myself. "Here we go!" I take one last look at my childhood house as we pull out of the driveway. Tears threaten my eyes as the amount of distance that will be between me and the only home I've ever known settles in.

We ride through town in silence and I take in as much as I can, memorising every detail. The playground a block from our house looks exactly the same as it did ten years ago. The same rusty swing chains and creaky merry-go-round. I catch a glimpse of the abandoned farmhouse through the trees flashing by. I can't believe Abby and I used to climb onto that roof, it looks like it's ready to cave in with the next gust of wind. We pass houses of old friends. It dawns on me that I'm graduated. I probably won't talk to some of these people ever again. Then we're on the onramp and the town I grew up in suddenly seems so small. I'm ready to move on.

We merge onto 94 west, I sneak a peek at Kodi in the back seat through the rear-view mirror. She has the biggest doggy smile I have ever seen plastered on her face. I smile too, any threat of nostalgic tears disappearing. The warm feeling of happiness is back. I feel it creeping throughout my body the same as last night. I throw a quick glance in Jen's direction, she's busy on her phone. I shift in my seat so I can see myself in the rear-view mirror. I gasp and almost swerve into the other lane.

"What the heck are you doing?" Jen says still staring at her phone.

"Sorry, didn't mean to swerve." I mumble as I peek into the mirror again to be certain I wasn't seeing things. My skin has a healthy-looking glow emitting from my face, and my eyes are extremely bright. There's no denying it, they're *glowing*.

Chapter Four

My legs are stiff when I finally get out of the car for the last time, it feels good to stretch them. I crank my head upwards to take in the full grandeur of my aunt's home. It's the largest house I've seen in real life. A beautiful river stone pillared structure that seems to blend in with the surrounding forest. The home is incredible, but the landscape it's nestled into is what takes my breath away. Tall pines surround me, shooting up towards the sky, well beyond the two-story home. I feel safe under their canopy of green. In the distance, I see the Teton range in all its glory. My breath catches as I drink them in, it's as though a physical weight has been lifted from my shoulders, leaving a gentle calmness in its place. I'm where I belong.

There isn't a neighbour in sight. Just wild space. I close my eyes as I aim my face towards the sun, letting the warmth wash over me. I hear running water somewhere nearby, Kodi is going to love that. Sage, and pine with a touch of moss fill my lungs. I smile, this is what heaven must smell like.

"And this must be Rosalia!" I jump, I hadn't heard the tiny old lady with her walker come outside. I smile at who I can only assume is Aunt Rose. She has streaky grey hair that's been folded into a neat bun at the nape of her neck and is dressed in blue jeans and a cosy ski sweater. She peers at me over her half-moon glasses, there's a twinkle in her pale blue eyes and a start of a smile on her lips. "You're glowing my dear," her voice low so only I hear her. I freeze, a panic of butterflies erupts in my stomach. I concentrate on roping in the warmth that I now realise isn't just from the sun. Were my eyes doing that thing again? What is happening to me? I gulp and send a quick glance around to see if anyone else is watching. Lucky for me, they're all busy pulling luggage out of the back of the suburban. I look back at my aunt who's still smiling, "Don't worry honey you don't have to hide that from me." She glances at my parents and Jen, "We have much to discuss, but that can wait until we have some privacy."

I stare at her, at a loss for words. I realise my mouth is gaping open and I close it. She's not freaking out. But she told me I was *glowing*. Why wasn't she freaked like Jen had been? Does she know what's happening to me?

Rose smiles, gently laying her hand on my arm. "Relax dear. You're safe. Now, I thought you were bringing a dog with you?"

I snap out of my shock and look around, there's no sign of her. "Kodi!" I yell into the trees. I hear leaves rustling in the distance, we only have to wait a few seconds before the soaking wet dog bursts out of the brush, her tail wagging at high speed. I laugh, "Well don't you look happy! I had hoped to introduce a clean and dry dog to Aunt Rose, but you'll have to do. Aunt Rose I'd like you to meet Kodiak, Kodiak meet Aunt Rose."

Rose clasps her hands together in delight. "What a beautiful dog!" She bends down and pats Kodi on her head, passing her a treat she's pulled from her sweater pocket. She straightens back up. "All right! Let me show everyone where you'll be staying. George and Katherine, I have you in the main house. Girls, you'll be up the driveway a little further, in the little guest cabin. I hope you don't mind close quarters! We'll go there first." She heaves herself into a golf cart that has a little truck bed for a back end, my dad loads our suitcases into it and then joins Rose in the cart's passenger seat. They head up the drive, leaving the rest of us to follow on foot.

As soon as we're past the main house the tiny cabin comes into view, nestled between some aspens. I can't help but smile, it's the definition of a snug cabin. "It's perfect." I declare as Rose leads us up the two steps to a little porch and opens the red door, revealing the musty room within. It houses a small kitchen in the front corner with a table for two, two twin beds, with a small dresser in between them, and two oversized armchairs in front of a little wood stove. The perfect place to cuddle up on a rainy day to read. My heart flutters, there's no other way to describe it, it's perfect.

My dad walks around the room knocking on the walls, looking at the ceiling, and inspecting each window. He pauses to turn the kitchen sink on, and then continues back to the door checking the deadbolt. "Don't forget to lock the door every night." He looks to Rose, "Is it safe for them to sleep with the windows open or will wild animals get in?"

Rose laughs, "It's perfectly safe to sleep with them open." She turns to me and my sister, "It's not much, but you should be comfortable. Don't worry about the kitchen, you'll be eating in the main house anyway." She points to the only door besides the one we entered through. "The bathroom is just through here. We're on septic, so don't flush anything besides toilet paper." She smiles, as my mom opens the door a crack to peep in before she goes on, "It still gets cold at night, so I'll send you back with some extra comforters after dinner. I'll also have Kheelan stop by sometime tomorrow to show you how to work the fireplace."

"Kheelan?" Jen asks as she wheels her suitcase to the back corner of the room.

"He watches over my horses and helps me out around the house with things Gerald used to do before he passed. I guess he's my handyman."

"Horses?" Jen's face lights up, "They're nearby?" I smile at my sister, Wyoming won't be as dull as she feared.

Rose smiles at her enthusiasm and nods. "If you listen carefully, you might be able to hear them, that's how close. Do you ride?"

"We haven't been in ages, but if that's something we could learn while I'm here, I know Lia has all summer, but I'd LOVE that."

"I'm sure Kheelan would be more than happy to get you both on a horse this week. All right, we'll leave you to it. Katherine, George let me show you to your room!"

"You girls come back to the main house once you're settled in, and don't let Kodi wander too far, there are bears in these woods." Mom reminds us as they open the door to Kodi lying on the little porch.

"Will do." Jen walks to the closest bed and flings herself onto it.

"How awesome is this?" I say as I open the windows to air the room out.

"I have a crazy thought."

"Mm?"

"What if I stay for the summer, too?"

I turn to face my sister. She's lying flat, looking up at the ceiling. "Are you being serious?"

She scoots onto her elbows to look at me, a huge smile on her face, "Yeah. How much fun would we have?"

"So much!" I bounce onto my own bed. "What about Wyoming being dull?" I smirk at her.

"I may have spoken too soon." She admits, a small smile tugging at her lips as she drops her elbows, flopping back onto the mattress.

I try to imagine this cabin on my own. It'd be pretty lonely. I smile, "Think Mom and Dad will go for it?"

"I'll think of a way."

* * *

"That was delicious! Thank you Rose." My dad calls towards the kitchen where Rose and my mom are finishing with dinner clean up. He plops down on the sofa next to Jen, holding his now full belly.

I cross the great room, pausing in front of the stone fireplace where the fire my dad built before dinner is still roaring, to pat Kodi. She didn't waste any time making herself at home. I'm drawn to the giant windows that take up the entire back wall, framing the Tetons. The sun is still visible just beyond them, turning them a brilliant golden orange. "I can't get over how beautiful it is here." I say to no one in particular. My sister and dad grunt their agreement from the couch. "Seriously, I think I could see these mountains every day for a thousand years, and they would still manage to take my breath away."

"I believe you'll be very happy here." I jump, Rose has snuck up on me again. How does she get around so quietly with that walker? "You'll be able to be yourself." She adds, her voice quiet.

I whip my head to look at my aunt, my brow furrowed in question.

"This painting, is it new?" My mom asks from across the room before I can question the old lady about her comments with underlying meanings. We both turn our heads in her direction, she's scrutinising a large canvas on the wall, a glass of red wine in her hand.

Rose winks and shuffles over to join her. "Oh that! I painted it right after your last visit."

"It seems familiar…" my mom's voice trails off as she takes a sip of wine.

"Well, it should! The dream you shared with me is what inspired it."

Curiosity pulls me over, what kind of dream did my mom have that inspired Rose to paint? "Oh, that's right!" My mom smiles as she reaches out and brushes her fingers along the painting. "I had completely forgotten about my Fairy dream."

Right as the words 'Fairy dream' leave her mouth the painting comes into my line of vision, I stop short. It's incredible. I can't believe Aunt Rose painted it. Her paint brush has managed to bring to life three beautiful Fairies. Their skin has a pale lavender tint to it and vibrant flowers adorn their long flowing hair. They're dancing around a fire, the way she's managed to capture the scene it's as though the flames are flickering. The Fairies themselves are full of movement, their sheer pastel dresses flaring out at their knees as though they're mid spin, showing their backs where the garments dip low revealing delicate, iridescent wings. What really catches my attention is their eyes. The need to get a closer look pulls me across the room.

"Do you like it?" Rose asks, watching my reaction closely.

"It's beautiful." My voice comes out a whisper, I raise my fingers and gently brush the canvas. "I was just noticing the eyes...They almost seem to be, glowing?"

"What?" My sister's attention is caught. She wanders over to join us. I watch her carefully as she stares at the painting. I turn my face away when she begins to turn to look at me, with questions in her eyes.

"Yes, they're glowing. They're Fairies." Rose says matter-of-factly. "Would you like to hear the fairy tale that inspired it?"

"I thought it was mom's dream?" Jen challenges, her eyes narrowing on the old woman.

Rose chuckles as she walks over to an armchair by the fireplace, "It was your mom's dream that reminded me of the tale. Would you like to hear it?"

"Yes," my mom says as she joins my dad on the couch. I cosy up on the floor next to Kodi, Jen lies next to me. I lean my head against the couch and turn my attention to Rose.

"It was a warm summers night." She begins, "The moon was full, and much brighter than usual as a young maiden made her way home through a thick forest. A strange noise drifted through the branches, making its way to her ears, causing her to pause. As she stood in the moonlight concentrating, she heard it again; certain now that it was music. Without realising it, she started to wander towards the sound, as though she were being pulled to it by a magical force. As she got closer, she could hear distinct voices singing, and lots of laughter. She had never heard anyone sing in such a beautiful manner, even though it was in a language she didn't recognise."

"Curiosity was the new force that drove her forward, and before long a clearing came into sight. The maiden could see giant orange flames dancing in the middle of the open space. She ducked behind a bush so she could watch without being spotted by the beautiful creatures that were skipping around the fire. They were fair girls with a slight green tinge to their skin," Rose pauses to look at my mother, "in your dream they had a purple tinge, which I prefer."

48

"Actually, only one was purple. One of them was green," my mother says thoughtfully, "I can't remember the third." She laughs, "that dream feels like it was a lifetime ago."

Rose smiles, resuming the story. "Their skin shimmered in the moonlight and their long hair flowed behind them as they skipped. They were the most beautiful beings the maiden had ever beheld. They all wore white sleeveless dresses that exposed their backs, from which the most beautiful wings extended out from their shoulder blades. They were as delicate as a moth's and as stunning as a shimmering pearl."

"The young maiden couldn't help but to gape at the scene before her. The three girls joined hands around the fire and smiled up at the moon as they finished singing their song. When they lowered their heads, the maiden had a clear view of the one closest to her and nearly gasped out loud. She was still smiling, her skin emitting a faint glow, but her green eyes were glowing brighter than emeralds in the sunlight."

My dad lets out a theatrical gasp, making me jump and sending himself into a fit of laughter. My mom jabs an elbow into his side to silence him. "Sorry, Aunt Rose," she says.

Rose smiles at my dad, "Frightened, the young maiden stumbled backward causing the brush around her to rustle, revealing herself to these terrifyingly beautiful creatures. She got up to run, but the breeze picked up and lifted her off her feet. She was carried on the wind to the three girls by the fire. 'Be still,' one said, her long blonde waves blowing in the wind that now held the maiden in place."

"Trembling, the maiden asked, 'Are you witches? Please don't kill me.'"

"The beautiful creatures laughed. 'Heavens no! We are *Fairies*.' The blonde answered. 'We only kill human men who have broken our hearts.' One with red hair added with a smirk."

"The third, a brunette, stepped forward and gazed into the maiden's eyes, as her blue ones flared up in an intense glow, and with this a wave of calm washed over the trembling maiden. 'You came upon us by no mistake, our song was sung to bring you to our fire. We've been observing

49

you for some time now. You interact with nature in a way most humans do not, that is why we have chosen you,' the blonde said. The maiden started to tremble again. Positive she was about to die. 'Fern, make her hold still,' the blonde demanded of the brunette Fairy."

"Fern stepped forward and gazed into the maiden's eyes. Once more they lit up, but this time she whispered, 'Do not move. You have been chosen to carry an extraordinary type of child. You are to be our vessel.' The maiden now paralysed could only watch as the three Fairies stepped forward and placed all six of their hands on her midsection. In seconds, all their fingers started to shine. The maiden felt a fire erupt inside her belly, and it began to spread like flames licking through her body. A new panic burst to life inside her. When the burn reached her fingertips, she was able to see that her skin was shimmering as well. A calmness overtook her, still aglow the maiden made her way back through the forest to her home. In a trance she made love to her husband."

"The next morning, she woke up disoriented, for she could have sworn she had just been in the forest, and didn't remember her journey back or what happened when she arrived home. She brushed it off as a strange dream and carried on with her life. Almost ten months later, unbeknownst to her or her husband, a half-Fairy child was born. Or as the Fairies would say, a Fairling was born."

When it is clear Aunt Rose has finished the story, Jen spins around to face our mom. "You had that dream? How do you know it was a dream?" She demands.

Both my parents laugh, "Because it was a dream. I probably had read one of Rose's Fairy books before bed or something." My mom says with a reassuring smile.

"When did we come here last?" Jen asks.

"A long time ago." My dad says. "You were just a baby."

I watch as my sister's brain starts calculating. This was not a story for Jen to hear. She turns to look at me, "Who does Lia get her blonde hair and green eyes from?"

"Oh, stop it!" My mom throws a pillow at my sister. "There are light eyed and light-haired people on your dad's side, you know this!"

My dad starts laughing, "Your sister is not a Fairy." My sister giggles as he rises to his feet stretching his arms over his head and letting out a loud yawn. "I think I'm gonna call it a night. Thank you Rose for the wonderful dinner and entertaining story. Girls, walk back safely, and don't forget to lock your door." My mom gets up to follow him, thanking Rose and making her way around to each of us for a hug and good night kiss before they head down the hall toward their bedroom.

"I'm going to go to the bathroom before we go outside. I don't wanna hear a stick crack and wet my pants!" Jen leaps up and heads down the hallway after my parents.

"Did the parents ever find out what their child was?" I ask my aunt.

"Some trust their memory, and know that their child is special, but most believe it's just a dream. The Fairlings are 'Awakened' when they come of age and realise on their own that they're special."

I breathe out a laugh, "You're talking as though these Fairy-children hybrids are real."

Aunt Rose just smiles, sympathy clear in her eyes. "It's hard for some to accept that they're special. The human half is to blame for that, I'm afraid." She pauses and glances at the painting on the wall. "When your mother recounted that dream of hers, I thought she was teasing me. She has always liked to laugh at me for believing in fairy tales."

"She probably did find the book with the story in it." I offer.

"That's what I convinced myself at the time. I even assured your mom that's all it was, a weird dream. I've regretted that reaction. Two days after they left my friend Maggie returned the book with that story to me. I had forgotten I'd lent it to her to read to her grandson the month before...When I received your birth announcement, I knew for sure. A head of blond hair, and your bright green eyes."

I study the old woman's face, she looks so stressed over this. "What are you saying, Aunt Rose?"

"Haven't you figured it out on your own?" She studies my face, "Someone has squelched your light for many years, but I can see you've recently been ignited. You must be feeling a bit off balance?"

"Someone squelched me?" I ask.

Rose nods. "I'm afraid so."

"I had a dream about someone warning me that someone close to me isn't *what* I thought they were."

"Did you figure out who this dream was warning you about?"

I nod. "I think so."

"How long did you know this person?"

"Two years," I whisper, remembering how I met Jesse just before I turned sixteen. I remember because my dad didn't want me dating until I was sixteen, but my mom helped me convince him...The dots begin to connect in my head.

"So that's why you didn't Awaken on time." Rose says, mostly to herself.

"Awaken?" My heart is pounding in my chest. Part of me wants to believe she's crazy but the other half is relieved that there's an explanation for all the weird things that have been happening to me.

Rose glances down the hall. We can hear my parents and Jen talking about comforters and blankets. "Rosalia, think about it," Rose says, her voice hurried, "where do you go when you need to clear your mind?"

I stare at her, my gut tells me she doesn't need me to say it out loud, she already knows it's the forest.

"You're happiest when you're in nature, because you're a *Fairling*." She whispers. "*Nature* is your *home*."

Jen is walking down the hallway, getting closer. "Sorry I took so long! Mom found us some extra bedding so we don't freeze to death." She stops at the entrance to the room, her head barely visible behind the pile of quilts in her arms. She looks back and forth between my wide-eyed expression, and Rose's sympathetic one, "Uh, everything ok?"

"Sorry dear! We were just talking boring flower shop stuff. I'd like to take Lia down there in a couple of days to take a look around. But I'll let you all enjoy some vacation time first." She smiles at both of us. "I'm so happy you're here. I'll leave the back door unlocked in case you need anything during the night." She pulls Jen into a hug and says good night, then shuffles over to me, pulling me into a tight embrace. "We'll talk more soon." She whispers into my ear.

* * *

Long after Jen's breathing has become deep and Kodi starts snoring softly from her bed in the corner, I'm still awake trying to sort through everything that's happened to me over the last week. The dream about weird beings—Fairies, I guess—discussing my Awakening, Aunt Rose's story about Fairlings Awakening at sixteen, the dream warning me about Jesse, the memory dream of Jesse's fire eyes, and then me witnessing a flash of them again at his house. And I can't forget my own glow-in-the-dark-freak-show-eyes. Is this all real or have I officially gone crazy?

What is squelching? I've never heard this word before, but it sounds horrible. I grab my phone off the nightstand, the glow of the screen is too bright in the complete darkness. I type into the search bar as quickly as I can, not wanting the light to wake my sister. My eyes scan the definition of squelch, *to forcefully silence or suppress.* I suck in a breath and lock my screen, darkness blanketing the room again. Why would Jesse want to forcefully silence or suppress me? What *is* he? What am I? I guess I know the answer to the second question. I'm a *Fairling.*

Do Fairies really exist though? Aunt Rose could be senile. My stomach does a somersault, she's not senile, and I'm not crazy. I let out the deep breath I was holding. Deep down I know I'm different, I've always known.

When I was a kid, I only had a few friends. Maybe it was because the other kids could sense something about me. In fifth grade, the handful I had dwindled down to zero when Timmy McCoy, a boy who lived a few houses down, started a petition that I was a witch. Anyone who signed it was swearing to never speak to me again. He told them if they didn't sign, they'd get warts on their faces. Everyone but me signed it. He went through all this trouble because he had been clever enough to observe that every time I walked under a street lamp, the light would turn off, or it would turn on if it was off to begin with. I didn't know why this happened, but I didn't believe it was because I was a witch. After that, life at school was miserable. I had to beg my mom every day that summer to let me transfer school districts. Thank God I finally got her to agree, or middle school and high school would have been torture.

Timmy wasn't the only one to notice things. Animals always seem to follow me, or act strange in my presence. Not just cats and dogs, but wild animals, and the friends I eventually did make noticed. I was fortunate that this oddity wasn't enough to scare them off, but kept them entertained instead. One time, my friend Abby couldn't stop laughing when we were out for a run together and a young buck ran along with us in the tree line for nearly half a mile. Another time, in the seventh grade, my entire field trip group was amused when we went to the zoo and a butterfly sat on my shoulder for forty-five minutes. My classmate Bianca did the honours of timing it. Or the time a couple of loons followed Jen and me around the lake while we were kayaking. That's only naming a few. Looking back, these events were probably huge red flags that I wasn't normal. That's the beauty of hindsight though.

"A Fairling," I whisper out loud, liking the feel of the word on my mouth. I wish I'd had more time to talk with Aunt Rose. Now that the panic has subsided, the questions are bouncing around in my head and I want answers. Instead, I'm lying awake while they pile up, unanswered.

Do Fairlings have a job to do? Are we created for a purpose? Am I part demon? I remember reading somewhere that Fairies are half angel and half demon. I shiver, I don't want to be part demon. I gaze up at the stars through the open window, it's amazing how many I can see out here, star dust and everything. I send up a quick prayer for guidance as a shooting star streaks across the sky, hoping God will still listen even if there is demon blood in my veins.

A horn trumpets through the trees, causing me to pause. That's all the time the grey skinned demons need to catch up to me. They're riding skeleton horses and gaining on me fast. My legs will only allow me to run in slow motion. I push harder, trying to make them move at a normal speed, but it's hopeless. I continue at a snail's pace. I look over my shoulder at the approaching monsters, fire burns from their eyes making my blood turn to ice.

"Rosalia," one says, his voice sounds unearthly and is too high-pitched, like fingernails on a chalk board. "Why are you running from us? We're your family, you're one of us!"

My foot catches on a rock and I fall hard to the ground, my palms stinging as I push myself into a sitting position. I try to get back to my feet, but my legs refuse to move at all now. Helplessness washes over me. The demons have caught up. My eyes dart from one terrifying face to the next. They've formed a circle. I'm surrounded.

The one who spoke is in front of me, black horns that resemble a ram's, curl out from his ashen grey forehead. My head aches as his blood red eyes bore into mine. Can he read my thoughts? I try to pull my eyes away, I want to look anywhere else but at his hideous face. I can't move. I'm paralysed. I search his face for any sign of humanity but the only thing that remotely resembles a human is his body shape.

A chill consumes my body as realisation dawns on me, they're going to kill me.

"They won't be able to hide you forever. We'll find you again, and I hope you're ready to join us when we do," the horned monster says. I can only stare back, crippled by fear. His mouth spreads open in what I can only assume is an attempt to smile, revealing wolf-like fangs. I begin to tremble. "Don't be scared. You'll recognise at least one friendly face." He scoots his horse to the side opening my view to what's beyond him.

A blood-curdling scream rips from my throat.

Chapter Five

With a surprised scream, my sister bolts upright in the bed next to me. "What's going on?" I don't move. I tell her everything's okay and to go back to sleep. She grumbles something unintelligible, followed by the sound of her body flopping back onto the mattress. I take deep breaths and concentrate on getting my heart rate to return to normal. It was just a nightmare. It didn't feel as real as the dreams I had last week. But knowing this doesn't stop the uncontrollable shivers from running through my body. The image of Jesse with those monsters is burned onto the back of my eyelids.

Light snores make their way from Jen's bed, she's already fallen back into sleep. I'm envious as I lay staring up at the wood grains of the ceiling beams, sleep nowhere in sight. I check the time on my phone, 5:52. Time to accept defeat. I roll out of bed and tiptoe across the room to the bathroom. I turn the shower on, once the temperature is up to par, I step under the stream. The hot water rushes over me, instantly calming my nerves and clearing my head. Determination takes over, I am going to start today on a positive note. This is the first day of my new life, after all.

I pull on some clothes, careful not to make too much noise. Luckily Jen's a heavy sleeper and doesn't stir. I finish lacing up my hiking boots, grab a light jacket, and quietly open the front door. I suck in a breath. The sun is beginning to rise, its beams casting golden rays through the early morning mist giving the forest a magical air. Excitement rings through my veins, this is home now. I pat my leg so Kodi follows.

The air is brisk, the perfect amount of cold. The kind that doesn't make you shiver, just adds a slight nip to your cheeks and freshens the air. I like it. The gravel crunches beneath my feet as Kodi and I make our way further up the driveway, deeper into our unexplored backyard. With each step I feel like I'm walking into my new life, leaving my old one behind. What happened with Jesse is beginning to feel more like a bad dream, one I can tuck away in the corner of my mind with the other nightmares.

Kodi's swishing tail leads the way. She stays a few yards ahead of me, acting like she knows exactly where she's going. As we make our way around a sharp bend, an old barn comes into view. Kodi wastes no time breaking into a run, disappearing inside. I groan and take off after her, not sure how she'll react to seeing horses for the first time. I have to double over when I enter the barn, the air is definitely thinner up here, and apparently, I'm out of shape. The heavy stench of manure doesn't help either.

I straighten up and déjà vu hits me like a ton of bricks. I cast my eyes around for Kodi, the barn door across the way is open, light spilling through onto the dusty floor planks—just like in my dream. I take a deep breath, my heart pounding. "Kodi! Where are you?" Why is my voice shaking? I walk further into the barn, but there's no sign of her.

"She's out here!" An already familiar voice yells from beyond the open doors.

My heart pumps faster and my palms begin to sweat as I make my way towards the sound of *his* voice. The cool air is a welcome change to the staleness of the barn when I finally walk through the doors. I dry my hands on my jeans and take a deep breath. His back is to me, crouched down petting Kodi. I don't need to see his face, I already know it's him. "I'm sorry," my voice comes out hoarse. I clear my throat. "She usually doesn't run off like that." I'm standing right behind him now.

"Not a problem, I love dogs." He stands up. He's taller than I expected, at least six three. He begins to turn around, my heart flutters. "You must be Rosalia, your aunt told me about—" He falters, staring down at me, his face mirroring the shock I feel, "—you." He finishes in a bare whisper his brows crinkling inwards towards each other.

Our eyes lock. His are just as blue as I remember. The now familiar warm feeling starts to spread outwards from my chest, panic following closely in its wake. I rip my eyes away from his and focus on the three horses that are grazing on the other side of the wooden fence, afraid my eyes are about to do their circus freak act again. "You can call me Lia," I turn my gaze back to him once I'm confident I'm not glowing. "Everyone does, except for my aunt, I guess."

"Lee-ah," he drawls with an easy smile that makes my heart do flips. He extends his hand, "I'm Kheelan. It's nice to finally meet you."

I wipe my hand against my jeans before I wrap my fingers around his, a jolt of recognition shoots up my arm. I gasp and stumble backwards. Kheelan catches me but drops my hand as soon as I regain my footing. His furrowed brow deepening. He studies my face for what feels like an eternity, I shift my focus back to the horses, uncomfortable under his scrutinising gaze. He opens his mouth but before he says anything he shakes his head slightly and closes it again, deciding against whatever it was he was going to say. Instead, he motions towards the horses, who are busy chomping on the grass a few feet away. "The brown one is Laila," he says, "Matoskah, or Mat, is the white one, and the grey one is Oberon."

Relieved we've silently agreed to ignore the weird moment, I look at the speckled grey horse who is closest to us, Oberon. He's beautiful. They all are, and I tell him that. I reach out my hand and nicker, hoping they'll come over.

"Oberon can be a little temperamental," Kheelan warns, "his name means king and I think he believes he's an actual king."

"He's magnificent enough to be a king." Oberon perks up, giving in to curiosity before the others, and trots to the fence to inspect my outstretched hands. He must approve of my smell because he closes the rest of the distance between us, resting his forehead against mine. I smile and reach up to pat his cheek. "Aren't you a sweet boy." Mat and Laila, seeing I'm not a threat, trot over to inspect the newcomer for themselves. I look over my shoulder at Kheelan, unable to stop the grin that's spreading across my face as the horses shower me with love. "Do you have any treats I can give them?"

Kheelan's eyes are wide, his mouth gaping open. "I can't believe Oberon just did that. I have never seen him take to a stranger so fast before."

I shrug, "Animals tend to like me." I turn my attention back to the horses, making sure to give them all equal amounts of love.

"Here," Kheelan grabs my hand, "they love these." I look at my palm, he's given me three baby carrots.

"Thanks," I mumble as I feed a carrot to each horse, lying them flat on my hand like I learned when I was younger. Their lips slime my palm one by one.

An impatient woof comes from behind us. Kodi is sitting expectantly, one paw raised.

Kheelan laughs. "Do you like carrots?"

Kodi's tail swishes back and forth on the dusty ground.

Kheelan looks at me, a silent question if it's okay to give her one. I smile and nod as he pulls an extra carrot out of his pocket and crouches down, handing it to her. "Sorry girl, I didn't mean to leave you out." He scratches behind her ear as she swallows the vegetable whole.

"She likes you." I say as he stands back up.

He smiles, the sun catching his eyes making them impossibly blue. My heart flips. "Is that unusual?" He asks.

I shrug. I guess she does like most people, just not Jesse…"She hated my ex."

"Sounds like she's just smart." He winks at me as he walks towards a red pickup truck, the bed full of hay bales. He pauses to look back, his hand on the door handle. "Animals tend to like me too, though." He opens the door and hops into the driver's seat. He rolls down the window, "I gotta get some work done around the property, but if you'll be around later, I'll stop by and show you how to work the stove in the cabin. Does five sound okay?"

"Sounds good, I'll be there."

His truck rumbles to life and he drives through the open pasture gate. His brake lights glow red as the vehicle comes to a stop, he leans out the window and looks back at me, "I'm glad you found me."

My mouth drops.

He laughs at my reaction, his eyes sparkling with mischief. "I'll see you later, Lia." I watch as his truck disappears in a cloud of dust, unable to move my feet. I think they may have grown roots.

* * *

Rose could be a professional tour guide. She has an entire day planned out for us and I welcome the distractions with open arms. It's like when you have so much to do you don't know where to start so you just take a nap, but instead of things I need to do its new information I need to process. Instead of processing, I'm just adding it to my mental shelf to deal with later. I'm determined to be a *normal* teenager, or at the very least to appear like one.

We start the day in the Town's Square for breakfast. Rose points out random 'historical sites' as we make our way down the wooden planked sidewalks towards the restaurant, her voice a bit too loud over our clomping feet. *"There's the spot where your great-uncle proposed to me,"* she aims her finger across the street towards an antler archway, *"and right here is where Maggie and I decided to open up the flower shop,"* she says coming to a stop in front of a small coffee shop, her eyes staring off into the distance, seeing a different time. I can't help but smile, her sharing a bit of her personal history makes this new place feel more like home.

The rest of the day we spend crammed into the suburban, Rose directs my dad where to go from the passenger seat while simultaneously overloading us with information as we wind our way through Grand Teton National Park. I only half listen as she drones on about the explorer John Colter, a grizzly bear named 399, Jenny Leigh and some guy they called *Beaver Dick.* I'm too lost in the scenery flashing by my window to pay attention. The landscape is unreal, like we've driven out of our normal world straight into a postcard. I'm thankful each time Jen interrupts Rose from her spot way in the back, insisting we stop at the pull out she sees up ahead. She only wants to stop so she can get the perfect shot for Instagram, but I like breathing it all in, the pine, the sage, the freshness. It doesn't matter that every time we pull over it's the same mountains just a new angle. Each time I take them in, the crisp air catches in my throat and my heart swells a little.

By the time we get back to Rose's I'm exhausted, and sick of being in the car. I glance at the clock on my phone, it's 4:45. My heart starts hammering. Kheelan will be coming by the cabin in fifteen minutes. I mumble an excuse and leave everyone at the main house, I'm not sure why I don't want my sister to come with me. I pick my way through the sparse trees by myself in the direction of the small cabin, my feet kicking up dirt from the path as I go. My once white sneakers are already forming a nice layer of Wyoming dust. A smile tugs on the corners of my mouth. It suits me. My mouth droops, will Jen feel the same way?

She brought up her idea of staying while we were seated around a weather-beaten picnic table on the shore of Jackson Lake, eating lunch. I was careful to keep my face neutral, my eyes focused on the still snowy Mount Moran across the choppy waters. "That's a lovely idea!" Rose had exclaimed before anyone else could react. "Let's speak with my caretaker Mindy when we get home this afternoon, I'm willing to bet she could get you set up with a job at the hospital no problem. You're going to school in the fall for nursing, isn't that right?" Rose peered over her half-moon glasses at Jen, who had pure delight radiating off her. Her grin covered her entire face as she nodded, glancing at my parents who forced smiles and shrugged their approval. My sister had prepared herself for an unneeded argument. They're probably relieved I'll have someone more responsible to keep an eye on me this summer.

The cabin appears in front of me. Kheelan will be here any second, my heart pumps harder. When I get inside, I sit down in the armchair to wait. I can't sit still, I pop back up to my feet and begin to pace, wiping my palms on my jeans. I wish I hadn't been too chicken to tell Jen about my encounter with him this morning. Maybe she would have had some insight that would make me feel less like throwing up right now. I come to a stop. Maybe I shouldn't tell her. I dreamt about him before I met him. Do I really need extra confirmation that I'm going crazy? Guilt knots my stomach at the thought of lying to my sister. I resume my pacing. It's not really lying, just withholding information that makes me sound crazy. It may not even warrant as withholding information. I come to a stop in front of the window. I'm probably making a bunch of nothings pile up into something. The shock of recognition I felt when I touched Kheelan is probably just static, the air is dry out here and Kheelan was happy I found him because it's his *job* to show me the stove. I let out a breath, yes, it's all explainable. Him quoting my dream is a simple coincidence, all common words used by people every day. A lone butterfly comes to life in my stomach. My *dream*, how do I explain away dreaming of him before I ever saw him?

A sharp knock on the door pulls me out of my internal battle. I whip around towards the sound. He's here, no one else would knock. I wipe my hands once more on my jeans and take a deep breath as I walk swiftly across the creaky floor to open the door.

"I hope you like lemonade." Kheelan flashes a smile, my heart flutters. He holds up a six pack of lemonade bottles. "I bear gifts, Teton County's finest huckleberry lemonade, in my opinion, anyway. And two keys, for you and your sister."

I manage a smile, "Who doesn't love lemonade?" I reach out and accept the gift, freeing his hands. "Thank you." I take a step back swinging the door open, letting him in. "Would you like one?" I offer as I walk towards the mini fridge to stow the rest of them.

"I'd love one." He clicks the door shut behind him, motioning towards the little table where he's left the keys. I feel his eyes on me as I open the two drawers rummaging for a bottle opener. "May I ask what you're looking for, maybe I can help?"

I glance over my shoulder at him, an amused smile plays across his mouth, he's laughing at me. "A bottle opener," I say.

He reaches out and grabs one of the bottles from my hands and twists the top off. I laugh and twist the lid off my own, leaning against the counter for support. "Smells good," I take a tentative sip, I'm not sure what I was expecting huckleberry to taste like, but I'm pleasantly surprised how well it's blueberry-like sweetness mixes with the tartness of the lemons. I smack my lips loudly in approval. My body goes rigid as the horror of what I've just done washes over me, he's going to think I'm the biggest dork. With that thought, uncontrollable laughter bubbles up in my chest, I force it back down. "I officially trust your opinion, this is delicious." My voice is too high, I take another sip and smack my lips again unable to stop myself. Inward groan. Someone needs to stop me.

Kheelan smiles politely, he's leaning against the support pillar in the middle of the space, "I'm glad you like it." He studies me with a thoughtful expression, "You're different from what I expected."

I let out a nervous laugh, oh God he thinks I'm demented. I clear my throat, and force my voice to sound normal, "Oh yeah? What were you expecting?"

"I'm not sure." He pushes off the pillar and walks towards the stove. "Want to wait for your sister before I show you how the wood burner works?"

I follow him across the small space. "I'm sure you don't want to wait around, I can just show her when she gets back."

"Well, the flue can be tricky, you'll want to make sure it's fully open before you guys start any fires, or you'll get smoked out pretty fast." I watch as he crouches down, his shirt stretching tight over his broad shoulders. He glances back at me to make sure I'm watching, the sunlight gleams into his eyes making them sparkle like sapphires, I feel my cheeks flush, and quickly shift my gaze to watch what his hands are doing.

His graceful fingers grasp the flue's lever and turn it halfway, he gives it a jiggle before turning it the rest of the way. I nod as he explains what he's doing, but it's hard to concentrate on his words. I'm transfixed by his fluid movements. He doesn't stop when the flue is open, reaching into the bin next to the stove to grab kindling and logs, stacking them expertly inside the opening. He crinkles newspaper and shoves it beneath his freshly constructed pyramid then strikes a match. Flames burst to life. He flashes a smile and plops into one of the armchairs to admire his handiwork.

Just as I make myself comfortable in the second chair, the front door opens and Kodi bounds in, stopping briefly at my legs for a pat before greeting our guest.

"Oh! Hello!" Jen's face lights up at the sight of Kheelan. "You must be the horse guy." She walks directly to him, not breaking eye contact once and extends her hand. "I'm Jen." Her confidence never ceases to amaze me, her voice didn't squeak once. How did I get stuck with all the awkward genes?

Kheelan takes a break from scratching Kodi's ears and takes her hand. "Pleased to meet you, Jen. I am the horse guy, but you can call me Kheelan for short."

A delighted laugh bubbles out of my sister as she glances at the bottles clutched in both of our hands. Without a word, she spins on her heel making her way to the small fridge where she helps herself to one.

A loud screech fills the room as she drags a kitchen chair over to where the two of us are sitting. Jen's presence puts us both at ease and the three of us fall into comfortable conversation as Kodi settles into her new favourite spot in front of the fire. I'm surprised how much I open up to him, talking more than Jen even, which is rare. He's easy to talk to, it feels like we've known each other our entire lives. We tell him what life was like growing up in Wisconsin, how we usually spend the summer up at our family's lake house. I even confide in him about how being up there is a reset button for my soul—how when I'm floating in the lake, breathing in the forest around me, I can almost see the stress of life float up and out of me. I stop short as I realise I've never said that out loud before. I sneak a glance at Jen, she's hanging on my every word.

"Wow." She says, her voice barely a whisper. "I never realised how important those trips were to you."

I smile at my sister, "My first happy place."

"It'd be nicer if there weren't so many mosquitos." Jen sticks out her tongue in disgust. "The flies are terrible, too." She informs Kheelan.

Kheelan's not looking at Jen though, he's watching me, his thoughtful expression back. "I get it. Being in the forest is calming for me, too."

"But the bugs!" Jen laughs and sets her empty lemonade bottle on the floor. She leans in towards the stove to warm her hands. "I'm happier in the city with lots of people around, but I promise to give it a fair chance this summer." She flashes a smile in my direction before turning her attention back to Kheelan. "What was life in Wyoming like for a young boy?"

He learned to ride when he was five, and has loved horses and all animals since before he can remember. He goes for long hikes when he needs to think, and when he turned sixteen, he became a vegetarian. Jen interrupts him to inform him that I've been a vegetarian for the past week because lasagna made me lose my biscuits and now I can't stand even the sight of meat. Blood rushes to my cheeks as the words leave her mouth, but Kheelan just smiles. He goes on to tell us that his dad was never in the picture, and that his mom and six-year-old brother were both killed in a car accident when he was only four. His grandmother is the one who raised him, Aunt Rose's friend and business partner, Maggie.

When he stops talking, I just stare at the fire. I didn't expect his life story to be so tragic. Jen stays quiet too, it might be the first time she's ever been at a loss for words. The crackling of the logs is the only thing filling the silence, which starts to stretch into an uncomfortable length. Finally, Kheelan stands up and stretches, his arms almost reaching the ceiling. I let out a sigh, he's beautiful.

Jen clears her throat, jolting me out of my trance. That annoying, know-it-all-smile of hers on her lips. I'm sure my cheeks are crimson. I drop my gaze to my feet, ashamed. Caught in the act of checking out the horse guy.

Kheelan fishes his phone out of his pocket and reads a text message as he collects our empty bottles and walks them over to the sink. He stops by the front door. He's ready to leave. I'm surprised by the disappointment that settles over me, but I take the cue and rise to my feet, "Thanks for the lemonade and keys, and for helping with the stove..." I let my voice trail off, I can feel Jen's eyes burning into me.

Kheelan laughs, amused by my awkwardness. "I don't know about you ladies, but I'm STARVING. Some friends of mine just texted. They're at this girl Emily's house grilling burgers," I hold back a gag at the mere mention of red meat, "and they're going to get a campfire going in a bit."

"Sounds fun!" Jen chirps.

Kheelan meets my eyes, "Want to come?" He smiles, "There's gonna be veggie burgers too, don't worry."

"We'd love to!" Jen answers fast, not giving me a chance to even open my mouth.

I shoot a glare in her direction. "What about Mom and Dad? They're probably expecting us at Aunt Rose's."

"Please." She stands up rolling her eyes. "They'll be thrilled to be rid of us for the evening. I'll text them now." Her thumbs move swiftly across her phone screen, and before I can object, I hear the swooshing noise of the text being sent. "All right, we'll just need a moment to freshen up." She ushers Kheelan out the door. "We'll only take a second!" She sings as she shuts the door behind him, whirling around to face me. Her mouth opens, but I'm faster.

"Don't!" I warn.

"But I caught you!"

"I said, don't!"

Jen laughs, "He's hot. I can't blame you for crushing." She examines me, "I think you should wear your forest green shirt, it brings out your eyes. And wear your hair down, your waves are gorgeous."

I smile, happy I'll have my bossy Jen with me all summer. I open my mouth, I should tell her that Kheelan is the guy from my dream. But I chicken out, "He is super-hot." I say instead. We both erupt into schoolgirl giggles.

* * *

The smell of campfire is heavy on the air, the musky smoke and pine needles making it a real summer's night as Kheelan leads us across a neatly manicured lawn and around to the back of a tiny blue house. As soon as we round the corner, a pretty brunette pops up from a plastic lawn chair tipping it backwards. She starts to squeal as she runs towards us. My mouth drops open as she throws herself into Kheelan's arms.

"Baaaaabe! You're finally here! What took you so long?" She asks pulling away so she can look up at him, pushing her bottom lip out into an exaggerated pout.

"I'm sorry, I had to work." He bends down and kisses her right on the mouth. "Forgive me?" He asks pulling away.

"One more," she whines, going up onto her tippy toes so she can push her mouth onto his again.

I can't look away. I need to look anywhere else, but instead I stare in horrified silence. I did not see this coming. Kheelan is the man from *my* dream, he's not supposed to be kissing other girls! I feel Jen grab my arm. I know she's holding back laughter and it's taking all her will power to not let any escape. We'll make fun of this poor girl mercilessly later when we're alone. There's nothing my sister hates more than baby talk. I take a deep breath as the initial shock wears off. I'm being crazy, it was a *dream*. Of *course* he has a girlfriend. He's funny, he's smart, and he's super sweet, and let's not forget, smoking hot. I hold back a groan, but *why* does he have to have a *girlfriend*?

"Hi! I'm Allie. You must be Rose's nieces." Baby talker's normal voice, which is still annoyingly high-pitched breaks my trance.

"Hey there!" Jen says. "I'm Jennifer, and this is my sister Rosalia."

"Rosalia," her eyes lock on mine. "you're the one staying for the summer? Wow. You're like really pretty. Isn't she pretty Kheelan?"

Kheelan's cheeks burn red, but he just shrugs in a noncommittal way. My heart sinks a little, but what was I expecting? For him to declare his love for me, the girl he's known for two seconds, in front of his girlfriend?

Allie latches onto my arm and starts dragging me away, clearly not wanting anyone who's *like really pretty* anywhere near *her* boyfriend.

"You HAVE to meet Tipton! He's a rodeo star," she says in a stage whisper, too close to my face, "and he's hilarious. Don't you think Tipton will love her, Kheelan?" She says over her shoulder, but doesn't wait for him to answer. She whips her head back towards the fire. "Tipton!" She calls out in a sing-song voice, I hate her already. I send a desperate 'save-me-now glare' over my shoulder at Jen, but she and Kheelan are too busy laughing to notice my plea for help as Allie pulls me further away from the only two people I know at this party.

Tipton monopolises my entire evening. I barely get a chance to talk to anyone else. He corners me against the back of the house leaving no room for escape as he bombards me with bad jokes and stories that make him look good at other's expenses. At one point, I excuse myself to use the bathroom but he's outside the door waiting for me when I finish. He even follows me to the grill when Kheelan announces the veggie burgers are ready. My eyes bore into the back of my sister's head, but she's engrossed in a conversation she's having with a girl who has black hair and tan skin. She doesn't even notice my absence, and Tipton doesn't notice my disinterest as he drones on about himself. It's obvious he's used to girls liking him. I guess he's kind of cute, in a baby-faced goofy sort of way. But he's horrible, and I hate how hard he's trying. Finally, when the fire is burning low, Jen grabs my arm and tells Tipton she's stealing me away.

"Thanks so much for saving me." I grumble, "A DECADE late."

"I'm sorry! It's just that I could tell he loves you so much, and I couldn't bear to break his heart any earlier." She laughs, "Kheelan is waiting by his truck, I'm gonna run inside to use the bathroom, I'll be right out."

"Yeah, yeah, yeah, you left me, abandoned me, for your own entertainment. Just admit it." I mumble heading towards the front of the house.

"You and Tipton seemed to be hitting it off?" Kheelan says, careful to keep his tone casual as I approach.

"He thinks he's pretty funny," I shrug. Being cornered all night by undesirable company has not left me in a very good mood.

"He's a really good guy." Kheelan says, glancing towards at the house. "He was probably just nervous and trying too hard."

I sigh, "I know Allie was hoping for sparks, but he's really not my type." Then, so I don't sound too mean, I add, "I don't think anyone's my type right now." *Except maybe you,* I want to say, but instead go with, "I just broke up with my boyfriend last week."

"It's probably for the best." I throw him a sharp look, but before I say anything he throws up his hands in defence, "I didn't mean for that to sound mean." He glances towards the house, again. "I don't know what you know or what your aunt has told you yet, but…" He trails off, lost in thought.

"What do you mean?" I ask, paying close attention to his face.

"About what you are." He turns his head, locking his eyes on mine, gauging my reaction. What does he mean *what I am*? I don't know what to say, I just stare at him, my mouth slightly open like an idiot. Does he know about *Fairlings*? "I know it's a lot to grasp." He goes on, his voice gentle. "Believe me, I've been there."

"You have?" My eyes narrow, surely we're not talking about the same thing right now.

"Maybe we can talk tomorrow, with Rose?"

Heat rises to my cheeks. I'm so sick of everyone talking in riddles, I could spit. "Why does everyone keep saying weird things to me?" I snap.

"I'm sorry, I shouldn't have said anything." He glances towards the house, Jen is making her way across the front lawn. He looks back at me, his eyes apologetic.

I don't try to hold back the exasperated groan as I stomp around the car and clamber into the backseat. I slam the door as hard as I can, so he knows I'm annoyed. Jen climbs into the front passenger seat, looking back at me, worry crumpling her brow. "Everything okay?" she mouths. I just nod, angling my body towards the window so she can't see my face.

It's a silent ride home. When Kheelan pulls up to our cabin, he hops out of the truck and runs around to open our doors, I don't know why him being the perfect gentleman annoys me so much. He hugs Jen good night first, and then tentatively turns to me. I let him pull me in, melting into his embrace. It feels good, *too* good. He has a girlfriend.

"We'll talk tomorrow." He whispers into my ear before he pulls away, looking down at me, his eyes unsure, but then he leans down and places a gentle kiss on my forehead. His lips are warm and have a calming effect on my mind while simultaneously sending my heart into overdrive. "Get some sleep, and welcome home." He says softly, then at a volume loud enough for Jen, "Good night ladies! Hope you had fun tonight!"

We stand on the porch and watch as he drives away. When his taillights are tiny red dots in the distance, Jen spins to face me. "Did he *kiss* you?"

I feel the blush start to creep up my neck. "Just a forehead peck, it was nothing."

"You like him." Her voice is full of accusation as she pushes the door open, Kodi wiggles through to greet us. "I don't blame you, he's a cool guy, but be careful. He has a *girlfriend*, I don't want to see you get hurt." She turns towards me, her face morphing into gossip mode. "I did a lot of observing tonight. You're not the only one who has the hots for him, that girl Emily, who by the way works at Aunt Rose's flower shop, don't worry you'll like her, she's super cool. Anyway, she *definitely* has a thing for Kheelan too. She tries to hide it, but I'm very perceptive when it comes to these things."

I offer a weak smile. "It's not a crush." I assure her, but by the roll of her eyes I know she doesn't believe me. "It's just that…" I take a deep breath and decide to follow her advice. Quick like a Band-Aid. I let the words tumble out at lightning speed before I can lose my nerve. "He's the guy from my dream."

Chapter Six

Soulmates. That's the term Jen kept using last night as she gushed on about me and Kheelan being meant for each other, no longer worried about the fact that he has a girlfriend or about me getting hurt. *Soulmates* is the only explanation for my mysterious dream about him. *'You found your destiny,'* she whispered one last time as she climbed into the suburban with my parents. They're headed to Bozeman to spend the night. She wants to scope out Montana State's campus. She still has her heart set on going to Madison but, 'it doesn't hurt to look'. I'm staying behind to go over my new role at the flower shop with Rose. But in reality, I'm on my way to the main house to demand some answers from her. But, of all the things I've learned since arriving in Wyoming that are bouncing around in my head, it's Jen's voice that is the loudest as I trudge down the path. *Soulmates.*

* * *

"When dealing with Fairies, you need to keep in mind that they are a different species. They are *not* human. They have a reputation for being cunning and conniving, and it's true. They're sneaky and like to get their way, no matter the cost," Rose begins. We're sitting at her patio table on her back deck with steaming cups of tea and a platter of freshly baked chocolate chip cookies, that smell amazing, between us. I'm relieved when Kheelan, instead of sitting by me, walks up the steps and situates himself against the deck railing, turning his face towards the mountains in the distance. Even with him a few feet away, my nerves are buzzing. Rose

71

confirmed my suspicions, he's like me. He's a *Fairling*. When Jen learns this titbit, she'll find a word stronger than *soulmates* to describe our connection. This thought brings a small smile to my lips, but I push it aside and focus my energy on my aunt's words. Her tired voice and deep laugh lines around her mouth and eyes give her an air of wisdom, making it easy to be pulled in.

"I heard once that Fairies are half demon and half angel, is that true?" I grab one of the cookies and break off a chunk, the chocolate's still gooey when I pop the bite into my mouth, "These cookies are delicious." I say around my mouthful, "Is that cinnamon?"

Rose chuckles, "I'm sorry to say, I had no part in baking them. Any secret ingredients will remain a secret." She winks, "As for your first question, there are many tales of how Fairies came to be." She lets out a sigh, "The most popular is that Fairies were thrown out of Heaven with Lucifer. They weren't really evil enough for Hell, but too mischievous for Heaven. They remained neutral in the fight between Heaven and Hell. In time, a realm of their own was formed, the *OtherWorld.* Which leads me to—"

"With Fairy-Blood, will we not be allowed into heaven?" I struggle to swallow the last bit of cookie, my throat suddenly dry, "I don't want to be evil." I wrap my fingers around the warm mug in front of me, trying to ebb the chill that has begun to creep through me.

Rose clicks her tongue, "Oh! I wouldn't worry about that. You're still human and you live on *this* plane. Live right and do good. I'm sure there will be a place for you. As far as being *evil,* not even close. You my child, are a child of The Light." She gives me a reassuring smile. "As I was saying, there's a story you need to hear. I think it'll answer a lot of your questions, but if you still have some when I'm finished, I promise to answer them to the best of my ability."

I nod my silent agreement.

Rose lifts her tea to her lips and takes a long drink. She pushes her mug to the side and heaves an enormous book from her lap onto the table with a loud thud. She flips through the pages looking for the story she's after. I settle deeper into my chair, leaning my head against the high back and close my eyes. The cool breeze soft on my eyelids. I'm all ears as she begins her tale.

"Legend has it the fairest King of the Fae was King Beaumont, whose blood was made from the mountain, he was of the Earth. Beaumont married a beautiful Fairy named Darya, who's blood was created from the sea, she was of water. Together, they created three children, twin daughters; Luna and Lucille, and one son, Dillon."

"When Luna grew to maturity, she fell in love with a Fairy named Herne DerJagër. They wed and had three children of their own. Lucille married Oliver AusFeuer, also bearing three."

"Dillon, although unwed, was Beaumont's only son and next in line to be the ruler of the OtherWorld. Since Fae are immortal, unless their life is taken, Beaumont had ruled the OtherWorld for thousands of years. He was beginning to grow weary and planned to step aside and allow his son to take the throne. Herne, Luna's power-hungry husband, didn't like this. He had three sons of his own, better suited to carry on the bloodline. He felt he was more fit to be King. Unbeknownst to the royal family at the time, he murdered Dillon."

"Filled with despair, the King decided his son-in-law Oliver would make a fair ruler, alongside his level-headed daughter Lucille. Herne once again was not pleased. In a fit of rage, Herne went on a rampage. He slaughtered Oliver, King Beaumont and Queen Darya. He intended to take the lives of his wife's sister and her three daughters, but Luna discovered her husband's hideous actions and was able to warn her twin. In learning the news of her family's fate, Lucille cast a powerful enchantment around the OtherWorld, banishing Herne, his kin, and followers."

"Devastated by her true love's actions, Luna gulped down a goblet filled with poison, ending her life. Lucille, left alone with her three small children, rose from the ashes of her destroyed kingdom as a very powerful and much beloved Queen."

"Herne defeated and nearly broken, managed to escape the worst of Queen Lucille's wrath. They were not seen or heard from for hundreds of years."

"When they finally reappeared in the mortal world, they no longer resembled their former selves. No one knows what happened during their travels, but they had morphed into dark and dangerously powerful creatures. They had fire for eyes, rode atop skeletal horses, and feasted upon human souls. They called themselves 'The Wild Hunt'. But Queen Lucille's enchantments held strong. The Wild Hunt was still unable to enter the OtherWorld."

"Angered that his powers still weren't enough to break his sister-in-law's magic, Herne declared a warning directed at the Queen; 'Hear me all—for what I am about to say concerns not just my own, but also the Fae who still identify with the so-called *Light*. I, Herne DerJagër, vow to you on this night; I will find a way back into the OtherWorld. When I do, it will be me who sits upon the Royal Throne with your precious sovereign and her daughters dead at my feet.' With that, the monster that had once been part of the Royal family disappeared in a cloud of smoke. That was the last the Fairies of the Light have seen or heard from Herne DerJagër."

Rose closes the book softly and looks up. "So he started his own kingdom?" I ask.

"Yes, they aren't in our world, or the OtherWorld, but in a place called the NetherWorld. I imagine it to be similar to Hell. The Hunters are able to come to Earth but only when there is no light, and they do come, every new moon." My aunt's voice goes low, a warning level, "The darkest nights are the most dangerous for both Fae and humans to be wandering the forest. The Hunt rides upon their skeletal horses, collecting human souls. Legend says if you hear their horn of doom, it's already too late."

"If they collect human souls, why is it dangerous for Fae?" I ask.

"It's worse for Fae." She says, her soft blue eyes bore into mine, willing me to hear her warning. "When they hunt Fae of the Light, they capture them and force them into an eternity of slavery in the NetherWorld."

A shiver runs down my spine at the thought of being enslaved for eternity in a place like Hell. "Definitely the bad guys," I say. This gets a chuckle from Kheelan. I jump. I'd forgotten he was here. "So you say I'm a Fairling of the Light, does that mean that these monsters in the NetherWorld have Fairlings too?"

Rose nods, "The Hunt can make Fairlings of sorts, though they call them *Underlings*, and they're created in a different way." She meets my eyes as she continues, "Unlike Fairlings who are created with Light and born naturally, The Hunt steals babies and transforms them in the NetherWorld. No one of the Light knows what the process entails, but I'm sure it's not pleasant. I have a hunch that this ex-boyfriend of yours may have been one of Herne's *Underlings*."

Goose bumps prick to life along my arms despite the warm sun. How terrible for those mothers to lose their babies. I think about how I never met Jesse's parents, I guess he didn't have any. Did he ever experience any sort of love or nurturing growing up? Then I think about his burning red eyes and the dream of monsters on horses, how much human is left in him? My head begins to nod on its own, "That would explain some things." I try to swallow away the fear clenching at my throat, was he planning to collect my soul? Or my families? I shudder at the thought. "He was in my life for *two* years," I say, "if they consume human souls, why didn't he eat mine?"

"You don't have a fully human soul." Rose says her voice matter-of-fact. "They consume souls, but with a Fairy or Fairling's soul they do something called *squelching*." My eyes shoot up at the sound of that word again. It peeks Kheelan's attention too, Rose takes a slow sip from her tea and continues, "Squelching is to keep someone who has Fae-Blood close and slowly leech the Light from their soul. It's how they keep Fairies enslaved in the NetherWorld. Since Fairy-Blood is able to regenerate it's Light, if done correctly, The Hunt can feed off one Fae for many years. Keeping them weak enough so they're not able to escape, but not so weak that they perish."

"You think Light from my soul was taken? Will I die sooner? Am I less of a Fairling now?" I fire my questions at her.

"Yes, I believe some of your Light was taken, but as I said, it will regenerate…Eventually." She smiles, "You are still just as much a Fairling." She pauses, her face thoughtful. My mind races. I'm a Fairling, but I'm weaker than I should be, all thanks to my boyfriend…*Ex-boyfriend.* "If the light hasn't been consumed yet," Rose's voice snaps me out of my reverie, "it could be taken back." Her voice fades, her gaze lost on the horizon.

"How would we know if it's been consumed yet?" I ask when she gives no sign of continuing her thought.

Rose shakes her head slowly. "We wouldn't. It's just a hunch, but Underlings don't require the Light since they are still part human themselves. My guess would be it was stolen for The Hunters. Two years' worth is a lot of Light, they're up to some sort of scheme." She lets out a long sigh, "You'll be weaker for some time."

"I think I should try to get it back for her," Kheelan says making me jump again. Why do I keep forgetting he's here?

"Brave offer, Kheelan. I'm afraid it would be too dangerous, especially by yourself." Rose says.

I watch his face bunch up in determination, his hands tight balls at his side. "I've been training, I'm ready."

My eyes flick between the two stubborn faces, neither wanting to budge on the subject. "It's my Light and I know Jesse, maybe I should be the one to try and get it back?"

Rose considers this, "The amount they have could be dangerous, and the time is nearing, according to the Queen."

"Okay what is up with that? The ominous remarks about *time,*" my annoyance level rising with my voice, "*We're running out of time,*" I mimic, "*the time is nearing, we fear we may not have enough time.*" I shoot glares at the stunned faces of my audience, "Running out of time for *what*? If I'm part of some big plan, it'd be handy to know the role I'm supposed to be playing." I look between the two astonished parties, both left speechless from my outburst. I roll my eyes, "Someone needs to tell me what you know, *we're running out of time*!" I add unable to help the laughter that bursts from me.

Rose studies me over the top of her glasses before giving in, "I don't know much. Kheelan, this is why I wanted you here today. The Fairy Queen has informed me about a prophecy. It states that three Fairlings will decide the Fate of the three worlds by finding the Lost Stave. The Fairies are adamant the Fairlings named are the two of you." She looks at Kheelan, her face dropping, "Declan would have been the third." She returns her eyes to me, "Declan is Kheelan's older brother, but he died many years ago in a very unfortunate tragedy."

I look towards Kheelan, his eyes are on the mountains, his jaw clenched tight. How are we supposed to decide the outcome of the three worlds? I don't even know what a Stave is. I'm not strong, I won't be able to fight if it comes to that. I can barely open a pickle jar. I shake my head, "That can't be right. I'm Lia Matthews, from Wisconsin. I'm not a warrior who can decide the fate of the worlds with a stave, whatever that is." A cool breeze blows out of the trees. I wrap my fingers around my mug, leeching any lingering heat into my hands.

Rose and Kheelan exchange a look, then Kheelan turns around, leaning against the railing again, his face grim. "You're stronger than you know." He says, "You're not an ordinary Fairling, my Grandma Maggie told me that you're the granddaughter of Queen Lucille. Your mother is Aspen, the Queen's eldest daughter. You are the *only* Fairling she's ever created."

The air goes still and suddenly it's hard to breathe. My hands collect a fresh sheen of sweat as my feet turn to ice. This is too much. "My mother is Katherine Matthews," I manage to choke out.

Aunt Rose reaches across the table and grabs a hold of my hands. "Of course she is dear, and your father is George. Kheelan meant to say *Fairy Mother*. Trust me you have both of your parent's DNA running through your veins, but you also have the powerful blood of Aspen AusFeuer-DieErde. This makes you an exceptional young woman."

I pull my hands free from Rose's, leaping to my feet. My chair skids backwards before toppling over, landing with a loud thud. I don't bother to put it upright, "I need to take a walk, clear my head. This is a lot to take in." I don't wait for permission. My vision has gone blurry, all I can see is the open lawn. The need to get to it is strong as I push past Kheelan and stumble down the few steps. Kodi appears at my side, her clear blue eyes bore into mine as she nudges my hand.

"Whatever you need dear." Rose is standing at the railing next to Kheelan, her hands fiddling nervously at a fallen leaf. "We do need to finish this conversation though. When you feel up to it, will you come back?"

I nod as I make my way into the forest, needing both the comfort and the privacy it offers. I don't have a destination in mind, I just walk, and keep walking. I'm blind to where I'm going, my sight has gone inwards replaying the story Rose told and sorting through all the revelations that followed. I can't believe that just a couple of weeks ago I had no idea what to do with my life, what path to take. Now my future has been laid out for me. The fates of not *one*, not even *two*, but *three* worlds are resting on my shoulders? I let out a frustrated scream, the sound absorbing into the trees and mossy ground around me and sending a family of birds scattering into the sky. What I wouldn't give to go back to being clueless. Life isn't fair.

Time stands still as I wander for what must be hours of wallowing in self-pity. Kodi stays by my side the entire time, not even tempted by the squirrels skittering around in the branches above. I've put all my trust in a *dog* to stop me before I walk off a cliff or straight into a den of wolves. I try to stop myself from thinking after a while. I'm tired of thinking. Instead, I concentrate on clearing my mind, but it doesn't work. I only stop walking when the barn is looming over me. I go around and greet the horses, petting each one in turn, telling them how pretty and handsome they are. That's when I feel his presence beside me.

"I dreamt of you," I say, "before we met." I steal a peak at his face, but he doesn't look surprised.

"I know," he admits. My mouth drops open, I whip around to look at him full on as he continues. "I dreamt of you, too."

I'm speechless.

He laughs, "It freaked me out too. I've never had anything like that happen before. When you showed up the other day, I worried I subconsciously sent you that dream or something." He smiles his eyes sparkling down at me, "My grandma is teaching me how to communicate with people through dreams. My other theory was that I dreamt up the perfect girl and the universe sent you to my doorstep..." He nudges me playfully with his shoulder.

I laugh, "I am rather dreamy." My first dream jumps to the forefront of my mind, "I don't think you sent it though. And I definitely know you didn't imagine me into existence," I laugh, "The Fates sent it to both of us."

He raises one eyebrow, I hurry to explain my dream to him, not skimping on any details. When I finish, he looks into my eyes with a meaningful purpose, his own shining electric. "Well," he starts, "I guess that makes a little more sense than my theory." He smiles, "A *destiny* dream, huh? Well, I for one am glad we found each other." He keeps his eyes locked on my face, as seconds tick by. I feel a blush start to creep up my neck towards my cheeks while the silence stretches on. Finally, he breaks it, "Wanna go for a ride?"

I grin. "Yes, but only if I get Oberon."

"Deal."

Riding is a dream. It feels like I've been riding Oberon my entire life. As soon as I'm in the saddle he becomes an extension of my body. Kheelan says I'm a natural, even for a Fairling. I agree when he says I was born to be on a horse. It feels right. Even still, he starts us out slow, giving some instruction on posture and form. Before long, we're galloping. The speed is exactly what I need, the rush it brings is like nothing I've ever felt before. I put all my trust into the beautiful beast and let my thoughts scatter like leaves in the wind behind us. Leaving my mind empty and light.

* * *

"Before you tell me more, I'd like to ask my questions." I'm sitting on Rose's couch my back against the armrest with my legs pulled up to my chest, facing my aunt who is seated at the other end of the sofa watching me. She looks worried, she probably thinks I'm on the verge of a mental breakdown. I can't blame her, I'm a little concerned about that myself.

"I will try my best to get them all answered." She says, her voice low and gentle. The same tone you use on a child who has finally stopped screaming.

"Thanks. First of all, this deciding the fate of the three worlds business, what's that mean?"

"I'm not sure. I can only guess. My guess would be whichever side has The Stave is the side that holds the power." My aunt says.

"What's a stave?" I say quietly, knowing it's probably a stupid question.

Rose smiles, "It's a magical staff, like a walking stick or giant wand. According to legend it's been missing for thousands of years, before even King Beaumont's time."

"How are we supposed to find something that's been missing for so long? Are we sure it even exists?" I sink into the couch as the impossibility of the situation weighs on me. I want to cry, instead I take a deep breath and ask my next question, "Is there *any* chance this prophecy thing could mean someone else? *Anyone* else?" I can't help the pleading tone that creeps into my voice.

Rose's pale blue eyes are sympathetic. "I'm not sure dear. Queen Lucille seemed quite certain that you're the one. I haven't heard the prophecy myself, I'm only half Fairling, so I'm certain I was told the minimal amount of details necessary to pass along to you and Kheelan. You're to start training at once, and I think you'll surprise yourself with what you're capable o—"

"—*You're* half Fairling? How does that work?" The question bursts out of me, the shock of Rose's revelation straightening my spine to attention as I take in my feeble looking aunt.

My reaction gets a hearty laugh out of her at least, her shoulders relaxing a bit. "Well, dear, my mother was a Fairling, but my father was a human, so here I am."

Duh. I should have been able to figure that one out on my own. I move on, not wanting to forget any of my questions. "I was late with Awakening." It's not a question, but I pause to let Rose nod in agreement. "And you knew, and this Queen lady knew I was a Fairling?" Rose nods again. "Why wait *two* years if time is of the essence?" I stop, this is the question that's been bothering me the most. If an Underling was squelching me this entire time, why didn't someone try to stop it sooner? Especially if I'm supposed to be deciding the fates of the worlds they live in? Wouldn't they want me to have as much power as possible?

"The Queen hadn't been in contact with me until the night before I called you." Rose explains, "She informed me that she had been having several council meetings with the Fates. She didn't give me many details to go on, just the bit about the prophecy and how they're certain that you, my niece, is the girl mentioned." She looks at me, her eyes brimming with remorse. "I had no idea you hadn't Awakened on your own until that night, dear. I promise."

I scoot down the couch and reach out for my aunt, pulling her into a hug. "I didn't mean to sound accusing." I murmur breathing in her perfume, Chanel number 5, as what she says fully sinks in. The *Fairy Queen* had contacted her, to chat about *me*? Unreal. I pull out of our embrace, "Why not the Fairies then? Why didn't they try to Awaken me?"

My aunt dabs a balled-up tissue at the corners of her eyes. "Fairies are selfish. I'm sure she didn't even care about your existence until the prophecy was brought to her immediate attention."

I stare into the flames crackling in the fireplace, mulling this over in my head. It doesn't matter how powerful Rose thinks I am, I know I'd be useless in any form of battle. I try to picture myself wielding a sword, or even perched on top of a building with a sniper rifle. I smile, there's no way.

Aunt Rose leans over and places her cold hand on top of mine, startling me out of my imaginings. "I know this is a lot to absorb, but you're taking it marvellously." She lets out a light laugh, "When Kheelan Awakened, he locked himself in his room and didn't speak to anyone for an entire week! He only came out to eat, then he'd go right back to his room, slamming and locking the door behind him! Maggie was beside herself with worry."

I laugh, it does make me feel better knowing that Kheelan, who always seems to have it together freaked out about all of this as well.

"Do you have any more questions, dear?" Rose asks.

I nod, "One more," I suck in a breath of air, knowing this is one of the weirdest things I'll ever ask. "What exactly are Fairlings? I know we're half Fairy, and that my eyes light up sometimes, but what else can we *do*?"

A grin spreads across Rose's face. "I thought you'd never ask!" Her eyes twinkle. "What you mentioned, your eyes lighting up we call that our *Glow*. Our Glow connects us to all living things, it's what makes Fairlings more in tune with nature. It may be hard to tell now because I'm so old, but we're a pretty bunch." A smile pulls at her lips, like she's remembering another time. "Humans are attracted to us. It's probably them sensing our Glow, some humans, who are more in touch with their gut instincts, may be frightened by the draw they feel." She pauses to think, the fire pulling her gaze. "You'll find you're faster, and stronger than you were before you Awakened, you'll heal faster too. We have the ability to heal others, with the light of our glow, we also have a strong intuition when it comes to medicinal plants for mixing salves and such." She turns her eyes back to me, "Fairlings have enhanced senses, they're nimble, more durable, and have a way with animals. I've never been invited to join a Fairling Clan because my blood isn't strong enough, so I don't know much about full Fairlings and their abilities. I did hear once that some can shape shift. Apparently, that gift is extremely rare."

I nod, absorbing her words. Excitement rings in my ears, I have *powers*, "Can we fly?" I ask.

Rose laughs, "Only full Fairies have wings. Although, I suppose a Fairling capable of shape-shifting would be able to turn into a bird and fly that way."

"Wow." I manage to whisper, deciding this whole Fairling thing might be pretty cool after all.

"Any more questions?" Rose asks. I shake my head, relief flashes through her eyes. "Good, I have a few more things I need to tell you, and then my official duty is done." She smiles broadly, it's clear this situation has been straining on her and she wants to get it over with.

I nod my head in agreement, but I don't think I can take anymore. How can there even be more?

"So Kheelan has an older brother named Declan. We all thought he died in the same car accident that killed his mother. However, the Royal Council believes that Herne had caught wind of the prophecy back then and tried to take both boys. Except he only succeeded in getting his hands on one." My heart stills. Does Kheelan know his brother might still be alive? He must be falling to pieces inside.

"If his brother is alive and a car crash didn't kill him, does that mean their mother was murdered by whoever took him?"

Rose takes a sip from her water, the ice clinking against the sides of her glass, "Yes, I'm afraid so. It was no accident."

I shudder. I can't imagine how confused Kheelan must have felt losing his mother and brother all at once. Having to move to a new town to live in a new house with his grandmother. And he was only four. My heart aches, and now he's reliving the whole nightmare, learning his mother's death was planned, and his brother might still be alive.

"Kheelan's father is a member of the Wild Hunt." Rose continues, reclaiming every bit of my attention.

"What?" I say astounded, "What does that make Kheelan? Is he not a Fairling?"

"Technically, he's a type of Underling." Rose confirms. My blood runs cold. "However," she goes on, "his father loved his mother, and the boys were created by love."

"I don't understand."

"It means they conceived the boys the old-fashioned way, except in his case one human, one Fairy. Still makes a Fairling. Same as you, except only one human's DNA." Rose smiles at the confusion still on my face. "He's not weaker, or stronger." She assures me, "And I've seen his glow, he is aligned with The Light. He's a beautiful blue. If he wasn't aligned with the Light, he'd glow a deep red, like fire. Your light can't lie."

"So they have his brother, he was created same as Kheelan. Are they squelching him?"

"No, he was taken when he was only six." Her voice goes quiet, "The fear is, they raised him in the darkness, distinguishing his light completely. If he's alive, he's a full fledge Underling now." She studies me, gaging my reaction to the information, but I'm a statue. Frozen in fear from this real-life ghost story. She continues, "If this is the case, and Declan is alive, the three who are to determine the fate of the worlds are split."

I force a laugh, it sounds more like a choking noise, "No pressure or anything."

Rose smiles, "That's it!" She says her voice oddly cheerful, "You officially know everything I know." She leaps to her feet, apparently happy to be done with her task. It's as though years melt away before my eyes, she really doesn't do well under stress. "One last thing," she starts pushing her walker towards the kitchen. "Your parents and sister are expected back tomorrow by lunch. I want to go over your training schedule before then. Some of the time they'll think you're at work, you'll have to make the early morning runs seem like your idea. We don't want to raise any questions." She stops and turns towards me, her face serious, all evidence of her smile gone, "They can't know you're a Fairling. It's too dangerous for humans."

My stomach drops, Jen already has noticed things. How am I supposed to keep such a huge part of my life hidden from the one person I tell everything to?

Chapter Seven

My parents start their journey home two days later, after a lot of hugs and tears, both happy and sad. Mindy, the sweet middle-aged woman who helps Rose around her house is successful with securing a job for Jen at the hospital. They're desperate for workers and she's able to start right away. She works mostly nights, which means she sleeps late every morning. She doesn't even notice the routine I settle into over the next few weeks, and it's a full one.

Each day starts with Kheelan dragging me out of bed at five in the morning to run five miles, then he forces me to spar for an hour. The only thing that gets me through it is knowing that Mindy will have enough food to feed a small village waiting for us to devour when we finish. Once our bellies are satisfied, we go our separate ways. Him to the stables, and I go to *Maggie's Roses,* Aunt Rose and Maggie's flower shop. After work, I take Kodiak for a hike. On rare days, Jen is able to join us before she goes into the hospital. My feet automatically start each hike the same way— going past the barn to see if Kheelan has finished for the day. I ignore the burst of happiness that lights up my chest on the days he's already waiting for us. He has a *girlfriend,* it doesn't *mean* anything, we're just *friends,* I'm constantly reminding the annoying voice in the back of my head. I go to Rose's house for dinner each evening, staying late at least three times a week for *'glow'* classes.

When we first start running, Kheelan is much faster than me. It's obvious he's slowing his normal pace a significant amount for my benefit. By the middle of the second week, he's the one pushing to keep up with me. I feel my legs growing stronger every day.

Combat is another story. I suck at it. I'm fast, but that's it. Or maybe Kheelan is that much better than me. Either way, I get my butt kicked every day. Kheelan is sweet to remind me almost as often that he's been training for years and reassures me I'll get better over time. I just need to *'keep practicing'*. I have a hunch that he caught on pretty fast though, everything he does seems to come easy. He makes all his movements look effortless and fluid, especially compared to my own, which are stiff and unnatural. I find I have to force my ears to stay on when he's demonstrating a new strike or counterstrike, otherwise I'm in danger of becoming only eyes, stuck in a daydream induced by his graceful motions and flexing muscles, which I find more beautiful than intimidating.

Then there's glow practice, trying to make my eyes light up on *purpose*. Turns out, it's not so easy when you want it to happen. For me at least, Kheelan, of course, makes it look easy. He's even able to concentrate his glow to singular body parts—which is how he was able to calm my mind the night after the campfire by kissing my forehead—he's a big show off. His favourites are making his hand glow for high fives, or his nose while he sings 'Kheelan the bright-nosed boy'—a parody he came up with using the melody of 'Rudolph the Red Nosed Reindeer'. These party tricks do nothing to boost my confidence, even though he swears to me every session that he wasn't able to control it at all when he first Awakened. Rose and Maggie are patient as saints with my lack of glowing, and Kheelan's goofing-off. I'm startled when I first meet Maggie by how similar her and Rose look, it's hard to believe they're not sisters. The most distinguishable difference being Maggie prefers to wear her hair in a long white braid down her back instead of in a neat bun like Rose.

"Breathe in the light and breathe out the shadows!" Maggie always chants while Rose has us meditating, trying to help us connect with our inner light. In two weeks, I haven't been able to muster even the slightest flicker. The two older women would never verbalise it, but I can tell this has them worried.

Glow practice leaves me mentally drained on top of my physical exhaustion. It takes all the strength I can muster to trudge along the path back to our little cabin each night. I try to wait up for Jen, but my heavy eyelids always win, sending me into a deep sleep with a nightmare featuring the Wild Hunt long before she gets home.

'Maggie's Rose' is an enchanting shop. It's a small cottage nestled on a tree lined street a few blocks from the main square with a small greenhouse out back. Besides Rose, Maggie, and now myself there's one other employee, Emily. She's my age, with a beautiful olive complexion, long shiny black hair, and observant chocolate eyes. Jen was right, we hit it off immediately, and I'm thrilled to have a friend. Jen's been so busy at work I'm lucky if I get to spend more than ten minutes with her. My new life revolves around Fairies, Fairlings, and The Wild Hunt. Going to the flower shop and hanging out with Emily is a nice, and much needed dose of normalcy. Rose and Maggie hardly make an appearance at the shop. When they do, they spend all their time in the greenhouse, so it's Emily who teaches me everything I need to know; the pricing of certain flowers, what colours complement well in a bouquet, how to use the cash register, the tending of the plants we grow in the greenhouse, and she even points out which of the regular customers are a pain-in-the-butt.

My favourite part about my new job is the naturals corner. Everything is made in house out of a recipe book written in Maggie's careful penmanship. I take the book home with me most nights, reading for as long as I'm able to keep my eyes open, drinking in as much knowledge about local plants and all their medicinal, and non-medicinal uses as I can. On my third day, I'm successful in making a poultice out of pitch, which I collected myself from the Lodgepole Pine, which helps to relieve muscle and joint aches. By the end of my second week, I'm turning sage brush leaves into a tonic to treat digestive disorders and sore throats without any help. By the start of my third week, I create my first original recipe using the sap of a Douglas Fir, lavender oil, and beeswax. It's an antiseptic salve for cuts and rashes. Maggie is delighted and insists I add it into the recipe book. Beaming with pride, I take extra care forming each letter, wanting my page to be as tidy as the others.

Running off the high of creating my first recipe, I'm beginning to feel confident in my ability to run all the shop operations with minimal help from Emily, which I prove by getting through the morning rush on my own. It's almost noon and one customer remains, a guy in a black leather jacket busy looking at our selection of lotions in the far corner of the shop.

Emily brushes past me as she returns from the back room, "That guy keeps looking at you." She hisses in my ear.

I glance up just as his head whips back to the lotion jar in his hand. "No, he's not. He's looking at the lotions."

Emily rolls her eyes, "He's cute. I think he was in here last week too…" Her voice trails off and she nudges me with her elbow her eyes gleaming with mischief, "WELP! I'm taking my lunch break. You're on your own for thirty minutes, don't burn the place down," she says, her voice too loud. She walks swiftly to the front door, not giving me a chance to object. She pauses to throw me a menacing look as she yanks the door open and disappears down the sidewalk. The tinkling of the bell is the only sound that remains in the shop, which suddenly feels too quiet.

I throw a nervous look in the direction of the stranger. Well, he's definitely looking at me now. My cheeks burn hot. God, I hope he didn't hear her antics! He's smirking though, which means he probably did. Nervous butterflies erupt in my stomach as he starts to walk towards the counter. "Don't throw up," I instruct myself under my breath.

The bells on the door tingle again, causing the stranger to pause mid-stride. Saved by the bell. I let out a breath of relief as we both turn our attention to the newcomer. I gulp, full on nausea replacing the butterflies as I register the new customer. It's Allie and she doesn't look happy. She zeros her sights in on me, beelining for the counter. I rack my brain, trying to figure out what I possibly could have done to make her look so angry, but I can't think of anything.

"What is going on between you and *my* boyfriend?" She demands, her eyes unblinking, stunning me into silence.

I open my mouth, but no words come, I probably look like a dying fish. I shoot a glance at our one-person audience, but he's gone. I realise

I'm holding my breath. I let it out slow, buying time to collect myself and figure out a response to her crazy allegation. "What do you mean?" I lamely ask.

"What I *mean* is I hardly see him anymore, and it seems like he's spending all of his spare time with *you*." She spits the words out with so much venom I stumble back a step. She doesn't slow down, "I hope you're happy being a home wrecker!" Her nostrils flare with rage.

I put my hands up in defence, "Whoa! First of all, I'm not a home wrecker. I *promise* nothing is going on between Kheelan and me, we're just friends." I hold her wild gaze, but guilt floods my stomach as all the times I've wished we were more than *just friends* flashes through my mind. *But you haven't acted on anything,* the small voice in the back of my mind reminds me, *you really are just friends.*

"Then why is he always hanging out with you and not me?" Her voice cracks, anger giving way to her pain. "Everything was perfect until you showed up." She glares through the tears that are beginning to well in her big brown eyes.

I hate awkward situations like this. I never know what to say. "I'm sorry," I offer, silently pleading with her not to cry. I can't deal with criers, especially when it's someone I don't even like that much. I reach over the counter and pat her shoulder. It feels weird, so I pull my hand back and busy myself by re-stacking the pile of receipts in front of me. "Have you tried talking to Kheelan?"

"No," she sniffles, "I don't want him to think I'm a crazy person. We've only been dating for a few months…" She trails off as a half laugh, half sob bubbles out of her.

I force a laugh, hoping she doesn't take it as me laughing at her. "Well, I guess it's good you got the crazy out with me then. I swear there's nothing going on between us."

Allie lets out a heavy sigh as she wipes her tears on her sleeve. "I'm sorry. I guess I may have overreacted. It's just that you're *so* beautiful and whenever I do get to see him, he goes on and on about how funny you are, and how smart you are." She shrugs, "And then I was just stewing about everything today and I guess I let my emotions boil over a little."

I weave my way around the counter and open my arms, offering a hug. I instantly regret it. She rushes into them and releases the waterworks. I don't know what to do, so I just stand there. A stone statue holding this girl who might as well be a stranger, while she gets her gooey tears all over my shirt.

That's how Emily finds us. "How'd it go?" She sings as she strolls through the shop's door, coming to a sudden halt, one eyebrow shooting up as she takes in the scene before her.

I meet her eyes over Allie's shoulder and mouth the word 'help'. But she just stands there staring, her eyebrow frozen in place, a look of horror rearranging her other features.

"I should go." Allie says, her words coming out fast. She wipes her eyes one last time as she mumbles another apology and pushes past Emily through the open door.

"What was *that*?" Emily's eyes are gleaming as she bursts into laughter.

"You don't want to know," I moan, "But apparently I'm a home wrecking hussy who is trying to steal Kheelan from her."

"Ha! That's fabulous. We've been in need of some drama around here. You were starting to get boring."

"Ha-ha," I say, unable to hold back my grin as we both head to the back of the shop where I retrieve the sandwich I packed for lunch out of the mini fridge.

Emily leans against the wall behind the register, folding her arms in a protective manner over her chest, her eyes lock on my face. "Is there anything going on between you and Kheelan?" She finally asks, her voice void of any emotion.

I throw her an exasperated look, and swallow my bite of sandwich, "Of course not!"

"No judgement from me, I would never think of you as a home-wrecking hussy," she promises. "He's hot! And after all, you're only," she pauses as she considers her next words, her eyes glued to my face as she finally finishes her sentence, "human." She doesn't blink, as though gauging my reaction.

I feel the blood leave my face as I stare back. Am I being paranoid, or did she pause way too long before saying human? And why did she say it like that? Like she wasn't sure I am one? I force a light laugh. I must be imagining things, people don't go around accusing people of not being human. "He is hot," I finally say while taking another big bite of my lunch before throwing the remaining crust into the trash can.

She bursts into laughter. "Wow! You're a terrible actress. You definitely need to practice keeping your expressions on lockdown. You're like an open book." She laughs harder, and then her face goes sombre. "What if I were part of The Hunt, or someone you needed to hide your identity from?"

I go rigid. How does she know about The Hunt? *Is* she someone I need to be hiding from?

"Relax!" She reaches out, resting her hand on my arm. "I'm not going to tell anyone. I've actually had my suspicions for a while." She smiles at me, "Did you know when you smell flowers, your skin glimmers? It's not super noticeable, but when the sun hits you the right way you can see it. Not to mention the effect you have on people. Has anyone ever *not* liked you before? I almost want to dislike you, just because no one else does. Allie should hate you, and yet she was here, crying in your arms *hugging* you. Then there's the fact that you can do every task perfectly, after being shown how to do it *once*." She grins, "And seriously, *no one* comes up with a working recipe after mixing for only two weeks."

My jaw drops to the floor. Is all of that true? Do I actually *glimmer* when I smell flower? That's *weird*. I've never been exceptional at school, am I really a fast learner? It's not like anything we do in the shop is difficult.

Emily shrugs, "I come from a very spiritual background, being Native American. My Grandfather used to tell me stories of the Forest People all the time. No offence, but it's not like you're trying to hide what you are."

I take a deep breath as everything she just said settles over me. I work to keep my voice neutral, "Forest People?"

"Sorry, I mean Fairies. I just hate saying 'Fairy tales', it makes it all sound so childish." She shrugs her shoulders again as though determined to prove that all of this is no big deal to her.

"I'm not a Fairy." I stammer, not sure how I should be reacting to all of this. Should I deny everything? Convince her she's crazy?

"Lia, my God! Please relax. You look terrified. Your aunt knows I know all about this stuff and you don't see her freaking out. I'm sorry, you're not a Fairy. I know Fairies can't stay human-sized for long periods of time. My guess would be you're a child of a Fairy or a half of *something.*"

"A Fairling," the confirmation comes out barely above a whisper. But as soon as it does, I'm flooded with relief. I decide I'm glad to be able to share this part of my life with someone. Keeping it from Jen is killing me.

"Good. So now that that's out of the way," Emily continues, "Is there something going on between you and Kheelan?"

"NO!" I insist. "He has a girlfriend and contrary to popular belief around this town, I am *not* a home wrecking hussy." I laugh.

"But you find him attractive?" She wiggles her eyebrows at me.

I laugh again, "I think everyone finds him attractive."

Something on my face must give me away. Emily raises her eyebrows, a knowing smile tugging her lips upwards, "And if he didn't have a girlfriend, would things be different?"

I shrug, "Maybe. Honestly, I thought he was the reason I was supposed to come to Wyoming. But it's turning out to be much bigger than just him."

"What do you mean the reason you were supposed to come here? Did you know him before?"

"No, that's the weird part. I never even saw a picture of him before. I had a dream about him right before Rose called to invite me out here." I laugh to ease the serious air that has settled over the room. "Jen, my sister, is convinced he's my *soulmate.*"

Emily's face darkens. "Soulmates? That sounds heavy. What do you think?"

"I think he has a girlfriend and my sister is crazy. It was just a dream." I look down at my hands and force another laugh, not liking the direction our conversation is going.

"What about that hot customer that was in here, did you give him your number?" Emily wiggles her eyebrows at me again, her face hopeful.

I don't have to force my laugh this time, "Allie did the honours of scaring him off before any words could be exchanged."

She smiles, "He'll be back," she says, "mark my word."

* * *

I'm not sure what to say to Kheelan, or if I should say anything at all about what happened with Allie. I decide it's easiest to skip walking by the barn today, save the decision for later. But Kodi has other plans and races ahead of me, forcing me to take our usual path. My heart leaps when we round the bend and see that Kheelan is waiting for us, leaning against his truck bed, his easy smile spreading over his face when he sees me. I decide his relationship is none of my business, it's up to Allie to talk to him. He tips his cowboy hat in greeting and falls into step beside me. We don't talk. I find comfort in his silent presence as we make our way through the forest, the only sound coming from the birds singing around us and our soft steps through the pine needled forest floor. I breathe deeply, letting the smell of pine and cedar ease my mind.

"I don't know about you," Kheelan says breaking the silence as we enter a clearing filled with wildflowers, "but I'm exhausted." He plops onto the ground and sprawls out, tucking his hands behind his head, grinning up at me. "What do you say to us just laying here and relaxing for a bit before Rose and Maggie exhaust our minds as well?"

I smile and give in, taking care to leave a respectable amount of space between us as I situate myself next to him. I stare at the perfectly blue sky above us, I can feel him watching me, but I don't turn my head. "What's wrong?" He finally asks. "You haven't said a word all day."

I sigh, "Sorry, there's just been so much on my mind." I turn my head slightly to smile at him what I hope to be a reassuring one.

"I find it's easiest to start with the heaviest thing that's weighing on you, and the rest will follow suit."

I let out a breath of a laugh, "You asked for it."

"Lay it on me, lady."

"Well, first of all, we're kicking our butts for these *beings* we've never even met before and these worlds we're not even a part of." I sigh, "I don't know. It just doesn't seem fair, we're only teenagers. We should be drinking beer and sneaking out, not training for an impossible mission."

"It is our world now," he says, his voice gentle.

"This is our world." I motion around us. "Earth. Not the OtherWorld and *definitely* not the NetherWorld. But they still expect us to save them all, single-handedly."

He chuckles nudging me with his shoulder, "Not single-handily, we've got each other so it's double-handily." He laughs at his joke then takes a deep breath, "Can I tell you something? But you have to promise not to laugh."

I sneak a glance at his face, it's dead pan. He's being serious, so I nod my agreement.

"You make me feel different. Sometimes I feel like I can't help but be happy when you're around, even if I'm so tired I just want to scream. Like right now." His eyes lock on mine. "You make me feel stronger too. It makes me believe that together we will be able to hunt down the Lost Stave."

My glow bursts to life in my chest. The warmth creeping through my limbs as an uncontrollable longing for him to kiss me sweeps through my body. I stomp the thought down and tear my eyes away from his, focusing on a puffy white cloud that's floating by as I concentrate on subduing the glow from spreading any further. When I manage to smother the warmth, I take a deep breath and pray my voice doesn't crack, "Speaking of happy,

Allie stopped by the flower shop today." I hope my words sting. I'm not the one who's supposed to be making him feel that way.

Kheelan turns his face back towards the sky, closing his eyes. A few beats pass before he speaks. "I don't know how to act around her anymore. Not since you arrived."

"You need to talk to her. She's going crazy."

"I know. I do love her," my heart stills at his words, I didn't realise he felt so strongly for her, "and she does make me feel happy, but all I can think about is how my world," he looks at me, his blue eyes determined for me to understand, "*our world,* isn't safe for her."

I turn my head away from him, busying myself by scanning for Kodi. She's a few yards away sniffing around at the tree line. My heart aches, both from jealousy of his love for her and because I feel bad for him, my *friend.* "None of this is fair," I say as the realisation hits me like a hammer to my gut. His situation is how both of our lives will be forever. "I guess we might as well say goodbye to any chance of a normal life now." I let out a frustrated groan, "And that's all I want, a normal life! I didn't ask for this. The stupid Fairies are forcing us into these roles. They've stolen such a huge part of our lives that we'll never get to experience now." The words burst out, surprising even me, but I mean every single one.

Kheelan bolts up and stares down at me, his eyes fierce. "Lia, this is our *purpose.* It's what we were born to do, fight for The Light. Sure, I'm sad about Allie, but I'm happy to commit my life to the Fae and to The Light. You should be too. It's our destiny." His eyes darken, a streak of white flashing through his iris causing the hairs on my neck stand on end.

I scramble to my feet as uneasiness grips me. I don't understand why. He's passionate, it's a *good* thing. Still my anxiety doesn't ease. I need to move. I can't stay still. "We," my voice comes out as a croak. I clear my throat, "we should go. I don't want to be late for glow practice."

* * *

96

"Try to concentrate on not concentrating," Rose instructs as she sits in a chair in front of Kheelan and myself. She has us sitting cross legged in her backyard. My eyes are shut but I can't get what I think I saw this afternoon out of my head. I slit them a crack to peek, Kheelan already has light pouring out of him, his eyes bright blue—irritation at how easy it is for him replaces my uneasiness. Of course they're blue, it's Kheelan. Strong, sturdy, loyal Kheelan. It was a trick of the light, that's all. And anyways *white* is the colour of the good side. It'd be different if I'd seen black or red.

I open my eyes the rest of the way to glare at my aunt, annoyance ringing through in my voice, "How am I supposed to not concentrate by concentrating on not concentrating?"

Rose chuckles at my remark. "I'm only trying to help dear," she pauses as she considers her next words. "All right, just clear your mind. Try to focus on your breathing. Breathe in every happy thought you can and exhale all the negative energy."

"There's something I've been wanting to try," Kheelan interjects, his light flickering off. He turns his body so he's facing me. "Turn and face me, Lia," he commands. I do as he says and place both my hands gently into his waiting palms. The familiar recognition that runs up my arms when we touch makes me smile. He smiles back and looks intently into my eyes. "I have a hunch," he says, "that we make each other a little stronger," I gaze into his warm blue eyes, not sure how I allowed myself to feel so much anxiety from their passion earlier today. I know Kheelan, and with everything I know about this new world we're a part of, the only thing I'm one hundred percent sure about is that he's good through and through. I keep my eyes fixed on his and let everything around us fade away. I think of the kiss we shared in our dream, the moment I first saw him, the soft kiss he placed on my forehead, the way his eyes seem bluer after we run, him breathing on top of me after he's pinned me in a sparring match, all these memories crash through my head all at once. My chest bursts. This time I don't try to stop it. I let it spread, encourage it as it creeps down my arms and up my neck. I can't stop the grin that spreads over my mouth, I finally called the glow. Kheelan rips his eyes away from mine and holds out our hands to examine them. "Huh," is all he says.

I look down to see what's so upsetting to him, my heart sinks and my light goes out. "You're so much brighter than me." Kheelan's light dissipates at my words. He looks up to Rose who hasn't made a sound. She doesn't need to. Her furrowed brow says it all.

She's quick to collect herself when she sees that we're both looking at her and feigns happiness that I finally called the glow. She says it's a major feat, I should go home and get some rest—Jen will be home soon and it would be good if the two of us could spend some time together. She worries about how much my sister has been working. She bids us good night and Kheelan walks with me in the direction of the small cabin. He doesn't say anything, I know he's as worried as Rose. It must be bad that I'm so much dimmer than him. I'm not as strong as they all thought.

We come to a stop in front of my cabin. The light is on inside, Jen must have gotten off early. I begin to say good night, but Kheelan cuts me off. "Your light is dimmer than I thought it would be, Lia." He finally voices his worry, combing his fingers through his dark waves as he looks up at the darkening sky. He lets out a long breath, lowering his gaze back to mine, "I think it's time we start making a plan to get your light back."

I nod, of course that's why I'm dimmer—Jesse had been stealing my light.

"It'll be a perilous mission," he continues, "but I think you'll be in more danger being so dim. You won't be able to defend yourself against a Hunter, or even an Underling if God forbid, one comes after you. Not to mention trying to recover the Lost Stave. We'll talk with Rose and my grandma, hopefully tomorrow. They aren't going to like it, but I saw Rose's face tonight. She knows just as much as I do, you're at risk." He studies my face. "Don't worry Lia, as long as I'm around nothing will hurt you," he promises. "Try to get some sleep." He bends forward and kisses the top of my head, sending calmness into my mind just as the cabin door opens. He turns and walks down the driveway towards the barn and his parked truck.

"Good night," I mutter at his retreating back. I turn and walk towards my sister's silhouette. As she comes into focus, I can see the ecstatic look on her face, excitement is practically oozing out of her. She saw him kiss my head and now her imagination is running wild.

Chapter Eight

I'm barely through the door and Jen is on top of me. "Something's going on between you two, and don't tell me I'm wrong!" Her eyes shining with hurt. "Why aren't you telling me things? I feel like you've become a stranger to me since we've been out here."

Guilt burns in my gut as I furiously blink back the tears that are threatening to spill. I hate lying to my sister, but I made a promise to Rose. I have to keep the Fairy aspect of my life a secret. To keep Jen safe. "It's not what you think," I finally say as I plop onto my bed.

"How do you know what I think? We haven't spoken in ages." My sister sits on the edge of her bed. Her eyes fixed on my face, full of unspoken accusations.

"We speak every day," I say. I don't look at her, I keep my eyes riveted on the aged wooden planks above me.

"Not really though, you've been going to bed before I get home and I know that's partially my fault. I've had to work late almost every day since I've started, but you're waking up so early too. I hate how little we see each other. I don't even know if you like it here." She goes quiet her shoulders slumping in defeat.

I turn my head to look at her, "I *love* it here. Seriously, I've never felt more like me," I wish I could tell her more.

She smiles, "Good. That makes me happy." But her face is drawn and tired. I know she senses there are things being left unsaid and it's killing me that I'm the reason for her dejection. "I'm learning a lot at the hospital. I think I've made the right decision with my major." She offers.

I scoot up and prop myself against my headboard. "Have you seen a lot of blood?" I wrinkle my nose at the thought of gruesome hospital scenes from movies.

Jen laughs, "I've seen some, but nothing too gory yet."

"No grizzly attacks?"

"No! Oh God, I didn't even think about how that's a possibility out here." She wrinkles her nose, "I hope I don't have to see that."

We sit in heavy silence for some time. My mind drifts to the prophecy, how we're supposed to find the stave and how hard it will be without my light. I want to tell my sister all of this. I yearn for her input, knowing she'd know exactly what to say to make me feel better. But a voice nags in the back of my mind, Kheelan's voice, reminding me that our world isn't safe for the people we love.

Jen's voice breaks through my thoughts, "What were you guys talking about out there? You and Kheelan?"

I shrug, "Nothing really."

Jen eyes me, "It looked serious." She lays down flat on her back. "He likes you. I can tell by the way he looks at you. Like you're the only person in the world who matters."

"He has a girlfriend." I feel like a broken record with how often I've had to say that recently.

"For now," she half smiles, "I'm being serious when I say he's your soulmate. You don't just dream about a person you've never met before and then meet him a week later." She turns her head in my direction. "Seriously. That's not something that happens outside of a supernatural movie." She waits for me to say something, but I don't. What can I say? She's right, it doesn't happen outside of supernatural movies. What she doesn't know is I happen to be living in one. She mumbles a good night and clicks the lamp on the nightstand off, simultaneously sending the cabin into pitch blackness and shattering my heart into a million pieces.

* * *

"Only one can live boy, and you must choose!" A shrill voice cackles, making the hairs on the back of my neck stand on end. I'm sitting on hot metal and the smell of sulphur stings my nostrils. I stand up, the ground wobbles sending me forward. My hands grasp the bars in front of me. I'm in a giant bird cage dangling above a pit of molten lava.

Uncontrollable screaming echoes around me. My eyes make their way around the enormous cavern, scanning the rough, rocky walls, until they land on the source of the noise. My heart drops into my stomach. It's Allie, suspended in a cage of her own a few yards from myself, tears mixed with mascara streaming down her face. What I thought were wordless wails erupting from her are actual words meant for someone below us, begging for them to help her. My eyes match the panicked rhythm of my heart as they dart around the space until finally finding who she's shouting to. Kheelan's face comes into focus mirroring my own fear as he stares up at us. He's standing at the edge of the lava pit, a golden sword hanging limply by his side.

"Rise and shine Rosalia! Glad you could join us." The familiar voice is like a trickle of ice down my spine. I tear my eyes away from Kheelan, searching for the horned man. I find him standing on a cliff just above Kheelan, his eyes full of menace, watching me. "I was just telling your dear friend how generous I'm feeling today." My eyes dart back to Kheelan, my heart's pounding quickens as the situation settles over me. I can't help him. I'm trapped. "Don't worry Fairling, I've decided to let him live! After all, I require a messenger for your dear Queen." He smiles revealing his revolting grey, pointy teeth. "I'm feeling extra generous. I've informed him that you, or the screaming girl could go with him." His smile widens, the red glow from the lava casting eerie shadows across his face, "But *only* one. He must choose which one of you will die."

"I can't," Kheelan chokes out.

"Then they'll both die!" The cage around me jolts downwards, Allie's screams cut off. I look at her, her eyes are wild staring back at me. Her cage has plummeted as well.

I whip my head back towards Kheelan, fresh panic bubbling up my throat wanting to come out as a scream. I force it down. He looks back at me, his eyes pleading for me to understand. "She's my girlfriend. I'm sorry, Lia." With his decision, my cage drops at an alarming speed towards the lava. The scream I tried to swallow comes back and finds its way through my lips as I crash towards the molten liquid.

I land hard on my bed.

I lay staring up at the stars through the window next to me, my heart hammering so loud I'm afraid it'll wake Jen. Kheelan promised to keep me safe, and even though he hasn't been in my life long, I trust him. I try to convince myself that he meant what he said, but my nightmare is too fresh. I know if Kheelan had to choose between my life and Allie's, he'd choose Allie. He loves her, I'm just a colleague to him.

* * *

"It'll be extremely dangerous," Rose warns. We're sitting around her dining room table with Kheelan and Maggie. Kheelan has just finished informing the older women that he and I plan on coming up with a strategy to get my light back. "But I know better than to try and talk you out of it," Rose continues, peering at Kheelan over the top of her reading glasses. She glances back down at a book that's open in front of her and spins it around, so the words are right side up for Kheelan and me. "I know you've already made up your mind, and to be honest I can't think of a better solution. Even though, I desperately wish I could." She pushes the book closer to us. "What I can do is make sure the two of you are as prepared as possible for whatever lies ahead."

"What is this?" Kheelan asks as he leans forward to study the pages. I crane my neck to get a better look over his shoulder. It's a children's book. The page has an illustration of two goat men skipping down a green hillside, one is looking up at the dark sky ahead of them, the other is looking over his shoulder, his forehead furrowed and his eyes weary.

"It's a Fairy tale." Maggie chimes in. "Those satyrs are on a very important quest to find a map." I whip my head up and look at the women before me. A children's book is how they're going to help us prepare? Maggie smiles and leans forward, reaching for my hands. "You look troubled." She says in her gentle tone that would normally soothe me.

I let out a low laugh as I meet her eyes, "It's a children's story." Everyone is watching me, waiting for me to continue. How is me pointing out that it's just a children's story not enough? I clear my throat, uncomfortable with all the attention. "I just don't see how it will help us prepare unless the next page has a how-to-kill-demons section."

Maggie bursts into laughter. "Oh, heavens child! That wouldn't be in a children's book!" The idea alone has her doubling over in fits of giggles. Kheelan catches my eye, his own dancing with laughter, a small smile playing on his lips. We get our laughs from how Maggie takes everything we say in the literal sense. "Could you imagine the nightmares they'd have?" Maggie continues wiping at the tears that are now streaming down her cheeks.

"Stop it you old loon! You're off your rocker!" Rose swats at her friend's arm, unable to hide her own smile at her friend's giddiness. "Lia is being sarcastic. She doesn't think a children's book can teach them anything." She turns her gaze to me, her smile fading as she waits for my confirmation.

I stare at my hands which I'm twisting nervously in my lap. I feel bad for being rude, but I nod. "Yeah, it's just a bedtime story for kids," I mumble.

"All stories come from truth." Maggie whispers. A troubled expression replacing the laughter on her face. "You must know that by now."

Everyone's eyes burn into me, I slouch down in my chair as the hot blush creeps up my neck all the way to my ears. "Sorry," I mutter, "please continue."

Kheelan smirks and intervenes, saving me from the limelight, "What kind of map are they looking for?" He asks, directing his attention at his grandmother.

Maggie smiles, "A map to their heart's desire."

Kheelan nods, does he think this story is going to help us? "Herne promises the heart's desire in exchange for human souls," he says.

I straighten in my seat. How does he know that?

"Exactly!" Rose exclaims. "I believe these satyrs are looking for a map that will lead them into the NetherWorld. And since none of us," she motions around the table, "know how to enter the NetherWorld, you'll need a map if you want to get Lia's light back."

I gulp the lump away before it can finish forming in my throat. Their way of helping us is by helping us go to hell? That's not very comforting, I glance around at everyone's faces, they all mirror my concern, which only makes me feel worse. "Where do they find the map?" I ask, breaking the silence that's growing unbearable.

"I don't know." Rose pulls the book back towards her and flips through a few pages, revealing that the last couple have been ripped out. "I haven't been able to find this story where these pages aren't missing. Someone has gone through great pains to make sure nobody knows how this story ends."

"Probably for good reason, but do we know anyone who might know the story anyway?" Kheelan asks, his brows knitting tightly together as he flips through the book, studying the pages we do have.

"Not that that I know of." Rose sighs as she closes the book. "In the meantime…" She trails off, her eyes clouding with worry.

"We'll train harder." Kheelan finishes for her. "I think it's time to start practicing with some weapons." He says mostly to himself, nodding his head in confirmation, "That's what we need to do."

"And Light Travel!" Maggie's voice rises with excitement. "I'll teach you how to Light Travel!"

Rose smiles at her friend, "Maggie is the only half Fairling who has been able to Light Travel." She says, brimming with pride. "You're both full Fairlings so you should be able to do it rather easily." She's almost able to hide the doubt that flashes across her face as her eyes meet mine.

"Wait a second." I say, "Maggie is half Fairling, too? Does that make Kheelan more Fairy than human? A Super Fairling or something?"

Kheelan snorts as laughter bursts out of him, "A super Fairling? I wish! But, no, my mother was all human, Grandma Maggie adopted her."

"That's disappointing," I nudge him with my elbow, "a Super Fairling would have made you a *little* cool." I flash an evil grin at him before directing my attention back to my aunt and Maggie. "Okay, second, what exactly is 'Light Travel'?" I raise my fingers in quotations at the foreign phrase they're throwing around so casually.

"When you call the glow, you're connected to all other life forces." Maggie begins, "If you reach out with your mind and feel around when you're in your state of glow, you'll feel the trees, plants, people, and animals. You can reach out to particular life forms and travel through the energy that's connecting you to them. Light Travel!"

"So…like teleporting?" Kheelan asks, excitement lighting up his eyes, "Why is this the first I'm hearing of this?"

Rose laughs, "In a sense, yes, it's like teleporting, but it's harder than it sounds. Call the glow now, if you can. See if you can feel the life around you."

"I still can't believe neither of you have mentioned this to me until now," Kheelan mutters not bothering to hide the annoyance in his voice. His hand finds mine under the table, his fingers are warm, his grip firm. I close my eyes and concentrate on the warmth in my chest and will it to spread throughout my body. I open my eyes. I'm in a ball of bright light and we're both glowing, I can't believe how much easier it is to call it by holding onto Kheelan. My heart sinks as I notice I'm still noticeably dimmer. What was expecting, to regenerate over night?

"Close your eyes Lia and try to feel." Rose instructs softly. I do as I'm instructed and reach out with my mind. I feel Kheelan's energy next to me, strong, serious, and sturdy. Rose and Maggie across the table both soft, gentle, and kind. I push harder and draw in a deep breath as a crushing rush of emotions pour over me. My glow flickers out. I open my eyes and turn towards Kheelan. His glow has gone out too. He looks just as overwhelmed.

Rose's smile is full of sympathy, "It can be quite overpowering. We'll need to increase your practice from three days a week to everyday if this is going to work."

"It has to work." Kheelan says, determination clouds his eyes, but they don't waver from my face. "The fate of the three realms depends on it."

* * *

The day is dragging. There have been two customers in the last three hours and I ran out of busy work about two and a half hours ago. Since then, I've been leaning on the counter taking turns between staring out the window, lost in my mind, and glancing at the clock to see if I can leave yet. I'm staring out the window, when it dawns on me. "EMILY!" I yell.

"Oh my gosh, whaaat?" Emily groans from the chair behind me. I jump, has she been there this whole time? "You don't have to scream, I'm right here." She's as bored as I am, and well past irritable.

I grin, "Sorry! I thought you were in the back. My bad. Anyway, your family is spiritual yeah?"

"Uh, my grandfather was. My parents are a different story, they're both pretty fucked if I'm being honest."

I groan inwardly at my word choice. She's not close with her parents and is sensitive to the term 'family'. Her grandpa is the one who raised her. When he passed away neither of her parents bothered to show up for his funeral and that was the last straw for her. She cut all lines of communication off, any hope of a family buried with her grandfather. Rose and Maggie have tried their best to fill the void in her life, but that's not something easily done. "Sorry," I mumble, "bad word choice." I clear my throat, "you said once that your grandfather used to tell you stories about the people from the woods, or whatever the word is you used for Fairies?" I'm unable to mask the excitement building in my voice. How

107

didn't this occur to me sooner? She's literally my only friend in this state—besides my sister and Kheelan and two eighty-something year olds.

"Yeah," she eyes me suspiciously. "Why?"

"Do you know any stories about goat men?" I pause, trying to remember the word Maggie used last night. "Err, satyrs?"

"Yeah, probably about a thousand, you'll need to be more specific. Satyrs are literally in every culture's Fairy tales." She yawns, bored with the topic.

"How about one where two of them are looking for a map to hell?"

This gets her attention. She straightens in her chair, "You mean 'A Quest to One's Desire'?"

"Yes, that's it!" Excitement buzzes through my veins. "Do you know how it e—" The bell on the door tingles, cutting me off mid word, announcing a customer.

"Good afternoon!" Emily plasters on her cheerful guest face as she stands. A mischievous grin instantly replacing her fake smile as her eyes land on the newcomer. It's the guy who's been in the shop before. My pulse quickens. Emily quickly turns back to me, her voice hushed, "Actually I'm pretty bored here. I think you can close. Your sister said something about making cupcakes this afternoon for the doctors she works with. I think I'm going to go help her." She winks over her shoulder as she disappears through the swinging door that leads to the back room. "You got this." I hear her yell through the door as it flaps in her wake.

I glare at the door, letting out a slow breath. I turn around to face him. He's tall and lean. Not skinny lean though, I can tell he has muscle beneath his black leather jacket, the white t-shirt he's wearing under it clings to his midsection giving away his firm abs. I tear my eyes away from his body as I feel a blush burn to life on my cheeks and focus on his face. My eyes go straight to his full lips. Why am I looking at his lips? My cheeks burn brighter. I must be the colour of a beet. I force my eyes up, he has messy black hair, a stark contrast to his fair skin. Butterflies erupt in my belly as he starts to walk towards me. Why does that keep happening?

"How—" I falter. He's taken off his sunglasses. I suck in a breath and concentrate on forming words, but I can't focus on anything besides his cerulean eyes. He smirks, my bumbling amuses him. I take another deep breath and force my eyes shut as I try again. "How can I help you?" I smile, opening my eyes, proud of myself for getting a full sentence out. But before he can say anything, I begin to ramble. I explain how the lotions along the wall are made in house, using only natural and organic ingredients. I also let him know we sell flowers, like that isn't obvious. I even start listing the flowers that are currently in season. I know I'm talking too fast, but I can't stop the words, they just keep pouring out of me. Finally, his laughter cuts me off, saving me from myself. *Why am I like this?*

"What's your name?" He asks before I can resume my nervous rambling.

"Lia," I tuck a strand of hair behind my ear. "What's the occasion? A birthday, or anniversary? Roses are popular for anniversaries, but I think lilies are nice for birthdays," I can't be stopped. Seriously, why am I like this?

He laughs again, "You're not from around here, are you?"

Oh God. Is it that obvious? "No, I'm from Wisconsin," I admit.

"Ahh, the state of cheese and beer," his eyes glance down my body sending a fresh wave of heat to my cheeks, before returning to my face. "I thought people from Wisconsin were supposed to be fat?" His smirk is back, pulling one half of his mouth up, bemusement lighting up his eyes.

"Excuse me?" I cross my arms over my chest, hiding as much as myself as I can, suddenly very self-conscious from his evaluating eyes.

"I meant that as a compliment! Because you're obviously not fat at all."

"Is there something I can help you with?" I ask, my voice all business. "If not, I've got to get back to work."

He makes a show of looking around the empty shop, laughter dancing in his eyes when he finishes and his gaze returns to my face. "I didn't mean to offend you. I'm sorry…" his voice trails off and he glances down at the sunglasses in his hand.

I don't say anything. I wait for him to say what he's come in for.

"Aww and now you hate me. I'm sorry. I'll make a mental note *not* to talk about a girl's weight, even if it's meant as a compliment."

I meet his eyes, a stray butterfly flits around my belly. I shoo it away with my mind. He's arrogant and I don't like him, I tell myself.

"Let me try again," he shoots me a winning smile, my heart stills before going into overdrive. He expects me to swoon at that smile, well I won't. "Hi Lia, it's nice to meet you. Would you like to grab a coffee with me sometime?"

I fight back the smile that's threatening to crack my icy stare. "Thank you, but I can't." I say, adding "sorry" as an afterthought. I shouldn't be too rude, he is a customer after all.

"You have a boyfriend?" He asks.

"No," I unfold my arms and start to pick at piece of tape that's stuck to the counter.

"Girlfriend?" I shake my head. He must not get turned down, like ever. I look up, my eyes fall straight to his lips, I suck in my own bottom lip. *Pull yourself together Lia.* I force my gaze up to meet his eyes again. Is *crystal blue* a colour?

He places a hand to his heart, mocking hurt. "Well, my deepest apologies for offending you, madame." He pantomimes tipping a top hat at me.

I offer a small smile, "There actually are a lot of fat people in Wisconsin, it's nothing personal. It's just that, I don't know why I'm telling you this, but if you must know, I just got out of a pretty bad relationship." I concentrate on the tape on the counter. *Pretty bad* is the understatement of the year. "Can I help you with some flowers?"

"Ahh yes, the 'it's not you, it's me'. Very good way to let someone down easy." He smiles in his overconfident way. "Maybe some other time," he winks as he looks at the flowers around us. "What's your favourite? Roses or lilies?" I must look confused. "You suggested earlier somewhere in your ramblings that I should get roses or lilies," his eyes find mine, full of laughter again. I'm impressed he was able to keep up with all that. I couldn't, and I was the one talking.

"Ooh right." I consider lying and telling him that roses are my favourite, so he'll spend more. But I can't pull my gaze away from his and the truth pours out. "Neither of those, actually, they're just popular choices. Peonies are my favourite."

"Peonies it is. One bouquet, please." He glances at his watch, "Do I get them now, or come back to pick them up later?"

"You can have them now. I'll only be a second." I spin around. "That'll be thirty dollars!" I call over my shoulder as I retreat into the backroom to gather what I need. When I come back out, two twenties are on the counter. I hand him the wrapped bouquet. He's halfway to the door before I can get the change out of the drawer.

"See you around, Lia." He flashes one last smile over his shoulder as he pushes through the shop's door.

My legs feel weak. I sink into the chair behind the register and stare out at the street. I need to get a grip.

* * *

I pull up the gravel drive to my cabin, Kheelan is sitting on my front steps looking tormented. I groan inwardly. What's happened? I shift my car into park and climb out. I approach him slowly. I don't say a word, just sit next to him, breathing in the fresh air. It rained earlier, leaving behind the smell of damp earth and moss and making the forest feel extra vibrant.

Kheelan says, "I spoke with Allie today."

"Judging by the look on your face, my guess would be that it didn't go well?"

"Not at all. We got into a huge fight." He looks up from his lap, his eyes are bloodshot. He's been crying. My heart aches for him, I want to gather him into my arms and make his sadness go away, but I don't let myself. "I don't know what to do. I can't be what she needs."

111

"I wish I had advice I could offer you," I give in and put my arm around him, squeezing him gently into a sideways hug.

He sucks in a quivering breath. "I was wondering if you'd come with me somewhere?"

"Of course," I say before I can think better of it, "I just have to let Kodi out to relieve herself, then I'm ready."

I open the door to find my sister and Emily at the tiny table frosting a tray full of cupcakes. Kodi races up to me in greeting. "Oh! Hello ladies, don't tell me you managed to bake all of those in this miniature kitchen?"

"Nah, we used Rose's oven. We're just frosting them here." Emily says. "I've been filling Jen in on the hot customer who keeps coming in to check you out." A wicked grin lights up her face.

Jen's eyes narrow at me, "Be careful, that's all I'm going to say." I pull the door closed behind me.

Emily laughs. "She's very much team Kheelan, but unfortunately for everyone, Kheelan is spoken for."

I throw a nervous glance at the door. "Shh, he's out there! I'm gonna go for a quick drive with him, I'll be back soon. Just wanted to make sure Kodi wasn't cooped up in here alone all day."

Jen's eyes light up, "Ohh have fun!" She throws a victorious smile at Emily and whispers, "Team Kheelan."

Emily rolls her eyes and mutters, "Team hot stranger."

I roll my eyes at both of them as I open the door to leave, "Team *no one*," I say walking out and shutting the door firmly behind me. I'm relieved Kheelan is already waiting in his truck, meaning he most likely didn't overhear anything.

We drive in silence for almost twenty minutes. I'm about to ask where he's taking me when he pulls into a drive. We're at Aspen Hill Cemetery. Creepy spot to go when you're sad about a girl.

"I'm upset about my fight with Allie," he confesses when he's parked his truck, "but today is hard for me every year." He draws in a breath. "Today is the anniversary of the day my mom and brother died—or I guess maybe just my mom."

112

I don't move, my hand is hovering over the door handle, but I don't open it. I'm not sure what I was expecting, but it wasn't this. "Kheelan," I whisper his name. "I had no idea, I'm so sorry."

He doesn't say anything, just gets out and starts walking towards a path. I scramble out of my seatbelt and follow him. I stay quiet as we walk towards the headstones. I don't know what to say or how to be comforting in a situation like this. I reach out hesitantly and take his hand. I give it a gentle squeeze, hoping it offers him some comfort. We walk this way for some time until he finally comes to a stop in front of two tiny gravestones:

"Elenor O'Connell
Loving mother, loving friend.
August 4th, 1973–July 11th, 2003"

"Declan Lane
Beloved grandson, and brother.
November 9th, 1997–July 11th, 2003"

"I wonder what happens to a grave if the person who's supposed to be beneath it turns out to be alive?" Kheelan muses, his voice flat. I barely manage a shrug in response. It's the second headstone, Elenor's, that has my hands trembling and eyes staring, unblinking. "My grandma must have been by already. I wasn't thinking, I should have brought some flowers, too." Kheelan says shifting his attention to his mother's stone. I nod my head slightly. He's right, someone has been to his mother's grave today, but I know it wasn't Maggie. The bouquet of peonies leaning against her headstone is all too familiar.

Chapter Nine

I can't get the peonies out of my head. I'm in denial about what they mean, but deep down I know it was Kheelan's brother who was in the flower shop. I spoke to an *Underling* and I thought he was *cute*. Bile rises in my throat at the memory of how his presence turned me into a bumbling schoolgirl. My heart goes still, he knows my *name* and where I work which means Herne knows my location. I should be dead by now. I probably will be soon, along with everyone I care about. Guilt and horror at the situation churns in my stomach as it dawns on me how bad this situation is. I should have told Kheelan the moment I saw the peonies. I'll tell him tonight. I let out a breath, relaxing a bit. Kheelan will know what to do. It only happened yesterday. We'll figure it out after dinner.

I walk through Aunt Rose's back door, Kodi pushes past me in the direction of the great room, beelining for the comfort of the fire as I follow the sound of voices into the dining room. Everyone is already sitting around the long mahogany table. "Sorry I'm late!"

"Oh, we were all early." Rose smiles and pats the empty seat next to her.

"Where's Jen?" I ask noting the empty seat between Kheelan and Emily who are across from me.

"Hospital called her in to pick up an extra shift." Rose says with a heavy sigh.

I groan, I live in a tiny cabin with my sister in the middle of nowhere, but I feel like we're thousands of miles apart. How can I miss someone who's in such close proximity? *Maybe because you're keeping the biggest part of your life a secret from her,* the nagging voice in the back of my head chimes. I Ignore it and focus on my more persistent grumbling stomach as I help myself to the mounding piles of food spread out between us, scooping healthy portions of everything I can reach onto my plate.

"So, you know the end of the story?" I ask Emily around a mouthful of food.

Her lips crinkle upwards in revulsion as her eyes land on my full mouth, she doesn't try to hide the disgust in her voice. "Let's wait until after the meal before discussing anything, and please don't speak with your mouth full."

I laugh. "Sorry," I mumble around my full mouth. She bulges her eyes at me and I just widen my grin, closing my lips in a silent gesture of understanding.

With appetites satisfied, the table cleared, and the sun long gone, Emily holds a captive audience. Even though she finished reciting the tale of 'A Quest to One's Desire' about two minutes ago. (She was very excited to see it in written form, she thought it was a folk tale that was only passed down orally—of course the ending is exactly that.) I found myself holding my breath as she neared the end of the written pages, thinking she'd falter, but she didn't miss a beat and continued on from memory. I could tell it dragged up memories of her grandfather and I felt a pang of guilt in my stomach for making her come here to relive it for us, but now the sadness in her eyes is transforming into discomfort. Fidgeting in her seat while twirling her sweatshirt strings tight around her index finger, her gaze flitting around the room. I want to save her from the obvious unease she's feeling from being the centre of attention, but I don't know what to say, and I guess no one else does either. I open my mouth and close it again, her final words still ringing in my ears, making it impossible for me to form any of my own. *It's so far away.*

"At least, that's the ending my grandfather always used," Emily's shaky voice shatters the heavy silence.

Another beat passes before Kheelan says. "So we want to find the Daoine Sidhe, in the heart of Ireland. Does anyone know where the heart of Ireland is, exactly?"

Something to do. The task snaps me out of my frozen state. I pull my phone out of my pocket and type in a quick search. "Tipperary," I say holding up my screen for everyone to see. "If we count an internet search as a reliable source."

"It's a starting point." Rose confirms. "That's far away, I hope you both have been practicing calling the Glow as much as possible?" She peers at me over the top of her glasses with a knowing look. I can't hide the guilt as I offer her a weak smile in response.

"Well," Emily jumps to her feet. She says she's cool with our world, but any mention of the Glow and she gets awkward and weird. "I hope I was some help, but it's late and I should get home."

"Thank you dear, you were a huge help." Rose assures her, "I'll see you at the shop tomorrow morning." She gives Emily's hand a quick squeeze as she rushes past in the direction of the exit.

I set my phone on the table and follow my friend to the front door. "I hope you're not too freaked by all of this?" I search her face, trying to gage the severity of the panic she must be feeling. She's the only friend I have to share this part of my life with and I don't want to scare her away.

"I'm not freaked, I promise. Actually, I find it all pretty awesome, it's just late and I need to get home." She grins at me. "You let me know if you need more stories, I'm here for you girl." She surprises me by pulling me into a hug, her out of character affection is reassuring. "See ya," she says pushing through the entrance way.

"See you tomorrow, Em, and thanks again." I say pulling the door shut.

The group has moved to the living room. I stop in the doorway to observe. Kheelan is sitting on the floor in the middle of the space, Maggie and Rose his ever-attentive audience are nestled together on the couch, even Kodi has woken up and has her icy eyes intently on him, her head cocking to one side as he transforms into an illuminated orb, his shape barely recognisable through the blaring light.

"Amazing!" Maggie leans forward, "Now send out those feelers. Concentrate on a tree outside of the barn, or on one of the horses," she instructs. "Living things have the strongest energy."

I'm a set of eyes in complete awe by how bright his glow is. Then he gets even brighter. I can no longer make out his form, he's just light. As I lift a hand to shield my eyes, the room goes dark. Floating spots of colour dance around the room from the sudden absence of his glow. Kheelan is gone. I can't stop the yelp of surprise that rips out of me.

"He's done it!" Rose whispers excitedly.

"You mean, he Light Travelled?" I ask, excitement shoving my fear aside as I walk across the room to join the two women on the couch. My eyes never straying from the spot Kheelan had just been, willing him to come back.

"Oh dear, I hope he can find his way back," Maggie says after a few minutes have gone by, adding a light laugh as an afterthought to lighten the mood.

"And hopefully he made it where he was intending to go." Rose adds, her voice flat. The room grows quieter, the heaviness of the situation and all the things that could have gone wrong weighing on our minds.

The seconds tick by loudly from the old grandfather clock in the corner. "Should we try to call him?" I ask, unable to bear any more silence or waiting. The words have barely left my mouth when Kodi jumps up and runs to the back door. Her tail going a mile a minute. A second later Kheelan is walking in, a massive grin across his face.

"Well?" Maggie leaps to her feet with surprising nimbleness for a woman of her age. "Did you do it? Did you get lost? Why did it take you so long to come back?" She rapid fires her questions at her grandson.

Kheelan laughs as he walks further into the room. "I did it," he confirms, pride ringing in his words. "Nearly gave Oberon a heart attack though. It took me a little while to calm him back down."

"Did you get lost coming back?" Rose asks from her spot on the couch. "You didn't return to the same spot."

Kheelan shrugs, "I remembered the aspen tree you have out back and concentrated on that. I wasn't so sure I wanted to concentrate on a human just yet. I could crush you." He meets my gaze, his blue eyes have a mischievous twinkle, sending a flush of tingling to my cheeks.

"Well, bravo!" Maggie exclaims, interrupting the moment by clapping her hands together, "I'm so proud of you." She teeters forward pulling her grandson into a tight embrace.

Rose turns towards me, a huge smile on her face. "Your turn Lia!"

Panic flutters through me. I look up at Kheelan wide-eyed, "Any pointers?" I ask trying not to sound as nervous as I feel.

"Don't go to the barn. The horses have had enough excitement for one day." He winks and reaches down for my hands, pulling me to my feet. "Sit crossed-legged, close your eyes, and clear your mind." He moves close to my ear, so only I can hear, his warm breath sending goosebumps down my arms, "I find it easiest to call the glow when I picture your face."

My heart catches in my throat. I nod mutely and do what he says, taking a seat on the floor. I draw in a shuddering breath and close my eyes. I try to clear my mind, which is no easy task when I can feel three sets of eyes burning into my back.

"Try for your cabin, or maybe the greenhouse at the shop." Rose suggests.

I breathe in, picturing the light fleeing from the lamps around the room, and out of the fire straight into my nose and throughout my body. When I breathe out, I imagine all the shadows and darkness leaving me, just like Maggie has taught us. I conjure Kheelan's face in my mind not leaving out a single detail. I picture his strong jaw, high cheekbones, his perfect wavy hair, and rosy lips. I remember the sparkle in his eyes just moments ago when he said he'd crush me. If only he knew how much he already is crushing me. I let out another breath but hold the image of his face firm, it's as though he's right in front of me. His eyes boring into me the way they always do, like they're looking straight into my soul. I remember the way his strong arms pulled me into him, in our shared dream so many weeks ago and the way his kiss shot straight to my core. A burst of warmth erupts in my chest. I hold onto the warmth and urge it down my limbs.

"Wonderful Rosalia!" Rose exclaims. "That's the fastest you've called it on your own! Well done, now reach out with your feelers for something familiar."

I feel with my mind, I decide to concentrate on the greenhouse behind the flower shop, my cabin is too close, it doesn't feel like a big enough challenge. My mind shoots off in a million directions, it takes all my concentration to rope in my feelers and concentrate on *the* direction, the one towards the greenhouse. It's as though I'm reaching through a tunnel filled with millions of roots, all of them trying to pull me in their direction, but I focus. I know I'm close when the familiar aroma—almost sickly-sweet cluster of different flowers—fills my head, bringing with it the welcome calm. I let it settle over my body, imagining I'm already there. There's a slight tugging in my gut—

A loud scream echoes around the room.

My eyes pop open. I squint through my own light, but Jen's pale face is clear as day. Her eyes wide and mouth nearly reaching the floor.

The slight tugging turns to full pull, I'm alone in darkness. I feel the humidity first. I breathe in deep, I did it. I'm in the greenhouse. My heart is hammering, how bad is this situation? Jen definitely saw me in my full state of Glow. Which means she saw me disappear and is probably freaking out big time right now. I need to get back, fast.

I settle back into position and begin to take my deep breaths. I do everything just as I had the first time. Retracing my mental steps. Except this time, the glow doesn't come. I start the process again, and then again—still nothing. I let out an exasperated scream and stand up, jumping up and down, shaking my arms out.

"You can do this. You've already done it before!" I say to myself in the darkness as I fold my legs into position. "Third times a charm." I whisper.

Still, I'm engulfed in only darkness. I feel the sting of tears threatening to spill. I wipe them away, furious with myself. I'm not going to give up.

After ten more tries, followed by ten more fails. I finally accept defeat. Jen has probably gotten all her stuff packed during this wasted time and the others are probably thinking I'm lost in a worm hole or something. I need to call someone to come pick me up. I pat the back pockets of my jeans, they're empty. I let out a frustrated moan. How do I not have my phone? I *always* have my phone.

My stomach turns to lead, I left it on the dining room table. And *of course* I don't have the shop keys on me to use the landline.

I walk in the direction of the square, praying one of the shops will still be open and they'll let me use their phone. Every step makes me grumpier. I'm so mad at myself. I feel like the biggest failure for not being able to travel back. What kind of an idiot doesn't think to grab their phone, or a jacket? Stupid Wyoming. How does it get this cold at night in the *summer*? I keep my eyes on the pavement in front of me, kicking at any fallen leaves that cross my path. I'm pouting, but there's no one around to witness me feeling sorry for myself, so I don't care.

An engine roars by. I keep trudging along with my arms tight around my shivering body, trying to infuse any extra warmth back into myself.

"What do we have here?" My feet go still. I can hear the smirk in his voice as butterflies flutter to life in my stomach at the sound of it. "Lia, is that you?"

He's the enemy, I remind myself willing the butterflies away. I whip my head around, my gaze landing on his form. His long legs are straddling a gleaming black motorcycle, his black hair messy from pulling off the helmet that he's clutching between his slender fingers. The butterflies try to stir back to life when my eyes meet his. I squash them and rip my focus away as I continue down the sidewalk. He's the bad guy I remind myself again. I should be running for my life, not calmly walking away.

"Lia! Wait." I hear him dismount his bike, his footsteps pounding the pavement to catch up to me.

My feet stop involuntarily and I turn around to face him.

An amused smile spreads over his face. "Having a rough night?" He asks, not bothering to hide his laughter.

"You could say that," I say through clenched teeth. I turn away from him and continue down the sidewalk picking up my pace. I need a phone before I freeze to death, or The Hunt shows up to consume the rest of my Light.

"Wait!" He jogs alongside me, catching my arm so I stop.

I jump back as electricity shoots up my arm. My brow furrows, confusion clouding my mind. I look at him, he's studying his hand, just as bewildered. He shakes his head, slowly drawing his gaze back to mine.

We don't say anything for a few moments, then his eyes become apologetic. "Look, I'm sorry for laughing. But come on! You're walking around with a big scowl on your face, shivering like it's the middle of winter, and to top it all off you're not even wearing any shoes. You have to admit it's pretty funny."

I look down at my feet. He's right, no shoes, just socks. I look back up, his face has softened and the sympathy in his eyes seems sincere. Without a word, he shrugs off his leather jacket and drapes it over my shoulders. A sigh escapes my lips as the welcomed warmth washes over me.

"Can I give you a ride somewhere?" He asks, his voice soft. I look up at him, I shouldn't trust him. He holds up his hands, "I promise to be the perfect gentleman."

My head is screaming at me to run, he was raised by The Hunt, maybe Herne himself. They want me dead. But my feet don't move. My eyes bore into his clear blue ones which only show worry. My gut overrules my brain and the words are out before I can think better of them. "Could you drive me to my aunt's?"

"Of course." I follow him back to his bike, my feet growing heavier with each step. He plops his helmet onto my head before I can change my mind, tightening the strap under my chin. He mistakes my hesitation for being nervous about getting on the motorcycle with him. "I promise I won't go fast." His voice is surprisingly gentle.

This is a different side to the arrogant guy from the flower shop. He hops on in one graceful motion and the engine roars to life. He twists around to pat the seat behind him. I offer a weak smile and pray this isn't the stupidest thing I've ever done as I climb on behind him.

"So," he shouts over the idling of the bike, "are you going to tell me how you ended up walking around the middle of town in short sleeves and no shoes?"

I ignore his question. Knowing he can't see my face gives me a surge of confidence. "Are you going to tell me why you were at Kheelan's mother's grave with those peonies yesterday?"

His shoulders tense. "You know Kheelan?"

I pause. Doesn't he know that already? Isn't that why he's here? To find me and Kheelan for the Hunt? "Yes," Is all I manage to get out.

"It's my mother's grave." I can barely hear him over the sound of the engine.

"You're Declan." It's not a question and I watch his profile closely.

"Yes," he turns to look me in my eyes.

"Did you come here to hurt Kheelan?" I try to keep my voice even, but a surge of protectiveness has washed over me and my heart is pounding in my ears.

"What?" His eyes widen in surprise, "He's my brother, why would I want to hurt him?" He studies my face, searching for something, but I concentrate on keeping it a blank slate. He was raised away from the Light, I shouldn't be feeling guilty for making him look so hurt. Finally, he turns forward. "Where does your aunt live?"

I give him quick directions.

He nods as he kicks the bike into gear. "Hold on."

I wrap my arms around his waist and try not to notice how firm his stomach feels under my hands.

"I'm not here to hurt anyone." Declan shouts over his shoulder after a few minutes of driving in silence. "I know what you are. I had my suspicions, that's why I came back to your shop. I was hoping you could lead me to my brother. I didn't know for sure until tonight, just now when we touched." He sneaks a quick glance at me over his shoulder before returning his eyes to the road. "By the way you're treating me, I'm guessing you think I'm part of The Hunt or something."

"Aren't you?" I shout back, "The Hunters raised you." I tighten my grip as he takes us around a bend in the road.

"Sure, they raised me, but I ran away."

"That doesn't mean much. How do I know you're not lying? They could have sent you here."

"I've had plenty of opportunity to hurt you and I haven't." He pulls to the side of the road and comes to a stop, cutting the engine. My pulse quickens and I scan my surroundings, searching for a familiar landmark, anything to let me know where I am. It's too dark, I can't find my bearings. Why did I get on the motorcycle? I knew who he was, and I still got on. Without any shoes too, that'll slow me down if I need to run, and running is my only option. Lord knows I'm not good at fighting. I begin to lift my leg over the seat, preparing for a quick dash.

Declan's faster, he jumps off and in one swift motion he grabs a hold of my arm, his grip unyielding. "I'm not going to hurt you." He repeats. "Please, just let me prove it."

I try to pull my arm back, but he keeps a firm grip. My limbs feel like jelly as fear pumps through my veins. We're in the middle of nowhere and he's much stronger than me. How can I get out of this? He closes his eyes and starts to take deep breaths. My heart rate slows. He's *glowing*, and he was able to call it faster than Kheelan even. His eyes open, finding mine. There's no fire, just a crisp pure blue light, almost white emanating.

We ride the rest of the way in silence. My thoughts bouncing around my head almost too fast to keep up with. Aunt Rose says Underlings can't call the glow, that the Light can't lie. If he were an Underling, he'd glow red as fire. Does this mean Declan is aligned with the Light? But how is that possible when he was raised in the Dark?

We turn into the driveway and come to a stop in front of Rose's house. Every light inside is flipped on. I can only imagine the panic buzzing around in there right now. They're probably worried sick. I dismount and pull off the helmet and his jacket, handing them back to Declan. I thank him for the ride and begin to walk towards the front door. He calls my name, I spin around.

"Could you do me a favour, and not tell Kheelan I'm in town? I need to be careful how I approach him. I'm afraid he'll react worse than you did." I nod my head. He's right, Kheelan won't react well to his long-lost brother popping up out of the blue. Especially with all that's been going on this summer.

"Sure," I say. Deciding Declan isn't a danger to Kheelan, not with the proof of his Glow. I'll let it stay between the brothers.

"Thanks." He smiles up at me, "Go put some shoes on." He plops his helmet over his head, and kicks his motorcycle into gear.

I watch him drive away until the red glow of his running light disappears into the darkness.

The door behind me swings open. "Lia!" Kheelan sighs with relief. "Thank God!" He closes the space between us, pulling me into a hug. "We were all so worried, and I think your sister might be in shock."

"I thought she might have seen me." My feet are numb as I follow him through the open door.

"She saw." Kheelan confirms. "Rose has filled her in on the basics of what's been going on in your life, but Jen hasn't said a word. I'm not even sure she's heard anything Rose has been saying. Her eyes haven't left the spot on the floor where you were sitting. Hopefully you being back will help calm her down a bit."

* * *

It goes better than I thought. Once we get Jen to accept the fact that I'm alive, and wasn't incinerated on the living room floor, she takes the supernatural stuff relatively well. She says she has known something strange was going on. She thought maybe I was a psychic, because of my dreams, or maybe had some kind of weird energy thing happening, a spirit haunting me, but never in her wildest dreams would she have believed I was an actual Fairling. She shoots Rose a knowing smile when she says the word out loud the first time, remembering the story she told us our first night here. *'I can't believe this is all real. My sister is magic!'* she had whispered to me, excitement lighting up her eyes.

Jen learns *everything*. About Jesse being an Underling—she makes a point to let everyone know she never liked him—my light being dim, and the prophecy. She asks questions for the better part of an hour, only stopping when Rose insists we talk about me and Kheelan going to Tipperary. I guess not being strong enough to make the return trip tonight makes getting my Light back even more urgent. We decide we'll leave next Friday at midnight. So actually, first thing Saturday morning, which marks mine and Kheelan's eighteenth birthday. Jen digs her elbow hard into my ribs when she hears this, turning her bright eyes towards me and mouthing *'soulmates'*. I give her a pointed look and then cast my panicked eyes around the room to make sure no one else saw. I'm relieved to find Kheelan has his full attention on the older two women, who are telling us a shared birthday probably explains our special connection, and since it's going to be a full moon, it'll make Light Traveling a little easier. Basically, I have one week to give my glow a needed rest and for Kheelan to get me comfortable with using weapons, in case they're needed on our journey. Even though they all assure me that they won't be—Ireland is a safe haven of sorts for Fairy-Bloods—Nevertheless, a skill that everyone agrees may be beneficial *soon*.

Jen immediately starts her questions back up on our walk back to our cabin. She doesn't even stop when we're both in bed and the lights are off.

"I knew I wasn't crazy. I knew I saw your eyes glowing when we were packing!" Her voice is giddy, she can't believe this is happening.

I laugh, "At that point I was sure *I* was crazy."

"I always knew you were special," she says, her voice getting serious.

"Oh yeah?" I turn on my side, my sisters face glowing in the moonlight.

"Yes," she nods her head in confirmation as she flips onto her side to face me. Her eyes gleaming. "You have an aura about you and people are drawn to it." Her teeth glimmer as she smiles. "People love you, love being around you because of the way you make them feel." She raises her shoulders up, her grin broadening, "Now we know how special you really are."

"I don't feel special." I say, "I still feel like me, normal, boring Lia."

"But you are, and you always have been. The world as we know it is on your shoulders, and Kheelan's." She pauses to consider. "And maybe his brother's—who may or may not be alive; but if he is, he's on the enemy's side. Either way it's up to you and Kheelan. That must make you feel *something*. Out of the billions of people on this planet, *you* were chosen."

"That's what I don't get. Why? I'm not special," I insist. I take a deep breath. "I'm scared," I whisper, "I'm scared of The Hunt, scared of Underlings, scared I won't be strong enough. My Light is dim, how am I going to even begin searching for the Lost Stave?"

"You're stronger than you know," Jen says, her voice full of confidence as she repeats Rose's famous line.

"That's what everyone keeps saying, but I still don't feel it. Kheelan Light Travelled to the barn and back so easily tonight—I couldn't even get home."

"How did you get home?"

I pause. I promised Declan I'd let him approach his brother on his own, but I don't want to lie to my sister, not when she finally knows everything. I take a deep breath and brace myself, "I was walking to the square to call Kheelan," I try to keep my voice casual, "and I ran into that guy Emily was talking about. The one who came into the flower shop a few times, and he offered me a ride home."

My sister's voice shakes as she begins to speak, "Lia, you were blessed with gifts," she takes a deep breath, steadying herself, "and given a very important task. Now is not the time to get distracted by a boy."

I force a laugh. "What, unless it's Kheelan?"

"Kheelan isn't just some *boy*. He's your *soulmate,* maybe even more. He's like you Lia, you're both Fairlings and you had a dream about him before you met him. You're both named in a prophecy. There is a higher power at work that's beyond any of us."

I want to tell her that Declan is like me too and is named in the same prophecy, but I don't. I just tell her not to worry, that I don't even like him. He's arrogant and rude most of the time, I just needed a ride and he happened to be there.

She flips to her other side so her back is to me, mumbling into her pillow, "Good. You need to stay focused."

Chapter Ten

"Swords look cool in movies," Kheelan begins, "but I'll warn you, they're heavy."

I step forward and wrap my fingers around the golden hilt of the blade he's holding out to me. The metal is cool against my skin and feels good in my hand, natural even. Then Kheelan lets go, taking a step back. My arm drops, the blade clanging against the barn floor. He wasn't exaggerating, it's *heavy*. I try to lift it in a cool swooping motion, like Mulan. All I manage to do is lift it waist high before the weight sends it crashing back down.

Jen bursts into fits of laughter from her stool in the corner. "Smooth."

Kheelan cracks a smile. "Don't say I didn't warn you."

"What else is there? I don't think the sword is a plausible choice," I join Jen's laughter, "at least for the time being."

"I think you're right." He takes the sword back, doing the motion I had attempted with perfect form.

"Show off," I mutter under my breath.

He laughs, "How about we try knives and archery next?"

"Yes, let's do that!" Jen hops off her stool, dragging it behind her as Kheelan leads us to the far side of the barn where he has set up a target.

He bends down and scoops something off the ground. Turning to me he asks, "Have you played darts before?"

I nod.

"Good, throwing a knife is similar. You point your elbow where you want the knife to go, like this," he demonstrates as he releases the knife at the target, missing the bullseye by less than half an inch. "Now you try."

He hands me a small silver knife, the metal gleaming in the dim light. "Hold the blade end," he positions my fingers, "and remember to keep your body forward and aim your elbow where you want the knife to go. One fluid motion."

I nod, zeroing my eyes and elbow in on the bullseye. The knife flips forward through the air and sticks into the target. I smile, it's nowhere near the centre, but it's *on* the target. I'll take it.

"Better than the sword at least." Jen chimes from her stool, the book she brought along laying untouched in her lap.

"Hey!" I snap, "You promised you'd be a *silent* spectator." Though, I can't hide the smile that springs to my lips, I like having my sister a part of all of this, even if it means extra teasing.

Jen smirks, "Sorry, you're right. I'm not here." She picks up her book and flips to her marked spot, but her eyes stay focused on the scene before her.

"You're a natural." Kheelan assures me with a grin.

I roll my eyes.

"I'm serious!" He insists. "Not many people can even hit the target let alone get it to stick to it on their first try."

I sigh, "Let me try again."

His grin widens, "This time try to aim for the *centre*." He retrieves the two knives from the cork and places one in my waiting hand.

"You think you're funny? Watch closely." I look at him out of the corner of my eye. "You might want to take notes." I flash a smile and let the knife fly.

"WHAT!" Kheelan's mouth drops open as the knife lodges itself into the board. "I didn't think you'd actually get it on your second try!" He lets out a whoop and picks me up, spinning me around. "That was amazing!" His eyes glisten.

I sneak a peek at Jen, she's pretending to read, but the small smile tugging at her lips gives her away.

I can't help my own smile as Kheelan sets me back on the ground. "Try again, this time from further away."

I walk to retrieve the knife from the target, accepting the two Kheelan offers me on my way back to position. I go an extra ten feet from the board. I concentrate on the target and I rapid fire all three knives in a row. Somehow managing to get them all to lodge within an inch of the bullseye.

"A natural," Kheelan beams. I smile up at his proud face. This weapon stuff is more fun than I thought it would be.

"Can I try shooting that next?" I point to a beautiful wooden long bow that's leaning against one of the stall doors.

"Absolutely, just try not to out shoot me in the first five minutes, please. I don't think my ego can take any more tonight."

"Sorry champ, I can't make any promises," I wink as I pick up the bow. I grasp it in my right hand and bend to pick up an arrow.

"Easy killer," Kheelan reaches out and grabs the bow. "You're right-handed, so you hold it in your left and draw with your right." He switches the bow to my left hand and brings my right hand to the string. He notches an arrow and places my hands where they're meant to be. "Guide it with your pointer finger." He whispers in my ear. I nod to show I understand. He grabs my shoulders and spins my body 180°, "Keep your feet pointed forward, you want the sides of them parallel with your target, then extend your left arm straight out, turning only your body." He stands behind me and guides my arm into position. His breath on my neck sends a ripple of shivers down my spine. "Now pull the string back like you're going to shoot, but don't release it yet." I do as he says. He gently pushes my right elbow lower, "Use your mouth as an anchor, of sorts. Your hand holding the bow string should be at that level, and that far back."

"Uh huh, got it. Can I release now? This is really hard to keep drawn."

Kheelan laughs, "Release it with your exhale."

I let the arrow fly, it misses the target and lodges itself deep into the wooden wall.

"Oh, thank God!" Kheelan bursts out laughing, "I don't know what I would have done if you got this perfect right off the bat too."

I laugh, "I gotta try again."

He smiles at my determination and hands me a second arrow. I glance over to see if my sister is watching, but her stool is empty. When did she sneak out?

* * *

Over the next week Kheelan and I fall into an easy routine. I suspect he's afraid of burning me out, literally. We only go running twice, and practice calling the glow once. We still walk Kodiak every day after work, then practice with the weapons in the barn. By the end of the week, I've managed to master the bow and throwing knives. I never miss a bullseye. Kheelan has me shooting and throwing from weird angels and awkward positions, trying to throw me off. But it doesn't work. I've found my strength and this causes Kheelan to beam with pride.

I expect Declan to make an appearance sometime during the week, but when Friday rolls around I haven't caught so much as a glimpse of him. Not even when I walk through town to pick up lunch on my breaks. So, after Kheelan leaves me on my doorstep, my forehead still tingling from the kiss he's placed on it with the promise to see me at midnight, I decide to go to the square to look for him. I convince myself the only reason is because I need to sincerely thank him for the ride he gave me last week and to apologise for how terrible I had treated him. But I know it's more than that. I *want* to see him.

I push through the crowd of tourists that have gathered for the nightly Wild West Shootout. Kodi right by my side, her leash an unneeded formality, as my eyes dart from face to face, but I don't find the one I'm looking for. I walk under an antler arch and across the square's park to the other side where there's less of a crowd. As I make my way down Broadway, I peer into the shops and restaurants, hoping to see his leather jacket. But I don't. I wander, my search turning into a stroll. I let Kodi stop and sniff and I find myself enjoying the cool breeze as much as she is. I glance up at Snow King Mountain, the sun is starting to dip behind it. It's getting late. The smell of fries from a nearby restaurant reach me,

131

making my stomach grumble. I pull out my phone to check the time and find I've been searching for almost two hours. I sigh, time to throw in the towel. I buy a sandwich from the New York City Sub Shop, load Kodi into the jeep, and start my drive back to Rose's. If Declan's still around in a couple of weeks when Kheelan and I get back to Wyoming, I'll thank him then.

* * *

It's 11:59. The moon is high, casting a halo of light around us. Kheelan bends down and pats Kodi on her head, asking if she's ready. Since his glow is stronger, he's going to hold her while we Light Travel. My stomach is in knots. I'm nervous it won't work correctly, that she'll get hurt, or he will. Rose and Maggie insisted we bring her along and that it'll be okay. Apparently Kodi is no normal dog. *FaeDog* is what they called her. In laymen terms, she has a good sense for 'this kind of stuff' and would be a necessary tool if we want to find the map or the Daoine Sidhe. I had asked what else made her different from normal dogs and Rose informed me that besides being able to track down supernatural things, she can also read minds. Well, *kind of.* She can't hear and understand our thoughts, but she can pick up on emotions more than the average dog. She also has superior night vision, and exceptional hearing. She can see things we can't, different planes and other dimensions which is how she'll be helpful with finding the Daoine Sidhe. FaeDogs are rare, so I guess I'm lucky Kodi found me.

"Come on Lia, study this." Kheelan snaps me back to the present. "We have thirty-seconds," I glance down at the picture of Tipperary he's holding out to me. I've already memorised it. The line of trees in the rolling green field, I've even practiced imagining how they feel, what to reach out for.

I tighten the strap of my knapsack that's slung over my shoulder, along with a quill of arrows and a bow. Kheelan has a sword strapped to his back, underneath his own backpack. I find myself wondering again how we'll go unnoticed, but I decide not to voice my worries for the umpteenth time and to trust him. He swears where we're going there won't be many people.

"Ready?" Rose asks, her voice cheerful. "Call to check in every day, and please, please, please, be careful!"

"We will," I promise as I draw her into a big hug. The sudden tightness in my throat surprises me as I breathe in the comforting perfume of my mentor.

I move into Jen's waiting arms. Clutching her tighter than necessary, wishing more than anything that I could bring her along. "Come back in one piece," she pleads into my ear.

"I'll try," I whisper back, "have fun in Wisconsin this week. Hug Mom and Dad for me."

"Five seconds," Kheelan says from behind me. I turn around to see him scooping Kodi into his arms like she weighs nothing. He gets her situated, cradling her against his chest like a baby. His eyes meet mine, "Ready?"

"Ready," I confirm, stepping in front of him so we're facing one another. We close our eyes and take our deep calming breaths. I hear Rose warning Jen to close her eyes. I feel the glow ignite in my chest and start to spread. I reach out with my mind to the landscape I've been memorising over the last week and let it consume me. When my glow flickers out, I open my eyes. Kheelan and Kodi are gone, and I'm still under the full moon with Rose, Maggie, and Jen.

"Oh dear," my aunt murmurs.

My stomach drops, and all I can do is stand motionless, letting defeat wash over me in a giant wave. I was so sure I was doing it, my Glow felt just as bright as the night I went to the greenhouse. I was positive I'd open my eyes to the rolling hills of Ireland. What did I do wrong? I close my eyes and start taking my deep breaths. I have to keep trying. I feel a hand on my arm and open my eyes to Maggie's face, worry creasing her brow. "It's too late dear. It's a big land, if you don't go together you could end up in different spots."

133

"But we memorised the same photo," I insist, "I can still catch up with him."

Maggie shakes her head. My heart sinks.

My phone starts to buzz, I answer it. "Kheelan! Are you okay?"

"Who is Kheelan?" My friend Bianca's voice from back home shouts into my ear. Music is blaring in the background, she must be at a party. "He sounds hot!"

"Sorry," I mumble. "I thought you were someone else."

"Clearly! Sorry to disappoint you, love. Just wanted to be the first one to wish you happy birthday! Welcome to adulthood!"

"Thanks, and you are the first." I try to make my voice sound cheerful.

"Good, three-year reigning champion! I'll let you go though, call this Kheelan guy. Make sure he gives you a happy birthday!" She bursts into laughter on the other end of the line, "Love you girl! You better call me tomorrow. I'm going to need details about what and *who* you've been up to out west!"

I force a light laugh, "Thanks, I promise we'll talk soon." As soon as I hit the end button Kheelan's name pops up on my screen and the phone starts vibrating in my hand. "Kheelan!" I answer, relief mixing with my sadness.

"We made it. I'm fine, Kodi's fine, so don't worry." He says, "Are you okay?"

"Thank God. Yeah, I'm fine, just bruised pride. I'm not sure what happened. I called the Glow, and everything felt like it did last time, except I opened my eyes and I was in the same spot." I sigh, turning my back to my small audience so they can't see me fighting back tears.

"Hey, don't worry, it's not your fault. You must not have enough light to travel this far." He takes a deep breath before going on, "Kodi and I will find what we need. Keep practicing in the barn and focus on resting your light. We'll be back before you know it."

"I should come help. I could look at flights, travel like a normal person."

"No, we're fine," he assures me. "I'm just looking for the Daoine Sidhe. They're the good guys. It's not like I'll be facing any Underlings or Hunters. When it's time to go to the NetherWorld, that's when I'll need you by my side." I can hear him smiling through the phone. "It's mostly sacred land out here, I'm safe. Promise."

"Okay," I agree, "but call me every day to check in and let me know what's going on and how Kodi's doing."

"I will," he says.

"Hug her for me and please take good care of her." A wave of loneliness hits me hard, it feels like my gut is being twisted as I realise my dog is gone and my sister is heading to Wisconsin for the week tomorrow. I take a shuddering breath. It's getting harder to hold back my tears.

"You know I will." The smile is back in his voice, "By the way, happy birthday."

"Happy birthday to you too, hurry up and find that map so you can come home and we can celebrate." My voice sounds like a dying frog.

"Hey," he says, hearing the catch in my voice. "Chin up, we'll be home soon." The line goes dead before I can say anything more. He must have spotty service over there.

I stuff my phone into my pocket and turn towards Rose. "I'm sorry Aunt Rose," I whisper as the tears finally win and start to stream down my face.

"Oh, come here dear." Rose clucks, pulling me into a hug. "You didn't do anything wrong," she assures me, stroking my hair down my back. "You had your power taken from you, and the power you have left is tired. You've been training hard."

"I should be helping them," I sob into her shoulder, "this whole trip, or quest or whatever you want to call it, is for me."

"I don't know if you know this, but," Rose pulls out of our hug to look me in my eyes, keeping a firm grip on my shoulders. "Kheelan would storm through hell for you," she smiles, "and I think he intends to do just that. Don't worry. Ireland is safe for Fairlings. Take the time Kheelan is gone to rest your light. Relax, and maybe have some fun."

I nod as she drops her hands from my shoulders and turns to walk back into her house, Maggie close at her heals. Jen comes up beside me and silently wraps her arm around me as she guides us in the direction of our cabin.

Chapter Eleven

I wake to the sound of Jen shuffling around the room. When I hear her zip her suitcase close, I crack my puffy eyes open, "I can't believe you're abandoning me on my birthday," I grumble into my pillow.

"I'm sorry! You were supposed to be away with Kheelan, so when Matt offered to go halfsies so I could be home for my birthday…"

I bolt upright, "You're still talking to Matt AND he paid for half your ticket?"

Jen grabs her book from the nightstand and shoves it into her purse, "I could have sworn I mentioned that." She coils up her phone charger and slips it in next to her book.

"Well, you didn't. You didn't tell me you'd be gone for so long either. Your birthday isn't until NEXT Friday!" I cross my arms over my chest and slump down in my bed pouting. "I'm going to be all alone *and* Rose doesn't want me to work. I'm going to be bored, and you're a big abandoner."

Jen sits on the edge of my bed, her brown eyes shining. "I am really sorry it's turned out this way. But Emily is still around, and Rose…Maybe you should stay up in the main house this week?" She shifts her weight and pulls out a tiny box from behind her. "I hope you're not too upset with me to refuse my birthday present?" A smile splits her face, "I went into town and got some donuts too, but open this first." She holds the small box out to me.

I smile, feeling my facade begin to crack. I reach out for the small package, "I'm really upset, and you're still an abandoner." I say as my fingers grasp the tiny box.

My sister laughs, "I'll be back a week from Monday! You'll barely have time to miss me."

"I already miss you," I mumble as I pull on the ribbon, untying the neat bow. I lift the lid off and look down to see a delicate gold chain with two little interlocked rings. I look up at my sister. "You didn't have to do this," I say, my voice catching in my throat. "It's beautiful."

"I'm glad you think so. I have one too." She brushes her hair aside to show her matching silver necklace. "SO, when you're busy moping and feeling sorry for yourself this week, or anytime you miss me, which will be a lot soon, since I'll be leaving for college…You can look at this and remember that even when you can't see me, you have a sister who loves you."

I smile. She has a way with words, and a way with giving thoughtful gifts. I make a mental note to have the best present I can find waiting for her when she gets back. Now I have something to do this week. "Help me put it on?" I twist around so she can clasp it at the nape of my neck. "Thank you, I love it." I say as she clips it into place, I press my fingers against the cool metal of the rings, already feeling comforted by its presence.

"Good!" She grins, "Now I only have time for a donut, then I have to go to the airport." Guilt floods her eyes but I stop her with a reassuring smile and tell her I'll be fine. I even offer to drive her, but Mindy needs to go into town anyway and it's on the way.

We sit in front of the tiny wood stove, the space by our feet where Kodi would normally be begging is empty. I push away the sad pang and focus on Jen's words as she gushes on about how good Matt has been since she's come to Wyoming. Always reaching out first and sending thoughtful texts. I can't help but smile, not because I'm happy about her getting back together with Matt—he's not a bad guy or anything, he's just blah—but I'm happy at how light and easy our conversation is. It feels like before everything changed, like we're normal, like I don't have the weight of the worlds on my shoulders.

* * *

I have a book open in my lap, a half-eaten donut resting on the chair's arm. Jen left almost an hour ago, but I haven't moved, or even read a sentence. I've been too busy feeling sorry for myself, staring out the window, watching the sun beams dance between the branches of the trees, absentmindedly twisting my finger around the chain around my neck.

A loud knock on the door makes me jump, sending my book crashing to the floor. My eyes dart around the room, I don't know what I'm looking for. A sign for who could be at my door? I take a breath, I'm being silly, it's Rose.

I slide across the wooden floor in my socks and paste a big smile on my face before I open the door, ready to greet my aunt with as much cheer as I can force. I swing the door open, my smile falters. It's not Rose.

Declan is standing on my porch, his hands shoved into the pockets of his jeans, the sunlight making his eyes seem almost silver. His smirk begins to creep across his lips as he takes in my pyjamas.

I don't move, frozen in horror by the situation. I don't know what to say. I haven't even attempted to comb my hair yet. To make matters worse, I'm wearing bright plaid pyjama shorts and an embarrassing Yoshi the dinosaur t-shirt. "Uhh…" is all I manage.

Declan laughs, "I heard it was your birthday…" His voice trails off, he watches as I hastily try to comb my fingers through my unruly hair.

"It is," I confirm.

He smiles, "Happy birthday."

"Thanks…" Is that all he came for? Should I close the door? Invite him in? I don't do either, I just stand awkwardly in the doorway, waiting for some kind of an explanation.

"I went to the shop looking for you," he finally offers. "Your friend Emily told me it was your birthday, and she mentioned she felt bad that she had to work and that you'd be alone." He shrugs, "I guess that sparkling personality of yours hasn't won you many friends."

My eyes bulge, did he come here to insult me? "Compliments for my birthday? Thanks so much," I start to close the door.

He reaches out and stops it. "I'm sorry!" He laughs, "Just a joke. I have something for you." He pulls an envelope out of his back pocket.

I raise my eyebrows in question.

"From Emily," he explains.

I reach out and take the envelope, sliding my finger into the corner and gently tearing it open. I pull out a silly card that says something about me being an old fart in big bubble letters. On the inside is a note scrawled in Emily's handwriting.

I heard what happened last night, and I'm so sorry I can't spend the day with you trying to cheer you up. But I give you second best, *drum roll, please!* Declan. He's my gift to you. I know what you're thinking, and no I'm not your pimp, not yet, (ha-ha, just kidding, sort of). But I know you're going to over think this, so let me stop you now. I'm only asking you spend the day with him and try to have some fun. I'm not asking you to date him or anything. Remember—half of you is still a regular teenage girl. Forget about fate, forget about your "destiny" and that damn prophecy for a few hours and have a HAPPY birthday!

Love you. xo-Em

I stand in the doorway, unsure what to do. If I send him away, what will I do all day? Continue to stare out the window and eat donuts? I sigh, glancing once more at Emily's words before I open the door wider and step aside, making room for him to enter.

He flashes me his cocky smile as he walks by, beelining for the chair I'd been sitting in. He wastes no time making himself comfortable. He picks up the half-eaten donut off the armrest and holds it up to me laughter in his eyes, "You gonna finish this?" He doesn't give me time to answer before shoving the entire thing in his mouth.

"Charming," I roll my eyes as I grab clothes out of my drawers and take them into the bathroom. I splash some water on my face and wrestle my hair into a braid. I decide to throw on a quick layer of lip gloss too—

it's my birthday after all, I should look halfway decent. I glance down at my bare feet as I emerge, "Sandals or hiking boots?" I ask.

"Hiking boots."

I plop on the end of my bed and pull my boots out from underneath it. "So, where are we going?" I ask as I lace up my shoes.

"You'll see." He stands up and walks out the door.

I hastily finish tying my boots and follow him out. I stop short. He's waiting for me at the passenger door of an old pickup truck. He opens the door for me as I approach the rusty thing.

"Your chariot awaits," he says with a wink.

"What happened to the bike?" I ask as I accept his waiting hand and heave myself into the monstrous vehicle.

"Resting at home, I thought you might be more comfortable in an enclosed vehicle. It's kind of a long drive," he says as he closes the door behind me, "I borrowed it from my landlord."

We drive for almost an hour and I am thankful for the rust bucket. Declan was right, a motorcycle would not have been an enjoyable ride, and talking would have been impossible. I can tell he shares my surprise with how fast we fall into a conversation.

He tells me about how he grew up with his father—in California! He laughs a little too hard when I'm surprised he wasn't brought up in the NetherWorld. He promises he had a relatively normal up bringing, he didn't learn about Fairlings or The Hunt until he was fifteen, right before he Awakened. A normal upbringing if you can ignore the fact that his father lied to him about being a member of the Wild Hunt, and that he led his son to believe that Kheelan and his mother had died in an accident when in truth they had been murdered at the order of his father's boss. Kheelan was lucky he was unconscious when the Hunter checked the car. Declan wasn't as fortunate, he was awake and thought to be the sole survivor, so the Hunter took him to his father.

A few weeks before Declan's Sixteenth birthday his father sat him down and told him the truth about who and what he was. It didn't sit well with him, and he decided he had to get away from his father's world. He ended up staying with his dad for a little over a year after that. He wanted to leave right away but knew he had to prepare for life on his own. He also wanted to learn as much as he could about the OtherWorld and NetherWorld.

Six months after his seventeenth birthday, he ran away, went to Florida. He moved into a shabby apartment he found on craigslist, got a job as a dishwasher, and began studying for his GED. When he was eighteen, he had a dream that changed his life. He dreamt that Kheelan was still alive and had begun to Awaken. His gut told him it was more than just a dream, he left Florida and has been searching the north-west for his brother ever since—for the better part of two years.

He keeps his story vague, and it takes all of my will power not to ask too many questions. He seems to have turned out so well, considering everything he's been through. I feel bad for being mean, I was only thinking about Kheelan with all the recent revelations. I never even considered the emotional roller coaster Declan has had to endure as well.

We turn onto a gravel road and silence settles over us as we wind our way upwards. We stay quiet as he parks the truck and we start across the parking area, making our way up the trail.

"All right, it's your turn," Declan declares, shattering the silence. "What brought you to Wyoming?"

I open my mouth, and I realise I'm about to recite my normal line of 'my aunt needed help with her flower shop'. But I pause, I can tell him the truth. I smile. "Same as you. I had a dream about Kheelan."

He looks at me sideways, "Well isn't that something." A few more beats of silence pass before he goes on, steering the conversation in a new direction. "I'd like to hear about that bad relationship you just got out of." A wicked grin spreads across his face.

I laugh, "Of course you do." I sigh, giving in. "I didn't know how bad it was until I got out here and learned about this supernatural world we're a part of."

"You mean you didn't learn about it when you Awakened?"

"I Awakened late." I sigh, I might as well spill, or he'll keep asking questions. "My ex-boyfriend was an Underling and he squelched me for two years," I shrug, hoping to downplay the severity of it a little. "It wasn't too bad, I didn't even know it was happening at the time." I focus on the narrow path ahead of us, ignoring his stare I can feel boring into my back.

Declan stops, "You were squelched before you even knew you were a Fairling?"

"I guess so," I say, turning to face him, he has an incredulous look on his face. "What's the matter?"

He kicks at a rock that's sticking out of the path. "As far as I know, it's pretty much impossible to know someone's a Fairling before they're Awake."

I narrow my eyes, "My Aunt Rose told me she knew as soon as she saw my birth announcement."

"Your Aunt Rose? As in my Grandma Maggie's friend?"

I nod.

"I remember her," he says thoughtfully. He looks up from the rock he's kicking. "She doesn't count though, she's already part of this world. She probably had some suspicions before you were even born." He brushes by me as he starts walking along the path again. I follow, keeping close to his heels.

"So how do you think Jesse knew I was a Fairling before I did then?" I ask, my stomach twisting into a nervous knot.

"Jesse?" His eyebrows knit together deep in thought. "I don't know. It's very bizarre."

Panic rises in my chest, "Do you think my parents and sister are in danger with him being close to them in Wisconsin?"

"He probably left when you did." He looks up at me, his eyes clouding, "What are we doing? It's your birthday and all we're doing is talking about depressing stuff. New rule, no more mentioning anything supernatural. We're supposed to be having fun, I have strict orders from Emily." He flashes his smile, my legs wobble.

I smile back, "You're right. We should live in the moment. Look how beautiful it is here." I step off the path onto a cliff edge that overlooks the valley below. It's a massive canyon with an ombre of greens cascading along the rocks, an array of wildflowers scattered like a paint brush was flung at the mossy ground.

"It takes your breath away," Declan agrees, his voice soft as he steps up beside me to admire the view.

"I feel like I'm living in a photograph." I let out a breath of a laugh, "Everywhere I look is so gorgeous out here. It feels too good to be true sometimes."

Declan looks down at me, a thoughtful expression on his face. "You know Lia, you're not as terrible as I thought you'd be."

I narrow my eyes, "Gee, thanks." Then I laugh and elbow him in his side, "You're tolerable too, I guess."

He lets out a surprised laugh, "Glad you think so. There's quite a bit of hike ahead of us still, but you'll love the waterfall at the end." He goes back to the trail, leading the way up the path. I follow. After a few minutes he looks over his shoulder at me, "What's Lia short for anyway?"

"Rosalia," I say.

"Rosalia," he smiles, "that's pretty," his eyes meet mine, "it suits you. Better than Lia." He declares.

I feel my cheeks flush at his compliment, I'm quick to turn my face away, hoping he doesn't notice the effect he has on me.

By the time we reach the waterfall the sun is high in the sky, and I'm dripping in sweat. It's worth it though. It's not a rushing waterfall, more like a faucet of water running off a cliff into a small pond, tapering into a stream that runs down through canyon. The pool is tucked into a cove, making it seem hidden, like it's the canyon's secret.

I bend down to splash water on my face, the cold sensation a shock as it drips down my face and arms, but refreshing. I straighten my legs, preparing to stretch, but before I can get my footing, two hands plant firmly in the middle of my back. I don't have time to react. I tumble forward, splashing into the freezing water. The pool isn't deep, I turn over and sit there, glaring up at Declan who is doubled over from laughing so hard.

"You butt head!" I yell, splashing water at him.

He laughs harder.

"At least help me up?" I ask, making sure innocence is dripping off my words.

He reaches out his hands, grabbing onto my outstretched ones. As soon as our fingers meet, I grasp as tightly as I can and pull with all my strength. Luckily, I catch him off guard and he loses his footing, toppling into the water beside me.

He sends a wave of water at my face with his hand, "I can't believe you did that!"

A snort of laughter erupts from me.

This gets him laughing again. "Did you just *snort*?" He asks through his hysterics.

I continue to giggle, only able to nod my head in confirmation. I can't remember the last time I snorted from laughing so hard. My eyes meet his which are dancing with laughter, and I realise how great it feels to be goofing around, I feel so much *lighter*.

Declan stands up first and offers me his hands to pull me up. "Truce?" I ask, not sure what else he has in store for me.

"Truce," he promises the corner of his mouth twitching upwards.

I reach up and grab his outstretched hands. He pulls me to my feet, but my foot catches on a rock and I trip forward. His arm loops around my waist as he catches me. Slow passing seconds tick by. "You steady?" He asks his warm breath so close to my face electric shivers shoot through my body. I raise my gaze, our eyes lock.

All I can manage is a nod, suddenly very aware at how close our bodies are. "Thanks for today." I whisper.

"You're welcome, Rosalia." his husky voice, mixed with him using my full name, sends my heart into overdrive. He raises his free hand towards my face and he gently grabs a small chunk of hair that's stuck to my forehead, tucking it behind my ear. His slender fingers linger near my cheek, his eyes never wavering from mine.

I suck in a shuddering breath as I lean in closer to him. I don't know what's come over me, but I'm not in control of my body. It's like an unknown force or a magnet is pulling our heads together. Our lips are a breath apart and butterflies are bouncing off the walls of my chest, my heartbeat thudding audibly. The familiar burst of warmth erupts in my core. I close my eyes in anticipation, I can feel his lips moving closer to mine—

"Hey! Could you guys move so we can take a picture of the waterfall?" Someone shouts from the path, shattering the moment around us.

Declan steps away from me and tilts his face towards the sky, reaching his hand up to tousle water off his hair. Disappointment settles in my stomach followed by a wave of confusion. Did I want to kiss *Declan*? Kheelan's face flashes in my mind and my disappointment turns to guilt. *Kheelan is your friend, who has a girlfriend.*

"Sure buddy, no problem," Declan shouts up to the strangers on the path, breaking me out of my internal battle of emotions.

Our chatter is minimal on our walk back to the truck, which leaves me with too much time alone in my head. The blissfulness of a normal afternoon gone. I can't stop thinking about Kheelan since he popped into my head. *After almost kissing his brother.* Where is he? What's he doing? Is he okay? Is Kodi okay? I decide I need to try calling him as soon as I get back home.

Once we're in the truck Declan turns on the radio, asking if I'm okay with the music. I grunt my approval and slouch down in the passenger seat, focusing my gaze out the window. If he's not interested in conversation, I'm not going to force it on him. I don't even know what to say. Should we talk about what almost occurred under the waterfall, or pretend it never happened? I'm not even sure how I feel. Did I want it to happen? I sneak a peek at him to get a hint of what he's feeling, but his eyes are focused on the road, jaw clenched in concentration.

* * *

Emily's perched on my porch step when we pull up the drive, a grin spreads across her face when she sees us together. I do my best to ignore her and turn towards Declan. "Thanks for taking me out today, I thought it was going to be a pretty crappy birthday, but I had a lot of fun." I reach for the door handle.

"You're welcome. I had fun too…" His eyes meet mine, he opens his mouth to say something, then he eyes Emily who is examining our exchange from the porch step with an unnerving intensity. He closes his mouth again, rethinking his words. "I'll see you around?" He asks, bringing his eyes back to mine.

Disappointment weighs in my stomach. What was I hoping he'd say? "Yeah, for sure," I say as I hop out of the truck.

"Happy birthday, Rosalia," I hear him say as the door shuts.

I trudge up the gravel towards Emily who has a twinkle in her eye. I hold up my hand, signalling her not to say a word. "It's my birthday, and my birthday wish is for you to not say anything about what you just saw, or for you to ask me anything about today."

"But—" She begins to protest.

"—Nope! Nothing," I smile wickedly at her. "It's the power I get to have as the birthday girl." This is going to kill her.

"Fiiiine," she groans, "happy freakin' birthday."

I laugh, "Thank you!"

She jumps up and latches onto my arm, pulling me towards the path to Rose's house. "My orders are to kidnap you and bring you to Rose's house. We're having a party, and let me tell you," she gushes as we walk, "it is going to be a rager. There will be the two of us, a middle-aged caretaker, and two old women who cannot hold their booze. Yes, that's right, they've already started drinking." She laughs at the picture she's painted for me. "Bet you didn't think eighteen would be *this* crazy."

I laugh, "Actually, that sounds kind of perfect."

It is perfect. Rose arranged for my parents and Jen to FaceTime, so I get to see them. Mindy prepares my favourite meal for us, lasagna with a side of garlic bread. She even remembers to make it vegetarian. Rose and Maggie got together earlier in the afternoon to have some wine and bake my cake, which leaves us with two very chatty older women and a rather impressive cake. It's a round white cake with a raspberry sauce between each of the six layers. They frosted it with a delicious lemon-lavender buttercream and covered the entire thing with glitter—which they assure us over and over again is edible—and topped it off with a big Tinker-Bell figurine surrounded by eighteen candles.

"I wish Kheelan were here to celebrate with us," Maggie says wistfully as she lights all the candles. I nod in agreement, but at the same time my heart does a flip flop in my chest as I realise that I'm also missing Declan's cheeky remarks and teasing smile.

"Now blow out that forest fire and make a wish!" Rose says as Maggie finishes lighting the last candle.

I grin and close my eyes, sucking in a big breath. As I let my air out, I wish for a normal life.

We remain at the table late into the night chatting about everything and nothing. Simply enjoying each other's company. The cake platter is the only dish that remains on the table. We gave up on using plates long ago, just grabbing bite-sized chunks throughout the night. When only crumbs remain, we decide it's time for bed.

It's midnight when I get to my cabin, that means it's six AM in Ireland. I decide to try calling anyway. I get his voicemail. I leave a brief message, wishing him a happy birthday again, and that I hope his day wasn't too terrible by himself.

Chapter Twelve

"No! I'm under strict orders. You are not allowed to work this week," Emily says as I walk through the shop's front door.

"Please? I'm going crazy in that tiny cabin by myself." I pop myself onto the counter. "I won't work, I'll just annoy you." I smile what I hope is my most winning one.

"Fine." She says, returning my smile with a wicked one. "But it's not your birthday anymore. You have to tell me about your day with Declan."

I laugh, I should have seen this coming. But talking about it might help me figure out how I'm feeling. So, I tell her everything. How the day with Declan was exactly what I needed. That I hadn't laughed that much in months. I tell her how he pushed me into the water and I pulled him in after me. I even tell her how he helped me up, that I stumbled on a rock, and he caught me. How we nearly kissed but another hiker interrupted us at the worst or maybe best possible moment. I tell her we only had idle small talk on the hike back, then didn't speak at all the entire drive home. She nods along hanging on my every word as I feed her the details.

"So you like him." She concludes.

I groan, "I don't know! That's why I needed to get out of the cabin. I can't figure out how I feel."

"You like him." She repeats firmer.

I sigh, "I honestly don't think I do. It was just a brief moment, and nothing happened anyway so it doesn't matter. Can I please help—"

The tinkling of the shop's bell cuts me off. I whip my head around, my heart soars out of my chest as Declan strides through the entrance. Speak of the devil. *Wow he looks good in blue.* His eyes shift back and forth from my face to Emily's. "Sorry to interrupt," he starts, "I was just hoping to have a quick word with you?" He meets my eyes.

I open my mouth, ready to send him off. I'm not ready to deal with this yet. I need more time to figure out what I'm feeling.

"She's all yours." Emily jumps to her feet sending an evil grin in my direction, as she hurries into the back.

I look at Declan, "What's up?"

"Not much, I was just thinking about going fishing this afternoon. I wouldn't mind some company, if you want to join me?" My pulse quickens. I hate that he has this effect on me. *I like Kheelan,* I remind myself, but I can't stop the smile that tugs at my lips as he waits for me to answer. It's cute and so out of character for him, how vulnerable he appears, standing there with hands crammed into his pockets, his eyes wide. "I can wait until you're done working," he adds as an afterthought.

"She's not working! She has the entire week off!" Emily shouts from the back.

His smile spreads easily across his face, hope lighting up his eyes, "Interested?"

I glance towards the swinging door and laugh. She'll be team hot stranger until the day she dies. "Sure," I say, sliding off the counter. Maybe fishing will distract me a little, even if it is with one of the people I'm trying *not* to think about. "I'm not baiting my own hooks though," I inform him as I walk around the register to poke my head into the back room.

Emily whips her head up from the accounting book, a playful smile already on her face. "Going fishing?"

"Yup, you're off the hook, I won't be hanging around to annoy you all day."

She returns her attention to the pages, her grin broadening, "You kids have fun," she sings.

* * *

We go to Jackson Lake, in Grand Teton National Park and rent a small fishing boat from the Colter Bay marina. I give casting a few tries, but when nothing bites instantly, I give up. I crack open my book and get cosy in the bottom of the boat, my legs draping lazily over the side. Declan doesn't bring up yesterday and neither do I. We fall into a comfortable silence, the only noise coming from the water lapping at the side of the boat and the occasional whir of his fishing pole. I rest my open book on my chest and close my eyes, leaning my head against the edge of the boat. I let the warmth of the sun wash over my face and I realise my mind hasn't been going a million miles a minute for the first time all day.

I roll my head to the side and watch as Declan reels the fishing line back in. I can see his muscles working through his shirt as the sinker drags through the water. I try to imagine what he's been through, what his life has been like. I can't. The idea of growing up without a mother sounds so lonely. Being separated from a sibling? Believing they both were dead. Despite the warm sun, the thought sends a shiver through me. Does he have anyone he's close to? He left his life in California and his father years ago. No wonder he's nervous about approaching his brother. He's terrified of being rejected. Kheelan is his last chance at having a family. I don't even want to think about what life without Jen would be like, I depend on her so much. Kheelan and Declan deserve that. They've missed out on so many important years, years when they could have really used a brother. "Do you think you'll tell Kheelan soon?" I ask.

His shoulders slump as he turns his head to look at me. "Yeah," he sighs, "I'm just not sure how to do it." He sits down placing the fishing rod along the bottom of the boat. "I know I need to, I should just get it over with. He's my brother, he'll be happy to see me. I'm just over thinking the whole situation and making it weird. Right?" He looks up at me, his clear blue eyes searching for answers. But I don't have any. "Where is Kheelan, anyway?"

I shift my eyes to the mountains behind him, "Ireland." I say as offhanded as I can manage.

"Ireland? Weren't you supposed to be with him?" Disappointment flashes across his face.

I raise an eyebrow, I'm about to tease him about being jealous, but something holds me back. "I was," I say instead. "But I wasn't able to Light Travel that far."

"He Light Travelled to Ireland?" Pride chases away any lingering disappointment from his eyes, "That's *really* impressive." He smiles, "What's happening in Ireland?"

I shrug, not really wanting to answer because I know he's not going to like it. "He's looking for something that will hopefully help get my light back."

Declan searches my face, probably hoping for a hint that I'm joking, or waiting for me to elaborate more. Finally, he says, "I know you're too stubborn for me to even try to talk you out of that." He sighs, "I don't like the idea at all. Your light will regenerate on its own. You don't need to put yourself in danger trying to recover it."

"Your grandma and my aunt don't think it will regenerate fast enough," I say.

"Fast enough for what?"

My eyes meet his as it dawns on me. No one has told him about the prophecy. He has no idea that his life will never be normal again. I swallow, I really don't want to be the one who tells him. I shift my gaze back to the mountains.

"Just tell me," he pleads.

I take a deep breath, breathing in the smell of the lake water and a trace of the worms we've been using as bait, "There's a prophecy. None of us know what it says exactly…We just know that the three of us are mentioned."

"And what, you just weren't going to tell me?" Declan's voice hardens.

I straighten up, "We thought you were on *their* side," I say.

"That's a load of bull, you've known for over a week now that I'm not on 'their' side." His fingers coming up to make air quotes around *their* as his eyes bore into mine, "Why didn't you tell me?"

I swallow around the lump that has lodged itself in my throat. Why didn't I? Because I felt normal around him and I wanted to hang onto that feeling for as long as possible? "I didn't think it was my place." My voice shakes. I stare down at the flip flops on my feet, unable to look him in the eye. He's right. I should have told him. I was being selfish. "The Queen contacted my aunt when they realised I hadn't Awakened on time. She told her that there was a prophecy that says three Fairlings will find the Lost Stave. You, me, and Kheelan." I bring my eyes up to his to find they've softened a little.

"And they didn't even try to find me?"

"Well, everyone thought you were dead. And I think the Fairies figured if you weren't, it was too late. That Herne had gotten to you." I say with a half-smile hoping to lighten the mood a little.

"Well, I'm not dead yet. When Kheelan gets back, I want to be included."

I nod and force my lips into a full smile, but my blood feels cold. Kheelan is a good guy, but he's *too* good. That's his weakness. He's so stubbornly good that he gets tunnel vision. When he learns his brother is alive, it'll be hard to convince him that he isn't an Underling working with The Hunt. A sinking feeling in my gut tells me that it'll take more than Declan showing his glow to gain his brother's full trust.

* * *

I haven't been able to get in touch with Kheelan. I'm sent straight to voicemail every time I try calling. When I verbalise my worries to Rose, she doesn't share my concerns. She's certain Kheelan is safe. She insists his battery probably died and the only thing worrying will get me is wrinkles. I know she's probably right, but it kills me not knowing what's going on. She won't even let me go to work to keep myself distracted.

'Fresh air and relaxation, doctor's orders!' She sings every time I suggest picking up a few shifts. That conversation always ends with me groaning in frustration and walking back to my tiny cabin.

If it weren't for Declan, I'd have lost my mind by now. The morning after fishing I open my door to his smiling face. He's holding up a kayak paddle. Without saying a word, I run back inside and change into a swimsuit. We fall into an unspoken agreement. Every day he's at my door with an activity for us to do. We become friends by default, our lives woven together through unseen forces.

Neither of us mention what almost happened at the waterfall, we just fall back into our usual banter, and we laugh, a *lot*. We fill our days with hiking, rafting, fishing, and national park exploring, which leaves me physically exhausted and with minimal time to worry about what's going on in Ireland. Not to mention how *normal* I feel when I'm with him. We don't talk about Fairies or The Hunt at all, we're just real people enjoying summer vacation together. Some days I'm even able to forget the fact that the fates of three worlds rest on my shoulders.

By the time I get home at the end of the day, my body is worn out, but that's when my mind wakes up. It's as though it needs to make up for the day where it was forced to be idle. I worry about Kheelan and my dog, wondering where they are, what they're doing, if they've found anything. I worry if we'll be able to get my light back, what happens if we don't find The Stave. And most nights I wonder about Jen's theory, if Kheelan and I really are soulmates. I miss him. His serious take on the prophecy, his sturdy presence on our afternoon walks, even his goofy jokes during our training sessions. Part of me believes my sister's theory. The same part of me *wants* it to be true. But for some reason every time I think the word *soulmate* lately, Declan's face flashes before my eyes, turning my heart into fluttering butterflies. I shoo the imaginary insects away by reminding myself that we're just friends. We've been hanging out every day for a week. I've *burped* in front of him. We're definitely just friends and I wouldn't want to do anything to mess up our newfound friendship. The cheeky black-haired boy has become my favourite part of every day.

I roll over and grab my phone off my nightstand, clicking Kheelan's name for a third time tonight. I'm sent straight to voicemail, *again*. It's been one week without any word. I decide I'm going to Aunt Rose in the morning as I switch off the lamp. We need to find a way to get in contact with him, make sure everything is okay.

* * *

I'm back in the canyon, soaking wet sitting in the pool at the base of the waterfall. My stomach is sore from laughing so hard. I look up to see Declan's outstretched hand offering to help me to my feet. I place my hand in his, the familiar warmth spreads up my arm as he pulls me to my feet in one swift motion. I don't get my footing, and trip forward. His free arm wraps around my waist, keeping me from falling. I look up, my gaze locks with his clear blue eyes. Our faces start to draw together like magnets. I close my eyes in anticipation.

Declan's arm disappears from around my waist. I stumble forward. My eyes snap open. He's gone. Can he do that? This is my dream. Then I realise the canyon and waterfall are missing too. I spin around, the walls of the cove, the pool, the trees, they're all gone. Left in their place, white nothingness.

Someone clears their throat. I whip around, my eyes finding the source. I can't stop the smile that spreads across my face as I drink in Kheelan's form. I run into his open arms. "Thank God!" I murmur into his shoulder, squeezing him as hard as I can. "I've been worried sick! You better be real!"

"I'm real," he assures me with a chuckle as he pulls out of our embrace, "Well, physically no. But I'm here, this isn't your subconscious dreaming me up." He glances at the spot I'd been standing moments earlier with my subconscious's version of Declan. I feel heat erupt in my cheeks. Had he seen that? "I'm not sure how much time we have, I'm not very good at this dream stuff. I've been trying every night. This is the first time it's worked."

"I'm glad you were able to. I was preparing to send out a search party first thing in the morning." I laugh thinking about how perfect his timing really is. "Are you okay? Is Kodi okay?"

"We're fine. I think I can mostly blame it on the time difference," he laughs. "I had to force myself back to sleep hoping to catch you. But it worked!" He grins down at me. "I miss you." He reaches out a hand and brushes my cheek. "Did you get my email?" His voice is barely a whisper.

I crinkle my brow, "Email? No. I'm sorry, I haven't checked my email in ages, what did it say?"

He tousles his hair, suddenly appearing nervous. "Don't worry about it. Nothing about the Daoine Sidhe or anything, just a note I sent on our birthday." He clears his throat, "Anyway, I fell in a stream last Saturday, phone is toast. That's why you haven't been able to get in touch. Also, bad news, I have no leads, nothing."

"I'm sorry I'm not there to help you," I offer. I wonder what his email says. Why won't he just tell me? I make a mental note to check it as soon as I wake up.

"Don't apologise, Lia. We're fine. I have one more idea, if it leads anywhere, it'll be another week, but if it's another dead end I'm coming home so we can regroup." He looks into my eyes, his face softening. "I really do miss you."

I smile, grabbing his hand, giving it a gentle squeeze. "I miss you too," I whisper. *He still has a girlfriend* the tiny voice reminds me. "Give Kodi hugs and kisses for me," I say, my throat tightening picturing her furry little face. We've never been apart for this long.

Kheelan pulls me into another hug, "I think she misses you too," he whispers into my ear. "What have you been up to?" he asks as he pulls out of our embrace. I catch him glancing over to where my dream version of his brother had been standing. He nudges his chin in that direction, "Who was that?"

My cheeks burn crimson, he had seen. I shrug, "Who was who? I can't even remember what I was dreaming about before you came." I lie.

Kheelan frowns, he opens his mouth about to say something, but before he gets the chance, he flickers. He glances over his shoulder at something I can't see. "I'm waking up. I think someone's coming, I better go." He throws one last smile in my direction, "I'll see you soon. Try not to worry. And check your email." He manages to say before vanishing completely.

* * *

Loud knocking fills the cabin. I groan pulling my blanket over my head, rolling over so my back faces the door. It's too early and I'm too comfortable. I'm not waking up.

The knocker takes the hint. I wake up a second time to a slit of sunlight pouring across my bed. I stretch smiling up at the blue sky that's peeking through the curtains. I bounce out of bed, feeling rejuvenated. I can't remember the last time I slept that well. Kheelan's dream visit really put my worries to rest.

I hum as I make my way to the bathroom, a loud clatter from the small kitchen stops me in my tracks. There's more rummaging. Fear prickles up my arms. Someone is *inside* my cabin. I tip toe up to the corner and peek my head around.

There's a man standing at my stove.

My heart leaps to my throat and a strangled squeal escapes out of my mouth, alerting the intruder of my presence.

He turns around, greeting me with his most winning smile.

I let out a sigh of both relief and annoyance.

"Good morning sleepyhead, there's coffee over there." Declan points at the counter with the spatula that's in his hand, where a pot waits. I scrunch my nose. "I thought so." He says, "There's some freshly squeezed orange juice too." He points to the other end of the counter, then turns back to the stove.

"If you wanted to kill me, you could have just pushed me off a cliff or drown me at any point this week," I grumble. "You didn't have to go through the trouble of breaking in hoping to give me a heart attack." I shuffle towards the waiting orange juice. My eyes don't leave Declan's back though, the current situation still settling.

Declan laughs. "I didn't want to wake you."

"So you broke in and…" My voice trails off as I take in the mess he's managed to make in the tiny kitchenette. "What exactly are you doing here?"

"Well, originally, I was here to pick you up. We were supposed to go to Pacific Creek today, remember?" He says as he flips something in the pan.

"I remember. Let me rephrase myself." I pause as I pour some juice into a glass. "How did you get in here? I had the door locked."

"Well, I figured when you didn't answer my knock, that you must be all tuckered out from the week of fresh air." His voice is teasing. "I decided I'd do something nice, since you're always accusing me of being a self-centred jerk." He flashes another smile over his shoulder, "So I let you sleep in while I made pancakes."

"Let me get this straight," I sit down at the small table, wrapping my fingers around my glass. "When someone doesn't open the door to let you into their home, you just break in?" I fight the smile tugging at my lips, struggling to keep my face neutral.

"Nah, just you." Laughing, he turns around, two plates in his hands. "I promise you're the only person I stalk, and you should think twice before you let just *anyone* see where you hide your key. You never know who could be stalking you," he wiggles his eyebrows at me. "But, if you're actually creeped out, I can throw these away," he motions to the plates with his chin, "go outside and knock like a civilized guest?" He walks towards the trash can, stepping on the pedal to flip the lid open.

"No, no, no!" I laugh, as my stomach growls on cue. "I want them!"

He smiles, setting a plate down in front of me and sitting down with his own, "That's what I thought."

I take a huge bite, instantly impressed as the flavours roll over my tongue. "WOW! These are actually really good."

"Don't sound so surprised," he says with a smirk.

"Well, I am surprised. I didn't know you could cook."

"You learn to do a lot of things when you live on your own," he says watching me with a bemused look on his face.

"I give you permission to break in any time you want as long as you make me pancakes." I shove another bite into my mouth.

"Does it have to be pancakes?" He asks.

I mock deep thought, "No, but it does have to be equally good, or better." I say around my mouthful.

"You're disgusting. Please finish eating before you say another word to me," he laughs.

I shoot him a wicked grin and shove another bite into my mouth, "What? Don't you like see-food?" I open my mouth displaying my breakfast for him.

He balls up his napkin and throws it at my face. "Like I said, you're disgusting!"

My phone blares from my bed side table, Jen's ringtone. I leap up sliding on my socked feet across the wooden floor to answer it. "Hello my dearest," I chirp into the receiver.

"Hey! You will never guess who I ran into," Jen says.

My heart drops. "Jesse?"

"Or you'll guess on the first try," she laughs. "He was asking all sorts of questions about you. Wondering where in Wyoming you are, if you're liking your job, what you've been up to. Very nosey."

My blood runs cold. "Did you tell him anything?"

"Of course not! I'm not stupid."

"Where are you now? He's not still around is he?" I ask, my heart racing.

"I'm at home. No. I saw him when I went to get brunch with some friends." Worry entering her voice, "What's going on? He's not dangerous to me, is he?"

"No." I sigh, "I don't know. I'm sorry. Just the thought of him puts me on edge I guess. Don't talk to him if you see him again."

"Did you want some syrup?" Declan asks from the table. "Forgot I brought some."

I cover the mouthpiece, "Sure, thanks."

"Who's that?" Jen asks.

"Oh, just Declan," I say as casually as I can while mentally preparing for her anger.

"Is anyone else there?" she asks, her voice oddly calm.

"No, it's just us. We're going to head to Pacific Creek in a little—"

"ROSALIA MATTHEWS! It is MORNING, what is a BOY doing in our one room cabin IN THE MORNING?" She screams over the phone.

I hear Declan chuckle. Oh God, he can hear her! My cheeks burn. "Would you shush." I hiss into the phone. "He didn't spend the night. We're just friends. He came over this morning because we had plans to hang out *in the morning.*"

"He better not have spent the night!" She practically screams.

"I just said he didn't," my voice rising to match hers.

"What are you doing?" She asks, "Seriously Lia. Don't be stupid. You don't need this boy in your life, especially now. You need to be focusing. Preparing. What about Kheelan?"

"I am focused." I say lamely.

"When's the last time you trained?" She asks. I don't respond, because I haven't trained since Kheelan was here. "He's distracting you Lia." Jen says as the line goes dead.

My mouth drops open. She hung up on me.

Chapter Thirteen

It's not until Declan drops me back at my cabin, after we spend the day fishing together at the creek, that I remember to check my email. Sure enough, there's one from Kheelan, time stamped last Saturday, 8:03 am.

Dear Lia, he starts with. *I'm so sorry you're alone on your birthday.*

As though I'm more alone than he was. I push away the guilt for being so distracted I didn't even see I had an email and read on.

I had hoped to talk to you in person, here in Ireland. Writing isn't really my thing. But I can't wait until I get back. I'm afraid I'll burst into pieces if I try. Allie and I broke up. That day we had the big fight, and you came with me to the cemetery. I didn't tell you then because I was afraid of how you'd react. Don't ask me why.

Why would he be afraid of my reaction? I would have been over the moon with joy at that news.

Our world isn't safe for her, he continues, *and that's part of the reason I ended things. But there's another reason, too, a bigger reason. I've fallen in love with someone else. Since the day I first laid eyes on you, actually since the night I first dreamt of you, I haven't been able to get you out of my head.*

My hands go cold. My heart stills. I force my eyes to finish reading.

I realise this probably seems out of the blue to you, but for me it's been a long time coming. Anyway, I love you. And I hope you have a happy birthday, Lia. Rest easy, and know that Kodi and I are safe, but missing you terribly. Hopefully we'll see you very soon.

Love,
Kheelan

My eyes unfocus, blurring as I stare at the phone in my hand. I read the email again. My heart drops into my stomach, I should be ecstatic. This is what I want, right? He's my *soulmate* and my *destiny*, and I love him? I sink onto my bed and try to force excitement into my heart as I read his words again. All they make me feel is guilt. I try to imagine the dream of Kheelan and the kiss we shared in it. Instead, it's Declan's face that comes to mind. Real, solid Declan, with beads of water dripping down his forehead, his face only inches from mine, laughter sparkling in his eyes.

Then the time stamp registers. It came Saturday morning. That was *before* Declan showed up at my door for the first time. *Before* we hiked to the waterfall. *Before* we almost kissed. Before my heart started to split into two. I wish I'd seen it that morning. Then I could feel happy right now, without it being laced with this horrible guilt.

* * *

Emily kicks her feet up on the register's counter, "Did you enjoy all the 'rest' Rose insisted you needed?" She raises her eyebrows, her eyes gleaming wickedly.

I have to concentrate on stopping the smile that tries to play across my lips. "Yes, it was some well-needed rest," I say, careful to keep my voice even and my expression neutral.

She barks out a laugh, "Yeah but you didn't do much resting did you? Say how's that guy, what's his name again? The one you almost kissed?" She pauses like she's deep in thought. "Declan?" She watches my face for a reaction.

I angle my body so she can't see my involuntary smile. "How should I know?" My voice dripping in innocence.

"Oh, come on!" She whines, "Life has been so dull. I'm in need of your juicy romance stories. Let me live vicariously through you. Surely you spending so much time with him means you decided you *like* him."

I turn back towards her, "Romance stories?" I laugh, "I'm sorry to disappoint, but I have nothing juicy to share. Declan and I have been hanging out, but just as friends." She wants juicy, I do have that. I could tell her about Kheelan's love letter of an email, but something holds me back.

"Yeah but, you obviously like him, or you wouldn't be spending so much time together. What *friendly* things do you guys talk about?" She asks, making the word friendly sound *too* friendly.

I shrug, "Just stuff." I have a strong urge to tell her who he is, but it doesn't feel like my secret to tell so I don't elaborate.

Her eyebrows shoot up, "You ignored the first part of my statement!" I shift my gaze away from her face. "You *so* like him!" She settles into her chair, a knowing smirk planting itself on her face.

"I didn't say that." I sigh, boosting myself onto the counter. "Sometimes I think I could, if I let myself…But it's complicated."

"How is it complicated?" She asks, her face full of doubt. "Jen?" It dawns on her, "The dream and her 'soulmate theory'?"

That, I think, and the fact that Kheelan confessed his love for me and oh yeah, Declan is his long-lost brother. But I don't say that, instead I just nod, "That's part of it. I don't really want to get into it here."

"Sometimes dreams are just that. Dreams. They're not real life."

I swallow and look away.

"Where has Kheelan been anyway? Did that story help with anything?" Emily asks before I cave and decide to spill my guts. I let out a breath, relieved for the subject change.

"He's in Ireland, but he should be back any day now." Emily's mouth drops and she stares at me wide-eyed, "We'll know if your story helped when he gets home, I guess." I busy myself by re-stacking the pile of receipts.

Her feet slam to the floor, "He's in IRELAND?" She's on the verge of shouting, "Why on earth is he in Ireland?"

I stare at her, receipts still in hand. I don't know what to say. I didn't expect this kind of reaction.

"Oh my God," Emily slumps back into her chair. "He's there looking for the stupid Daoine Sidhe, and the map from the story, isn't he?"

"Yeah," I say surprising myself with how quiet my voice comes out. It sounds so silly hearing it out loud. "I was supposed to go with him, remember? But my Glow wasn't strong enough, so he's looking for a way into the NetherWorld so we can try to get it back."

She rolls her eyes, "I knew you failed at travelling somewhere with him, but I just thought you were going..." She pauses, "I don't know where I thought you were going, but I definitely didn't think *Ireland.* It's a story, for children. Fairy tales are stories for kids to learn from, they're not history hidden in a picture book." She lets out an exasperated laugh. "I can't believe he actually went to Ireland. It's a metaphor people! To show kids that if something seems too good to be true, it probably is!"

"Well, it seemed like a good idea until you just put it that way," I say lamely. "I guess the fate of the world depends on a low-lighted Fairling. That's not very promising."

"I do have a theory about getting to the NetherWorld though!" Emily perks up leaning towards me, excitement all over her face. "You know how there's a bunch of Fairy tales that say mortals can only enter the OtherWorld on nights when the moon is full?"

"Uh...No," I say. "Then again, I don't know many Fairy tales, so I'm a bad person to ask."

"Well, it's in a bunch of them." She says in her know-it-all tone. "My theory is, you enter the OtherWorld on the *brightest* night of the month because they're the good guys. So," her eyes light up, "I think mortals would enter the NetherWorld on the *darkest* night of the month. Because, you know they're the baddies." She smiles, obviously proud of her reasoning. "I'd be willing to bet you could enter the NetherWorld during a new moon."

"That makes sense." I agree, "But how do we get into the NetherWorld during the new moon?" I shoot back.

"That!" She laughs, "That's a good question." She leans back in her chair, kicking her feet back onto the counter. "Hopefully Kheelan finds that answer in the hills of Ireland." She chuckles to herself as she closes her eyes.

* * *

My heart skips a beat as I pull into the driveway. I throw my car into park and my fingers fumble to unbuckle my seatbelt. I throw the car door open and jump out, crouching down and spreading my arms open wide. "Where's my good girl?" Kodi bounds into my waiting arms. I hug her with all my might and cover her head with kisses. "I'm so sorry I wasn't able to go with you," I say in my puppy dog voice I reserve for only her. "I missed you so much, yes I did!"

"She was a very good girl." Kheelan says as he stands from his seat on the porch step. My heart does a pitter patter in my chest as he makes his way towards me. "I think she helped find something pretty important—"

"—That's great!" I say looking down at Kodi's happy face, "Did you find the map? You're *such* a good girl!"

Kheelan laughs at my display of affection towards my dog, "Not exactly."

A noisy engine and wheels disrupting the gravel interrupt him. I groan inwardly, perfect timing.

Declan dismounts his bike, pulling his helmet off, Kodi races up to inspect the newcomer. He bends down and scratches behind her ears. "Hello there, pooch! You must be the famous Kodiak. Your mother speaks of almost nothing else." He looks up at me with a smirk.

"Hey! That's not true, I have plenty of other stuff I talk about." I'm suddenly very aware of Kheelan, I throw a nervous glance his way. He's watching us, his brow furrowed.

"Hey there, I'm Kheelan." He says stepping forward offering his hand to Declan.

"Kheelan," Declan notices his brother for the first time. His eyes mist a little as he accepts his brother's hand, his chest puffs up as he takes in a big breath. "It's me, Declan."

Kheelan freezes in place. His eyes cloud over, but he doesn't let go of his brother's hand. It's awkward standing here watching them in their long-lost brother moment. I take a few steps backwards and motion to Kodi, but she doesn't see. "Come on Kodi, let's go see Aunt Rose," I finally say, turning to make my way towards the main house.

"Hold it!" Kheelan shouts. He jogs to catch up to me, grabbing onto my elbow. "We need to talk. Right now." He shoots a look in his brother's direction before adding, "Alone."

I nod, glancing at Declan who bobs his in agreement. Kheelan lets out an exasperated sigh at our exchange and pulls me by my elbow towards the cabin.

"Just give us one minute," I say shooting a silent apology towards Declan.

"Take your time." I hear him say as Kheelan slams the door behind us.

Kheelan spins around to face me, I gulp. Anger burns in his eyes as he stares down at me. "What are you thinking Lia? That's who was in your dream the other night." It's not a question. Hurt seeps into his eyes mixing with his anger.

"He's not bad." I try to assure him.

Kheelan ignores me and continues scolding. "Have you been spending time with him?"

I nod.

"*Alone?*" His voice Is reaching hysterics.

I nod again.

"He was raised by a member of the HUNT, Lia."

I back up, wanting more distance between us. "It's not what you think. Just talk to him, he'll explain everything."

He ignores me, throwing his hands up in the air, "How could you be so *stupid*? You just finished being squelched by an Underling, so what? Did you think to yourself, *hmm better start dating another one*!"

Anger rolls through me. "I'm not stupid," I say through clenched teeth. "You're the one being stupid by refusing to *listen*." I put as much fury as I can muster into the glare I shoot his way. "And for the record, it's none of your business who I do or do not date! But no, I'm not *dating* your brother. I'm not *dating* anyone!"

"Do. Not. Call. Him. My. Brother." He snarls through barred teeth.

"He *is* your brother!" My frustration boils over as my voice reaches new heights. "You need to calm down and LISTEN! He is NOT an Underling!"

Kheelan lets out a big breath and studies my face, his own softening. "I'm sorry for yelling." He's careful to keep his tone calm. "But what do you have to base this on? Did Declan tell you he's not an Underling?" His voice takes on a mocking edge. "Because that's exactly what an *Underling* would say."

I roll my eyes, "You really do think I'm stupid." I'm unable to mask the hurt in my voice. "But yeah, he told me. But I also have seen his glow—guess what? It's identical to yours." I shove by him and open the door. "I'm glad you made it back safe, and I did miss you, and I do want to talk about your email, but I don't want to see you right now. I'm taking my dog up to see Rose." I walk out. Declan jumps up from the porch step, worry all over his face. He follows me down to the driveway, he definitely heard our entire conversation.

"I think he may talk to you now," I say under my breath.

He surprises me by pulling me into a hug. "Thank you for backing me in there," he whispers into my hair, sending goosebumps down my neck. "It means more than you know."

I draw away from him, searching his eyes for something, but I'm not sure what. "Please don't prove me wrong." I look back towards the cabin, Kheelan is standing in the shadow of the doorway, his eyes boring down at us.

* * *

"You have no idea how badly I've needed this," I say taking a long sip from my lemonade, I set it back on the little table that separates my lounge chair from Emily's. "Just us girls," I recline back and stretch my arms behind my head, smiling up at the sky. It's a perfect day, not a cloud in sight.

"We just need Jen, and it'd be perfect." Emily agrees, "When does she get back? We need to celebrate both of your birthdays."

"What day is it?" I ask holding my hand up to block the sun as I turn to look at my friend.

"Monday," she says.

"Today then, but I'm not sure what time. She hasn't been answering my calls. I'm on her shit list since she heard Declan in the background last time she called," I say half laughing but really, I'm hurt. I didn't get to wish her a happy birthday because of this. I left her a message Friday, and that was her calling me back Saturday morning, but she got mad before I got the chance. My hand shoots up to the necklace around my neck. She may be mad, but she's still my sister and has to love me.

"Ha, that girl will always be one hundred percent team Kheelan." Emily twists in her chair so she's facing me, diving into gossip mode. "Speaking of...I heard he got back yesterday." She lowers her sunglasses to eye me suggestively, "How was the reunion?"

"Not like I imagined," I say. It's the truth. I imagined more smiles, maybe some kissing. I had planned to discuss his email as soon as he got home. I wanted to thank him for his kind words, beg him for forgiveness for not seeing it sooner. Let him know I feel the same way.

"You gotta give me more than that."

"We got into a fight straight away and I haven't seen him since." I shrug, "Hopefully that means he's been spending time with Declan."

Her mouth drops open. "Why on earth would you want the two guys you like," she holds up her hand, stopping my denial before it reaches my lips. "The two guys you like," she says again, "to spend time together?" She stares me down as she sucks lemonade through her crazy straw.

"Well," I brace myself, and concentrate on keeping my tone casual. "They're brothers." Lemonade sprays out of Emily's nose and mouth, and all over me. "Gross!" I wipe the slime off my arms.

"They're BROTHERS? How long have you known? Did you know this before they did? I can't believe you didn't tell me!"

I roll my eyes. "Quiet down, drama queen. Declan knew, but it wasn't my secret to tell. He wanted to confront Kheelan first, so I kept it to myself for a couple of weeks. But believe me, it's been killing—" my phone begins to ring, I glance down at my screen. It's my sister. I smile and hold my phone up for Emily to see. "Guess she got over it!" I hit the green button and put it on speaker. "Hello lovely! We were just missing you!"

The other end of the phone remains silent.

"HELLO?" I try louder. Stupid cell reception is garbage out here.

"Lia?" Jen's panicked voice crackles through the phone. "Lia, I'm scared. They made me call you, but don't come for me. That's what they want!" My sister's voice is shaky as she relays the message. My eyes lock on Emily, her face mirroring my worry.

"Jen, what's going on?" I say, my hands beginning to tremble.

There's a loud thump followed by more silence. The hairs on my neck prick to life.

"Jen?" I try again. "Jen, what are you talking about? *Who* made you call me? Where are you?"

The line remains silent.

"Jen! Are you there? You need to tell me where you are!" I'm getting hysterical. I take deep breaths and try to stay calm. I won't be any help if I have a panic attack.

Agonising seconds tick by with nothing from the other end, but the call is still connected, so I don't hang up. Emily and I stare at each other wide-eyed in the heavy silence. Finally, I can't take it, "JEN!" I scream into the phone, full panic gripping me.

"Rosalia," a chilling voice answers. "I'd tell you not to come looking for your dear sister," the speaker lets out a low laugh that sends a chill straight into my heart, "but that's exactly what I want you to do."

"Where do you have her?" My voice comes out strangled, suddenly it's hard to pull air into my lungs.

"I look forward to meeting you. Ciao!" The line goes dead. A silent tear rolls down my cheek and plops onto the now blank screen that's clenched in my trembling hand.

"I think a Hunter has my sister," I whisper.

Emily jumps to her feet taking charge. "Call Declan. I'll try Kheelan." Her phone is already out and she begins to dial.

I nod and numbly begin to scroll through my phone until I find Declan's name. I'm sent straight to voicemail. I don't leave a message, I hang up. I need to do something. I stand up and rush inside my cabin. I grab my bow and a quiver filled with arrows. I tear a piece of paper off the kitchen counter and scribble a quick note for Rose, with instructions on how to care for Kodiak. Making it to Wisconsin on my own is a push, I know for certain I won't be able to bring my dog along.

I walk down the path towards Rose's, not noticing the tree branches that have over grown the past few weeks scraping against my arms. Kodi stays close to my heels. Determination and adrenaline hum through my veins, pushing me forward. Emily trails behind us, "Kheelan didn't answer, but I left him a message." She does a small jog to get next to me. "What are you planning Lia?" Her voice full of worry.

"I'm going to get my sister." I say matter-of-factly.

"You don't even know where she is." She tries to reason, "I think we should wait for the guys, or go down to the shop and talk to Rose and Maggie. It could be a trap."

"Every second counts, Emily. I'm not going to go on a wild goose chase to find people who aren't in harm's way just so they can try to talk me out of going." I look at my friend, "It probably is a trap, but I'm not going to abandon my sister. At least me going on my own won't put anyone else in danger."

"How are we going to find her?"

"There's no we in this." I say, "But I plan to start at my old house. Hopefully there will be some sort of clue I can go off from there."

"Your old house, as in Wisconsin? How do you plan on getting there? Your glow isn't strong enough, you said so yourself." I know she's trying

170

to look out for me, but I will not be talked out of this. My mind is already set.

"I have to at least try, Em." Tears burn the rims of my eyes. I take a deep breath to keep them at bay.

"You shouldn't go alone."

I shrug as I let myself into Rose's house, placing my note on the kitchen counter. I bend down and tell Kodi I have to go check on Jen and that I'll be back as soon as I can. I hug her tight and kiss the top of her head. If I succeed and make it to Wisconsin, this could be the last time I see my dog. Kodi gazes at me with her cool blue eyes, she whines and nuzzles into me. A single tear escapes my eye. "Keep Aunt Rose safe, girl," I choke out as I give her one last pat.

Determination to save Jen gets me back on my feet and out the back door. I hear Kodi whine out one last protest as the door shuts behind me, shattering my heart. I breathe in the piney air and send up a quick prayer that this won't be the last time I see her.

I situate myself in the grass. Emily stays silent as she watches from a few feet away as I sling my bow over one shoulder, and my quiver over the other. I cross my legs and begin the process of clearing my head as I breathe in and out, slow and controlled. I smile as the familiar warmth washes over me, something that was such an enormous task a few weeks ago, now comes so naturally.

I envision the big maple tree in our front yard. The spindly branches Jen and I used to climb when we were younger. The way the leaves make a perfect canopy, shielding us from any eyes below. My glow flickers off, I open my eyes. Dread floods my gut. I'm still in Rose's yard. Emily looks up from her phone and offers me a sympathetic smile.

I close my eyes and start the process again. This time imagining the smell of the leaves and the feel of the breeze. When my light flickers out a second time, I only dare to slit one eye open. A groan escapes my lips. I haven't gone anywhere. I let out a frustrated sigh and begin once again. I'm not giving up. This time I imagine Jen's laughing face under the tree. A fresh crown of dandelions woven into her hair. I feel my glow brighten at the memory. I cling to it. I can see it so clearly, even the little scatter of freckles that pop up across her nose and cheeks in the summertime. I can smell the lilies of the valley mom always had in her front garden. I feel the tug in my gut. I concentrate my feelers I *feel* the life of the tree as the suction grips me, then something latches onto my arm.

Chapter Fourteen

I open my eyes to my childhood home, something like relief mixed with anxiety overtakes me. I look down at my right arm. Emily's hand is stilled grasped tightly around it, her knuckles shining white. I follow her arm up to her body and finally to her head. I let out a breath. "What were you thinking? I could have split you into two for cripes sake!"

"For cripes sake? Who even talks like that?" Emily giggles, choking on it halfway when she sees my expression. "I'm sorry. It's just that I couldn't stand the thought of you facing whatever you're about to face on your own. I know we've only known each other for a couple of months, but you're my best friend. You're stuck with me." She elbows me playfully, "Let the adventure begin!" She forces a smile, but her eyes mirror the terror I'm feeling.

"I'm not strong enough to protect you." I warn as I walk towards my house. Even still, I find her presence comforting.

"I don't need you to protect me." She says, her feet crunching through the dry grass behind me.

I punch in the code and the roller door creaks up, revealing an empty garage. We walk through the house, but it's empty too. There's no sign of a struggle, everything is where it's meant to be. I pull out my phone and dial my mom's number.

"Hello?" She picks up after one ring.

"Mom," I breathe out, happy to hear her voice. "Where are you? Is Jen with you?"

"Hi Rosy! No, your father and I are up north, she had plans with friends last night, so we drove up yesterday afternoon."

"Oh," I say, unable to keep the disappointment out of my voice. "I'm having a hard time getting a hold of her."

I hear a rustling of paper from the other end of the phone. "Honey she's probably on her flight by now. Let me see," more rustling, "yes, it says here she'll be landing in an hour and a half."

"Okay thanks, Mom. I gotta go though. I'll talk to you later." My mom barely gets in a goodbye before I end the call. "That was wishful thinking," I say. "At least my parents are safe," I add under my breath. I try Jen's number again. I'm sent straight to voicemail. I look up at Emily, her eyes are watching me, waiting for instructions.

"Now what?" She asks, looking around taking in my family home.

"I guess we could check Jesse's house?" The thought alone sends my insides into turmoil.

Emily eyes the bow slung across my shoulders, her eyes dart around the kitchen before landing on the knife block. She reaches out and grabs hold of the biggest one, securing it to her belt. "Let's go," she says her voice strained.

Since there aren't any cars in the garage we hop on mine and Jen's old bikes. I lead the way as we make the two-mile trek to Jesse's house. I can feel the stares as we pass though the quiet suburban streets, the weird girl on a purple bike with a bow slung across her body, but I don't care. All I can think about is Jen, and the horrible things they could be doing to her. I pray we're not too late, and pedal faster. Fear and determination driving me forward.

* * *

As usual Jesse's curtains are drawn tight and the residence looks dark and dreary—creepy, like the place could be haunted. How had I never noticed how eerie it is when we were dating? We stash our bikes in some bushes along the side of the house. Almost tiptoeing we make our way to the front door.

I stretch my finger towards the doorbell, Emily grabs my arm pulling me away. "Are you crazy?" She hisses, "Even if Jesse doesn't have Jen, he's still an *Underling*. Do you really want to announce our presence? And if he does have Jen, the element of surprise may be our only chance."

I nod, thankful my friend is here to stop my natural stupidity. I reach my hand out again, this time towards the doorknob. I turn it slowly. It's unlocked. I push it open as gentle as possible. It creaks. I freeze. My heart is pounding in my ears, I see Emily out of my peripheral pull the knife from her belt. I lift my own bow off my shoulder and notch an arrow into place. Together we creep through the door.

We tiptoe through the entire house. Every room is dark and dusty, and there's a stale cigarette smell lingering in the air. When we make it back to the front door, ready to give up I notice a crack of light coming from under the basement door. The one place we haven't checked. I motion to Emily, holding my finger over my lips I point to it. We silently make our way to the closed door.

We stand and listen for a second. I don't hear anything. I lift my hand at a snail's pace, afraid to make any noise. I hold my breath as I turn the knob and pull the door open. I creep down the steps, Emily so close behind me I can feel her. Halfway down I come to a halt as voices drift up to us. My heart is going to pound out of my chest. Neither of us move, we just stare at each other eyes wide as we listen.

"Have patience Father, it'll work. We're playing on Lia's biggest weakness, *love*." The speaker snorts in disgust. Jesse. Even now, knowing what he is, my heart sinks.

"How long is it going to take for her to come for this sickening mortal? It's unnatural for us to keep it alive." The chilling high pitched voice from the phone call responds, sending a fresh wave of shivers through me.

I let out a slow breath, at least I've found Jen and for the moment, she's still alive. The small amount of relief this minuscule fact gives me mixes with the dread that's already occupying my stomach space, the combination makes me want to throw up. But fear of being discovered keeps my bile down. My mind races. How am I going to get Jen away from these monsters, and then get her and Emily back to safety?

"Twenty hours," Jesse says, his voice ringing with confidence. "My guess is, she's already on her way and I guarantee she isn't going the speed limit." He laughs, "It's her beloved big sister, her *best friend.*"

A slapping noise followed by someone spitting echoes up the stairwell. I move forward, hatred bubbling in my veins. Emily grabs my upper arm holding me back. "Save that for when we need it," she hisses in my ear.

I look at her confused, she points to my bare forearms. "You're lighting up." She mouths.

She's right, my skin is burning a faint orange colour. Nothing like my glow, more like embers. This is new.

"Quiet Jesse! Stop breathing." The cold voice demands, "I heard something." Agonising silence beats through the room. Fear that they'll hear my heart racing courses through me, causing it to beat even louder. "Yes, I can sense her. It looks like your little Fairling is faster than you thought. She's on the stairs. Go fetch her."

My skin turns to ice as horror floods my body, extinguishing my ember skin. I motion for Emily to start back up the stairs. She barely makes it around the corner when Jesse's voice roots my feet to the top step. "Lia?" He says, feigning surprise. "Is that really you?"

I turn around slowly, trying to mask my fear before revealing my face to my ex-boyfriend. My eyes land on his once familiar features, memories flood through me shattering my heart all over again. I take a deep breath and remind myself that none of it was real, it was all a lie. I focus on turning my sadness and fear into hatred and strength.

"It's good to see you *Awake*," he smirks as he begins to climb the steps towards me, the old wood creaking under his weight. "You wear it well."

I don't say anything. I know I should turn and run but my feet won't listen to my brain. My arms are dead weight at my sides, but I manage to raise my bow, aiming the pointed arrow straight at his heart. He stops, he's only a few steps away from me, no chance I'd miss. I pull the string back.

"Sorry Lia, I can't let you do that." He moves fast, a ball of smoke appearing between his hands, his eyes burst into fiery red flames as he thrusts the blackness towards me. I let the string go right as everything goes dark.

* * *

My head is heavy, my mind foggy. I can't move. My hands are bound behind my back and my ankles are secured tightly to the legs of the hard chair I'm seated in. My heart pounds in panic as the recent events rush back to me. Emily. Jen. My eyes snap open, I can't see anything. I'm in complete darkness. I pull at the ropes that are binding me with all my strength, to no avail. I'm trapped. "Hello?" I whisper into the darkness.

No one responds. A tiny bubble of hope rises in my chest. Maybe Emily managed to get away.

A door to my right shoves open, slamming into the brick wall behind it. I squint as light pours in around a large silhouette of a man towering over me. His large hand reaches up and pulls on something dangling from the ceiling. A lightbulb bursts to life revealing my cell.

My eyes take a moment to adjust, once they do I long for the darkness to return. The man, if he can even be considered a man, has situated himself in a gaudy velvet armchair in front of me. Only a couple of feet separate us. He's dressed in a well-made black suit with thin grey pinstripes, his chest barrels out from under his bulky neck. My eyes make my way to his face and I freeze. His eyes are blood red, which is a terrifying contrast to his ashen grey skin and slicked back silver hair. He smiles, his inky black lips spreading unnaturally wide revealing the pointed wolf-like teeth beneath. "Welcome back Rosalia," his voice unnerves me, it doesn't match his body. "You were out for quite some time. You had us *worried*." I shudder as the oily words come out of his mouth. His smile doesn't falter as he watches me intently, stroking the purple velvet of his arm rests with his black fingernails.

177

"Where's my sister?" I spit out, surprising myself with how brave my voice sounds.

The grey man chuckles as he looks towards the open door. "You were right, Jesse. She really does love that mundane mortal. Such a nauseating weakness," he turns his face towards me, a curious glint in his crimson eyes.

I shift my focus away. I don't like him examining me, so I busy myself with taking in my surroundings, or lack thereof. I'm in what's probably meant to be a utility closet in the basement. Concrete floor, cinder brick walls, all painted black. The only furniture is the simple wooden chair I'm tied to, and the ugly purple throne the grey-skinned man occupies. My eyes land on Jesse, who's hovering in the doorway. "Why are you doing this Jess?" I ask, forcing myself to meet his eyes.

He keeps his gaze steady, his face not revealing anything he may be feeling. "I'm not doing anything. You did this to yourself, Lia."

A bark like laugh escapes me. "Oh really? I tied myself to a chair in a creepy dark room?"

He glares back, he's never been a fan of sarcasm. "No, I told you not to go to Wyoming."

"So you kidnapped my sister because I moved to a different state? Wouldn't it have been easier just to kidnap me before I left? Seems like—"

"Children, please. You're giving me a migraine." The Grey-skinned man complains. His eyes bore into my face. "Who knows you're in Wisconsin?"

"No one," the lie comes out without having to think about it.

"Tsk, tsk, little Fairling, I'll give you another chance." His pointy smile creeps back onto his face sending a chill down my spine, "Who knows you're in Wisconsin?"

"No one," I meet his eyes this time, determined not to give anything away.

He leans forward, "Did you know when a Fairling lies their cheeks flush pink?" His breath is cold and smells like blood. I lean as far back in

178

my chair as I can, wanting to put as much distance between us as possible. "Who knows you're here?" He growls for a third time.

I stare into his eyes and jut my chin out. If he can tell when I'm lying, I won't speak.

"Going to be stubborn? Fine. More fun for me," his red eyes burn bright as fire, a searing heat shoots into my eyes filling my skull with a scorching pain. I try to close them, but they're held tight in his gaze. His hands clasp around my skull, his icy fingers a shocking contrast to the flames licking away inside my head. I can feel him creeping around in my mind. I need to stop him, to protect everyone.

I force my eyes shut, but the fire continues to rip through my head, I worry my eyelids are melting. I try to clear my mind. I need to call to my light, it's the only thing I can think of. I take deep breaths trying to slow my heart rate. I picture Kheelan's face, it worked at Aunt Rose's. I try to concentrate on remembering his soft eyes, and strong eyebrows, but Declan's face still wet from the waterfall pushes the image from my mind. His silvery blue eyes refracting light, his face so close I can see the individual drops of water spattered across his nose. The glow bursts in my chest and begins to spread outwards, I can feel it's even dimmer than normal. Still, I hold on tight to the flicker and I will it to my head, where the grey man is still probing around with his searing fire and burning cold hands.

Relief spreads over me as soon as the light reaches my skull. It worked. The burn has been extinguished. The grey man howls out in pain. I open my eyes concentrating on holding my Glow. He has his head cradled in his hands and is doubled over between his legs. Jesse is backed into a corner making an effort not to look at me. Good. I'm not useless, after all. I wonder if I'd be able to Light Travel?

"You little bitch." The Grey man hisses through his fingers.

"Did you see anything, Flint?" Jesse asks from his corner. He glances in my direction before quickly looking away. "Lia, turn it off, I'm going to be sick."

"Not a chance," I manage to spit out between my teeth. Sweat is beading up on my forehead but I need to hold it as long as I can. I picture everyone I love, everyone I need to keep safe. I fill my heart with them. My sister, my parents, Rose, Maggie, Emily, Kheelan and Declan, even Kodiak. My light swells, the room is blazing. I smile, my glow has never been this bright before. I need to get Jen and get us both out of here. "Tell me where my sister is." My voice comes out strong.

"One person knows," Flint says to Jesse, ignoring my demand. "A mortal. Nothing to worry about." He calmly gets to his feet and crosses the space so he's towering above me, pure hatred radiating out of his eyes. "As for you, you really shouldn't have done that." He places one hand on my forehead, my scream is instant. The pain unlike anything I've ever experienced. Like plunging into icy water and being stabbed by needles all over my body. My glow sparks out as he starts to reach his other hand towards my collarbone, I squirm trying to get away. My chair wobbles, but his grip is unyielding.

"FLINT," Jesse's voice booms from his corner, a sudden air of authority in his tone. "If you take a drop of her light, Herne will know. Do you want him angrier with you than he already is?" Flint's hand stops centimetres from my chest. I watch as his eyes flicker between his regular blood red and his burning fire. He's frozen as an inner battle between what he wants and what his orders must be rages inside him. Finally, he lowers his hand and rips the one on my head back to his side. The biting chill begins to subside. I let out a slow breath as he begins to turn back towards his chair. He hesitates. Before I can register what's happening, he spins back around, his hand crashing hard across my face.

A fresh wave of ice plunges through my skull, this time mixed with the sting of unbelievable force as his hand makes contact with my head. I fly backwards, taking the chair with me as I topple to the ground. My skull smashes against the concrete floor, with a sickening crack. I'm only semi aware of the taste of blood that's flooding my mouth as my vision blots out.

180

*   *   *

This time when I come to, Flint doesn't waste time with fake pleasantries. I open my eyes to the black floor. My chair has been righted, but I'm hunched over. There's a dull throb on the side of my head where my skull smacked the cement, and I'm aware of the wetness of my hair which I know can't be a good sign. The side of my face where Flint struck me is starting to swell, making it hard to see out of my left eye. I try to flex my jaw, but that only worsens the pain. I lift my head and find Flint sitting in his chair watching me, his face an eerie calm.

"Sore?" He asks, an amused smile playing at his lips. "You're lucky I didn't squelch you. IF I hadn't gotten specific orders not to, I would have. The pain you're experiencing now would feel like a tender caress in comparison."

All I can do is stare at him as confusion settles over me. He's making it seem like being squelched is painful, but I hadn't even known it was being done to me. "Being squelched doesn't hurt," I wince as the words come out. I shouldn't have said that.

Flint smirks and leans towards me, resting his arms on his knees so his eyes are level with mine. "And I suppose you have first-hand experience with squelching in the short time you've been awake?"

"Yes," I mutter. "Jesse stole my light." I straighten as best I can, trying to sit tall. "I'd like it back by the way, along with my sister."

This makes Flint laugh. *Really* laugh. He doubles over, grabbing on to his armrests to stop himself from falling out of his chair. That's not the reaction I was expecting. I steal a glance in Jesses direction, he's laughing too. What's so funny?

"Oh Rosalia, thank you for that! I don't get to laugh enough." Flint reaches up and wipes dirty tears from his eyes. Then he notices the astonished look on my face. "OH!" Another sputter of laughter shoots out of him, "You're being serious. You actually thought you were being squelched? Adorable."

A cold numbness drips down my body.

181

"Your new Fairling friends didn't tell you otherwise?" He leans forward again, his eyes unwavering. He waits for me to respond. But I keep my lips tight. He reaches out and slaps me, causing a fresh wave of pain. "Answer me!" His voice sinister.

I gulp. "They thought I had been squelched," I whisper.

"And what led them to believe this?" He asks, his eyes hungry. I stare back at him. He raises his hand, preparing to strike me again.

"Because I Awakened so late, and my light is so dim." I say through gritted teeth.

He barks out a noise that makes my skin crawl, something bordering between laughter and excitement. "Fairlings are fools! You know *nothing* about the sweet art of *squelching*. It's a shame I can't demonstrate for you, provide you a proper lesson." He smiles wickedly. "However, I can assure you sweet little Fairling, you have never been squelched a day in your life. Your light is how it should be. You're just naturally weak."

I feel dizzy as his words sink in. There's no light to steal back. Whatever Kheelan found in Ireland is useless, it won't help us, I won't get stronger. I'm weak, and we'll never find The Lost Stave because of it. Or, I'll be dead before we can even look. I wonder what will become of the worlds, of my family.

"I was misting you," Jesse steps out of the shadows. "You can't squelch someone who isn't awake. I was just misting you so you wouldn't Awaken, and I would have been successful if you wouldn't have been whisked away to Wyoming."

I can feel Flint's eyes boring into me, watching as I turn all the new information over in my head. I look up at him, an evil grin is covering his face. "Sorry little Fairling, you're weak. Kheelan on the other hand, I have a feeling he isn't. He's the one we want."

My heart skips a beat, *no*. They can't hurt him. I won't let them. A new determination shoots through my limbs and I struggle against my binds, a fruitless attempt to loosen them.

Flint chuckles, watching my useless battle against the ropes. "You have spirit, I like that. But it's too late, we already sent an Underling to look after little Kheelan. Us taking your *human* sister," he says human like it's a bad taste in his mouth, "was merely a way to get him to come quietly, so to speak."

I go still. There's an Underling by Kheelan? I thought me coming to Wisconsin alone was keeping him safe. But I fell for the trick and left him alone. Fear clenches my heart, is that why Emily couldn't get through to him? Because he's hurt?

Flint's grin widens, showing off every single one of his dirty pointed teeth. "Oh wait, you know the Underling we sent," he pauses watching my reaction carefully.

I fight to keep my face neutral but a fresh wave of dread fills me.

"Right before you kicked me out of your mind, I saw his face." His eyes gleam.

My blood has turned to ice, I struggle to keep my poker face intact.

"Declan, Forrest's boy." I didn't think it was possible for his grin to widen, but somehow it does.

My heart drops into the pit of my stomach. I have never felt betrayal this deep before. Worse than Jesse even. How could I be so stupid? How did he fake his glow? And to think I *pushed* Kheelan to talk to him. I basically handed him over on a silver platter. Tears spring to my eyes. *Kheelan.*

"I love watching your emotions dance across your face. So many of them!" Flint cackles. "You seemed rather cosy with young Declan. Where were you? At a waterfall?" He claps his hands together in mock delight, "How *romantic!*" He stares at me, a flicker of flame dancing across his iris's, his pointy smile returning. "You don't *love* him, do you?"

My face must give something away because he doubles over in laughter again. Panting to catch his breath when he finally rights himself.

"Ahh Rosalia, I get it, why Jesse wanted to keep you around now. You're funny. But, that's enough. No more questions from you. Here's what's going to happen." His voice has returned to normal, all traces of laughter gone from his eyes. "We need you to call Kheelan and tell him where you are. Then, we'll let your sister go free, simple as that."

"How do I know Jen is still alive?" I barley manage to form the words, my tongue suddenly too thick.

His hand moves too fast, I don't see the strike coming. "I said no more questions from you!" I slump down in my chair as a fresh trickle of warm blood drips down my cheek. "It hurts that you don't trust me." His ugly grey face morphs into an exaggerated pout when I manage to straighten back up in my chair. "You're right though, you don't know." He turns his head to the dark corner behind him. "Jesse, fetch the girl."

Jesse nods and exits the room. We sit in silence, me desperately trying to think of a way out of this mess, and Flint watching me with no shame. I try to ignore him, I need to figure out a way to save Jen, find Emily, and keep Kheelan far away from this monster. I need to get back to Wyoming and beg for his forgiveness. The only problem is, I can't think of one plausible scenario where I can achieve all four.

I whip my head to the door as Jesse re-enters, he's pulling a stretcher behind him. My sister lays motionless, immersed in a misty cloud. She looks like she could be sleeping. I breathe a slight sigh of relief when I see her chest rise and fall. She's breathing, she's alive. Then I take in the rest of her condition. Her bottom lip is cracked and covered in dried blood, her right eye surrounded by a ring of black and blue bruises, so swollen I can't see her eyelashes. A new wave a hate and anger scorches through my veins. I feel my skin begin to bubble, I don't need to look down to know I'm hot as an ember.

"None of that," Flint warns, eyeing my orange skin warily. Was that fear that flashed across his face?

I breath in, getting my emotions under control, letting my skin cool. I have to be careful.

"That's better," Flint says, looking me over with new interest burning in his eyes. "Maybe you're not so weak, after all." Words start pouring out of him. Something about joining the Hunt, about power and the worlds, but I tune him out. I've just realised the rope around my wrists is looser. *My flare up burned the rope.* I start to formulate a plan in my head. No doubt a suicide mission, but I have to at least *try*. I nod my head, pretending like I'm listening, to keep Flint talking while I work at freeing my hands behind my back.

My hands snap apart. Excitement rings through me, it takes all my will power to keep my face blank. "I would *never* join the Hunt." I say to Flint, keeping my hands behind my back. "I would rather die."

"That can be arranged," he says dryly. "You've seen the human." He motions lazily at Jen's mutilated form. "Now hand us Kheelan and she goes free."

"I'm afraid I can't do that," I say.

"Then you can sit here and watch as I consume your sister's soul." He begins to stand. My heart reverberates through my chest, as a cold sweat breaks out all over my body. It's now or never. I need to act fast. I squeeze my eyes shut and concentrate, letting my guard crumble. I think about Declan's betrayal, I picture Jen's mutilated face, I remember all the lies Jesse fed me over the years, the fact that he kept me from Awakening, kept me shadowed and confused about who I really am. I think about how the Fairies expect me to risk my life and the lives of my loved ones to save a world I'm not a part of, not really. I think about what I've done to Kheelan. All these thoughts flash through my head in seconds and I let them feed my burning anger, I urge the fire though my veins as I ignite in a scorching flame. The smell of burning rope from my ankles drifts up to my nostrils and I jump to my feet not allowing myself to think twice. I hurl myself forward my hands stretched out in front of me, burning hot embers.

Flint isn't expecting it, which gives me a slight upper hand. I take advantage of his surprise and grasp at his face, wanting to inflict as much damage as possible. Agonised screams screech out of him as my hands burn into his flesh, the smell of melting skin burns at my nostrils sending my stomach in to turmoil, it takes all my control not to throw up. When I'm confident I've immobilised him, I spin around anticipating Jesse's attack. Except Jesse isn't there. I stare at the open door unsure of what to do next.

Between Flints cries I hear a loud crash from the main part of the basement. I push Jen's stretcher through the door and do a quick scan. The walls are lined with shelves, all cluttered with junk piled all the way up to the unfinished ceiling, where wires to the floor above are exposed. There are dark stains all over the concrete floor, I shiver thinking what could have caused them. On the far side of the room are the stairs, the source of the noise blocking my way out. Emily is on top of a furious, red-eyed Jesse, a knife to his throat.

I'm paralysed from the shock of what I'm seeing. How has she managed to overpower him? A chill washes over me as I realise Flint's screams have come to a sudden stop. It snaps me out of my daze. I finish my scan of the room, my eyes finally landing on what I need. My bow and arrows, I rush to the shelf they're resting on and snatch them up, whipping back around as I notch an arrow. I turn towards the room I just exited. Flint is hunched in the doorway, his face melted and deformed, the amount of blood oozing out of him is repulsive. He's struggling to stay upright, he has his arms above his head, rage burning in his eyes. I let my arrow fly right as he brings his arms crashing down, a giant fireball launches across the room. I barely dodge out of the way in time. Rolling on the ground to avoid becoming torched.

Everything slows down. I watch from the ground as my arrow soars through the air, straight for Flint's chest. I brace myself for the impact, unsure how it'll feel knowing I killed someone. But before my arrow makes contact, he disappears, leaving only a faint trace of smoke in the air. My arrow lodges into the doorframe.

I whip my head around to see the damage the fire ball has caused, there's an enormous, scorched circle on the brick wall. I shudder thinking what could have happened if I was a second slower. A yelp pulls my attention to the bottom of the stairs. I half expect to see Emily in flames, even though I know the ball went nowhere near her and the Underling. Instead, what I see is my friend lying motionless next to a very bloody Jesse.

186

Thinking quick I dash to the stretcher my sister's on, hoisting her onto my back. The weird mist moves with her. I surprise myself with how quickly I'm able to carry her over to where Emily lays motionless, her arms and neck starting to blister from burns. The stories I've heard about adrenaline fuelling superhuman strength must have some ring of truth. I lay Jen down next to my friend so I can assess the damage. I barely spare a glance for Jesse, it's clear he's not going anywhere any time soon. He might even be dead. The thought doesn't make me feel anything.

A soft moan comes out of Emily.

"Shh," I whisper, "don't move, you're hurt. It looks like he was able to burn you pretty badly." I push hair off her forehead. "Don't worry," I smile down at her as she opens her eyes. "Nothing Maggie and Rose won't be able to mend." I glance behind me. We need to get out of here. "Are you okay to walk because we need to go, like *now*."

She doesn't say anything, just struggles to her feet, brushing my hands away. "I'm fine. Trust me, I've had worse."

I just stare at her. "Worse? How? You're covered in burns." I say as I watch my friend somehow manage to get Jen hoisted up. I leap to my feet to support the other half of my sister and we begin our way up the stairs towards our freedom.

"Sorry I beat your ex-boyfriend up so bad," she laughs.

"I think you may have killed him," I say.

"Nah, he's just unconscious. You half human types are hard to kill." She takes in my condition, quickly adding, "Which is a good thing, sometimes."

I glance down the steps behind us, Jesse's beginning to twitch. We've made it to the top of the stairs. "Do you think you can get her outside on your own? I'm going to go tie him up so he can't follow us."

Emily nods and heaves Jen onto her back.

"Have you been able to get through to Kheelan?" I ask. Emily shakes her head no. "Try Maggie and Rose." I say as I start back down the stairs. "Tell them not to trust Declan!" I say over my shoulder. Emily crinkles her brow in confusion. "I'll explain in a sec."

I take the remainder of the steps two at a time. Exhaustion hitting me as I make it to the bottom, any lingering adrenaline burning off. I stare down at Jesse's bloody body. I muster my remaining strength and grab a hold of his ankles, dragging his limp body across the basement. I manage to get him into my chair, situating him so he doesn't flop over. I dash into the main room of the basement and dig through the shelves until I find the spool of rope they must have used on me. I run back into the dark room and get to work securing his feet and hands.

As I finish tying my last knot, a groan seeps out of him. I stand up and stare down at his familiar face. Features I once upon a time found adorable. Now, they make my skin crawl.

"I hope you know you just signed your death sentence, Lia," he says, his voice full of venom.

I open my mouth, but before I can get any words out someone grabs me from behind.

"So you're the little Fairling that Flint couldn't handle?" A rough voice coos into my ear.

Fear trickles through my body. I try to stop the panic. I need to call the Glow right now. I try to clear my mind.

"Not much of a girl," a second voice muses, walking around to my front, drinking me in from head to foot. He has the same grey skin as Flint, and when he opens his mouth to speak, I see the same pointed teeth, but his hair is jet black, hanging limply around his shoulders. There's a predatory hunger in his eyes that makes me wish I was wearing more layers. I close my eyes, not wanting to look at him, wishing he'd stop looking at me like I was something to eat. I need to picture Kheelan, I need to call the Glow. "Are you sure we can't taste just a tiny bit of her Light, Blaise?" The long-haired man sneers.

I can't manage a flicker. Hopelessness fills me. My light isn't coming. I'm too weak. I can only hope Emily gets herself and Jen to safety.

"No, our orders are to take her straight to Herne," the man called Blaise says from behind me, his voice firm.

At their leaders name I start to fight with all my might, straining against Blaise's strong arms. I cannot be taken to Herne. Being taken to Herne means being taken to the NetherWorld. My struggles only make the two men laugh, Blaise tightens his hold on me, making my shoulders scream in protest as he rips them backwards.

I open my mouth, preparing to scream a warning up to Emily, hoping she's out on the lawn by now and isn't about to come back looking for me. Before any noise is able to escape my mouth, the grey man in front of me opens his hands and blows a puff of dark smoke in my face, silencing me.

I feel myself slip out of consciousness as soon as the cloud reaches my face. My body going limp in the Hunter's arms, and for the third time today I'm engulfed in blackness.

Chapter Fifteen

I'm in and out of consciousness. Every time I come to, I can't open my eyes. It's as though my eyelids have been glued shut, they're so swollen. I'm semi aware that my face is pressed against a hard, rough surface and that I'm cold. But I can't move, my limbs are too heavy. Somewhere in the cloudiness of my mind I know I should be terrified. I'm in the NetherWorld, I can feel it in the heavy, damp air surrounding me that smells like dirty pennies. Each time my mind is about to grasp the severity of my situation I slip back into the silent darkness.

Footsteps clatter by a few times, but I can't move to see who or what it is, so I lay in my helpless heap and wait to slip back into the safety of my own oblivion.

"Rosalia," a piercing voice slips into my mind.

I'm able to slit my eyes open a sliver. I'm lying on concrete, all I can see are thick jail-like bars a couple of feet from my face.

"Rosalia," the voice sings again.

I lift my head, my cheek peeling away from the clammy floor. I'm careful not to move too fast, my head and limbs still weighted and aching.

"ROSALIA!" The voice bellows. "Wake up." The sing-song tone turning into fierce command.

I somehow manage to sit up. My head is throbbing, and the metallic smell of blood is stuck in my nostrils. I try not to think about the damage that's been done to my face, but I can't stop my fingers from flitting up to investigate. My cheek where Flint struck me is crusty and swollen, I drag my fingers higher to where my head struck the floor. My hair is thick and matted. I take a deep shuddering breath as my current circumstance settles over me, I'm a prisoner of the NetherWorld.

I scan the dim stone walls of my cell, looking for the source of the voice, but I'm alone. I clamber to my feet, my legs wobbling under my weight, how long have I been in here? I shuffle over to the bars of my cage to peer down the dark passageway, maybe the speaker is hidden in the shadows. I lean forward wrapping my fingers around the bars, I expect the metal to feel cold, but instead a searing burn sizzles up my hands and through my arms. My howl comes out coarse as I crumple to the ground cradling my melted appendages. I scramble away from the bars until my back is pressed up against the concrete wall. I turn my palms over to get a good look at the damage. Angry bar-shaped welts have already formed and are beginning to blister. A slow tear leaks out of my eye, despair clutching my heart, dragging me down the wall.

I take a deep breath and straighten back up. Feeling sorry for myself isn't going to get me out of my current predicament. I need to start with what I know, list the facts.

One, I'm in the NetherWorld. I don't need confirmation, I can feel it. A heavy darkness that no amount of light could chase away, and the damp coldness chilling me to the centre of my bones. Not to mention the *smell*, the dirty penny odour has commingled with a faint hint of sulphur that has made its way to my cell from somewhere further down the passage. I shudder at the thought of what's causing it. My nightmare of the lava pit flashing to the forefront of my mind, I shake the thought away. I need to stay focused.

Two, I'm a prisoner of The Wild Hunt, probably about to be squelched and enslaved for all of eternity.

Three, no one knows I'm here.

Four, I have to get out on my own.

I close my eyes and start what has become my routine over the summer. Deep breaths, while concentrating on clearing my mind. I try to picture Kheelan, his bright blue eyes and honest face, but all I'm able to conjure is Declan's teasing smile and silvery blue ones. My brain clouds

191

as a fresh wave of betrayal and guilt hits me, a sob rips out of my throat. I let my body slump to the ground and I curl up in a ball, surrendering to the anguish as silent sobs shake through my body.

Declan seemed so sincere when he talked about wanting to protect his brother, why didn't I see through it? I could have stopped this. I could have kept Kheelan safe. But no, I was blinded by a cute smile and charming sense of humour. Now I'm stuck in a jail cell in the NetherWorld, powerless to help the one person I can trust. Kheelan could be dead or in a cell of his own and it's all my fault.

The light doesn't lie Rose's words ring through my head. How had he managed to call the light? Rose was sure an Underling couldn't conjure the Glow. *Rose was also sure you were squelched* the nagging voice in the back of my head points out. I sigh, as dear as she is, I have to accept the fact that my half-Fairling aunt and mentor doesn't know much about the world of the Fae.

* * *

"Aww did the iron bars burn the little Fairy-Blood?" The same cold voice coos.

My eyes shoot open. I must have cried myself to sleep. I'm still curled into a ball, my palms carefully placed so they're facing upwards. I pull myself off the ground so I'm sitting upright and raise my gaze to the source of the voice. I recognise his gleaming horns instantly, the star from my nightmares these past few months. That doesn't stop his burning coals of eyes and chilling black smile from making me flinch. My obvious revulsion only causes his smile to broaden, exposing more of his black vampire-like fangs. He likes being feared.

"Don't be afraid, my little light." He lies, "I don't want you dead, at least not at the moment. You being alive and at full," he pauses to take in my current state; swollen face, burned hands, broken heart and soul. "Strength," he finally finishes with, an amused twinkle in his eyes.

I stare up at him, unblinking. Hate and fear bubbling through my body, but no words come to me. What could I possibly say to make this situation any better? Even if I wasn't too scared to speak, I know my voice would betray me, I don't want him to know how much I actually fear him.

"I can see the hate in your eyes, Rosalia." The way he says my name makes it sound slimy, sending a tremble down my spine. "That's good," Herne continues, "Let hate take over and fuel you. It's the most powerful emotion." He looks at my face, not bothering to hide his disgust. "You look like a child," he snorts. Then his disgust turns to curiosity, "I guess looks can be deceiving though, you've proven that much to my Huntsmen."

"What do you want?" I finally manage, wanting nothing more than for him to leave me alone. I need to think, plan. I have no idea how much time has gone by since Jesse's basement. The thought makes my stomach turn. Did Emily and Jen manage to make it to safety? Is Kheelan ok? Kodiak? Aunt Rose, Maggie? I can't bear the thought of any one of them being hurt, or worse. Bile burns my throat at the mere possibility.

Herne flashes his repulsive black teeth again. "You," he says simply. "I want you to join my Hunt. You'd make history Rosalia, the first Huntswoman."

"What makes you think I have any interest in joining the Hunt?" I ask, letting the disgust drip from my voice.

His smile vanishes, "What makes you want to fight for Queen Lucille and her daughters?" He snarls back, "Have you ever met your Fairy Mother? Or any of the Fairies for that matter?" His slimy smile stretches his lips too tight when I don't respond. He's revolting, I have to look away. I concentrate on the spider web of cracks on the concrete floor in front of me. "I didn't think so," he continues after some time, "I wouldn't hold your breath either. They're selfish and lazy, they only use their Fairlings to do their dirty work, so they don't have to." He squats down so he's level with me, "Look at me," he demands.

I keep my gaze fixated on the cracks.

"LOOK AT ME." His voice shakes the walls. I slowly raise my head until I'm looking into the crimson eyes of the creature grasping my cell bars, the metal having no effect on him. "We treat Underlings like family." His voice returns to syrup, "They're our own and we take care of them." He rises back to his full height, "One big, happy family." He stares down at me for a moment, waiting for a response, but I keep my lips tight. "No need to answer now. Weigh your options; do you want to be a pawn on a chess board, or be part of a family?" With his final word a puff of black smoke fills my cell, sending me into a coughing fit. When the air clears, he's gone, and I'm alone.

* * *

Twice a day, at least my guess is twice a day. There's no sign of daylight or any other way to show that time is passing, but two times a *day* a man who has a head of a pig shows up, and with a grunt he slides a bowl of sloppy mush through a flap at the bottom of my cell door, along with a glass of water. Besides this minuscule amount of interaction, I don't see another living thing. When I receive my third bowl of mush, I decide to start keeping track of the passing time, every 'morning' I scratch a tiny tally mark into the cement floor with the handle of my spoon.

I try to call the light, but it never works, so I pass the time by sleeping. Dreamless, fitful sleeps. Each time I wake, I feel more tired than when I went to sleep. The darkness of this place is draining my energy faster than I can regenerate it.

By my count it's a week into my imprisonment, when I finally dream. I'm standing in a dark forest, there's no moon, the dark of the night heavier than normal. A familiar voice rustles through the leaves from somewhere in the distance making me go cold. Declan.

"This way Kheelan!" I hear him shout. Fear grips my heart. I try to call out to Kheelan, tell him to run. I shout a warning that his brother is an Underling. No sound comes out of me. I try again, pulling from my gut to really make my voice travel through the thick darkness of the woods as I bellow. Nothing. Tears run down my cheeks as I keep trying to call out.

A blur of a shadow swooshes past me, in the direction Declan's voice had come from. The branches around me rustle, but all I can see are the shadows of the trees.

"Is it the dog?" I hear Kheelan ask from somewhere far away.

My heart pumps harder, "KODIAK!" I try to scream, but again, nothing comes out. I break into a run, even my foot falls slamming through the dead leaves and twigs that blanket the forest floor don't make a sound. I brush the frustrated tears off my cheeks and force my legs to move faster, *don't touch my dog*.

Finally, silhouettes enter my line of vision, I hear Kodi's familiar bark, "I'm coming girl!" I try to say, but of course the darkness swallows it before it leaves me.

Dark mist suddenly lifts from the forest's floor, stopping me in my tracks. I hesitate for a moment before pushing through it. They aren't much further, I need to get to them. The mist keeps rising and thickening until I'm in black nothingness. The forest. The voices. Kodiak. All of it, gone.

The dream gives me a new surge of determination. I spend the rest of that day meditating, hoping it'll help me call the light, but it doesn't. Each time I sleep a dreamless sleep after that, my hope drains a little bit more. Days pass and no more dreams come. I wake to a darkening mind, depression taking a firm grip on me. Negative thoughts fill my head, and I let them chew away from the inside out. By the middle of the second week in the cell, I'm a stone statue. I stare at the wall, sometimes I get up to pace, but I tire so quickly I have to sit back down after just a few steps.

I begin talking to myself. Deep in my mind I realise this isn't healthy, but still, I talk to myself. Sometimes it's to bounce crazy ideas around about ways to escape, but mostly I just need to hear my voice, to know I'm not dead.

I gulp the water in one mouthful as soon as the pig man slides it across the floor towards me, it's never enough to ease the burning dryness in my throat or to give my cracked and bleeding lips any relief. I eat the mush just as fast, it's repulsive, instantly rising in my throat as soon as I swallow but I know I need it to stay alive, I use all my will power to keep it in my stomach, where it belongs.

On the fourteenth day, I can't get off the ground. Terror rings through me. It's like my body won't listen to my brain's commands. I try to stand, but my legs can't bear any of my weight anymore. I try to drag myself across the floor when my mush comes, but I can't even make it the few feet. So I stare at the walls. My eyes feel too wide, I know I'm not blinking enough, but I can't seem to make myself do even this small task. Words I can't even decipher tumble out of me with each breath, implausible plans of escape.

On the fifteenth day Herne reappears, in the same black cloud of smoke he left in two weeks prior. I stare at him, my eyes still too wide, they shouldn't be so open.

I'm not sure if he's really here or if my mind has created a hallucination of him. Words bounce around in my head, mostly angry ones. I know I don't like this guy but none of the things I want to say make it to my mouth. I just stare at the creature before me, all rational thought lost in the darkness of my mind.

"Looks like time has quieted your spirit," Herne says, with a twinkle of delight. "Maybe a little too much."

I open my mouth, hoping words will find their way out, but all I manage is a dry croaking noise.

"Looks like I'll need to have a servant get you," he assesses me from head to toe, "cleaned up." His high-pitched cackle reverberates though my skull, I wish my hands to my ears to block out the noise, but they stay limp at my side refusing to move.

I open my mouth again, surely words will find their way out this time.

Herne holds up a claw like finger, my mouth flops shut. "Don't speak. I didn't come here for conversation, merely to inform you that you'll be attending a dinner party this evening. You're the guest of honour!" He slaps his grey taloned hands together in feigned excitement, but his face remains void of any emotion. "A servant will help you prepare." As quick as he appeared, he's gone again. Leaving only a whisper of smoke in his wake.

I close my eyes and shake my head. When I open them again, the smoke is gone. Was that real?

I try to stand up, to look down the passageway but my legs give out half way up. I curl up into a tight ball. Death breathing down my neck.

I'm not sure if I'm awake or dreaming, maybe I'm somewhere in between. The line between the two states have become a blur, I try to rouse myself, but I can't. I hear metal clinking, echoing off the walls. That has to be real. I'm awake.

I'm weightless and floating away. This has to be a dream. I'm sleeping.

"Doesn't look good, this one might be too far gone." A tongue clicks, "Such a shame, she was a Fairling, like you."

Maybe I'm dead.

The world blinks to life around me. I'm standing on the edge of a cliff, there's a river rushing over the edge next to me. I lean forward to peer down the rock ledge. The water falls at least three stories, forming a small pool within a protective cove of giant boulders. I bring my gaze back up and drink in the ombré of vibrant greens to mossy ones the trees create in the canyon and rolling hills in the distance. I take a deep breath in, the air doesn't feel right in my lungs, it's not fresh. I'm dead.

The crunch of rocks alerts me I'm not alone. I turn my head, it's Declan and he's dressed in a tuxedo, a single black rose pinched between his fingers. He smiles down at me. "I'm so glad you're here," he says.

My heart flutters to life, my lips pull automatically into a smile.

Wait. I'm not supposed to be happy to see him. My smile drops. "Where are we? This isn't right. Where's Kheelan? Am I dead?"

"You need to jump," he says, ignoring my questions.

I shake my head, "We're way too high and that's the pool..." The memories flood over me, "Our pool..." I whisper, "It's too shallow."

"Trust me," he says.

His eyes send a warmth through me and I want to nod, tell him I do trust him. *No*, that's not true, "I can't," I say instead. "You tricked me. *Lied* to me."

"You have to. It's the only way." He grabs my hand and closes my fingers around the black rose, the thorns tear into my flesh. He's behind me in an instant, his hands gripping my shoulders firmly. He spins me around in one swift motion to face him. "You have to," he whispers again. "Trust me." His face is pleading as he pulls me towards him and kisses me hard on the mouth. Butterflies erupt in my chest their wings spreading through my limbs, waking my body. He tightens his hold on me, then the pressure of his hands disappears as quickly as they found me.

I'm falling backwards. I stare up at him, he's standing over the ledge watching me plummet towards the water below. He wears a mask of eerie calm. All I can do is watch him get smaller as I fall. I open my mouth to scream but before I can make a noise the icy black water is splashing up around me and pulling me into its depths. The water rushes into my open mouth and down my throat, choking me as it fills my lungs. I try to kick towards what I think is the surface, but the black liquid is crushing me. The harder I kick the more it fights back, pulling me deeper. I kick my legs as hard as I can, reaching my arms above my head pulling with all my strength in a last attempt to save my life. I need air.

Chapter Sixteen

My head breaks the surface. I manage to get a swallow of air before the burning in my lungs turns into coughing. Thick black liquid sprays from my mouth with every convulsion. My ribs ache when I finally collect myself. I realise I'm not in the pool at the bottom of the waterfall, I'm not in the canyon at all. I'm in a large wooden barrel of a tub, submerged in a sticky black liquid. I look around, baffled, "But the waterfall..." My throat is raw.

"A vision," a sharp voice responds. "Your mind coming back. You were a little, how do I put this delicately," the voice pauses, "*broken*."

The voice is too loud, reverberating around the cavernous room and pounding into my ears. I press my sticky fingers into my forehead trying to ease the headache that begins to throb in my temples, my eyes search for the speaker. The room looks like a set out of a mediaeval film. Heavy red curtains drawn tightly over what I can only assume are windows tied shut with chunky gold ropes looped into knots the size of baseballs. The castle-like walls tower up to a raftered ceiling, three crystal chandeliers dangle from the big wooden beams over each of the barrel tubs. The wall in front of me has two large vanities, both home to identical golden framed mirrors. I find the speaker in the reflection of the mirror closest to me sauntering through the massive double doors on the far side of the room, her black gown billowing in her wake, on *fire*. I close my eyes hard and open them taking a second look. It's her brilliant fiery-orange hair fanning out like a veil. Her red lipstick and eyes darkly lined in charcoal are a shocking contrast to her colourless skin.

"Who are you, what is this place?" I ask as she walks up to the side of my tub.

"Zila, these are my private quarters." Her voice is void of any emotion as she grabs my wrist to feel my pulse.

"I was in a cage," I say, under my breath, mostly to myself, but my sense of reality is a bit hazy and I need the confirmation.

"Yes, you have been our prisoner for two weeks, here in the NetherWorld." Zila tinkers with something on the edge of my tub that I can't see. "Herne got carried away, and here I am stuck cleaning up another one of his messes." She tugs hard on something, my entire barrel rocks, the murky liquid sloshing over the edges. I grab onto the rim to steady myself.

"Dinner?" I ask, my eyes meet her cold black ones. "Herne came to see me and said something about a dinner party. Was that real?"

Zila chuckles, her eyes warming a fraction. Hope blossoms in my chest. Maybe she'll take pity on me. "I'm surprised you remember that, you were mostly dead when the servants brought you to me. But yes, it was real."

I need to keep talking, she may be my only chance of getting out of here. She's Herne's *sister* a small voice whispers in my head. My stomach twists, I don't have another option. "I saw myself at the top of a waterfall, I fell into a black pool of water."

"You were put into this elixir," she waves a well-manicured hand at the liquid surrounding my body. "Everyone's mind mends in its own way." She shrugs, "You must have a weird thing with waterfalls, I'm not going to try to understand the inner workings of a *Fairy-Blood.*" She spits out the last words with so much venom, I recoil into the far side of the tub. My little flicker of hope extinguished. She's not on my side. She kicks the side of the barrel, I tighten my grip on the sides as the liquid begins to gurgle out the bottom. "Looks like you'll live. Go rinse over there." She points to the barrel next to me.

I get to my feet slowly, afraid they won't hold my weight. They're shaky from lack of use, but I'm standing. Horror clenches my chest when

I look down at the black syrup dripping off my body, I'm naked. I hastily cover as much of myself as I can, stealing a glance in Zila's direction, she's busy emptying the drawers onto the counter of one of the vanities. I climb out of the tub, taking care not to slip from the black goo that's dripping off my legs and feet as I walk down the unsteady steps while trying to keep as much of myself covered as possible in the process.

I make my way to the next tub, I try to hurry, the stone floor is freezing but I'm like a new-born calf learning to walk with how bad my legs are trembling under the pressure of my weight. When I finally reach the second tub, I can't help the moan of pleasure that comes out of me as I dip into it. The warm water almost makes me forget where I am as I eagerly wash my hair and clean my body.

When I finish, Zila snaps her fingers, the click echoing through the silence. I wonder if I'm supposed to do something when she snaps? My silent question is answered when a small woman pushes through the heavy doors, something black clutched to her chest. She moves so quickly she looks like a scurrying mouse. She slides to a stop at the edge of my tub, holding out a fluffy black robe for me to step into. Her eyes are the lightest blue I've ever seen, almost white. I notice a single tear trickle down her cheek as she wraps me in the welcoming warmth. She whispers something to me, but it's in a language I've never heard before. I shake my head to let her know I don't understand. She opens her mouth again, but Zila interrupts before she can say more.

"That will be all, *bug*." Her frosty voice cuts though the space like a knife, causing my back to stiffen as though she's scraped her fingernails down a chalkboard. The woman turns to exit, exposing dingy shredded wings extending from between her shoulder blades. I swallow back my fear as the comprehension dawns on me. I watch in silent horror as she disappears through the doors she entered. A squelched Fairy doomed to an eternity of servitude. Will I share her fate?

Zila plops me down in front of a vanity without a word and gets to work. She doesn't speak again, pursing her lips tighter and shaking her head if I try asking any questions. So I stop trying and sit rigid in the chair.

I try my best not to move as she tugs and pulls at my hair, and somehow manage not to flinch when she starts to glop makeup onto my face.

When she finishes zipping me into a black dress she disappears in a puff of smoke. I really hate how they do that. I stare into the mirror, a sickening feeling settling in my gut as I see how bad my health really is. My eyes are sunken, the makeup Zila caked on unable to hide the huge black circles. My bruises are gone, or what's left of them were successfully hidden with foundation. Under different circumstances I would probably like the gown the Dark Fairy has dressed me in, it's elegant, but as my current circumstance has it, I'm a prisoner of the NetherWorld. The satin fabric hangs off my newly defined bones in a grotesque way. I twist my body to get a look at the swooping back, blanching at my protruding spine.

I'm alone. *I'm alone and I'm looking at myself in a mirror.* What is wrong with me? I rush as fast as I can, which isn't fast at all, the elixir has restored some of my strength but I'm still weak and malnourished. The window is closest, I throw the drapes back. It's a stone wall. I gather up the length of my dress into my fist and make my way towards the door. I'm not even halfway there when it swings inward, revealing the man with a pig's head. He's bigger than I remember, taking up the entire doorway.

"Come with me." He grunts closing the distance between us. He latches his cold clammy hand around my upper arm and drags me into the corridor. He keeps his grip firm as he pulls me forcefully along.

We wind through twisting passageways, I see more squelched fairies, but none of them seem to notice us. Their eyes are glassy and completely drained of colour. It's like they're unaware of their surroundings, or maybe they've turned inward to avoid what's become their reality. My heart clenches at the thought of them having to endure this for all eternity. I wish I could break free from the man holding me. I wish I could grab every last one of them and get them out of here. Give them the freedom they deserve. But his grip is too strong and I'm too weak. Instead, I'll probably share their fate.

I try to keep track of where we're going, but we make too many turns and I lose track after the first few. This place is like a labyrinth. At last, we come to a stop. We stand before a stone archway, my escort grunts and shoves his head towards the opening, shoving me in front of him as we enter the already full room.

The chattering comes to a sudden halt and my heart stalls. Before me is a long table, my eyes do a quick scan. I count seven grey-skinned men, whom I can only presume are The Hunt. Herne, with his magnificent horns is seated at the head of the table, the rest are situated down either side. I recognise two of them, the long haired one who brought me here, and Flint, I have to fight the smile that begins to tug at my lips when I see his face is still mangled. He's nearly unrecognisable, more closely resembling a melting wax figure than whatever he was before.

The pig faced man pushes me across the room, his fingers moist on my exposed back. He thrusts me into one of two empty chairs, to the left of Herne, with a grunt he turns to exit, his job complete.

"Porcus!" Herne scolds. "That's no way to treat our guest of *honour*." The horned devil clucks his tongue in disapproval. He reaches out and runs his claw like hand over my arm where Porcus' had gripped me, a painful chill trickles up my limb. "You've bruised her!"

"My apologies, your Majesty," he grunts, quickening his shuffle to get out of the room. If he were a dog, his tail would be between his legs. Then again, maybe pigs do that too. I force the thought out of my mind, I don't want to think about his back end.

"Rosalia, we welcome you!" I turn my attention to Herne's hideous form. My eyes are instantly drawn to his gnarled clawed hand, his knobby fingers clutching a staff so tightly the skin over his knuckles is taught and shining. My sight zeros in on a ruby gleaming menacingly at the top of his stick, I'm mesmerised. Something about it nags in the cobwebs of my mind, but I can't put a finger on it. "Good to see you up and about again." His pointy black grin rips my focus away from the stone.

I try to look him in the eye, wanting to seem strong, but I can't bear the grotesqueness. My focus drops to my hands wringing nervously in my lap. I rack my brain for any idea on how I can get myself out of this literal hell. None come.

"We're just waiting for one more, then we will begin the feast," Herne announces to the room, "and Rosalia here, will let us know her decision."

I sneak a glance at their leader. His eyes are burning flames flickering around the table to each of his followers, his smile frozen in place. I shift my eyes back to my hands, before his gaze lands on me. He doesn't really think I'd consider joining The Hunt, does he? Would pretending interest be my best chance of survival? *Keep your friends close, but your enemies closer.* I gulp trying to keep the nervous bubbles in my stomach from surfacing. How could I pretend to be one of them when I can't even look at them for longer than a few seconds without feeling sick? Kheelan would know the right thing to do. Kheelan would also never pretend to be someone he's not.

"Where is your son, Forrest? You know I hate to be kept waiting." Herne's annoyed voice echoes as he collapses into his chair.

"I'm here." A breathless voice says from the doorway. "Sorry I'm late, your highness." An icy shiver trickles down the back of my neck at the familiarity. I raise my head slowly. I'm afraid for the confirmation but the need to see with my own eyes is too strong. The speaker is doubled over in a deep bow. I'd know that messy black hair anywhere. My body feels numb as he straightens out of his bow. I've been dwelling on his betrayal for weeks, but the wound feels fresh with Declan so close.

He meets my glare for an instant, an unrecognisable emotion flickers across his face before he rips his gaze away, and makes his way to the only remaining seat, directly across from me. I can't speak, not with the entire Hunt surrounding me, but there are words I'd like to shout at the boy I once trusted. Instead, I ignore him. I fixate on the empty platter-sized pewter plate in front of me.

I jump as food appears out of thin air, piling up on everyone's plates. My stomach grumbles loudly, I haven't had a real meal in weeks. Then the smell hits me hard, raw meat. It happens too fast for me to try to stop it. I lean over the side of my chair, a bit of mush from my morning meal, but mostly the black sludge from my bath showers out of me, spattering all over the ground. I don't move. I don't know what to do. I do know I'm afraid to sit back up and face the monsters that surround me, sure they'll take offence and punish me in some twisted way.

The Hunters break the silence in a loud burst of laughter. I straighten back up in my chair, wiping the back of my hand across my mouth. I hate that my eyes instinctively go to Declan. He's gone rigid, his eyes locked on me, bulging in…Fear? No, it must be disgust. I force myself to look at Herne, he's taking a slow drink from his goblet, his calculating eyes are also fixed on me. I cast my gaze down, scared of what's coming. I risk another peek at him when I hear his goblet clunk onto the table. The laughter teeters off. Herne wipes what looks like blood from his mouth, my stomach churns. I close my eyes and concentrate on not being sick.

"I need a bug!" Herne howls, "Bring the *Fairling* some *plants*. And clean up this mess." His voice drips with disgust. I force my eyes open. His are burning into me. "Your diet will need to be adjusted over time." His tone matching his cold stare.

A squelched Fairy scurries into the room with a bucket and rags clenched in his frail hands. He doesn't lift his head, keeping his eyes glued to the floor as he focuses on his task of cleaning my mess. The Hunters don't even glance in his direction. But I watch his bony limbs in horrified silence. Wishing again that I could find a way to help them.

The Hunters don't speak while they eat, but it's not quiet. The chamber fills with the sounds of slurping and gargling as they shovel spoonfuls of bloody meat into their mouths, pushing the next mouthful in before swallowing the previous one. It's repulsive. I find myself watching Declan. He keeps his eyes down, focusing on his food. I note that all he does is push it around, he doesn't take a single bite. No one else seems to notice. They're all too self-absorbed with their own eating. I notice though and wonder at the meaning as I nibble the roll a second squelched Fairy brought me. She placed it delicately in front of me, murmuring in the same language the Fairy in Zila's chambers used. I couldn't understand her, but I got the impression it was an apology. Probably for not being able to find any plants in this castle. I know I should be gobbling the roll down and asking for more. It's the most substance I've been offered since being here. But I can't bring myself to take more than a nibble at a time. The stench of blood is too thick in the air, making it impossible for my stomach to settle. *Why isn't Declan eating?*

When the last of the dishes are whisked away, Herne rises to his feet, his staff shining magnificently at his side. Again, I can't help but steal a glance in Declan's direction. His attention is on his leader. "Gentlefae! I thank you for being here tonight, it's a rather exciting occasion," he roars, his voice taking command of the space. He looks at Declan, then at me, his expression what I assume must be joy, looks unnatural on his pointy features. "We have *two* from the Great Prophecy dining with The Hunt tonight!" The room erupts into loud cheers and stomping.

I keep my eyes downward.

"Declan, my boy, any luck on finding the third?" My head snaps up. My heart pounds in my ears, *Kheelan.*

"No, your Majesty. I'm sorry, I've failed." Declan says, bowing his head in shame. My mouth drops open. I stare at the top of his head. Why is he lying? He knows exactly where Kheelan is. My stare draws his eyes for a split second, but his expression is carefully blank, he looks back to his leader.

"But you will find him." Herne says his voice ice.

Declan nods his head in agreement.

"How do you know to trust him?" One of the Hunters asks, "He's run away before. How do we know he's loyal?"

"He didn't run away!" Another insists.

"Of course you want to believe the best of your son, Forrest." The first speaker says. "But he was gone for nearly three years, without a word. Then we get our hands on this one," he motions at me with his nose. "Suddenly he's back?"

"He was searching for his brother, to reunite the family." Forrest says. "Your Majesty, it was to please you." He turns his eyes to Herne.

Herne nods, his horns casting an ominous shadow on the wall behind him. "Yes, so he says. Do not worry Damien, we have ways for one to prove their loyalty. The boy will prove his before we send him back to the middle realm." He straightens, a spark returning to his fiery eyes. "Imagine though, all three fighting for our side. Queen Lucille will be beside herself when I take her throne and rule all three worlds!" His cackles ricochet around me, the room erupting into more thunderous applause. I wish I could cover my ears. "We won't be stuck in the dark any longer! Imagine, being able to wander all the realms even in the day light and feel the warmth of the suns once again!" He shouts over the noise. This makes them cheer even louder.

Herne waits for the excitement to die down before he turns back to Declan. "How were you unable to find your brother? He's quite close with the girl." He sweeps his hand in my direction.

Declan gulps, throwing a brief glance in my direction, "I got close, but he didn't trust me and got away after Rosalia was taken. I wasn't able to find him again, so I thought it was time to come home, and admit I need help."

He is on their side.

"This girl," Herne says, turning his hungry eyes to me, "she is our ticket. We will use her to lure him in. No honourable man can resist saving a damsel in distress!" He pauses, allowing his lackeys to laugh before continuing with a half-smile, "Then we'll win him over with the promise of his family reunited, and of course infinite power once we have all three realms under my command."

"Excuse me, your majesty," a familiar high pitched voice pipes up. "I think Damien is right. We shouldn't trust this boy's word." I turn my head to Flint's mangled face as he gestures in Declan's direction.

"As I said he will prove his loyalty."

"May I suggest we do that soon? I witnessed a rather nauseating memory when I was interrogating the girl." The wounds I gave him have made him a bigger nightmare and I can't help but jump back as he snarls in my direction.

"What memory?" Herne says through clenched teeth. Clearly, he doesn't like receiving new information in front of an audience.

"One where he seemed rather," Flint pauses for effect, a sneer pulling his burnt lips tight, blood trickling from the cracking skin, "*intimate* with her."

Herne whips his head around and bores his eyes into Declan, his iris burning into flames, "Do not lie to me boy," his voice roars, "I'll know if you do. Do you have feelings for this Fairling?"

"No, your Majesty." Declan keeps his voice level, never breaking eye contact with the horned man. "It was a strategy. I hoped to return with both of them, a gift for you."

I look down, wishing my hair was loose so I could hide my face. I don't want these monsters to see the flush of embarrassment and rage spreading across my cheeks. My stomach is a solid mass, at least Kheelan was smart.

"That's my boy!" Herne lets out a laugh. "I guess that leaves us one last task for the evening." He addresses the long table. "When Rosalia first came to us, I offered her a spot among us." I keep my eyes on my lap. "Tonight, the young Fairling is prepared to give us her answer. So my little light," I feel the eyes burning into the back of my neck.

I don't look up.

"Look at me when I speak to you." He hisses.

I still don't move.

"LOOK AT ME!" He bellows. Thunder crackles, and a bright light flashes around the room.

Pain sears in my neck, forcing my head up. My eyes land on the staff in his hand, which is still glowing. Did he just control my movements? I gulp and focus my eyes on his forehead. One last act of rebellion, I won't look into his fire pits he calls eyes.

"That's better," the horned devil forces a smile on his face. "Will you join us?"

"This is the world you've created." I say, surprising myself with how steady my voice sounds. On the inside I'm a nervous wreck. "Is this what will become of the OtherWorld? Of Earth?" I force my eyes to slide down his forehead and meet his empty ones.

His eyes narrow, a half-amused smile parts his lips, "You think *I* created this world?" He asks, flames dancing in his pupils. "You're mistaken," he says. "It was your darling Queen who created this world. She forced us into it. We were Fairies, just like her when she banished us. She turned her back on so many of her own kind. Do you think we *wanted* to feast on souls?" His voice drops low, a new wave of fear washes over me as he leans forward, his eyes boring into mine, "She moulded us into the monsters that we are. She's a grand puppet master. She has minions waiting in the shadows to do her dirty tasks at a snap of her finger. She would never get her own hands dirty, wouldn't want to tarnish her shiny facade. Nothing persuades quite like *gold* in the OtherWorld and the royal family has an everlasting supply." His lips pull apart barring his gruesome teeth as he goes on, "It's Lucille who's behind the NetherWorld. Lucille who's behind you and all the other Fairlings and even the bugs in our servitude. You're all just too *stupid* to see your own strings and who's grasp they're in."

I sit in stunned silence. Could his words be true? If they are, how good can the Fairies of The Light really be?

His smile splits into a full grin as his eyes study my features. "Once all I wanted was to rule." He continues in wake of my silence, "I didn't agree with the amount of control the current regimen wanted to place upon the Fae. A lot of the fae agreed with my views, but the stories have painted me into a terrible creature, they've turned me into the villain." He straightens back up, looking around at the hunters seated at his table. "At the time it was just politics. Now I want more." He says to the room, "I want all who turned their backs on us to suffer as we've been forced to suffer. I want to watch them become less than *nothing*. I want to watch their faces crumple as everything they love and hold dear is plucked from their lives and destroyed in front of them. Until they're left in complete and utter darkness like the eternal fate they've tried to doom us to."

209

The room breaks into a loud applause once again, whooping and cheering at Herne's words. My blood has turned to ice. Maybe the Fairy Queen has banished them from The Light, but this monster in power of all three worlds would be much more devastating.

When the room quiets, Herne's eyes find mine once again, "Will you join us?" He repeats.

"Do I have another choice?" The words slip through my gritted teeth before I can consider them.

Herne's chuckle ripples around the table with all of his Hunters. "Other options you ask?" He strokes his chin with his gnarled fingers, forcing his features into a thoughtful expression. "Well, I suppose I can offer two other options." He throws an amused look around the table, making sure his men are enjoying his theatrics. "One, you can return to your cell and rot." His men chuckle, his smile broadens, "Or two, we can squelch your light and allow you to enter into an eternity of servitude with all the other *bugs*." His voice goes cold and his eyes harden as they lock on me. "So what will it be, *Fairling*?"

My tiny bubble of hope explodes. I take a deep breath, my chance of survival depends on my acting skills. My breath quivers on my exhale, that's not promising.

Chapter Seventeen

They believe me when I tell them I wish to join The Hunt, or at least decide to humour me knowing I'm worth more alive, at least for now. Instead of being taken to my cell, I'm led to an actual room. Guards are stationed outside my door, and the room has no windows. I'm still a prisoner.

My new accommodations are dark, like everything in this world. The only light is from a tiny lamp on the nightstand. Even though there aren't any windows, heavy black drapes with a flourish of golden embroidery still hang on either side of the large four-poster bed, which is covered with a gold satin comforter. In normal circumstances, the room wouldn't be inviting, but as soon as the door closes and the dead bolt slides into place from the other side, I collapse onto the big bed, my exhaustion, both mental and physical, finally catching up to me. I'm in a deep dreamless sleep within seconds.

* * *

A loud succession of knocking startles me awake. I'm still in my dinner attire, laying on top the slippery golden covers. Groggy I clamber off the bed and pad over to the door. I can't open it. It locks from the outside. "It opens from your side," I say through the door not bothering to hide my annoyance.

"Just a courtesy knock," the rough voice of one of the guards responds before the door clicks open.

Declan's standing on the other side. His eyes lock on mine, and before I say anything he begins to speak with an urgent edge to his voice, "Good evening, Rosalia. Herne has granted me permission to take you outside and show you the gardens." He shoots a nervous glance at the guard to his right before adding, "If you'd like to join me, that is."

I narrow my eyes. What game is he playing?

"You need to trust me," his voice drops and his eyes bore into mine like he's trying to say more.

I open my mouth to respond. I want to tell him that I *don't* trust him, but he cuts me off before any words form.

"It's a *moonless* night." His eyebrows go up and eyes widen, like he's trying to convey something. My head is heavy and still groggy, but for some reason this detail resonates with me and I step into the hall with him. He smiles, relief relaxing his features. "Should be a lot of stars out," he flashes a smile at the guard and grabs my hand to pull me down the corridor. "I won't keep her out late buddy, I promise."

When we round the corner, I yank my hand free and stop walking. "What's going on?" I demand, knowing my whisper is too loud the moment it leaves me. "You better be able to answer some questions, like *right now*."

"Not here, Rosalia," Declan glances around, his brow crinkling. "Let's just get outside." His eyes return to mine pleading, "*Trust* me."

I feel like telling him repeating those two words over and over, isn't going to make me magically start trusting him. I search his eyes, hoping to find unspoken answers, I can't help but notice they're more of a blue-grey tonight. Sincerity radiates out of them, my head nods in agreement, without my permission. My hand squeezes his back as he leads me through the dark passageways and into the night.

The air is sharp, pungent. Instead of a breath of fresh air like I was expecting, I get a heavy one, laced with mildew. I shiver, wrapping my arms around myself. Why didn't I look for a change of clothes? The dress Zila put me in isn't practical for a garden stroll, or anything besides maybe a school dance. It's darker here, I realise. I look up at the sky, Declan was right, there's no moon, there aren't many stars though either.

He leads me through the grounds, the stepping stones like ice on my bare feet. The gardens aren't beautiful, looking at them make me feel sad. It's a wasteland of death. The plants all dry and crinkled, withered, and their colours drained. I stop, their *colours*. I take in the trees, and grass, they're the same. Everything is in varying shades of grey, all dried up and dead. "There's no colour," I whisper, a fresh wave of sadness hitting me like a tidal wave as another shiver sizzles through my body.

Declan unzips his hoody and shrugs it off, draping it over my shoulders. I slip my arms into the sleeves, welcoming the warmth that seeps into me. "That's right, and if you were to stay long enough, you'd lose your colour too. I'm sure you noticed how all of The Hunt have grey skin?"

I look at him, horrified. "How long does that take?"

"Let's go this way." He gently grabs my elbow and steers me down a path that leads away from the castle. "I saw a nice stream on my way in, it should allow us a little privacy."

We walk in silence, the only sound the patter of our feet on the path of stepping stones. After a few minutes, the sound of trickling water reaches my ears, and after a few more paces a tiny stream bubbling over rocks comes into view. There's a grey bench on its bank, Declan leads me to it. He sits down next to me and drapes his arm around my shoulders, ignoring my protest. He leans his head towards my ear and whispers. "I'm here to get you out. Are you strong enough to Light Travel?"

"It's no use," I hiss back, "I've tried, I can't even get a flicker here."

"But now you have me to help you."

"Why are you helping me? You're an Underling. Herne would have known if you were lying."

"Rosalia, I promise I have never lied to you." His eyes, the only bit of colour in the world around us shine with sincerity.

"How could you lie to Herne?" I ask, "Flint was in my head, I couldn't hide anything."

"With the light," he glances over his shoulder to make sure we're still alone. "I'll teach you sometime. But we really need to get out of here."

I draw in a shuddering breath. My heart wants to believe him, but a dark voice in my head tells me not to. It tells me not to let anyone close. Silent tears roll down my cheeks. I brush them away, irritated by their existence. "I need to get out of this place." I decide out loud. "Happiness, love, hope, *trust,* all positive emotions, they don't exist here," I whisper. "I can't even remember what those emotions feel like anymore. I think my mind has cracked these past couple of weeks." I look up at him, he's blurry from the tears. "My colour is missing, just like the flower's."

"Weeks?" Declan's eyes search my face. "How long do you think you've been here?"

"Two weeks," I shrug, looking up, his face full of worry. "You know that, I tried calling you the day they took me."

"Rose…" Declan whispers the first part of my name, "That was only four days ago."

My mouth drops open, "That's impossible."

"Shit." He says tilting his head back, looking up at the sky. "I knew time worked differently in this world, but damn." He lowers his head and looks at me, tears shimmering in his eyes. "I was sick thinking about you enduring four days down here, but two weeks! I am so sorry I didn't get here sooner." He burrows his face into his hands, leaning forward onto his knees. "We had to wait for a moonless night," he mumbles into his hands.

My heart swells. The first trace of a positive emotion I've experienced since being in this realm. Declan does care about me. His tortured expression confirms it. I offer a weak smile and reach for his hand. "Thank you for coming for me." I look into his eyes, as relief spreads through my body. I never wanted to hate him, it didn't feel right, it was unnatural. Then the rest of what he says sinks in. "You said *we,* did someone come with you?"

"No, but trust me, Kheelan wanted to. We decided me coming alone would stand a better chance of them believing I had decided to come back to join them."

My smile feels alien on my face, like I haven't used it in years instead of just weeks, or *days*. "So the two of you are working as a team, hey? Getting along?" I playfully nudge him with my elbow.

Declan laughs, "You're incredible. Leave it to you to pick *that* detail out of this situation."

I grin, "So it's the new moon tonight. That means tonight is our only chance of getting out of here? Until next month anyway," I say getting us back on track.

"Yes, as far as we know. I'm going to need your help though. My glow alone won't be strong enough."

I stare into his eyes, fear gripping my heart. I'm not strong enough, and I tell him. I tell him I was never squelched either, I'm just weak.

He grabs my face with both hands, looking deep into my soul, searching. He rests his forehead against mine, "You are strong enough. You're the strongest person I know, Rosalia. You just survived over two weeks in hell, literally. How many people can say they've done that? I'm not saying this will be easy. There's no light in the NetherWorld, so all of it has to come from you. Just hold on to me, and remember to think of home."

I nod weakly, and latch onto his upper arms. I stare back into his blue eyes, and try to clear my mind. I picture the mountains behind Aunt Rose's. I think of Kodiak, and Jen. I imagine the feel of fresh air on my skin. I think of Kheelan. But mostly I think of the man right here with me. How I know all the way to my core that he loves me. He came to hell, *for me.* There's a familiar flicker in my chest. Declan smiles, "That's it," he says as he starts to glow bright.

There's commotion up by the castle, breaking my concentration. My spark dies with it. I look behind us and see guards rushing in our direction, shouting about the light coming out of Declan. Panic beats through my veins as I try to reclaim my focus. I stare at Declan, panic radiating off me.

"You can do this Rosalia." He says, emitting no sign of panic, he's a picture of calm.

Tears roll down my face as I try to find my glow. But nothing comes. "I can't," I sob. The guards are getting closer, sending a new ripple of panic through my body, my stomach bubbling with nausea. I stare desperately into Declan's glowing eyes, I need to get him out of here. I can't even imagine what they'll do to him if they catch him now.

I love him.

The spark flickers to life in my chest.

"That's my girl," Declan whispers, "think of home."

The guards are only a few yards away. I can hear them clear as day, shouting to one another about seizing us before we get away. I see fear flicker through Declan's eyes. His hands tighten their grip on my face as he pulls me to his own, kissing me full on the mouth.

A firework explodes inside me, and the two of us are encapsulated in a giant orb of light as I melt into his kiss. I close my eyes and let the warmth wash throughout my body. The versions I've dreamt up of this moment don't compare. Besides the location, it's perfect. Better than any kiss I've experienced in my eighteen years. The first kiss to cause my stomach to drop to my toes, and my heart to sprout wings. The world shifts around us. I feel like a shooting star with my heart about to explode from happiness.

Declan releases my face and pulls away, but I keep a firm hold on his arms, my eyes shut tight. I don't want the moment to end, the moment ending means us getting arrested and dragged back into the castle to be tortured.

A bird sings somewhere in the distance. I pause. A bird? I can't hear the shouts of the guards. I'm not cold. I feel sunlight on my face! I open my eyes a sliver, sunlight pours in. I grin.

"You can stop glowing now." Declan says, a sheepish grin lingering on his lips.

I laugh as I switch my concentration to turning my glow *off.*

"Sorry about the kiss," he mumbles, "it was my desperate attempt to push your glow along." He flashes his cocky grin at me, "I'm glad it worked." His face sobers up, "But don't take it the wrong way. I know about you and Kheelan and I'm not looking to step on any toes." He traces an X over his heart, "Promise it won't happen again. It was purely for survival." He keeps his eyes on the ground, a slight blush tinging his cheeks pink.

My heart plummets at his words, tears springing to my eyes. *It won't happen again?* Then the rest of his words register. Kheelan. A fresh wave of guilt floods me. But I push it away, too relieved to be home, to be *alive*. I throw myself into his arms and start to cry. "You saved my life," I say into his neck.

I feel him hesitate but finally he wraps his arms around me and strokes my back. "I'd do it a thousand more times," he whispers into my hair. "You ready to go home now?"

"What do you mean? Where are we?" I pull away from him, but I don't let go. I didn't realise how much I missed human contact the last two weeks. I look around, the scene is familiar, but it's not Aunt Rose's house like I expected. We're at the bottom of what I've come to think of as our waterfall. "Oops," I murmur.

"I'm pretty sure I felt one of the guards in my head, which means they were in yours too. They probably know where we are," his eyes are full of regret as he looks down at me.

Panic seeps back over my flesh, "If they saw where we went, they'll be coming for us?" I just escaped the NetherWorld, something that is supposed to be impossible. I have no intention of ever returning. I tighten my grip on Declan's arms. Fear shaking my body.

Declan pulls me into a hug. "It's okay, you're safe. I'm gonna get you out of here." He strokes his hand over my hair that's managed to work its way out of Zila's elaborate up-do. "It's daylight, the Hunters can't follow us."

I let out a sigh of relief. "So we have time to rest before Light Traveling again?" I say as the fatigue of the last few weeks, or *days,* I still can't wrap my head around that, settles on me.

"We don't have to worry about Hunters for a while," he confirms, his voice soft as he brushes a stray piece of hair off my forehead, "but we do need to worry about Underlings." He assesses my face, his brows furrowing with worry. "They'll have weapons, and we'll be out numbered."

I nod, "I'll find the strength." A fight will be harder than traveling.

Declan circles both his arms around my waist, preparing for us to travel together. He opens his mouth to say something, but a loud cracking noise stops him.

I whip my head in the direction the noise came from and suck in a gulp of air. Jesse is standing in the shadows of the canyon wall, an evil grin contorting his features. "I was hoping to see you again, Lia," he says. "I wasn't very fond of the state you left me in last time." A blade switches open in his hand. Flames dance menacingly across its surface before fading into the jet-black metal. I gulp, that's no ordinary dagger.

Declan reacts instantly while I stand frozen in place. He shakes out of our embrace and steps in front of me, acting as a human shield from my ex-boyfriend. He reaches into his pocket and pulls out what looks like a pocket knife. When he flicks it open, instead of a black dagger like Jesse's, a golden sword appears in his hand glowing fiercely. His always ready smirk appears on his face, "Hello Jesse, long time."

Jesse stumbles into the stones behind him, shock replacing his grin. He wasn't expecting us to be armed. Neither was I. He glances at the watch on his left wrist, *the watch I gave him for his last birthday*. I glare over Declan's shoulder at him, wanting to tell him to take it off. He looks to the shadow next to him, then back at his watch. He's waiting for someone. I go up on to my tip toes to whisper this into Declan's ear, but another crackling through the air drowns out my words.

Another Underling appears in the shadows. I stare in horror as another crackle fills the silence and a flash of flames announces a third.

"Lia," Declan breathes over his shoulder, "RUN."

I hesitate for a moment, but I know staying and being unarmed won't help him, and will only add to his disadvantage. I turn to run, but it's a steep incline and my foot catches on the length of my dress, I stumble, sliding down the canyon. I hear metal clanking from above me. *Think.* I scan my surroundings, looking for anything I can use as a weapon. I need to go back and help him. A jagged rock a few feet down the slope catches my eye. I grab a hold of a big tree root and lower myself towards it. I reach out with my free hand, my fingertips nearly brush the rock. I inch down the incline cursing my stupid dress. My fingers are on it and I'm tightening my grip as something heavy knocks me forward.

A sharp pain shoots through my skull as my forehead comes crashing down on the rocks. I lose my grip on my root and get caught in a slide, tumbling the rest of the way down the slope. I lay motionless for an instant trying to process what just happened. I smell my own blood. A warm trickle making its way down my face. I start to lift myself up, but strong hands finish the job, flipping me onto my back.

One of the Underlings is on top of me. His eyes are so dark I can't see his pupils, it's unnerving. His mouse brown hair is stringy and slicked across his forehead, his impish grin reveals yellowing teeth. He drops to his knees, crushing my arms into the rocky soil and pinning me in place. In one swift motion, he has a black dagger similar to Jesse's pressing into my throat.

I suck in a sharp breath as the hot blade makes contact with my skin.

"So you're what I almost got stuck with as a sister-in-law?" The Underling asks, his voice husky and deep. His smile turns into more of a snarl as he leans down, breathing his onion breath onto my face. "You pissed off my little brother though, I don't think he's willing to take you back anymore. Personally, I don't get the fascination some Underlings have with Fairlings. I Find you all rather repulsive."

I dig my head into the ground trying to get away from his rancid hot air. Deciding to use our close proximity to my advantage I bring my head up as hard and fast as I can. It collides with the Underling's face, a searing pain splits my skull and spots of colour explode across my vision.

He yells out in pain, but doesn't move or loosen his hold on me. Anger takes over his features and he crushes more weight onto me, sharp rocks piercing through the hoodie into the flesh on my back. "You little bitch."

He hisses into my face, pressing his scorching knife deeper into my neck. The smell of burning flesh sizzles up, masking the stench of his breath.

I stop my struggle, knowing if I move the blade will pierce my already burning skin. I lie perfectly still, but he doesn't stop pushing his knife deeper. His eyes hateful as they burn into me. He's going to kill me. My skin gives way, and a small gasp escapes my mouth as thick warm blood begins to stream down my neck. I try to free my arms, but the Underlings weight is too much. All I can do is lay there and look up at his nasty face as he stares intently at his blade and my leaking throat. His face twists into confusion, and the pressure from his knife lessons. An inner battle raging inside of him over whether he should kill me or not. With my own struggle quieting, I notice the forest around us has gone eerily still. The sound of clashing metal no longer bouncing off the canyon walls. My heart falters, Declan.

I try to turn my head to get a better look up the slope I fell down, but the movement causes the knife to burn into my flesh. The Underling on top of me doesn't seem to notice the absence of sound. The furrow in his brow only deepening as his internal battle rages on.

My heart flutters when Declan appears soundlessly behind him. In one swift movement, he raises his golden sword above his head and plunges it into the Underling's back.

A hissing noise pierces my ears, and the weight on me disappears. A cloud of black ash in the place where Jesse's brother had been. It hovers above me for a moment before raining down, covering me in soot. His dagger clatters onto the rocky ground.

I lie in the soot coughing. Then I realise why I'm coughing, because the *ashes of a dead body* have just fallen all over me, and into my mouth. I scramble to my feet spitting the ash out of my mouth and brushing at what's clinging to my limbs. That wasn't the best idea. I've lost a lot of blood from my head wound and the cut on my throat. Spots begin to cover my vision, my head too light. Declan appears next to me in a flash, catching me before I can fall.

He tucks his sword away with one hand, his nose scrunching up as he leans in to examine my neck. Fear registers across his face and he lowers me to the ground, sitting so my head rests in his lap. He takes off his shirt and balls it up applying pressure to my oozing cut. "You're bleeding pretty bad. I'm going to try to get us out of here."

His blue eyes clouded with worry are the last thing I see before the black spots blot out the rest of my sight.

Chapter Eighteen

"Rosalia," cool fingers brush the hair from my forehead. "Rosalia," Declan repeats my name. "Please be okay…" He adds, his voice barely audible.

I open my eyes. I'm lying on a lumpy mattress, Declan leaning over me. He smiles when he sees I'm awake. "How are you feeling?" He brushes the last bit of hair off my face.

I scoot up so I'm sitting, my back against the headboard. We're in a wood panelled room, there's a mini fridge and a sink in one corner and a door that must lead to a bathroom. There are clothes draped over the chairs at the table by the window, and piles of old food cartons are scattered everywhere. Has someone been living here?

"Where are we?" My voice comes out rough and a searing pain burns through my throat. My eyes bulge and my hands flutter to my neck as the memory of the burning dagger floods back.

Declan reaches out and stops my hands. "You shouldn't touch it." His voice is thick. "I've bandaged it as best I can, but those aren't normal blades." He gulps turning his head away, as tears spring to his eyes. "I think whatever they're made out of is eating away at your flesh still." Fear rings through my veins. He takes a deep breath, his cheeks puffing out as he exhales before he returns his eyes to me. "This is where I've been staying the last couple of months." He looks around the cluttered area, "The Pony Express Motel. Sorry I didn't have time to clean before you arrived." He flashes the briefest of smiles before his worried expression settles back onto his face. I must look pretty bad.

I stare at him unblinking, none of his words registering after hearing that my flesh is being eaten away. "Eating my flesh?" I manage to whisper. I gulp at the realisation of what this could mean. "Am I going to die?"

"Not if I have a say in it." His jaw sets in determination. "Try to rest, I'll figure out our next move."

Even with death looming over me, I'm able to fall back into oblivion. I dream in flashes, short scenes one after the other. Each one making less sense than the one before.

I'm standing in a dark meadow. Billions of stars shining bright in the inky sky above me. The field is filled with fireflies lighting up in vibrant variations of yellows, blues, reds and even greens. A blue one lands on my shoulder and like a switch being flipped, it's daytime.

The meadow is gone. Now I'm standing at the edge of an emerald pool in the middle of a thick forest. There's a beautiful blonde Fairy treading in the water, only her eyes and the tips of her wings visible above the luminous water. She's watching me with a growing intensity, her green eyes glowing, reflecting off the water, illuminating the air around her. She dips below the surface, out of sight.

I'm standing before the table of peculiar beings. All their eyes are on me and I'm trembling. With nerves or fear, I can't tell. The Fairy Queen opens her mouth to speak.

I wake up.

"They sent three Underlings after us. I managed to kill two of them, but one got away." Declan's voice reaches me in hushed tones. *He killed two of them? I wonder if Jesse is dead?* I push the thought away, it doesn't matter. He tried to kill us. There's a moment of silence before Declan says, "She took us to Darby Canyon." Another pause, "I don't know why. I'm just thankful she was able to get us out, I'm not powerful enough to go between the realms."

I open my eyes. Declan is standing across the room talking on the phone. He's looking out the window, his back is to me so he doesn't see that I'm awake.

"Tell her they were daggers," he says to the person on the other end of the line. "I don't know what they were made of, but Rosalia's hurt. Her wound seems to be getting worse." He nods his head in response to what the other person is saying. "You're sure it's safe there? That's why I brought her here. I didn't want to lead them to the house." He nods again. "No, she can't Light Travel. You'll have to pick us up." He turns around, a smile spreads across his face when he sees I'm awake. "Thanks man, we'll see you soon." He ends the call and shoves his phone into his pocket.

"Who was that?" I ask suddenly very aware that I'm in Declan's bed. I swing my legs off the side so I'm sitting on the edge, hating that I'm still wearing the stupid gown.

"Kheelan. He's coming to get us since my bike is still at your aunt's." He starts going around the room whisking the empty food cartons into a small garbage bag.

"Won't they know to look for us at Rose's?" I ask.

"That's what I thought too." Declan shrugs as he drops the trash by the door. He grabs a duffle bag and starts shoving clothes into it. "Apparently her house is built on sacred ground."

"Ah of course, sacred ground. Who doesn't build their homes on sacred ground these days?" I say with a grin.

Declan throws a smile over his shoulder, which is quickly replaced by his furrow when his eyes land on me.

"Is it really that bad?" I ask, dread pulling my heart into my stomach.

"The black is spreading outward from the wound," he says as he begins to collect his belongings faster. "It's past the bandage now."

I stand up and make my way to the bathroom, fear making me feel like I'm moving in slow motion. I dread what I'm about to see.

A stranger stares back at me out of the mirror. My face is covered in scratches. I have an egg-sized bump swelling out of my forehead where I made contact with the Underlings skull. All minor wounds. I know they'll heal in a couple of weeks. The sight of my neck makes the air catch in my throat. Declan has cut some fabric into strips and carefully wrapped my wound. The white cotton, now stained with dried blood seems to have done the trick, I've stopped bleeding.

I'm relieved to see the fine gold chain from Jen still secure around my neck, she'll laugh when I tell her it withstood hell. *I wonder if she's awake for me to tell her?*

I'm careful as I unwrap Declan's handy work, I need to see what's under it. I stifle the horrified scream that tries to come out as I study the damage. I have a four-inch blistering scab running from the side of my neck down to my collar bone. As ugly as the cut-burn is, it's not what makes my limbs incapable of moving. Coming off the wound in spidery, vein-like lines is an inky black pattern that's beginning to wrap around my neck, stretching towards my chest. I hesitantly place my fingers onto the markings, they feel strange. Physically, they're smooth, like my skin has been tattooed to look that way, but it makes me feel odd as my fingertips brush over them, like uncontrollable despair seeping out of the lines into my hands. I pull them away and stare at my fingers in wonder as the sadness creeps up my arm.

"Kheelan should be here soon." Declan says from the doorway.

I jump, I didn't hear him come in. He's watching me, concern deepening the furrow between his brows. He steps into the room and wordlessly takes the bandages from my limp hands and starts to wrap them back around my wound. I don't protest. I stand still and watch in the mirror as his hands redress my injury. I can feel the despair creeping from my arm into my body, the lines on my neck pulsating, as though they're celebrating a victory.

A car door slams just as Declan finishes up his handy work. I turn to see Kheelan's familiar red truck parked in front of the window, Kheelan himself rushes by and through the door. He beelines for me across the room, collecting me into his arms. "Thank God," he breathes into my hair.

I smile up at him as he pulls away and starts to inspect my injuries. I suddenly feel shy under his gaze, it feels like months have passed since I last saw him. His eyes land on my neck, a furrow of concern, identical to his brothers makes itself at home between his brows.

"I'm fine." I insist, brushing his worried fingers away. "Where's my sister, and Emily?" I hold my breath waiting for his answer.

"They're safe." He says, not meeting my eyes. "We should get out of here. We'll talk more when we get to Rose's." He picks up one of Declan's bags and heads out the door tossing the bag into the bed of his truck as he walks around to the driver's side.

I eye Declan, sending the silent question with my eyes. What's up with Kheelan's vague answer?

He responds out loud, "I'm sure we'll get all sorts of answers as soon as we get to your aunt's. He says they're safe, so wipe that worried look off your face." He smiles and pulls me into a one-armed hug as he leads me to the door, throwing his remaining duffle bag strap over his shoulder.

I force a smile, but I'm not reassured. Something in the way Kheelan dodged my question isn't settling right. It's not like him to avoid a question. Something's wrong, and he doesn't want to be the one to tell me.

* * *

I peer down at my sister's sleeping body. Her face is peaceful. If I didn't know better, I'd think she were in a natural sleep. But I know better. I know her body shouldn't seem so small and frail. Seeing my big sister, the person I've looked up to for my entire life looking so vulnerable and broken shatters my heart. It takes all my strength to keep my tears at bay.

Maggie and Rose were able to mend all of the exterior wounds Jesse and Flint inflicted, I'm impressed with how fast they have faded, all that's left is a faint trace of a black eye. Mindy got her hooked up to a TPN the instant Emily returned with her, so at least she's not starving to death. The older women fill me in on all the different techniques they've tried so far to wake her, but they haven't had any success. Whatever is keeping her asleep is beyond everyone's abilities.

"How can we wake you up, Jen?" I whisper to the unresponsive body, hysteria threatening to burst my seams.

"We've tried everything we can think of," Emily says from behind me. My heart jumps in relief as I spin around to greet my friend. She looks good as new. Rose and Maggie are miracle workers.

"Thank God you're okay!" I say pulling her into a tight hug. "Thank you so much for getting Jen out."

"Of course." She looks at me, her big brown eyes brimming with tears, "I'm sorry. I never should have left you in the basement by yourself. I should've—"

"—Don't. I'm glad you left. It would've been so much worse if you hadn't." A strangled choke comes out of me at the idea of my best friend and sister being killed because of me. "Seriously. The thought of you and Jen getting out kept me somewhat sane while I was there." I suck in a deep breath to clear my tears and turn back to my sister's still body. "I owe you my life for saving her, Em."

"Don't mention it," she says, uncomfortable with the direction our conversation is heading. Emotional talks aren't her thing. "Anyway, Maggie sent me to find you. The salve she's been working on for your neck is ready."

* * *

"Tell us what happened." Maggie says when I enter Rose's office. Everyone has already gathered. She begins dabbing something gooey onto my neck, spreading it out to cover all the black lines. The smell hits me like a pound of bricks. A stifling scent of pine needles mixed with rotten eggs. I crinkle my nose and back away. She pushes me into the chair across the desk from Rose.

I sigh and try to breathe through my mouth. It doesn't help, tasting it is much worse. Then the words pour out of me. I don't hold back and it feels good to get it all out. I start with the phone call from Jen and end with waking up at the motel. I only leave out the details of my vision while being healed and the kiss Declan and I shared. Not wanting Kheelan to know those minor details. When I finish, my voice feels raw and the room has gone so quiet you could hear a pin drop. Everyone is stone still. Even the people who had a role in my tale. Declan is sitting motionless on the leather couch, leaning onto his thighs, his eyes fixed on the oriental rug beneath his feet. Kheelan's eyes are on me, his mouth slightly open. Emily who had been hovering in the doorway for most of my recounting, unsure if she belonged, now slumps into an armchair near the door, a look of wonder on her face. Maggie having capped her salve long ago stands behind Rose, her hands hovering near her chest.

Rose breaks the silence first. "Wow. So there's no light to retrieve after all. You just had to find it within you." She studies me for some time, before continuing, "I'm glad you found your strength and am so happy to have you home." She chokes, clearing her throat to collect herself, getting back to business. "We were able to identify the material of this blade to be *Tenebris*." She says her voice still shaky as she places the Underling's knife on the wooden desktop between us. The knife gives off an ominous air.

"A what kind of blade?" Kheelan asks, his eyes still glued on me, probably horrified by the markings spreading across my neck.

"Tenebris, it's dark magic. We're fortunate that Declan was smart enough to grab it or we wouldn't have known how to treat the wound. There isn't a cure." Rose's shiny blue eyes land on me, "Not in this world anyway."

"Only in the NetherWorld?" I manage to get the guess out, but only in a bare whisper. I reach out my hand and pick up the blade in front of me. A loud humming rings in my ears and the lines on my neck pulsate. I release it. The knife clatters back onto the desk. The humming and pulsing stop as soon as I lose contact with the metal. I raise my wide eyes up to my aunt in question, she's watching me with interest, but it's clear she hadn't heard the humming. She hasn't been poisoned by the dark magic.

"Yes, I'm sure there is. However, we thought the OtherWorld would be the more desirable place to find one."

"So we wait until the full moon and somehow get into the OtherWorld?" Declan asks, "Then what? Hope her Majesty will be so kind as to help her? Or will we stumble upon a magic flower?" He gets to his feet and starts pacing. "There has to be something we can do now, without *their* help. We don't want her having to owe them anything."

Maggie looks at her long-lost grandson, sadness drooping her face and shoulders as she watches him. He stops at the bookshelves, searching the titles. "My salve will slow the spread," she says, "but it's not enough. She won't make it to the full moon. It's two weeks away."

Declan's face crumples. He's quick to cover it with a mask of determination, "No. That can't be all we can do." I reach my hand towards him, wanting to reassure him, comfort him. I hate seeing him hurt like this. He doesn't see. He's made up his mind and beelines for the door. It shuts heavily behind him. We all sit in stunned silence as the front door slams, shaking the walls. I hear his motorcycle roar to life disrupting the gravel as he speeds down the drive.

"We'll have to ask the Fae for their help." Maggie continues, her eyes still on the spot where Declan had been moments before. "Without their help, you'll die."

Rose's bottom lip begins to quiver at the word Fae, tears bursting out of her as soon as her friend finishes speaking.

"We'll do everything in our power to make sure you don't." Maggie tries to give a reassuring smile, nodding her head vigorously, but she's having a hard time holding it together as well. Her voice cracks as she continues, "We'll send a message to the Fairy Council with your FaeDog. It's risky with the way time works in the other realms, but I'm afraid it's our only option." She places her hand gently on her friend's shoulder.

A million questions race through my head, but only one makes itself coherent enough to come out of my mouth. "How will Kodi know where to go?"

Rose smiles, dabbing a handkerchief at her eyes. "She has natural instincts. That's how the boys were able to find a way into the NetherWorld to get you out. Kheelan learned in Ireland that natural portals to the other realms are located in places where Earths energies are high. Where we are, the Yellowstone region, it's an energy hot-spot. Kodiak was able to find the entrance for Declan. Getting home is the tricky part. But the Fae will probably help her, they're kind to animals."

I look down at Kodi, she hasn't left my side since I've been back. She lifts her head and looks up at me, as though she knows we're talking about her. I reach down and pat her on the head. "Such a good girl," I whisper. She's saved my life more than once now. I'm in debt to a dog.

"There are a few things you've missed while you were away dear." Rose sniffles. "For one, your parents are worried sick about you and your sister."

My parents. How self-absorbed am I? I hadn't even thought about them. Not once since I've gotten out of hell and all the while they were living in their own kind of hell. "Do they know?"

"No, that would be dangerous." Rose sighs, "I didn't like it, but I lied. I told them that Jen got back safely and the two of you have been running around having so much fun that you haven't had time to call, so I was calling on your behalf to let them know you're safe."

"But they're still worried?" I ask.

"They keep calling your sister's phone, and I'm guessing yours too, wherever that may be. You'll need to call them. Although I'm sure they'll want to talk to Jennifer too…" Her voice trails off and tears begin to carve their way down her cheeks. "We'll need the Fae to wake her up. But we'll have to tread that subject carefully. They won't want to help a human."

I watch as my aunt slouches back into her armchair, her tiny frame radiating exhaustion. Guilt wells in my chest. Her life has gotten so much more complicated since I arrived in Wyoming. "I'm worried they won't want to help you either." The old woman admits. "Fairies are selfish. They don't feel any sort of maternal instincts towards their Fairlings. Not the way humans do with their children. Declan is right, if they agree to heal you, they'll want payment."

"What kind of payment?" Kheelan asks after the silence stretches on for an unbearable amount of time.

"I'm not sure." Rose's voice begins to shake. I swallow, glancing around the room. Only Kheelan, Maggie, Rose and myself are left. I guess

Emily slipped out after Declan. I hate that I'm putting everyone through this.

Kheelan stands and walks to the desk. "What about the prophecy? It names all three of us." His voice is surprisingly cool and even.

"We did think about that," Maggie says, "with the state Lia is in," she glances at her friend, "we are certain it's going to happen soon. We're hoping this is all part of the great web of destiny."

"So what's the plan?" Kheelan asks. "What can I do?"

"Everyone is to stay in the main house. It's on sacred land, so we're safe." Maggie instructs. "Even I'll be staying here. Declan will need to as well, if we can track him down. Lia dear, you need to lay low until we hear back from the Fairies. Bed rest." I open my mouth to protest, but she cuts me off. "Doctor's orders."

"Which doctor?" I challenge.

"Me," she says sternly.

"You're not a doctor!" I protest. "Anyway, I feel fine. I don't need more rest. Let me help." I look around at the concerned faces watching me.

"She's a witch doctor," Kheelan says with a bemused smile, "you should listen to her, or she'll give you warts."

I giggle as the two older women nod their heads agreeing with him.

"Off to bed!" Maggie demands. "We'll get our letter attached and sent away at once."

I nod and slide off my chair to kneel next to Kodi. "Thank you, girl. You are going to deserve weeks of doggy fun after this whole mess is over." I kiss her on the top of her head and rise to my feet. "All right." I look at Rose, "Which room will be my dungeon?"

Rose chuckles, "Oh hush. I hope you find it a little more welcoming than the one at Herne's palace. I have you set up in the dandelion room, there's a bathroom attached with both a tub and a shower." She takes in my current state, "I think getting cleaned up will help you feel better. Kheelan, would you be a dear and help Lia get settled?"

"Certainly," Kheelan offers me his arm, a grin spreading across his face at his formality. "Right this way, m'lady!"

I laugh, accepting his arm. "Thank you, fine sir." I say in my best British accent.

* * *

I feel like a new person. Clean and nestled in the big fluffy bed, buried beneath a giant down comforter. Kheelan is in an oversized yellow striped chair next to my bed, his feet kicked up onto the side of the mattress. The room, which Rose has appropriately named 'the dandelion room' is every shade of yellow imaginable. In theory, this doesn't sound appealing, but somehow being engulfed in the cheery colour is comforting. We decide the best way to pass the time while I'm on my ordered bed rest is to have some movie marathons. Kheelan managed to find an old TV in the garage, and got it set up in my room. Now we're kicking off our first marathon.

"Thanks for joining me on my sentence," I say looking at him out of the corner of my eye.

"There's nowhere else I'd rather be," he says turning his head to look at me full on.

"Thanks for getting me out of the NetherWorld, too," I add, "I'm not sure I've gotten the chance to properly thank you for that."

"I didn't do much, it was mostly Declan." He says turning his head back to the glaring tv screen. "I wanted to apologise about the fight we had when I first got back from Ireland."

"You don't need to apologise." I say, "You've more than made—"

"—I need to. I shouldn't have let myself lose control." He turns his face to me, his eyes pleading. "It's just that I feel so strongly about you. I couldn't stand the thought of you being in danger the entire time I was gone."

"It's okay," I whisper.

"You were right though, so thank you for helping bring me and my brother back together." He places his hand on top of mine, "Seriously, thank you."

"You're welcome." I mumble, I'm the one who's trying to thank him, and here he is getting me all choked with his sweet words. "Let me thank you though! You got me out of the NetherWorld," I stop him before he can insist he didn't do much again, "AND because of you Jen and Emily are safe."

"That was all Emily," Kheelan says, a touch of pride in his voice. "She got Jen out of the Underling's house and hidden away before she called me. It was my grandma after that. I was able to help with the light a little bit, but it was Grandma Maggie who did the heavy lifting."

"Well, thank you. I appreciate it." I feel the tears beginning to well up, I turn my attention to the movie. "Now I just hope I can get my sister to wake up. Do you think I could persuade my Fairy-Mother to help?"

"Your sister is safe." Kheelan says, taking his feet off my bed and angling his body towards me. "You need to worry about yourself right now, Lia. It feels like you aren't grasping what's happening to you. Did you hear Maggie? You're *dying*."

I shrug, "There's nothing I can do about that, so there's no point dwelling on it too much. Of course I'm scared, but right now I'm more scared for Jen."

"You're incredible." Kheelan smiles, shaking his head at me in disbelief. "Leave it to you to brush off death," he laughs.

It's infectious and I laugh too, "You make me sound much braver than I feel."

"You're magic," he says, his face serious.

"I don't feel magical either," I whisper keeping my eyes locked on the screen, embarrassed by the turn of conversation.

"Everything about you is magic." His voice is soft, "Your laugh, your smell, you. You have no idea the effect you have on people." I sneak a peek at his face, his eyes are shining. "I love you," he says. "I know you never responded to my email, and I realise that probably wasn't the best way to spring it on you but…I love you." His words trail off.

I meet his eyes, his warm blue eyes, I know I should say *I love you too*. It's what he wants me to say, it's what I wanted to say just a few weeks ago. But, I'm speechless as a turmoil of emotions and feelings churn in my chest. How *do* I feel about him? I love him, but is it the right kind of love? Declan and the exploding kiss we shared flashes in front of my eyes. The thought sends my heart soaring. *But he said that can never happen again,* I remind myself. My fingers spring to my neck finding the cool chain, *wake up Jen, I need you.* I think as I twirl the interlocked rings between my fingers.

Kheelan gulps when I don't say anything, "When you were missing for those few days…I was a mess. That's when I knew it was more than a crush." He rushes, needing to get everything he wants to say out. "With the dream before we even met, our shared birthday, not to mention your mere presence making me stronger. We're meant to be together, Lia. You're my fate, and I'm yours too."

"I—" I stammer, "I—I don't know what to say."

"Don't try to tell me this is one-sided." A tinge of anger creeps into his voice.

"Of course it isn't," I whisper. "You make me feel stronger too, and there is a part of me that believes fate has pushed us together."

"But?" Kheelan says. "You've started to have feelings for someone else." He guesses, his voice low and defeated.

"Maybe," I whisper. "I don't know how I'm supposed to feel, there's a whirlwind of emotions inside of me right now and I haven't had a chance to sort through any of them yet."

"Look around, Lia. Who's here for you right now?"

I stare into his earnest eyes, silently pleading for me to love him back. How did I end up in this situation? It's *Kheelan*, the *perfect* guy. "You are," I whisper.

Maggie pops her head through the crack of the door, "The message has been sent! Now we wait!"

"That's great!" I turn back to Kheelan, with a smile of hope.

"Fantastic," he mutters peeling his gaze away from mine and rising to his feet, "I'm going to go check on the horses. I'll be back later." He bends down and places a gentle kiss on my forehead, his lips lingering a beat longer than normal. "I'll be back later," he says again as he straightens back up, "we'll talk some more then."

I watch his back as he exits the room, my heart ready to burst into a million pieces. I groan and pull the comforter over my face.

Chapter Nineteen

Kodi returns the same evening, without a response. I take this as a bad sign. I want to start making my rounds, say my goodbyes to my favourite spots, but Rose and Maggie insist I stick to my bed rest. They're still holding out hope that the Fairies will respond. I've lost all hope. If they wanted to help, they would've sent something back with my dog. No response, in my eyes, equals no help.

Between Rose and Maggie, I'm slathered with the pungent salve three times a day. I start to worry I'm going to lose or at least weaken my sense of smell from the powerful odour, but then I remember I'm dying, so that doesn't matter anyway. I spend most of my time in the living room, cosy on the couch or situated behind the big oak desk in the study reading anything I can get my hands on. I scour through every folklore, Fairy-tale, and mythological story I can find, hoping to find a sliver of a hint on how we can get Jen to wake up. The closest one I can find is Sleeping Beauty. I know it's ridiculous, still, I kiss my sister's forehead every night, just in case.

Kheelan comes by every afternoon when he finishes his work, and we watch another movie. He doesn't bring up his email again, or the three words he said to me the day I got back to this world. There's an air between us now, a heavy veil of things left unsaid. To the outside eye nothing has changed, but I can feel the shift and it makes my heart heavy, mixing with the tangled knot of hurt and anger that's in my heart about Declan's absence. No one's sure where he goes every day, and he shrugs off any questions directed his way, answering vaguely that he's researching. Most days he's gone before I wake up, not returning until after I've gone to sleep. Some nights I wake to the slight creek of my bedroom door, when I slit my eyes open, I see Declan's silhouette standing in the doorway. I can't see his face, so I can't guess at what's going through his mind. My heart always leaps with happiness when I see him, but I'm hurt by his daily absence. He's shutting me out, so I don't let him know I'm awake, I pretend to be fast asleep until he gives up and quietly closes the door behind him.

I'm thankful for Kheelan's almost constant company, even if our friendship isn't completely back to normal yet. We'll get there, eventually. Emily stops by a lot as well. At first, she insists movies are lame, but by the third day she begins shushing us if we talk at all. Their company lessens my anxiety about Jen. The not knowing would normally cause me to go crazy, it would keep me up all night. But I've been cut with a Tenebris blade, and the black lines that are worming their way over my flesh, sucking the life out of me, feeding and growing, leave me exhausted.

My fifth morning back, I wake up short of breath. I stand in the bathroom staring at my form in the mirror. The black lines spread more last night than all the other nights combined. My neck is now wholly covered by the markings, the swirls creeping onto my chin and running down my torso to my belly button, and my arms as low as my elbows. I twist so I can see the reflection of my back, confirming it has spread evenly. I gulp, just last night they had barely gone past my collarbone. The spread is speeding up, and with my chest covered, it's hard to breathe.

I grab my phone and panic dial Emily. I don't know why. I guess deep down I know she's the only one who can calm me down, she always manages to keep a level head.

She answers on the first ring. Her voice croaks with sleep across the line, "What's happened?"

"I think I need you to come see for yourself." I can't pull my eyes away from my reflection.

"Is everything okay?" The huskiness of sleep dissipating into worry.

"I don't think so." It's better not to sugar coat it, "The lines have spread…a lot."

"I'll be right over." The line goes dead.

It feels like an eternity waiting for her, I pass the time by tracing the markings on my arms. If they weren't killing me, they'd be kind of pretty. Tattoos of swirling doodles, or tribal rights earned for bravery in battle. I smile, liking the second idea more.

Pounding on my door snaps me out of my tracing daze, I throw on a bathrobe and open the door to see Emily with Maggie in tow. Maggie is all business brushing past me into the bathroom, heaving a big carpet bag onto the counter. Bottles clinking inside as the bag lands on the granite surface.

"Let's see." Maggie instructs, pulling the jar of salve out of the bag.

I hesitate.

"Not a time for modesty, Lia!" Maggie says with an air of exasperation.

I close my eyes and open my robe for her to see. Emily lets out a gasp from behind the older woman.

"Oh, my," Is all Maggie has to say about it as she starts to rub the salve onto my skin in vigorous circles. I have to brace myself against the counter so I don't tip over from her force.

When she finishes, she caps the jar and busies herself rearranging the insides of her make-shift doctor's bag. Emily walks to the bedroom positioning herself in front of the window, gazing out at the mountains deep in thought. I can't take the silence. I need one of them to confirm what I already know. So I break it, "It's over my heart. I'm going to die soon." It's not a question, but I still watch Maggie carefully, needing her confirmation before I let the horror really set in.

Maggie's hands still, her blue eyes find my face, tears brimming the edges. "We can pray that's not the case."

"I can feel it," I say. "It's hard to breathe today."

Maggie stays silent, a tear escapes her eye, tracing its way down her cheek. She doesn't bother wiping it away.

"Please don't give up on Jen if I do die. I can't bear the thought of my parents having to lose both of us."

Maggie just nods, as more tears stream down her face. She walks out of the bathroom, closing the door gently behind her, allowing me to get dressed in private. Their hushed tones drift through the door, but I don't try to listen, I don't want to hear their pity. I know I should be scared, I should at least be feeling *something*, but I feel empty, hollow. I pull a sundress over my head, and take a deep breath, my lungs don't expand like they should. It feels like they've been shoved into a jar that's too small, not allowing them to fully inflate. I look at myself in the mirror. The thin black lines a stark contrast against my fair skin, their swirling pattern making them seem like they're in motion. Which, I guess they probably are, creeping, spreading, squeezing the life force out of me.

When I emerge from the bathroom, Maggie is gone. Emily has perched herself on the side of my bed, she looks sad but has a brave mask on, for my benefit. She forces a hopeful smile, "I thought of something."

"Yeah, what's that?" I ask as I sit down next to her.

"Have you tried calling the glow since you were cut?" She asks.

I pause to think. "No, I guess I haven't. Declan transported us both from the canyon to the motel, and I guess I just haven't needed to since," I add with a shrug.

"I think you should try."

I nod, understanding her train of thought. "I don't think it'll make it go away," I tell her, not wanting her to get her hopes up.

"I don't either," she agrees. "I just think it might help hold it at bay, or something. I don't know. But *maybe* it'll help." Her brown eyes are earnest, "It doesn't hurt to try."

"That's true."

"Try it," she demands.

I smile, glad to see she's still her bossy self, even in our current situation. I scoot to the centre of the bed and position myself so I'm sitting crossed legged with my hands resting on my knees, palms up. I close my eyes and try to clear my mind. "I can feel you watching me," I mutter.

"Sorry, I'm sorry! I'll go." I hear her hop off the bed and make her way to the door. Once I hear the gentle click of it latching behind her, I begin to breathe in and out letting all my thoughts and worries leave my head. It doesn't come easy. But I don't give up. A good fifteen minutes pass before I feel the familiar flicker of warmth burst in my chest. I hold on to it, willing it to spread. It won't budge. The ball of light is faint and stuck in my chest. I keep it aglow for as long as I can before giving into the defeat, falling backwards into my pillows, completely wiped.

I gulp in air, somehow winded from barely calling the glow. I bolt upright. My breaths are coming easier! I scramble off the bed and race back to the mirror. Disappointment extinguishes my excitement as soon as I see the reflection of my arms and neck, they're still covered in the thin black lines. I lift my dress over my head and toss it to the side so I can get a look at my torso. There are still lines on my belly and winding down my rib cage, but in the centre, it's clear. A perfect circle of snow-white skin. I gape in wonderment. It *worked*, kind of.

There's a quiet knocking on my bedroom door. I pull my dress back over my head and go to open it, Kheelan and Emily are standing in the hallway wearing matching expressions of hope. Both their faces drop as they take in my exposed skin.

"It didn't work." Emily says.

"You weren't able to call the glow," Kheelan guesses. "Maybe I can help…"

I shake my head as a yawn rips out of me. I've managed to reach a new level of exhaustion. "It kind of worked." I get out before a second yawn hits. "The lines are gone here." I outline the circle on top of my clothes for them to see.

"That's fantastic!" Emily says. "Keep calling the glow as often as you can, maybe it'll stop it from spreading!"

"I couldn't fully call it," I admit. "Just in this area," I trace the circle again.

"You don't look so good." Kheelan's brows crinkle as he steps towards me.

"Gee, thanks," I say as I start making my way back to bed.

"Seriously, do you need to lie down? You look really pale."

* * *

I'm peering down at the table of peculiar beings, once again. This time, Kodi's there. She's sitting just behind the Fairy Queen, who's holding our message in her withered hands.

"The girl is dying." The Queen announces to her small audience which consists of the antlered man, and the lady with the birds from my previous dream, and an additional three Fairies.

"We must help. Our fate depends on her." The antlered man says.

"Fate?" the lady with the birds questions. "How, may I ask Quill, do you know that it isn't her fate to die? We shouldn't intervene."

"We know it isn't her fate because of the prophecy, Robin." Quill shoots back, angry red splotches popping up on his cheeks.

"You don't know the full extent of the prophecy." Robin strokes one of her birds who has landed on her outstretched finger. "Her death could be her role."

"Yes," one of the Fairies pipes in. Her blonde hair falling in perfect ripples around her shoulders as she nods her head in agreement. "Her death could be what sparks the son of the Hunter to fight harder. It was Herne's lackeys who did this to her, after all."

"You wish to allow your only Fairling to die?" Quill whips his head towards the blonde fairy, his mouth open in disbelief.

My jaw drops and I stare at the beautiful creature, my *Fairy Mother*. She shrugs her shoulders nonchalantly, her bright green eyes showing no emotion except maybe a touch of boredom as they hold the antlered man's gaze, "She is just a Fairling." The pang of hurt that flashes through me surprises me more than her lack of sentiment.

"Take care to remember that she has strong blood, Aspen." The Queen's attention focuses on her daughter, "Which can be useful."

241

"Yes, the strongest of the three named. I know, she is mine," Aspen says.

"Yet you believe the best role for her would be to die now?" The Queen asks.

"I didn't say that. Maybe she should be spared. I don't know. I merely agree that her death could also be beneficial to the cause." She shrugs again, and glances at the door like she'd rather be anywhere else than here talking about her only Fairling's numbered days.

"Call the Fates, Quill." The Queen demands.

"Yes, Your Majesty," Quill hops out of his chair, his bare feet slapping against the wooden planks as he lands in the centre of the table. He squats down cupping his hands into a ball, whispering words too softly for me to hear. Steam begins to pour out from between his fingers. He places his hands on the table and slowly pulls them apart, revealing a glowing ball of mist. The clouds swirl and grow, when they're the size of a basketball Quill mutters and it stops expanding. He jumps off the table and reclaims his seat, just as the familiar faces of the haggard triplets appear in the misty glow.

"Thank you for joining us," the Queen greets the Fates. "We have run into a little snag and require your assistance once again." The Queen waits for the sisters to acknowledge that they can hear her. "The girl from the prophecy is dying, and soon if we don't act on her behalf."

The sister with the frantic eyes answers, "Her future is uncertain," she stares past the Queen, into nothingness, "all we can see is darkness, and despair. She's been cut by a Tenebris."

"You cannot see if we are meant to save her or not?" The Queen asks, frustration causing her tone to rise.

"No, Your Majesty, Tenebris is a dark force. All we can see is death. If the court is going to intervene, you must decide fast. Her destiny has been blanketed in the black mist of mortality." The ball dissolves, her last words hang in the air leaving the table in a heavy stillness.

A sad whine breaks the silence. Everyone's eyes move in unison, focusing on the source. Kodi lets out another whine, her cool blue eyes staring intently at them all. She stands and nudges the Queen's elbow.

She peers down the length of her nose at Kodi's black face, "Smart dog." A small smile appears on her lips. "Very well, summon the girl. We'll figure out what to do with her when she arrives."

* * *

I wake to evening sunlight streaming through the dandelion room's open drapes, warm on my face. But a shiver of cold is stuck in my bones, I pull the comforter tighter around me and try to take a deep breath, it's like someone has piled weights on my chest and they're crushing the air out of me instead of letting it in.

I clamber off my bed, keeping the quilt wrapped around my shoulders as I make my way through the hallways towards the voices. I move slow, it feels like my soul is being dragged down by despair, the weight of it crushing me. I push on, needing to be by people, knowing being around others will help. I find Maggie, Rose, and Kheelan seated around the dining table, speaking in hushed tones. I clear my throat to announce my presence, they all turn their heads towards me, identical expressions of worry crinkle over their faces.

"I had a weird dream." I start, the emptiness of my words jostles something in me, but mostly I feel nothing and my voice reflects that.

"Come and tell us," Rose pats the empty seat next to her.

I sit down and recount as much as I can remember about what I had seen in my dream. All three of them sit and listen, nodding to indicate they're following, but no one interrupts me. When I finish, I look up from my lap. Kheelan's expression is full of hope, but Maggie and Rose wear identical blank expressions.

"Have you had any other dreams?" Maggie asks after a silent beat.

I nod, remembering the flashes of dreams I had right after Declan and I had escaped from the NetherWorld. I describe them, knowing they barely qualify as real dreams.

"Those sound like they could be visions of the OtherWorld." Rose looks over her glasses at me, leaning in to inspect the black lines climbing up my face. "With those visions, and the dream you had this afternoon I think it's safe to assume you'll be leaving our world very soon." She offers a weak smile, "You're going to the OtherWorld."

I drink in my aunt's worried expression and try to muster up some kind of feeling. I know I should be nervous, scared, *something*, but all I feel is myself slipping further away.

* * *

The sun is setting behind the Tetons, an orangish-pink glow filters through the windows of the dining room. Mindy has cleared our dinner dishes long ago, but we remain at the table. They're discussing the coming ski season. I don't contribute, I just listen, knowing I should be relishing in the normalcy of their chatter, it's the first time in a long time that we haven't been focused on me dying, the Fairies, or The Hunt, just talking about the change of season. The dark cloud in my mind reminds me I may not be around to see what winter is like in Wyoming, but I push the thought away.

Kodi lets out a yelp from the great room, making Kheelan stop mid-sentence. My spine straightens. Kheelan is quick to his feet and disappears out of sight.

"Everything's okay," his voice calls from the other room. "She was just startled," he says coming back into the room holding a rolled-up piece of paper in the air. Kodi dashes into the room, to sit by my side. "This shot out of the fire." His grin is wide, taking up his entire face.

Rose jumps to her feet. "It must be from the Fairies!" She snatches it out of his hand. "It's addressed to you, dear." She looks at me over her half-moon glasses, "Do you mind?"

"Be my guest," I say as Kodi jumps into my lap sniffing the markings on my skin in her now normal, frenzied way. She lets out a small whimper as she nuzzles her head into my lap. I pat her head, I hope it's reassuring to her, but I know she can smell the poison coursing through my body.

"Rosalia DieErde," Aunt Rose begins as she unfurls the ancient looking piece of parchment. "Queen Lucille of the OtherWorld, and the Royal Council request your presence. Your Royal Highness has received your request from the FaeDog. Although no official decision has been made regarding your case, Your Royal Highness has agreed to grant you access to the OtherWorld for her and a panel to hear your case. A messenger will come for you tonight. Meet him in the clearing of the forest where you were created, at the stroke of midnight. Do not be late. Sincerely, Robin, a hand of the Queen." Rose looks up when she finishes reading, a glimmer of hope in her eyes for the first time all week.

"Do you know the clearing?" I ask.

She nods. "It's not too far from here."

"I'm going with you," Kheelan insists.

I look into his loving blue eyes and smile, my rock since I was thrown into this world. I find myself nodding in agreement. I don't want to go alone. Jen's voice rings in my head, *he's your fate* and it's not the first time this week. Usually when the thought crosses my mind it's pushed away by the image of Declan's laughing face, his eyes sparkling in the mischievous way that only his do, the kiss we shared. I shake the image away this time though, Declan has been disappearing every day, I've barely seen him. I look at Kheelan and really see him for the first time in a long time. His steady gaze, and stable demeanour, the one who's been by my side these past few days, my *soulmate.*

"This is great news!" Maggie claps her hands together, forcing me to rip my eyes away from her grandson. "We should get to work. You'll have to be careful how you address the Fairies. It needs to be convincing. And you should take them some milk and bread!" She beams at the two of us. "You're going to survive."

All I can do is offer her a weak smile. I have no idea how to speak to Fairies, let alone how to convince anyone that my life is worth saving.

"You said before they'll want something in return? A bargain of some kind?" Kheelan asks his grandma.

"That's a very high possibility," Rose answers, then she chuckles, "I don't think in modern times milk and bread is an accepted bargaining tool anymore, Maggie." She turns back to Kheelan, "This is all new territory, even for us old ladies. Neither of us have ever met a Fairy, let alone travelled to the OtherWorld." She meets my eyes, "The Queen has only contacted me the one time, and it was through a dream."

"From what we have read about Fairies, they like to make deals," Maggie continues, picking up where her friend left off. "They're not a species known for handing out favours for free."

"What do you think they'll want from me?" I ask, but the words don't come easy. I'm out of breath again. I take a few shallow breaths and continue, "I don't have anything to offer, and Jen waking up is more important than me living."

"Both your lives are important," Kheelan says with too much force. "There has to be a way to heal you and to wake up your sister. I won't let you bargain for only her life, you must promise me you'll fight for your own survival Lia."

I look up from the letter that's been sitting on the table, startled by the amount of anger present in his outburst. "Of course I'll fight for my own life." I whisper. "But if it's one or the other, I have to pick my sister."

His eyes soften, "I know you will, that's what scares me."

I reach across the table and grab a hold of his hand, I give it a gentle squeeze but don't let go. "We have a few hours before we have to meet this messenger, what do you think I should say?" I ask Maggie and Rose, but my eyes don't leave Kheelan's face.

"You need to rest. You look terrible." Maggie says pulling out her jar of salve as she hobbles towards me and begins slathering it over my skin. "Rose and I will write down some notes for you."

"I'll help you to your room. You really do look awful." Kheelan says offering me a hand to help me to my feet.

"You're really sweet, has anyone ever told you that?" I ask as I scoot Kodi off my lap and stand up. I let Kheelan wrap his arm around my waist and escort me down the hall to the yellow room. I don't even protest when he lifts me into bed, that's how weak I feel.

He pulls the comforter up to my chin. I'm already half asleep when he bends down to kiss my forehead, whispering "I love you" before tiptoeing out of my room.

I smile faintly, *I love you too,* I think before sleep pulls me the rest of the way in.

* * *

I wake to a cold hand brushing the hair away from my face and feeling my forehead. "Is it time to go already?" I grumble, not opening my eyes.

"Where are we going?" A soft voice asks.

My eyes shoot open at the familiar sound. Declan is perched on the edge of my bed, moonlight casting a soft glow off his face. The sight of him makes my heart flip in my chest. Then I remember I'm mad at him. "Where have you been?" I demand, trying to force anger into my voice with no success.

"Researching," he says. "Where are you planning on going?" He asks again.

"Researching *what*?" I demand, ignoring his question.

"How to save you," he says like that should have been obvious. "I'm not about to rely on the *Fairies* to save you."

"You could have just told us that," I grumble, "instead of being so mysterious about it."

"I'm sorry," he whispers, "I've been light travelling everywhere I can think of hoping to find a book on dark magic that might have a smidgen of information on curing a Tenebris cut. Today I was in New Orleans." He places his hand on my forehead, checking my temperature. I don't expect the eruption of butterflies in my chest at the slight contact, a far cry from the emotional numbness I've been feeling all day. "Where are you going?" He asks again.

"I'm going to the OtherWorld. The Fairies have agreed to see me."

"When?" His voice hardening.

"Midnight," I say.

He glances at the watch on his wrist, "That's in less than an hour. Are they sending you alone?"

"No, Kheelan is coming."

"I'm going to go ahead and assume there's nothing I can say that will persuade you not to go?" His voice and eyes pleading in the moonlight.

"Did you do some ground breaking research and find a cure for me?" I ask.

He shakes his head sadly.

"Then I'm out of options," I say. "I can barely breathe." My breath comes out in a wheeze as though to prove my point.

"I'm coming too." He stands up and heads to the door, pausing in the frame, "I'm gonna find Kheelan. Then I guess we're off to make a deal with the lesser of the devils and get you good as new." He winks as he walks away, but his shoulders are slouched, not happy with the idea of making any bargains with unearthly creatures, even if they are the 'good guys'.

* * *

The clearing is the same one that Kheelan and I had lain in earlier this summer. The afternoon when his passion for the Light had shone in his eyes, terrifying me. I almost laugh out loud at the memory. It had been one of the scariest moments of my life up to that point. If only I knew what lay ahead of me. What still may lay ahead of me.

We arrive early. Kodiak refused to come with us. She didn't want any of us to go at all, but after some coaxing, she allowed it. I'm standing between the two brothers, the forest around us dark and silent. I don't feel nervous or hopeful, just unsettled. I know they're the *good ones*, but that doesn't stop Herne's description of the Queen being a puppet master from flitting around in my head or my stomach from being a tangle of knots.

Kheelan pushes a button on his watch, illuminating the face. "11:59," he announces.

Declan and I bob our heads in acknowledgement. I scan the clearing around us. There's no sign of life other than the three of us. "Maybe we're in the wrong clearing?"

"I have a feeling they'll be very punctual," Kheelan says, "and they still have ten seconds…"

"Ten, nine, eight…" Declan whispers. I can hear the mocking smirk on his face.

My laugh cuts off when he gets to the end of his count down. A tiny dot of light appears in the middle of the clearing right as he whispers, 'blast off.' It starts off the size of a firefly but keeps growing, until it's taking up most of the clearing. I raise my hands to shield my eyes from the blaring white light.

"Good evening, young Fairlings," a voice greets us from somewhere inside the light.

"Good evening?" I stammer back. Unsure how to address whoever it is.

I'm surprised when it's the antlered man from my dream who emerges out of the brightness, he's shorter than I expected, coming up to only my shoulder, even with his antlers. A big smile across his face reveals large square teeth, "Wow! Look at you Rosalia," he says, his smile not wavering. "I didn't know what to expect, but it definitely wasn't this! Tenebris is an extraordinary substance. Very interesting…" He's close enough to shake our hands now, but shows no sign of such a greeting. He just leans in staring at my freakish swirls.

I don't say anything, I'm speechless. Seeing a man with antlers step out of a ball of light is rather offsetting.

"I'm Declan." Declan steps forward, his hand outstretched.

249

The antlered man looks at his outstretched arm, not sure what to do with it. "I'm Quill, a hand of Queen Lucille, Queen of the Fae and ruler of the OtherWorld." He responds without touching Declan.

Declan nods, lowering his hand. "Right. This is my brother, Kheelan." He motions to Kheelan who's standing to my right.

"Pleasure." Quill says, his voice dry. "We need to go. Portals don't stay open forever."

I glance at Declan, he looks unsure about following this antlered creature into a ball of light. I turn my gaze to Kheelan, he smiles, reassuring me. I feel his hand clasp tightly around my own. He gives me a gentle squeeze as he walks forward, pulling me with him into the blinding light.

Chapter Twenty

It's like walking through a wind tunnel. My hair fans out behind me, my hoody clinging tight to my torso. I clutch Kheelan's hand tighter, glad to have something to hold on to. Then it's calm. My hair falls into place around my shoulders and the forest bursts to life with rustling leaves and bird songs. When my eyes adjust from the sudden brightness, I'm unable to take in our new surroundings fast enough. It's the same clearing; but it's *not* the same clearing. An explosion of vibrant colours dances around us, some I don't have a name for. The sun's rays weave through the leaves overhead, warming my skin. It feels different, warm like Earth's sun, but more cosy than hot, like the rays are wrapping around me in a welcoming hug. Something in my gut tells me I wouldn't get a sun burn here.

I fill my lungs with crisp air, the first full breath in so many days. It smells like a dream, I can't put my finger on it. Like fresh laundry but natural, the *cleanest* air. A burst of lightness rings through my body, a genuine smile lifting the corners of my mouth. I'm *feeling*. A light squeeze on my palm drags my gaze to Kheelan's wide eyes, taking in the exotic plants and animals around us.

"It's amazing," I whisper.

"This place is unimaginable," he murmurs.

Declan walks up behind us, "Incredible," he breathes.

"Yes, yes, very pretty. We must hurry though. We have to walk through the entirety of this enchanted wood, and through the night! Being late will not weigh in the girl's favour." Quill's voice carries from the other side of the clearing where he's waiting for us to follow.

This snaps the boys to attention and they rush in the direction of the antlered man. Kheelan keeps a firm grip on my hand pulling me along behind him.

Quill walks swiftly as he leads us through the forest. He doesn't hesitate as he weaves his way through the thick trees and moss-covered ground, as though he's walked these paths a million times before, which he probably has. We're moving so fast I almost don't notice the trees around us growing. They're towering hundreds of feet above our heads now, the upper canopy feels worlds away. The leaves and flower petals drifting on the breeze, are as big as I am. My jaw drops and my eyes bug out, they aren't petals or leaves at all. They're *Fairies*.

"We're shrinking," Kheelan whispers into my ear. Of course we're shrinking, why would the entire world around us be growing? I can't help but laugh, a giddy excitement zinging through me, my inner child jumping for joy at the marvel of it all.

Not everything seems magical and happy though. At one point, we pass a lone Fairy who's collecting plants from the forest floor. When she sees us, she becomes still as a statue, her eyes lock onto mine, glowing fierce. I tighten my grip on Kheelan's hand and quicken my pace. A shiver runs up my spine as her intense stare follows us. I only feel my shoulders start to relax when she's long out of sight.

There's so much greenery that I can't name here. I try to memorise the shapes of their leaves, the colour of their flowers. But I can't take them in fast enough. I wish I could get my hands on them. Take some back to the green house. Find a cure for Jen. "There have to be so many medicinal uses for these plants." I muse out loud.

"Careful young Fairling, plants in the OtherWorld are not like the ones on Earth." Quill says from a few paces ahead of us. I'm not sure how he heard me.

"Do you not use plants for remedies?" I ask him.

"Of course we do. But here, you must get the plants permission. The same plant that can save your life could also end it, depending on its mood."

I view the forest with a new eye, careful not to brush against any leaves. *Permission*? Do plants think and have free will in this world?

It feels like we've been walking for hours when we finally break out of the tree line and enter a meadow. The sunlight gone. I look up to the sky and note there are two very full moons. Billions of bright stars fill in the inky blackness around them, leaving barely any room in between, providing us with plenty of light to walk by. Fireflies blink to life as we push through the tall grass. Yellow ones, like we have at home, but also blue ones, red, green, purple and more of the colours I don't have names for. My breath catches at the exotic beauty of it all. The perfect sky and floating multi-coloured lights. I've never seen anything so magical. I point them out to Declan and Kheelan, muttering about the flash of the dream I had in the motel room.

As we approach the far side of the meadow the sky begins to lighten. It's not a sunrise, I realise. It's like we're walking out of the night and into the dawn. When mountains reveal themselves in the distance covered in the full light of day, I sneak a peek over my shoulder to confirm my suspicions, the night sky is still behind us. There's a clear line between the night and morning. I smile. That's what Quill had meant by walking through the night. I send out a silent goodbye to the fireflies that are still winking at me in the distance, wishing I could spend more time in the meadow. Alas, we're here for a business, not pleasure. I force my eyes back towards the day as a fresh wave of nerves ripples through me, we're going to meet the Fairy Queen.

Quill comes to a sudden stop in front of a small dirt mound. "We're here." He announces. I look around, outside of our small group there isn't another soul in sight. Quill reaches out a hand and places it on my shoulder. "May your light shine bright," he tilts his head forward until his forehead is rested on mine.

"Err...thank you." I somehow manage not to squirm at the stranger's sudden intimate contact.

Declan lets out a breath of a chuckle, Kheelan squeezes my hand in encouragement.

"Now what?" Declan asks, tearing his eyes away from mine and Kheelan's intertwined fingers to meet Quills eyes.

I drop Kheelan's hand, pretending to itch my nose.

"Just down here." Quill says lifting his foot high into the air, he brings it back down fast and hard onto a rock on the ground in front of him. I wince, that had to hurt. I watch in amazement as a hole appears in the face of the mound. It expands, revealing a tunnel within. "This way!" he says jumping off the mound and entering the shaft. Kheelan steps through after him, and I follow with Declan close behind.

After Declan steps into the tunnel, the opening closes behind him, putting us into pitch blackness. I bump into Kheelan, our leader has come to a sudden stop. "Hmm…" I hear the antlered man think, "Might be a bit dark down here for you." He whispers words I can't make out, a ball of light appears in his palms. "Ah! Much better," he says as he begins to lead the way through the passage, the light casting creepy shadows off his antlers and the roots dangling from the ceiling. I try not to think about spiders or anything else that might be creeping or crawling around with us down here.

The space is narrow, requiring us to walk single file. I try to step carefully, the ground beneath our feet is littered with rocks and large roots randomly protruding out of the soil, not to mention the occasional low dangling root from above, adding more hazards to our commute. A few catch me off guard, smacking me in the face, followed closely by laughter from behind me. At one point my foot catches on a root and I stumble, Declan's there in an instant. This time only a whisper of a laugh escapes his lips, the air tickles my neck as he grips me, keeping me upright. Whispering to make sure I'm okay before letting go.

I'm relieved when the tunnel opens into a proper passageway with torches lighting the path before us. Quill comes to a stop in front of a grand oak door. "Only Rosalia." He says, resting a hand on the brass knob.

Declan and Kheelan open their mouths to protest, but he holds up a hand silencing them. "Only Rosalia," he repeats, "wait here. I'll announce the girl and then escort you both to a place where you can wait." He motions for me to follow.

The room is familiar to me, it's the one from my dreams. The long wooden table stretches out before me, surrounded by faces I also recognise. The lady with the birds is seated to the right of the Queen who's at the head of the table. The brunette and red-haired Fairies are on either side of my Fairy Mother who is situated at the end furthest from me. The light glimmering off their tinted skin is mesmerising.

"Your Majesty," Quill's voice takes on a formal high-pitched tone, "may I present Rosalia AusFeuer-DieErde, Fairling of Aspen AusFeuer-DieErde."

I force a smile, my eyes flit around to each face of my intimidating audience. I rub my palms against my jeans, hoping Quill's refusal to accept Declan's hand in the meadow means that they don't shake hands in this realm, because mine are slick with nervousness.

"Thank you, Quill. Please have a seat so we can begin." Queen Lucille says, barely looking at me.

"Your Majesty, pray forgive me," his voice pleading, "the Hunter's sons have accompanied us and are waiting just outside the door. I must take them to a room to wait."

"Both of the sons are here?" The Queen asks, a spark bringing her eyes to life.

"That's correct, your Majesty." He lifts his eyes to look at his leader.

"Before you take them away, bring them in. I'd like to see the three together." Her eyes gleam greedily.

Quill nods once, spinning on his feet to open the door behind us. I step out of the way to make room for the boys to enter.

Kheelan walks up next to me, slipping something into my hand. "I almost forgot to give this to you," he whispers in my ear.

I look into my hand, it's a hot pink post-it noted, folded up. I eye him with the silent question. *What is it?*

"Speaking points from the old ladies," he mouths.

I nod looking back at the table of beings.

"So, these are the prophesied three?" The brunette Fairy scoffs from her end of the table. "They look like children."

"They are children Fern." Her red-haired sister says, her voice bored.

"Rosalia," the Queen says, I jump at the sound of my name on her voice. "You do not look well." She observes, moving her eyes down my body.

"No, your Majesty," my voice quavers.

"Take the sons away. We shall begin." The Queen demands.

Quill bows low as he backs out of the open door. I throw my eyes at the three departing, I don't want them to leave me here with these strangers. With strangers who don't like me and might decide I'm better off dead. Kheelan reaches out and gives my hand a squeeze of encouragement as he follows Quill through the door. Declan offers a weak smile, he doesn't like this anymore than I do.

"It must be hard to talk at this point?" The woman with the birds flying around her head asks me, pulling my gaze back to the table. The door clicks shut behind me.

I nod.

"And hard to breathe?" She asks.

I nod again. "Easier in this realm though," I say, but my voice sounds like a dying frog.

"Come here, child. I need to take a look inside you." The Queen says, her voice gentle.

I take four shaky steps forward until I'm standing next to her chair. The Queen rises to her feet and turns to face me. The top of her beehive hairdo barley reaching my shoulders.

"If you could kneel."

I sink to my knees, and finally bring myself to look at the Queen's face. I notice her skin, though not tinted in an unusual colour, still shimmers, like she's made out of pearl. She smiles at me, the creases around her eyes and mouth deepening. It's a warm smile, the kind only a grandmother can give. My breath catches as it dawns on me, she *is* my grandmother, kind of.

Her blue eyes are so pale there's almost no colour to them at all, but somehow, they still feel warm as they bore into mine. "No need to be frightened," she whispers. "It won't hurt." She reaches out with both of her hands and grasps my face tightly between them.

She keeps her eyes firmly on mine, as hers burst into a glow of pure white. Warmness pours in through my eyes and fills my head. I can feel the Queen prodding around with her mind. It's uncomfortable but doesn't hurt. Nothing like when Flint did it in Jesse's basement.

The Queen lets out a snort as she pulls away from my face. "She cares about a mortal's survival more than her own."

The blonde Fairy makes a disgusted noise from the far end of the room, I snap my head in her direction. My Fairy Mother is looking at me as though I'm something icky she stepped in. My heart clenches.

"She has a pure heart, and her light is bright, just as I expected." The Queen says pulling my attention back to her. She's looking at the blonde Fairy as she speaks. "She's much like you, Aspen."

Aspen meets my eyes. I search hers for any sign of empathy, or feeling at all towards me, her Fairling daughter. But I don't find what I'm looking for in her cool gaze. She looks back to her mother with a shrug. "Her hair is like mine, and her eyes are similar."

The Queen's gaze lingers on her daughter for a few slow passing seconds before she decides to ignore her comment. She addresses the entire room, "Both of the Hunter's sons are in love with her."

I rip my eyes from my Fairy Mother's face and spin back to the Queen in front of me, my mouth dropping open at her blatant words. How did she get *that* out of *my* head? My cheeks warm in embarrassment.

A small smile plays across her lips, and she winks down at me. "Quill is back outside the door now, go to him. He'll take you outside. I'm going to share with the others what I saw in you, then we'll decide your fate."

I nod, a lump forming in my throat making it impossible for me to say anything. I feel like I should say something compelling. Convince them that I should live. Then I remember the piece of paper balled up in my hand. My fingers shake as I unfold it, revealing Maggie's spiky handwriting, *speak from your heart.* That's not helpful. I guess all I can do is hope that the Queen liked what she saw.

The Queen was right, Quill is waiting for me when I exit the room. I follow him in silence as he weaves us through the underground maze. I'm thankful when the ground starts to incline under my feet and sunlight pours in up ahead. I follow Quill up a steep staircase and we emerge into a big courtyard, the burst of fresh air and sunlight warm and welcome on my face.

"I'll be back to collect you when we're finished deliberating," Quill says.

I keep my eyes closed, my face pointed toward the sky, "Where are Kheelan and Declan?"

There's no answer.

I open my eyes, Quill is gone. I scan the courtyard, there are a handful of Fairies, most gathered in small clusters talking, some children weaving through the wildflowers and soaring to the top limbs of the scattered trees, playing some sort of game. But I don't see my friends.

I make my way towards a small pond in the far corner of the space. Deciding it'll be nice to lie down for a bit and enjoy the weather, after all I could be in the last moments of my life.

I settle into the soft green grass and lie back, letting the warmth wash over my body. I feel the heat coming from both sides of my face. I crack my eyes and squint up at the sky. There are three suns shining down on me. How didn't I notice that before? I smile, closing my eyes again as another burst of happiness blossoms in my chest. This place is *magic* I think as I begin to drift off.

The hairs on the back of my neck prick to life, startling me out of my stupor. I bolt into a sitting position, am I being watched? I glance around, no one seems to be paying me any attention. Then my eyes find the source. One of the Fairy children has stopped playing the game and is watching me with big purple eyes, hovering above the middle of the pond. A smile covers her face when my eyes land on her and she begins to soar towards me, dragging her bare toes through the water.

She lands with a soft thud in front of me, her little white dress ruffling around her legs in the gentle breeze. She brushes her blonde curls out of her face, revealing tiny pointed ears. I smile as she situates herself right in front of me, too close for social norms.

"Hi Lia!" She breaths, her breath smells like a freshly cut bouquet of flowers, her voice reminding me of a wind chime. "Wow," she whispers leaning closer to my face. "Those lines are beautiful." She stops her nose a couple inches from my own, flashing her brilliant violet eyes into mine. "I can see you love your sister. But she's *human*." She crinkles her nose at the word human. Then she surprises me by reaching out her little hand and placing it on my forearm her fingers glowing. "Don't be sad."

A burst of warm happiness shoots up my arm straight into my heart. I pull away from her touch, examining my arm where her fingers had been. There's nothing there. I look up at her and force a smile. Not sure how to react to this. "Thanks…" I finally manage, my voice like sandpaper in comparison to hers. "And you're right, I do love my sister. That's part of the reason I feel so sad. I'm dying, and she's stuck in a sleeping state. I won't be able to wake her up before I go."

The child just nods. "I know." She clambers into my lap and places both of her tiny lilac hands on my cheeks. "I have the gift of sight." Her proud words come out like a song. "You aren't going to die though, they've already decided." She smiles, her tiny white teeth shine like pearls as light pours out of her, she's entered a full state of glow.

"You can see that?" I ask, not bothering to worry that a strange child is climbing all over me and touching my face.

Her light dims so only her purple eyes remain aglow as she nods her head, her blonde curls bouncing around her heart-shaped face. "They're going to heal you!" She squeals in delight. Then her face drops. "They aren't going to wake up Jennifer though. Fairies don't like humans. They chased us out of their World." She pauses for a thoughtful moment, "I wonder if I'd like humans?" She reaches out and grabs my face again. "I've never met one. You're part human though, and I like you."

I smile weakly, but my body feels heavy at her news. "Thank you." I manage to whisper. I knew they wouldn't give Jen a second thought, but hearing a Fairy confirm it, even if she is just a child, is like taking a punch to the gut. My posture slumps, "What's your name?" I ask, realising we skipped a step because this child already knows everything about me.

She giggles, "Tilia." She drops her hands into her lap, a thoughtful expression on her face. Suddenly a wide grin spreads from ear to ear. She leans close and whispers, "You don't need the Queen to wake up your sister!" She hops out of my lap and runs off.

"Wait!" I call out, she's a few yards away but stops and turns towards me. "What do you mean?"

Her purple eyes are bright and her smile widens stretching across her tiny face. She doesn't speak, she just lifts a tiny hand and points towards the far wall of the courtyard. I follow the direction of her finger, my eyes landing on some branches that are dangling over the wall, tiny blue bulbs are nestled between its leaves, pulsing with light. I open my mouth to question her further but before I can get any words out, she mouths one word, *MAGIC.* With a giggle she takes off into flight, over the wall.

I stumble to my feet as something like hope rings through my body. I begin to make my way across the yard, I finally have an answer, I know how to wake up Jen! I make it all of three steps when Quill appears at my side. I jump, my alarmed yelp breaking the peacefulness of the lawn.

"Sorry to startle you, but the council has come to a decision."

I send one last longing look at the bright berries, my bubble of hope bursting in my chest. Then I begrudgingly follow the antlered man back into the dark tunnels beneath us.

Chapter Twenty-One

A hush falls over the room upon my re-entrance, the kind that hangs heavy and can be felt in the air around. Everyone's eyes are on me. I try to swallow the lump that's returned to my throat as I look around, hoping to find an expression that's reassuring. I'm met with grim faces. My stomach sinks, the Fairy child tricked me. I twirl my finger around the necklace Jen gave me and shift my weight from foot to foot. Why isn't anyone saying anything? I focus on my feet, not liking the unblinking stares studying me with unabashed curiosity.

The silence drags on. It dawns on me that time isn't a concern in this realm. The Fairies can probably sit motionless without saying a word for hours. The thought makes me shudder. "So, where are Declan and Kheelan?" My raspy whisper shatters the silence.

The Queen smiles, "You'll be able to see them for a brief moment, before the healing process begins."

My heart skips a beat, "You've decided to heal me?" Why can't I manage to make my voice louder than a whisper?

"It took some convincing," the Queen's eyes sparkle. "Until today I was the only being, besides the seer who spoke the prophecy, who had heard it in full. Alas I shared with the others and in the end it's what weighed heavily in your favour switching the vote from split to unanimous."

They heard the Prophecy. Curiosity itches at me. Am I allowed to ask what it says, or would they think that rude and change their mind?

The Queen smiles again, as though my thoughts are written across my forehead for her to read. "We thought it'd be best for you to hear it too, so you can fully understand your fate."

I nod.

"Who would like to do the honours?" She asks holding up a long piece of yellowed parchment.

"I will." My Fairy Mother's voice is soft from the far end of the table. I look up and meet her sharp green eyes. They haven't softened towards me. I wonder if the votes were really unanimously in my favour.

The Queen whispers words in a language I don't understand and sends the parchment floating down the length of the table to her daughter.

Aspen's spindly fingers snatch it out of the air. She flattens the paper, my pulse quickens as she begins to read.

"Here and now the chosen I'll state,
Once spoken they are locked in fate.
The Fairling of the Queen's offspring,
And brothers from a Hunter's fling.
By oneself thy will not survive,
Three needed in order to thrive.
'Fore the sun is fully covered,
The Lost Stave shall be recovered.
Restore balance between the realms,
Before the darkness overwhelms.
Not everything is black and white,
It takes all three to judge what's right.
Strongest minds will turn for power,
Watch for this in final hour.
To stop tyranny there's a price,
One shall parish in sacrifice."

When she finishes, her eyes find mine, "You're meant to recover the Lost Stave, and since you haven't done that yet we feel it's not the right time for you to die."

Her words feel like a slap in my face. I take a step back towards the door, the words of the prophecy playing over and over in my head as I commit them to memory. One of us is going to *die* for a stave? How did Rose describe it? Like a fancy walking stick? One of us is going to die, for a *walking stick*.

"Aspen, do not be so harsh." The Queen interjects. "We will heal you, but we need to be sure the prophecy won't be altered." She pauses, "Herne has the Lost Stave. I had suspicions it was he who had stolen it, but I saw it in your head. He had it with him at that feast."

The ruby staff by his side, the one I had trouble ripping my eyes from. That's the Lost Stave, my hands begin to tremble as her words register. The Lost Stave is in the NetherWorld.

"You were able to Light Travel out of the NetherWorld, between realms on your own, you're the one—"

"—Not exactly." The room sucks in a collective breath. I glance around at the astonished faces, before breathing in my own sharp breath. I just interrupted royalty. "Forgive me, your highness." I sputter. "I only wanted to point out that Declan helped me escape the NetherWorld."

She waves off my apology and looks at me, her eyes steady. "You did it on your own. Yes, he stirred your Light, but it was you who got the two of you out. A remarkable achievement for any Fairling, but especially extraordinary for one who has Awakened so late. Your blood is strong." She folds her hands together and leans onto the table. "With the knowledge we gathered today, we have decided to heal you. After reviewing the prophecy, it's clear that all three of you will be needed." She leans back in her chair, a sinister smile curving her lips upward. I clench my pants to stop my hands from trembling. "In exchange for the healing process, we'll need something from you."

I manage to nod my head. I knew this was coming, but the idea still makes me nauseous. What will they ask of me? Is recovering their stave from the NetherWorld not enough?

"You don't want to go back to the NetherWorld." The Queen says, it's not a question.

"No," I whisper. "I *can't* go back to that place."

"Then you will die, probably within the next twenty-four hours." She watches my face carefully as the impact of her words settle in. I feel the little colour that I have left drain from my face. "Do you want to live or die?" She asks, her voice cool.

The thought of having to go back to the NetherWorld makes me long for death, it's the better of the two options. I finger my necklace. *Jen needs me*, "I want to live." I say, my voice nearly inaudible. "Wouldn't a full Fairy have a better chance of survival?" I ask knowing they don't care about me, I'm just a tool to get them what they want.

The Queen looks at me unblinking. "Fae cannot enter the NetherWorld, we die instantly." My mind flashes to the squelched fairies throughout the NetherWorld, they certainly were not in good health, but definitely not dead. The cold tone of her lie sends a shiver down my spine. Perhaps Herne's words weren't so far from the truth after all. Her eyes soften a bit, "Every spell cast has two sides." She explains. "Ying and Yang, black and white, dark and light, positive and negative, opposing magnets, whatever you want to call it. When I created the magic banishing Herne and his followers from the OtherWorld, it generated the realm of the NetherWorld. The opposite of the OtherWorld, the dark to our light. Just as we cannot enter the NetherWorld, the Dark Fairies cannot enter the OtherWorld, as long as my magic holds." She pauses, "But you have shown us that's not the case for Fairlings. Which could prove to be a handy tool."

"What about the squelched fairies?" I ask, my voice a mere whisper, "Could they be rescued from that realm with the power of The Stave?" Herne must not realise the power he holds.

"Those Fairies, and what The Stave is capable of is of no concern to you, *Fairling.* Your job is only to retrieve it." The Queen snarls.

I stumble back, my foot catches and I trip backwards into the cold roughness of the stone wall, my heart pounding. *These are the good guys,* I remind myself. "What do you need from me?" I ask, my voice shaking. "Just my promise that I'll get The Stave out of the NetherWorld and return it to you?"

My Fairy Mother is the one who answers. "You'll take a binding oath. That's the price if you want us to heal you, it gives us an added insurance that the prophecy will work in our advantage."

"A binding oath?" I look towards the woman who's blood I share but can't bring myself to look her in the eyes, so I focus on her porcelain forehead.

"It changes your fate." She says, "If you don't hold up your end of the bargain, you die."

I gulp, glancing around the room of emotionless faces that are watching our exchange. "Will I go as soon as I'm healed?" I ask, turning my attention back to the Queen.

"The eve of the eclipse," her voice back to its normal tone.

I nod, *'fore the sun is fully covered.* That's soon. The weight of the worlds drop onto my shoulders, it's a miracle I'm not sinking into ground. They aren't saving me. They're only prolonging my life so they can fully utilise me first. They need me to die at the right moment, and today isn't that moment. I take a deep breath, now is not the time to feel sorry for myself. I need to be brave. Extra time might be all I need to wake up Jen. "Okay." I finally say. "I'll take the binding oath."

The Queen's eyes burn greedily, the pressure I feel intensifies. She turns to Quill who is now seated to her left. "Will you do the honours?"

"Yes, your majesty," he bows his head and rises from his seat. "Rosalia, you'll need to come closer."

I force my feet to take the steps to close the distance between myself and the Queen. The old Fairy stands and raises her hands in front of her face, her palms facing me. I kneel and mirror her actions.

Quill nods his approval, "Your hands will need to maintain contact until we've finished. When I finish my part, you both need to speak the words *this is binding*."

We both nod to show we understand. The Queen shuffles forward, sending a tiny spark up my arms as our palms meet.

Quill steps towards us, his hands hovering in front of him, a glowing mist shoots out of his fingertips and surrounds our hands in a comfortable warmth. He whispers words in the same language from before. I wish I understood what he's saying, instead all I can do is watch as the foreign words transform the mist from a clean white to a foreboding red bringing with it an intense heat. I swallow and glance in the Queens direction to gauge her reaction. Her eyes are closed, a satisfied smile still lingering on her lips. I look back at our hands, the mist has returned to white.

"Say the words now." Quill instructs.

"This is binding." We both say, the queens voice comes out strong, overpowering my stammer. The mist disperses, shooting up both our arms and into our bodies. A shiver runs down my spine. My fate is set.

The Queen returns to her throne, but avoids looking at me.

"Will you wake my sister?" I ask, hating how timid I sound.

The Queen shakes her head no, still not looking in my direction. It's like my stomach is full of rocks. "Take her to see the Hunter's sons." The Queen demands. "I trust they were instructed on where to be at this time?"

"Yes, your majesty, they'll be in the courtyard." Quill answers.

"Don't allow them to linger. She needs to be taken to the large healing pond at once."

Quill nods curtly and walks to the door, pausing only to make sure I'm following.

I'm close at his heels. Wanting to get as far away from this room as possible.

My heart pounds in anticipation. Quill has led me back to the same courtyard. I *have* to get my hands on some of those berries. It may be Jen's only hope.

Kheelan and Declan jump up from under a tree in the middle of the grass as soon as we enter the yard and rush in our direction.

"Make it quick," Quill says. "I'll wait here."

I walk as fast as I can towards the boys. We reach each other mid-way but I keep walking, towards the far side of the lawn. I don't want the antlered man to be able to hear us. When I feel we're safely out of earshot I stop and turn to face them. Their faces wear identical expressions of concern, they want to know the outcome.

"Well?" Declan urges.

"They're going to heal me."

Kheelan lets out a breath of relief. "That's great!"

Declan asks, "What's the price?"

"Nothing too bad," I lie, avoiding his eyes. "I'll tell you everything later. Quill said we need to keep this short. I have to go to some healing pond right away." I look up, his blue eyes are boring into mine. He doesn't believe me. I quickly change the subject. Glancing over my shoulder to make sure Quill is still where he's meant to be. "They won't wake up Jen."

They both nod, they expected this.

"I was in this courtyard before, while they deliberated my case." I rush on, wanting to get it out before I have to leave. "I met a Fairy child." I throw my eyes around the space hoping to spot her, but she's not here. "She called herself a seer. She told me that they would save me but not Jen." I glance back at Quill, he's talking to a middle-aged Fairy man. Good, he's not paying attention to us. "She said we could save Jen without their help though." I point to the branches dangling over the wall a few yards away from us.

They turn their attention to the pulsating blue berries. "Are you sure this kid knew what she was talking about?" Kheelan asks, a furrow forming between his eyes.

"No," I admit, "but we have nothing else. She was right about the decision regarding me. We need to at least *try*." I peek over my shoulder again. Quill's friend is gone, he's watching us with an urgent look in his eyes. "I have to go. *Please* try to get some of those berries. This may be our only chance." I turn and start to make my way back towards the antlered man. A hand grasps onto mine. I half turn, meeting Declan's worried eyes.

"What's the price?" He asks again.

I just shrug and rip my eyes from him, focusing on the blades of grass under my feet, "Like I said, nothing too bad. I'll tell you guys about it later. Please just get some of those berries." My eyes return to his. My heart twists at the agony on his face. I offer a weak smile. "Nothing is worse than the alternative, right?" I take a step backward, "I have to go get fixed up now. I'll see you soon." I glance at Kheelan to show I mean him too. He's watching our exchange, something I can't quite put my finger on burning hot in his eyes. I flinch and release Declan's hand as I spin around and make my way back to Quill.

"We need to go, and they are not permitted to come," Quill says as soon as I'm within ear shot.

I turn my head to see who he's pointing to. Declan and Kheelan are right behind me. I jump, how did I not hear them?

"You can see her when the process is complete." He directs at the boys.

"Can one of us go with her at least?" Kheelan asks.

"No." There's a new edge of authority to his voice. "We must go. Rosalia, come," he demands, leading the way down the staircase.

I mouth the word BERRIES at the brothers as I follow him into the tunnel. Praying they're able to get their hands on some.

Quill leads us through the labyrinth of passageways with a new sense of urgency. I thought his pace was fast before but now I struggle to keep up. Without the fresh air of the outdoors, I can't seem to suck in enough oxygen, breathing almost impossible, but he ignores my requests to slow down. After what feels like an eternity, the tunnel begins to open up, revealing a ceiling that's at least two stories above us.

We come to giant double doors. I double over, gasping to catch my breath. When I get my breathing back to somewhat normal, I slowly straighten back up and take in the grand mahogany doors that gleam before me. They're covered in intricate carvings of Fairies and other magical beings and animals. I've never seen such fine details before. I trace my fingers over an image of Fairies dancing around a fire, it reminds me of the painting at Aunt Rose's. A sudden tightness clenches my throat. I want to go home.

I go to reach for the knob but, there isn't one. I turn to Quill. "How?"

He holds up his hand, "Magic." He says, answering my question before I can fully form it. He flashes me his unusual square smile and positions himself in front of the doors.

I watch as he extends his index finger, a long golden nail sprouting from the tip, glistening in the light.

A gasp breathes out of me.

He smirks as he stretches his arm high above his head and touches his golden nail to the centre of the woodwork. He begins to drag it downward. I cover my ears as the screeching echoes through the open space. He continues to drag his nail down the entire length of the wooden expanse, squatting to reach the floor.

The line glimmers for a moment before spreading open like a curtain, revealing an underground lake the colour of sun lit emeralds.

Quill turns to me. "This is where we part ways, young Fairling. I wish you the best of luck in your future venture, I hope to meet again soon. May your light shine bright," he bends himself into a deep bow, "it has been an honour escorting you."

"Thank you." My voice catches, I had no idea he felt any kind of fondness towards me. I step through the new opening and turn to say a final good bye to our OtherWorld guide, but the doorway is gone, I'm alone.

Now what? I look around the cavern, the stone walls are speckled with gemstones and curve upward creating a dome over the pool. There's no one else here. I seat myself on a large rock at the edge of the lake, the excitement of the day fading, leaving me worn. I stare into the water which seems to be emitting its own light and let its lapping sounds lull me into a daze. I replay the prophecy over and over in my mind, not wanting to forget any of it. Each line seems to be darker than the one before. The last two stick out the most though, one of us is going to die to save a stupid stick.

Someone clears their throat, I jump, whipping my head around searching for the source. My eyes land on Aspen, my Fairy Mother, standing a few yards away, watching me with an odd expression, the tips of her magnificent wings glimmer from her back, framing her perfect face. The green hue of the room makes her seem more supernatural than usual, her skin gleaming greener, like forest leaves on a sunny day.

I offer a weak smile, "Hi." I slide off the rock so I'm standing.

She scowls, "Let's get this over with."

My face drops. Why did you create me in the first place? I want to ask, but instead I say, "What do I need to do?"

She lets out a long sigh, annoyed. "You were created by my Light." She says, "So my Light is needed to drive the darkness that's entered your blood out of you." She slides the straps of her dress off her shoulders, the garment ripples to the ground around her feet, she carefully steps out of it, kicking it to the side.

I avert my eyes, blood surging to my cheeks, giving away my embarrassment at her nakedness.

"Undress." She demands. "You'll need to submerge yourself in the water. Hold your breath, until you can feel my Light. I'll have to fill the entire pool, so it'll take some time. When you do feel it, you must take a deep breath while still fully submerged."

"I'll drown." I say, not sure why I need to state the obvious fact that I can't breathe under water.

"Don't be stupid. Of course you aren't going to drown. You're not in your realm, this is the OtherWorld." She looks at me, her eyes full of scorn. "Stop looking like a frightened puppy. This is going to save you. You'll only die if you don't do as I say. Now undress." She spits out the demand through clenched teeth.

My hands are shaking so badly I'm afraid I won't be able to get my clothes off, but somehow, I manage. I try to keep my body hidden behind my arms as I turn back to face Aspen who's watching me like I'm some sort of specimen.

"Good," her voice is bored. "Enter the water, I'll begin once you're in position."

I nod and walk to the edge of the lake, the warm water surprises me, I was expecting a shock of cold. I wade out until the water is up to my shoulders. I glance back at the shore, my Fairy Mother is still watching me with an unsettling intensity burning in her eyes. I take a deep breath, expanding my lungs as best I can before I drop beneath the water.

My eyes open, the water stinging at first, but I want to watch. Aspens legs enter the pool. She stops when she's waist deep and places her hands on the surface. My lungs are already screaming for more air, but I ignore it and focus on what my Fairy Mother is doing. Light gleams out of her entire body as golden waterfalls, that look like sparks, begin to pour out of her hands into the pool. It's like her arms have become giant Fourth of July sparklers. The light streams out at a steady pace, each spark darting in a different direction, as soon as it reaches the water. They move around quickly, multiplying as they go. The lake is beginning to fill.

I close my eyes when the water becomes too bright. Without the distraction of seeing what's happening, it's harder to ignore the growing burn in my chest. My heart is pounding in my ears, my lungs demanding I take a breath. Just when I think I can't take anymore a high-pitched ringing starts in my ears. I clench my fists into tight balls, digging my fingernails into the fleshy part of my palm. I can't surface. Another few agonising heartbeats pass when finally, the Fairy's Light reaches me. The heat of her Light instantly slows my heart rate back to normal and sends a calmness through me. I know it's time, I need to suck in the breath now. *They need you alive a little longer* I remind myself, this won't drown you. I open my mouth and suck in the light-filled water as though taking a deep breath of air. I feel like I'm swallowing the sun, the hot water pours down my throat and fills my lungs. The warmth spreads into my heart and begins to pump throughout my body.

I go rigid. My arms and legs shooting straight out as the light takes over my frame. It feels like I'm on fire. I shouldn't have trusted her. She's not helping me, she's *killing* me. I scream and try to move my limbs to take me to the surface, but they stay stiff, only bubbles escape. The tiny bit of air I had left now expelled from my body. One last flash of searing white pain shoots through me, then darkness.

* * *

The pain is gone. I feel only peace being engulfed in this warm blackness. Aspen created me and destroyed me, a nice clean circle of life. I thought death would be more than just my thoughts in nothingness. Shouldn't I be seeing dead relatives?

"Hello?" I call out.

Only my echo responds.

"Can anyone hear me?"

Again, no response.

A yawn rips thought me. Should I feel tired if I'm dead? I lay down on the hard black nothing, curling myself into a tight ball, a cold shiver runs through my body. I pull my knees tighter to my chest.

A sudden gleam of brightness bursts to life around me. I realise, it's coming from *me*. I'm a ball of light. I float over vast meadows, giant mountains, and gleaming lakes. Sometimes the Fairy child from the courtyard appears next to me, giggling out words of encouragement, her purple eyes bright and lavender skin glistening in the light, before racing off in a different direction.

I come to a stop in a meadow where thousands of butterflies land on me sending a fresh wave of burning through me. When I can't take anymore, I scream out in protest causing them to scatter. The burning remains.

I continue on as the ball of light. For hours, maybe days before I stop again. This time I come to a rest atop the soft moss carpeting of the forest floor. Bugs land on me covering the entire ball that I am, I wish for arms to brush them off. Their butts begin to glow, they're fireflies. The burn I feel coursing through me is extinguished and with their job done, the insects fly away.

I'm back in the darkness. The ball of light experience must have been my journey to the afterlife, now I'm here. I can feel that time doesn't exist, even the concept of it is slipping away. What does a minute feel like? Or an hour, or a day? A year?

"Do you love her?" A voice asks, snapping me out of my musings.

I open my mouth to respond, love who? I want to say. But before I'm able to, a second voice responds. "Yeah, I do. I'm sorry…"

I look around hoping to find who the voices belong to. I'm still surrounded by blackness. But I must not be alone! I open my mouth to call out to them, tell them I'm here too. My voice is gone. I try to reach my hands up to my throat, *I don't have hands. I don't have a body. How are they talking?*

"What do we do?" The first voice asks again.

"I didn't mean to step on your toes. I know she cares about you though." The second voice says.

There's a long pause, "She loves you, too." The first voice responds, "I guess we'll leave it up to Lia."

They're talking about me, this stirs something deep within me, I recognise these voices. My memories seem to be getting more distant.

"You come first. Can we make a promise not to let anything get weird between us, no matter what happens? I just got my little brother back and I don't want to lose you again."

"Yeah," the first voice says gruffly. "Promise." His voice so low I can barely hear him. "She's been sleeping for over ten hours. Should we try to wake her up?"

"That blonde Fairy said not to do that. She'll wake up when she's done healing, at least she's still breathing." They seem to be moving further away from me.

He said *I'm healing.*

"I never should have gone to Ireland." The words come out bitter, as the voices fade out of earshot, leaving me alone in the darkness again.

* * *

Happiness bursts through my chest, rousing my mind. I grin I'm *feeling*. Then my five senses hit me all at once. Pin pricks tingle through me as sunlight wakens my limbs. I sniff away a sneeze as an overwhelming flower scent fills my sinuses. My name reverberates through my skull.

"Rosalia?" I hear again, excitement ringing through Declan's voice. "Kheelan, wake up! She's moving."

I groan. His shouts are too close to my ears. I open my eyes, sunlight pours in. I snap them back shut.

"Rosalia?" Declan says again, this time his voice more controlled.

"Why is it so bright?" I grumble.

Declan makes a sound of relief mingled with amusement. "There are three suns here. This place is actually crazy beautiful, you really shouldn't have slept the entire time, lazy bones." He pokes at my ribs.

I slit my eyes open to peek at him. I can't help the smile that comes at the sight of his face hovering over mine, blocking the light of the suns.

"You're *glowing*," he whispers, amusement dancing in his blue eyes.

I suck in a breath, he's right. I pause, I suck in another breath. I can breathe! I feel myself glow brighter. A laugh escapes my lips. "I can't get it to stop!" I feel another sneeze tickling at my nose. "Did someone spill perfume?" I ask lifting my head. That's when I notice that my hands have sunk into a foamy substance, I pull them up to inspect my fingers. They're covered in…Pollen? I look up at Declan, confusion settling between my brows. I feel my glow flicker out. "Where on Earth are we?"

"Technically, nowhere," a smirk settles on his face. "Because we're not on Earth, we're in the OtherWorld."

I roll my eyes, "You know what I mean!" I push him aside and sit up. We're surround by light pink, what are *those*? I reach out and touch the closest one to me. It's velvety surface under my fingertips send recognition buzzing through me. "Are we in a flower?"

Declan burst out laughing. "Yeah, we are. A giant peony to be exact, I requested that since I know they're your favourite." He smiles, his crystal blue eyes sparkling. "Pretty bizarre, huh? We're in their nursery. Which is what they call a field of flowers that they have the Fairy children sleep in when it gets dark, which doesn't seem to happen as often as it does in our world."

Laughter bubbles from my lips, as the situation washes over me. This place is unreal! I lift my arms and look down at myself. The robe I've been wrapped in is covered in pollen. "I'm going to be sneezing for days!"

Declan's smirk turns into a wicked grin as he scoops up a handful of pollen, "It's good to have you back!" He says as he dumps the orange powder all over my head. "I missed that smile of yours the past couple of weeks."

"Hey!" I protest shaking my head and brushing the pollen from my hair, then his words sink in and I freeze. "Did you say *weeks*?" My voice comes out too loud. This only causes him to laugh louder. But I don't join in. If I've been out for weeks, that means the eclipse is soon, *really* soon, maybe today, maybe we missed it. I'm not ready to go back to the NetherWorld *now*.

He must note the panic in my eyes because his laughter teeters out. "Oh! No, no, no…" Realisation dawns on him and a light laugh comes out, "You've only been asleep for like," he glances at his watch, "fifteen hours. I just meant I've missed your smile because your real smile I haven't seen since before the NetherWorld."

I can't help the involuntary flinch at the mention of the NetherWorld.

He cocks his head at my reaction, narrowing his eyes, but doesn't say anything, "It's good to have you back…" He leans over the edge of the flower. "KHEELAN!" He shouts. "Wake up, Rosalia is awake!"

Unintelligible grumbling makes its way up to us. Then a messy-haired Kheelan appears as he clambers over the highest petal's edge. "The lines are still visible though," he says scrutinising my neck. "How do you feel?"

"Great," I smile, it's good to feel like me again. I didn't realise how disconnected from myself I had become after being cut by the Tenebris. "I actually *feel* happy and I can *breathe* which is incredible! I'll never take that for granted again."

"I'm sure the markings will fade the rest of the way in time." Declan says, reaching out and lightly touching the lines on my neck. "They already have faded significantly."

Kheelan nods in agreement, but the worry doesn't leave his eyes.

The berries! My eyes bulge and my hands flit to my neck. Relief washes over me as my fingers find the delicate chain from Jen still intact. "Were you guys able to get the—"

Declan's hand clasps over my mouth before I can say more.

"We'll talk when we get home." Kheelan says, throwing a nervous glance over the top of the flower.

I crinkle my brow and throw them each an annoyed look. "When can we go?" I ask.

"The blonde chick said once you woke up, we could go." Declan says.

"So do we just Light Travel out of here?" I ask looking back and forth between both of their faces.

Kheelan laughs. "That's what I thought, but no they said you have to save your strength to hold up your end of the oath." He looks at me pointedly, letting me know I'll be spilling it all once we get home. "They gave us this," he pulls a small box out of his pocket and removes the lid showing a tiny silver bell.

"What's it do?" I ask.

"Not sure, she just said to ring it when we're ready to go home. I'm assuming that antlered dude will come and get us then." He shrugs.

"I hate that." Declan says, "Ringing for someone like they're a servant."

I stretch and scramble to my feet. My legs wobble. Declan and Kheelan both leap up to keep me steady. I smile at them. "This place is incredible, magical, really great. But I want to go *home*."

"Me too," Declan says, "something about Fairies really gives me the creeps."

Kheelan throws a look at his brother, shushing him. He picks up the bell and sways it back and forth. It makes no sound, but Kheelan bursts into light. I quickly grab onto his arm, Declan does the same.

Chapter Twenty-Two

It's not like Light Travel. There's no pulling in my gut. I don't even have time to picture where we need to go. I watch Declan and Kheelan start to dissolve into thin air, I look down at my own hand which is clenched tightly around Kheelan's arm, I'm disappearing too. My vision goes white. The world blinks to life around me, we're standing in the same clearing we had been in when we first met Quill. I wonder how long ago that was? Kheelan's hand is suspended in the air as though he's ringing the bell, but it's gone.

The sun is high in the sky, marking mid-day. There's a subtle change in the atmosphere, like time is moving how it should be again. We trek towards Rose's house, the only sound the soft crunching of pine needles and leaves under our feet.

Kheelan scoots up beside me and scoops my hand into his with ease, like it's natural, us holding hands. I sneak a peek at Declan, he's watching but his expression is unreadable. Guilt twists my stomach. The conversation I heard while I was healing, could it have been real? I wish I could split my heart into two and give half to each of them. *I don't want to hurt anyone.* I slip my hand out of Kheelan's and wrap my arms around myself, pretending to fight off a shiver.

When Rose's house appears in the distance, happiness ignites in my chest.

"By the way," Declan says, "we got the berries."

A smile covers my face. My light spreads fast. Before I can even register it's started, I'm in full Glow. My eyes bulge as I try to extinguish it.

Both boys burst into laughter.

I fight to put it out but only manage to dim it. I laugh helplessly as we continue through the forest, faint light still emitting from my skin. At least we live in the middle of nowhere.

"I was worried you hadn't completely healed because you can still see some of the lines, but if the glow is coming that easy, I think it's safe to say I was wrong!" Kheelan says between fits of laughter.

"I couldn't even feel it coming! I'm going to have to learn to control that."

"I'm glad you're happy," Declan says with a grin.

I smile, "Thank you for getting them. I hope they work."

Kodi comes tearing out the back door as we step out of the tree line. I squat close to the ground and she leaps into my waiting arms. I squeeze her tight and let her lick my face. Without warning I'm back in a full state of Glow. I laugh as I sprawl out on the soft grass and let my dog tumble all over me.

Declan and Kheelan are laughing again, they're going to get their kicks out of the new uncontrollable glow worm Lia. I concentrate on dousing my light.

Aunt Rose walks down the deck steps, a broad smile across her face. "I'm so glad to see all of you!" She pulls me into a tight hug.

"I was afraid I'd never see you again." I admit in a whisper as I squeeze her back. "How's Jen doing?" I ask as we pull out of our embrace.

"The same," Rose says.

"I'm going to go see her." I throw a look at Kheelan and Declan, so they know they're meant to come with me.

"She's in the library," Rose says. "I'll call Maggie and Emily. They've both been worried sick!"

Excitement is buzzing through my veins. It's taking all of my self-control to keep my pace normal and not to break into a run down the hallway.

Declan catches up to me and pulls on my arm before I open the door to the library. "What was your payment?" He asks, his hand on top of mine to keep me from turning the knob.

I sigh and meet his eyes. "I agreed to return to the NetherWorld." I push his hand off mine and open the door, beelining to my sister's side.

I look down at her motionless form, she looks serene. Her black eye is fully healed, making it easier to believe she's just sleeping.

"Why would you agree to that?" Declan whispers from my side. As though speaking too loudly will wake Jen up. *If only.*

"It's in the prophecy anyway. We're meant to recover The Lost Stave. Turns out Herne has it. I just took an oath to solidify the prophecy more." I shrug, "I didn't really have a choice. They said I'd die in less than twenty-four hours if they didn't heal me."

"Did you hear the full prophecy?" Kheelan steps up on the other side of me.

"Yeah, it's pretty dark," I admit.

"Do you remember any of it?" He asks.

I nod. "I remember all of it." Although having the words stuck on repeat in the back of mind isn't very comforting. "Let me see the berries," I say.

Declan pulls three cherry-sized berries out of his pocket. They're still glowing, but not as brightly as when they were on the tree.

"I'll go get something to mash them." Kheelan says as he darts through the open door.

Declan is examining my face, I raise my eyes to meet his. "I really didn't have a choice."

"I know." He whispers, his eyes sad. "You know, you're still glowing kind of." The corner of his mouth lifts. "I think you may have to avoid humans for a while. You look pretty supernatural." He brushes my hair behind my ear. "It's beautiful though." Butterflies burst to life in my chest. At the same time his hand stills, as though realising what he's doing. He drops it to his side, tearing his eyes away from my face. Returning his focus to Jen.

I open my mouth, I want to explain the confusion I'm feeling. How I feel like I owe Kheelan, because of my dream and *destiny*. But before I can say anything Kheelan jogs back into the room. "I got this bowl." He says, "I thought we could mush them up in it."

I nod and dump the berries into it. As Kheelan starts mashing with a fork he has in his other hand, I explain the emerald pool to them and how my Fairy Mother filled it with her Light. The burning pain and the nothingness that followed.

"Hmm," Kheelan says when I finish. "I wonder if that process put *more* Fairy into you. Who's the super Fairling now?" He laughs elbowing me gently in the side.

I smile, remembering the conversation from earlier this summer. I was so sure he was some kind of Super-Fairling. He's so much better at everything than me.

Kheelan holds out the bowl filled with glowing berry mush. I look up at him, "Do I just shove it in her mouth then?"

He shrugs. "Your guess is as good as mine."

I gently pry my sister's mouth open with one hand and scoop up some mush with the other. I put as much of the glop as I can between her lips. We all stare at her face expectantly.

Nothing happens.

"Maybe it takes a while?" Kheelan suggests.

"Or maybe that kid tricked me." I say, my hope diminishing. We stand there for a moment gazing at Jens motionless body. Still, nothing happens.

"Can we hear the prophecy?" Declan finally asks after so much time has passed, we all know Jen isn't waking up.

I nod and follow them to the sofa facing the bookcase. I take a deep breath and begin to recite our doom from memory, *"Here and now the chosen I state,"* I say, closing my eyes to concentrate. Wanting to remember every word correctly.

"Once spoken they are locked in fate.
The Fairling of the Queen's offspring,

And brothers from a Hunter's fling.
By oneself thy will not survive,
Three needed in order to thrive.
'Fore the sun is fully covered,
The Lost Stave shall be recovered.
Restore balance between the realms,
Before the darkness overwhelms.
Not everything is black and white,
It takes all three to judge what's right.
Strongest minds will turn for power,
Watch for this in final hour.
To stop tyranny there's a price,
One shall perish in sacrifice."

Silence rings heavy in the air when the last word leaves my lips. Both boys are watching me.

"So, The Lost Stave is that stick Herne is always carrying around?" Declan asks.

I nod. "The Queen saw it through me when she looked into my mind."

"'Fore the sun is fully covered," Kheelan says, "that's the Eclipse."

I nod again.

"One of us is going to die." Declan says, his voice so soft I almost don't hear him.

I look at both of the guys in front of me, the idea of losing either of them rips my insides apart. "In an act of sacrifice," I repeat, the full meaning dawning on me. "I should go to the NetherWorld alone." I say, glad my voice sounds braver than I feel.

"By oneself thy won't survive." Kheelan recites the prophecy's words at me. "Three needed in order to thrive." He looks at me pointedly, "That means all three of us need to go. That's why they saved you."

I open my mouth to argue but I'm cut off by a dry cough.

"Lia?" A raspy voice says. I whip around. Jen is sitting up in the hospital bed, her face bunched in confusion, berry juice running down her chin. My eyes lock on hers, my jaw drops.

"Whoa," Declan breathes.

I can't speak. I can't move. What have we *done*?

"How are you feeling, Jen?" Kheelan asks his voice the same as when he's trying to keep one of the horses calm. He gets to his feet and walks towards my sister slowly. Like he's approaching a monster.

This snaps me out of it. I pull my jaw off the ground. He's approaching my *sister*. She's not a monster. But I can't tear my eyes away from hers. Once such a soft brown, now marbled with a pulsating neon blue.

I gulp and get to my feet, taking a shaky step towards her.

Jen's eyes are frantic as they dart from each of our faces and around the room. "Are we in Wyoming?" She asks, her voice rising in panic. "How did I get here? And why are you all looking at me like that?"

"It's okay." Kheelan says his hands out in front of him to demonstrate that everyone should stay calm. "Some stuff has happened that might come as a shock to you…"

"What are you talking about? Lia, what's going on?" Jen starts pulling at the tubes hooked to her arm.

"Don't tug, you'll hurt yourself!" I place my hand over hers and look into her eyes. I focus on the familiar brown bits. "You've been asleep for," I pause, what day is it? "Awhile." I finish with. "What's the last thing you remember?"

My sister's face scrunches in concentration, "I was home in Wisconsin. Mom and Dad went back up to the lake house a day early," she squeezes her eyes shut and pushes her fingers into her temples. "I was annoyed that they weren't going drive me to the airport." She says, "I was mad at you." Her eyes shoot open glowing fiercely as they land on Declan, "And *you* were with my sister in the *morning*."

"Do you remember calling me?" I ask quickly pulling her accusatory glare away from Declan. I throw a quick glance at Kheelan but he's keeping his face carefully neutral as he digests my sister's words. I turn back to Jen, "With Jesse?" Declan scoots back towards the couch, out of Jen's line of sight.

Her eyebrows knit together. "Why would I be with Jesse and why would we call you together?"

I glance at Kheelan. He looks nervous. "Maybe you should see if you can find Rose?" I suggest. He nods and backs out of the room. His eyes not wavering from my sister's face.

"Lia, you're scaring me. What's wrong? What's going on?"

My tongue feels thick in my mouth. How do I tell my sister that I got her out of one enchantment and possibly threw her into a different one? I swallow, my hands are trembling again. I don't know that, I remind myself. It could be a temporary thing that only affects her eyes, she's still the same Jen. "Like I said, you've been asleep for a while. Jesse and one of The Wild Hunt put you into a sleep like state. We couldn't get you to wake up," I take a deep breath, "until today. We got some berries from the OtherWorld." Her eyes bulge at the mention of the realm. "I'll tell you about that bit later," I say, "but anyway, they worked. You're awake."

"Why is everyone acting like they're afraid of me?" Her voice starts to tremble. "What else did these berries do?"

I open my mouth but nothing comes out. I close it again, and throw a glance towards Declan, he just shrugs. I look back at my sister, her eyes a lightning storm. "No one's afraid of you," I focus on keeping my voice calm.

"How long was I out for? What day is it?" She's getting close to sounding hysterical.

I look towards Declan again, and again he just shrugs. I look back to my sister about to admit that even I don't know what day it is. But just as I open my mouth our aunt bustles in. "It's August 18th, dear."

My head snaps back to Declan. His face is ghostly white. The Eclipse is in *three* days.

Rose shuffles past me, she doesn't hesitate, or look the least bit scared by my sister's eyes. She goes right up to her and gathers her into a hug.

Guilt clenches my stomach. I didn't even hug my sister, my scared, close to hysterical sister. I just stood here staring at her freaky eyes, *afraid* of her. The same sister who loved me despite my own freaky glow eyes. I blink back the sudden sting of tears.

"You must be hungry dear. Maggie is already in the kitchen cooking up a feast for you. Kheelan, come help Jennifer up." Rose's knobby fingers expertly unhook the tubes from my sister's arms as Kheelan rushes forward to ease Jen to the ground. She leans most of her weight into him, but he doesn't flinch away.

I rush to her other side and wrap my arm firmly around her waist. We steer her towards the dining room. "Are you going to tell me what else the berries did?" She whispers. "I know somethings wrong, you all were looking at me like you saw a ghost or something."

I look down at my feet, shame burning my cheeks. "Sorry," I mumble. "But they kind of marbled your eyes."

Jen stops walking. "What do you mean *marbled*?"

"Well, the berries were this really bright blue colour that kind of pulsated with light..." I begin to explain. Her eyes pulse as if on cue. She's not happy. "And now your eyes have some of that running through them." The words come out in a rush.

"Maybe it's just a temporary effect." Kheelan offers. "How do you feel?"

"Honestly? I feel weird." Her eyes brim with moistness and she looks at me earnestly. "Do you think they could have changed more than just my eye colour?"

"You've been asleep for a long time. I think it's only natural for you to feel a little off right now. I think eating is a good start."

* * *

Maggie brings out a feast, and that's not an exaggeration. She places a platter of baked chicken on the table, a big bowl of left-over eggplant lasagna, fresh garlic bread, she even whips up some vegetarian spaghetti

Bolognese, and a few kinds of salad. The boys dig into everything, avoiding only the chicken. I even take a healthy serving. Jen doesn't touch a thing.

I try to get her to take a bite of bread. She just wrinkles her nose at it. I look around the table for help. Everyone's watching, Declan and Kheelan look as worried as I feel, both Maggie and Rose have pursed lips. They're waiting to speak their minds until Jen isn't around.

I swallow, my throat suddenly too small, returning my pleading eyes to my sister. "You need to eat something." I try again.

She shakes her head. "I'm not hungry. I think I need to lie down for a bit."

"But that's what you've been doing for weeks—"

"—Let her, Rosalia." Rose interjects, her voice uncharacteristically firm.

"Do you want me to go with you?" I ask my sister.

She shakes her head, "No I'd like to be alone."

I turn my face away so she can't see how hurt I am. She's going through enough. I don't need her feeling bad for me on top of it.

Kheelan jumps to his feet. "Let me help you to your room at least." He offers his arm. She smiles at him and accepts. Kheelan looks to Rose, a silent question as to where she'll sleep.

"My room," I say, not meeting my aunt's eyes. But from my peripheral, I am able to see her nod in agreement.

When Kheelan and Jen are out of ear shot, Maggie's eyes go fierce as she stares down me and Declan from across the table. "What did you give her?"

I swallow, "Some berries from the OtherWorld."

"What. *Kind.* Of. Berries?" She says each word with so much force I cower back into my chair wishing it could swallow me whole.

"I don't know." I whisper. "Blue ones. A Fairy child told me they'd wake her up."

"Ah good, so we're taking advice from children now." Rose says, her voice just as cold.

Tears prick to life in my eyes. "I didn't think they could do more harm than what was already done…"

"That's exactly the problem," Maggie says. "You didn't *think*."

"Hey!" Declan interjects. "Lay off her. We don't know if there are any bad side effects from the berries yet. Jen could be feeling off kilter because she's been under a weird enchantment from the Huntsman."

I squeeze his hand under the table. Thankful for his support.

"She woke up," I say. "Surely that's better than staying asleep for the rest of her life?" I scoot my chair back and stand up. "I'm going to take the dog for a walk." At the word walk Kodi appears out of nowhere, wiggling her body in excitement.

"Do you want me to come with?" Declan asks.

"No, maybe fill your grandma and my aunt in on the prophecy. Let them know how we have to go back to the NetherWorld in three days." I hear both women suck in a breath at my words, but I don't look at them. I keep my shoulders straight and walk out of the room.

* * *

I go to the horses. The sight of them sets my skin aglow, but my full light doesn't come. My insides are churning with worry. What if the berries do end up doing more harm than good? I don't think I could live with myself. I may not even live long enough to know. Oberon gallops to the fence, as though sensing something is wrong. He presses his forehead against mine. Our secret hug. I smile, "Hey there, handsome. Did you miss me?" I press my lips to his velvety nose. "I think I messed up boy and I don't know how to fix it," I whisper.

"Do you always talk to horses?"

I whip around, Kheelan is walking out of the barn a smile spreading across his face. I smile back. "Only as often as you do."

"I wanted to talk to you." He says leaning against the rough wood of the fence, his eyes glimmering in the sun. "We never really got the chance to talk about those words I said."

I focus my attention on Kodi who is busy pouncing around in the field where the horses graze, I laugh at her attempt at hunting mice.

"I meant them, Lia." Kheelan continues when I don't say anything. "I love you, and I know you love me too, but I really need to hear you say it." His voice is pleading.

I turn my head towards him. This is what he wants to talk about right now? Not the fact that something is happening to my sister? Something no one can explain. And it's because of something I did. Or the fact that we have to go to the NetherWorld in less than three days to retrieve The Lost Stave? And oh yeah, one of us has to die. But he's worried about having a girlfriend.

I narrow my eyes. "Forgive me, but I've had a few other things on my mind." I don't mean for my voice to come out so sharp.

"Like Declan?" He spits out.

My face hardens.

"I'm sorry," his voice gentler, "It's just… I don't want to die with—"

"—You're not going to die." I cut him off. The thought of losing him fills my heart with ice. I can't let him die.

He takes a step closer to me, hope igniting his eyes. A small smile plays at his lips. Before I can say more, he grabs onto my shoulders and turns me so I'm facing him. His hair falls across his forehead as he looks down at me. "I don't want to die," he repeats, "without doing this at least one time."

He presses his mouth onto mine, the fence digs into my back. My mouth responds to the familiarity of the kiss from my dream. It feels so long ago now. I let myself begin to melt into him.

Kodi's bark snaps me back to reality. I wriggle out of Kheelan's embrace and stumble away from him. My eyes go straight to the open barn doors where I see a flicker of movement, but nothings there. It must have been the shadows of the trees blowing in the wind.

Kheelan fills the distance between us reaching for me again. I step back. "I'm sorry Kheelan. I can't."

His eyes cloud over, "Declan." He says his brother's name without the inflection that it's a question.

I don't confirm or deny it. But he's right. I haven't been able to get Declan's kiss out of my head. "I'm sorry," I whisper.

"Lia, we're soulmates. Explain the dream. We both dreamt of each other before even knowing of each other's existence. That has to mean *something*. We're each other's *fate*. You can't change fate."

"I can't explain the dream," I say. "But the Fairies *can* change fate." My voice comes out stronger, "They did Kheelan, they changed mine, or maybe the underling did. Either way, I'm supposed to be dead right now, yet here I am alive and kicking for three more days." I suck in a deep breath and force myself to look him in the eyes. "I do love you. But we're going to the NetherWorld really soon. And forgive me, but figuring out which *boy* I like isn't my top priority at the moment. I'm more worried about trying to keep all three of us alive. Oh yeah and the sister I may have poisoned."

I don't wait for him to respond. I walk in the direction Kodi ran off, moving as fast as I can without running, leaving him standing there looking shattered. My heart aches. It takes all my will power not to look back, not to turn around and run back into his arms and accept my destiny.

* * *

I wander aimlessly. I don't know where to go. I consider calling Emily, inviting myself over to her house, but she'll have too many questions. I'm not in the mood for talking. I know I can't go back to the horses, Kheelan will be there the rest of the day. If I go back to the house, I'll have Rose and Maggie to deal with. My guilt is weighing me down enough, I'm not ready for them to pile on more. Going back to the house also means facing my wrongdoing head on. In the form of brown and blue eyes. So, I wander. How did I let myself get so desperate to find an answer that I gave Jen a fist full of berries I don't even know the name of? I kick some rocks out of my path. I was grasping for a solution and let myself be led blindly by a *child*. This may be the dumbest thing I've ever done.

I let out an exasperated scream. Kodi splashes out of the creek and bounds toward me.

"I'm glad I'm not fishing, that would've scared them all away."

I scream again, this time startled, spinning around looking for where his voice came from. I find him, propped up against the base of a tree a few feet from the creek bed. His eyes fixed on the water in front of him.

"Sorry," I mumble, "I didn't see you there."

Declan lets out a dry laugh. "A trend of the day, it seems."

My eyes snap in his direction. What does he mean by that? "Why aren't you fishing?"

"It was my plan, but when I went to the barn to grab a rod, I got a little distracted."

My heart slows with the weight of dread. How much had he seen? "I'm sorry," my voice cracks. "I didn't know he was going to do that. I should have stopped it sooner."

Declan's eyes finally turn toward me, a flicker of hope. "You stopped it?"

I nod plopping onto the grass next to him. I lean back on my elbows and watch Kodi digging around in the stream for rocks.

A smirk tugs at the corners of his mouth, but he doesn't say anything more on the topic. He looks at me though, concern in his eyes. "How are you doing?"

"Fine," I lie.

"Rosalia, it's me. You don't have to be tough in front of me. You just found out you have to go back to the NetherWorld." He places his head in his hands. "The idea about having to go back is killing me. I was only there for a few hours. I can't even begin to imagine what you're feeling." He looks up, his blue eyes tortured.

"I know," I whisper. "I keep trying not to think about it, but it's almost all I do. And when I'm able to get it out of my mind, I'm thinking about

Jen. What if I did more harm than good waking her up?" My voice catches in my throat.

"Don't say that. There's no way you could have known. No way any of us could have known."

"That's the problem, I just shoved berries in her mouth. Berries! Berries are *always* poisonous in the movies. And I just shoved a handful of them in her mouth." I don't bother to wipe at the tears that begin to carve their way down my cheeks. "I was so desperate I didn't even think about it."

Declan scoots across the grass and pulls me into his arms. "Rose and Maggie had tried everything in their power to wake her up," he murmurs into my hair. "The Fairies weren't going to help her. She wouldn't have woken up." He brushes his hands over my hair down my back. The comfort of this simple motion is enough to unleash all my bottled-up emotions. He continues to hold me tight, stroking my back in a steady rhythm as the sobs rip through my body.

When I run out of tears, I pull myself up, but stay inside Declan's arms. "Sorry," I murmur. Wiping at the last of my tears.

"Don't apologise." His voice is soft.

"She's not herself. Those berries changed her. Not just her eyes. Something more, her entire demeanour or the air about her feels different."

He squeezes my shoulder. "Let's just hope it's her feeling disoriented from being under The Hunt's enchantment for so long." His tone is strained though, he doesn't believe his own words.

I nod, settling into the crook of his arm. The sun is starting to dip below the mountains, another day over. I swallow, another day closer. "I can't go back there," I choke out. "I'm not powerful enough. There's no way I'm going to survive a second trip. I was just lucky the first time."

"You're the strongest person I know." Declan says, his voice sure. "You found out about this world less than three months ago. Three months! And already you've been tortured by a member of The Wild Hunt, held captive in the NetherWorld, you *escaped* the NetherWorld and saved me at the same time. You got cut by a Tenebris blade. Were on deaths doorstep. You went to the OtherWorld and stood in front of the royal court. Then you survived their healing process, which according to that blonde Fairy doesn't happen often. She warned us you would probably die from it. But you didn't, because you're *strong*. Now look at you, you can barely keep your light at bay! You're *strong*."

I look down at my arms. He's right a faint light is emitting from me. I smile. "Ok maybe I'm capable of going back, but I really don't want to."

He squeezes me tighter. "Neither do I. But this time you aren't going to be alone. I'm going to be by your side the entire time, and I'm going to see to it that you survive your second trip. And you will because one, you're amazing. And two, there's no way in hell," he smirks. "Pun intended," his smirk broadens into a grin, "I am going to let anything happen to you. I'll die before I let any of those monsters lay a hand on you."

The prophecy runs through my mind. I shake my head. "Promise me you won't make any sacrifices on my account."

"You know I can't promise that." He looks deep into my eyes, like he's searching for something.

"I don't want to return to this world without you." My voice barely a breath, but I know he hears and I know he knows I mean it.

"You'd prefer it to be Kheelan?" Declan's voice thickens.

I shake my head. My throat tightening at the idea of Kheelan dying, "Of course not. I don't want it to be either of you."

"Well, I don't want it to be either of you." He shoots back.

I offer a small smile. "Locked in fate." I say, the weight the words from the prophecy carry are heavy.

"They changed your fate. Or the Underling did." A hopeful spark lights his eyes. "You would have died without that healing pond and their entire prophecy wouldn't have come true. Maybe the prophecy is null now that your fate has been altered."

I shake my head sadly. Maybe that would have been true, before the oath. "They saw to it that wouldn't happen," I say. "The binding oath," I shudder as it all sinks in.

Declan's eyes cloud over with anger. "The Tenebris changed your fate, and those bastards didn't care about your life at all. They only care that you stay alive long enough to carry out your so-called purpose and die when it's most convenient for them."

I shift my body so I'm facing him. "I'm the one who's meant to be dead. Not you. Not Kheelan. Please try to remember that."

His jaw clenches, but he doesn't say anything.

Chapter Twenty-Three

I gaze down at my sleeping sister. It's nothing like when she was under Flint's sorcery, then she at least looked peaceful. Now, her eyes move rapidly beneath her eyelids and she's thrashing around like she can't get comfortable. I reach out a hand and lay it gently on her shoulder, her skin shudders under my touch, like a horse trying to rid itself of a fly. I jump back and stare at my hand. How did she do that? I pull back the covers and crawl in next to her. She's still my sister and tomorrow is a new day. I whisper a quick prayer that she'll be back to herself after having a little time to process everything she's been through.

* * *

A musical giggling fills my head. Big purple eyes appear directly in front of my face, I stumble backwards falling hard onto my back side. Fireflies blink to life around me. I'm under a velvet black sky lit up by the moons and stars, the field of night in the OtherWorld. Tilia's purple eyes are gleaming mischievously, her small wings fluttering madly, working hard to keep her a few feet off the ground. Eye level with me.

"I tricked you." She bubbles, a wicked grin spreading over her face.

"What do you mean?"

"I told you I like your sister Jen." Her smile disappears, "But I don't." The playfulness from her voice is gone.

My blood runs cold. "You've never met her."

"I don't need to. Remember? I'm a seer." Her purple eyes flash fierce.

"If you were a good one, you would've seen how kind she is," I say, my own voice hardening.

Her delicate features bunch up into a scowl. "I am a good one!" Her voice booms across the meadow, the grass around us rippling and the fireflies scattering away from us. "She was *too* perfect." She snarls.

She flutters around me, circling. I scramble back to my feet and turn with her, not letting her get out of my line of sight.

"Wanna know the rest of my trick?" Her sickening sweet voice is back with a smile to match.

I don't say anything. I just watch her, unblinking as her wings work tirelessly to keep her afloat, my stomach growing heavier with every flap.

"I tricked you into giving her *Demato* berries, without asking the tree."

"Demato berries," I whisper the name out loud, committing the word to memory. Then the rest of her statement registers and dread fills my limbs. Quill had mentioned that plants aren't the same as they are on Earth. We were supposed to *ask for its permission.*

Her grin widens and her entire face lights up. "Have you given them to her yet?"

I swallow.

"I know you took them. I watched the other Fairlings get them." She buzzes in close to my face.

I want to swat her away like a pesky fly, but I restrain myself. She may be my only source of information for these berries. "What do Demato berries do?" I ask through gritted teeth.

"You gave them to her, didn't you?" Excitement vibrates through her body. "They change people." Somehow her smile broadens further.

"Change people? How?"

She giggles again, "Depends. Of course, in this instance *I* can see. But I wouldn't want to ruin the surprise!"

"Then will you tell me why? Why did you *want* to hurt my sister?"

She goes perfectly still. Her tiny feet land gracefully in the grass. She stares up at me with her violet eyes. "I don't want to hurt her." She says, "You needed her to change."

"I needed her to wake up." I spit out.

"Don't. Interrupt me." Her cheeks flush a deep plum. "*Changing* was the only way." She says her voice straining to stay steady.

"Only way for what?"

"For me to be the sister you love most. You looked at her like she was without fault, like she could do no wrong. How could anyone compete with that?"

"But you're not my sister."

She stares at me, her eyes glowing vibrant in the dark. "My mother is Aspen DieErde-AusLuft, next in line to be Queen of the OtherWorld."

Cold pin pricks run the length of my body. I thought I was her only daughter. *Only Fairling,* the small voice in the back of my head points out. Tilia is a full Fairy.

"I always wanted a sister!" Tilia giggles throwing her arms around my waist.

I don't hug her back as the reality settles in. She poisoned Jen. "What's the cure for the Demato berry?" I ask, my voice vacant.

Tilia releases me and steps back. Her big eyes brimming with tears. She brushes them away. "There isn't one. The berry's powers will pump through her body, kind of like a parasite. And like a parasite it'll keep expanding until she's *different.*"

"You stole my sister." My voice comes out a choke.

"I'm right here." She reaches out her tiny hand, but before she can touch me her image begins to flicker. The meadow around me flickers with her until it wholly disappears and I'm alone.

"Rosalia, DieErde," a voice says, my name echoing around the empty space. Hearing my name with my Fairy Mother's last name, Tilia's last name makes my skin crawl. I recognise the voice. It's the lady with the fluttering birds from the Queen's council. Her face blinks to life in front of me, very Wizard of Oz-like. "I have a message from Her Royal Highness, Queen Lucille."

All I can do is nod. I don't want any more news. Finding out I poisoned my sister is enough for one night. I will myself to wake up.

"You won't be able to wake while I'm here." Robin's voice turns icy. "I'm here to remind you of the binding oath you took with Her Royal Highness."

"I remember," I mutter.

"When the royal mark appears on your arm, you have twenty-four hours to go to the NetherWorld, or the effects of an oath unfulfilled will begin."

I gulp, "Will it appear soon?"

She nods.

"How will I get to the NetherWorld when it appears?" I ask. "It won't be a new moon."

"You are strong enough, especially now that you've been reborn from the emerald waters, to travel between the realms. Light travel. You won't be able to enter the castle's grounds, you'll need to go to this place," an image of sinister black mountains flashes before my eyes, a barren valley situated between them. "When you pass through the wood, you'll be able to see Herne's palace."

"And if I'm unable to do it?" I ask, trying to keep the tremor out of my voice.

"Then the broken oath will kill you, Herne will discover the powers of The Stave and the delicate balance between the realms will cease to exist. Darkness will take over before the Eclipse has passed."

I open my mouth, but before I can get any words out, she's gone and I'm lying in my bed, alone.

Alone.

I whip my head in the direction Jen should be. Confirming what I can already feel, she's gone.

I don't wake anyone else. I tell myself it's fine, she slept all afternoon, so it's natural she woke up early. Still my dream nags on my mind as my bare feet pad down the long hallways of my aunt's big house.

I whisper Jen's name into the darkness.

I get no response.

"I'm overreacting," I say out loud, but even hearing it doesn't convince me. Tilia got in my head, her words a constant hum, like a mosquito that won't stop buzzing in my ears, *parasite*. Can parasites ever be a good thing? I think back to biology, parasites almost always harm their hosts, but it's unwise for them to kill their hosts…I think that's it. So, she won't die, she'll just be different, maybe only a *little* different.

Kodi whining piques my attention. I follow her soft cries through the house. She's sitting in the doorway of the dining room, her blue eyes round and fixed on something in the kitchen.

Then I hear what has her upset. It sounds like dishes clattering to the ground, something shatters. My heart starts hammering in my chest cavity when I hear the low rumbles. An animal has gotten into the house. I instantly imagine the worst. A grizzly bear rummaging through the cupboards with her cubs, then going full mama bear when she hears Kodi's whines.

"Shh girl, come here." I whisper.

She doesn't move.

I inch forward, careful not to make any sound. I reach out my hand, just as my fingers grasp her collar, another loud crash pulls my eyes up. A moon beam casting through the centre of the kitchen makes it easy to see. There are no wild animals, just a girl hunching over something in the middle of the floor.

The fridge door is ajar, the small light bulb like a spotlight on Jen's head as she ravenously tears through the contents of the fridge which are scattered around her across the black and white tiles.

The refrigerator begins to beep, from being left open. My sisters head snaps up at inhuman speed. Her eyes lock on the device. The light casts a shadow across her face, but it doesn't disguise the extreme glow emitting from the blue in her irises.

She leaps from the ground and slams the door shut. My eyes go to where she'd been moments before. A packet of raw ground beef lies ripped open, most of its contents gone.

I take a tentative step back, trying to pull Kodi with me. She refuses to budge. Her focus locked on my sister. I gulp as I run through my options in my head. I don't want to fight her. And from what I just witnessed with the fridge door, she might try to attack me. I need to go wake Declan and Kheelan.

I take more steps backward. I can't tear my eyes away from Jen, who's returned to her position in the middle of the space, crouching over the meat, shoving handfuls of the bloody mince into her mouth. My back bumps into a dining chair, the legs scrape loudly over the hard floor. I freeze.

Jen whips around, her gleaming eyes zero in on me. Time slows. Red juice trickles down her chin, she cocks her head to one side considering me. Then time catches back up, she lunges at me before I can react.

My head smashes against the hard floor as the full force of her tackle topples me to the ground. I don't even have to reach for the fire, the heat of burning embers ripples through my skin in automatic defence. My sister yelps and rolls off me.

I peel myself from the ground so I'm sitting next to Jen, who's curled up in a small ball, soft sobs rolling through her body. The light gone from her eyes. I lay a gentle hand on her back, the only way I know how to show comfort as I wait for her tears to subside. Guilt rips through my insides. This is happening to her because of me.

Finally, her body stills. One last sniffle and she says, "What's happening to me?"

My heart sinks. *I poisoned you.* I know that's what I should say, instead I shrug and brush the hair from her face revealing the dried crusty meat juice around her mouth and on her cheeks. "I'll figure something out, I promise." But I can barely get the words out.

We stay still for a while, Jen curled up on the dining room floor. At some point her head ends up in my lap, and I absentmindedly begin to stroke her hair. Our worlds are so different from three months ago, I yearn for the normalcy.

299

"We should clean up," Jen finally says after some time. She stumbles to her feet, her limbs shaking.

"Were you aware?" I ask following her through the kitchen door.

"What do you mean?" Her eyes meet mine, the moon reflecting off the blue in them.

"I mean when you were throwing the food all over and eating the beef." I say flipping on the light.

"Kind of," she says getting to her knees to gather the food off the floor. "I wasn't in control of my body, I was just kind of trapped inside my head having to watch it all happen." Her eyes brim with tears. "I'm sorry I tried to hurt you."

I'm sorry I poisoned you. "I'm sorry I burnt you, that kind of just happened, I didn't mean for it to. Since the Fairies healed me, my abilities are kind of," I pause, searching for the right words. "Right at the surface."

"What happened when I was asleep?" She asks.

I force a weak smile. "A lot." I fill her in on everything she's missed as we work side by side getting Rose's kitchen back to its pristine form. It almost feels like the old days when we were kids and we'd stay up late giggling over nothing. Except we're cleaning up a mess my sister made by ravaging a package of raw meat on the kitchen floor.

* * *

The sun is high when I finally wake. I poke at Jen asking her if she wants some breakfast. She swats me away and rolls over, dead to the world.

I stumble down the hall towards the kitchen. Besides the shards of broken dishes in the garbage, you wouldn't know the events of the night before even happened. I grab a muffin and follow the sound of voices out to the deck.

Maggie and Rose are seated at the patio table, I follow their gaze to the open stretch of lawn where Kheelan and Declan are engaged in a sword fight. I shuffle to the table, happy to be a spectator.

Declan's eyes brighten as they land on me, and with a swooping motion he disarms his younger brother, forcing him to surrender.

Show off. But I can't stop the smile from tugging at my lips.

"Where's your sister?" Rose asks turning her attention to me.

"Sleeping," I mumble concentrating on the muffin in my hands.

"Something happened." Maggie says, her voice too loud.

I nod, "There was an incident last night."

The boys clamber up the deck steps, their laughter fading when they see our grim faces. I smile tightly and begrudgingly recount the events of the previous night.

"We need to figure out what those berries were," Rose says.

My dream rushes back. I glance down at my arms, but there's no mark. "Demato berries," I say in barely a whisper.

Every one's attention focuses on me. I feel the blood rush to my cheeks. I take a deep breath and fill them in on my two visitors I received in my dream last night. I leave out the part about Tilia being Aspen's daughter, I'm not sure why but it feels too personal.

"Busy night," Declan smirks.

I let out a gentle laugh. "Yeah, guess so."

"We'll try adjusting Jen's diet," Rose says. "Hopefully that'll keep whatever's in her at bay while we focus on the more urgent matter." She casts her eyes around our group, "Which I think we can all agree is the three of you going to the NetherWorld to retrieve The Lost Stave."

"Lia is supposed to be strong enough to travel the three of you between the realms." Maggie says, her eyes gleaming with excitement. "So today, let's see what you are all capable of."

Kheelan grins in my direction but doesn't quite meet my eyes, "Let the trials begin!"

* * *

My feet kick up dust from the dry ground, my muscles flexing as they push me forward with ease. The strained and heavy breathing from the boys struggling to keep up fades into the distance behind me as I push on. I run with ease, when I reach the creek, I stop. My breathing normal. I feel good, *really good.* When the boys catch up their own breathing is laboured, both of them needing to double over to catch their breath.

I grin, "That felt good."

"Speak for yourself," Kheelan wheezes.

Declan straightens up to look me over, "I was sprinting as hard as I could, and it still wasn't enough to keep up with you. And here you are not looking the least bit tired, like you had a leisurely stroll all the way here." He looks at his brother. "Don't tell me you're not impressed?"

"I'm very impressed." Kheelan says straightening up. "Still doesn't make me *like* losing to a girl." He elbows me playfully in the side.

I broaden my grin. "Rematch?" I don't wait for either of them to respond, taking off in the direction of the house. This time I don't hear them on my heels, and I don't hold back, I push harder. The wind whips my hair out behind me and fills my lungs which expand and contract with ease as I pull in even breaths. It's like I've been a sprinter my entire life. When the back deck comes into view, I see Kodi jump up. She bounds down the steps towards me, her entire body wiggling. I drop to my knees as she crashes into me, knocking me backwards. Laughter bursts out of me and I don't try to reel in the warmth as it spreads throughout my body, engulfing both of us in my bright Light. Kodiak doesn't seem to mind it as she continues to lick my face.

"Bravo!" I hear the ladies cheer from the deck. I beam up at their faces. Rose looks relieved, like I might stand a chance. I might be able to make it home from the NetherWorld again. Maggie's laughter disappears, I follow her gaze to her two grandsons walking up the lawn, worry deepening her brow.

"All right show off," Kheelan says hovering above me, they sun turning him into a silhouette. "Could you turn off your light for a second so we can see what else you can do?"

I concentrate on extinguishing my glow. When his face comes into focus his teasing smile looks forced. The guilt from yesterday crashes over me in a fresh wave.

I straighten my shoulders and get to my feet. "You guys wanna see the burn I was telling you about?"

They gather around me. We're lucky to be surrounded by such a thick forest, with the closest neighbour being almost a mile away, we don't have to worry about prying eyes.

I take a deep breath and think about the things that enrage me. I picture Herne, his curling horns and gnarled claws, Flint and his burning eyes scorching into me, and the long-haired Hunter with his slimy words. I remember the despairing weight the NetherWorld brings, the burning iron of my cell bars, and the rage I felt when I saw the Squelched Fairies, the colour and life drained from their eyes, wings ripped to shreds. I even think about the Royal Council, how they've delayed my death to better suit their needs and how they brushed off the severity of the Fae that have been squelched, the torture they're enduring in the NetherWorld. Finally, Tilia's bright purple eyes flash in my mind, and I feel the embers bubble to life across my skin. A collective gasp ripples around me, I open my eyes. Everyone is wearing identical masks of horror.

"I've never seen such a thing," Maggie murmurs, taking a step away from me.

I swallow, they're all looking at me like I'm a freak. "Maybe it's only something full Fairlings can do?" My voice comes out a plea as I dose the burn. I don't like the way they're all looking at me, like I'm not fully aligned with the Light.

Declan tries first. I tell him to focus on things he hates, things that he doesn't agree with, like how we have to go back to the NetherWorld in a couple of days. I explain that we call the Light through pure and happy thoughts. But we're not just one emotion, some of the things we feel are negative. That's what we have to call upon for the Burn. He gives it a solid effort, but after fifteen minutes all he's able to do is call the glow. He shrugs it off, not seeming too concerned by it, saying I must be special.

Kheelan's determined not to be out done. His brow furrows in concentration, and he squeezes his eyes shut. I repeat what I told Declan. He tries for longer, his forehead has a sheen of sweat when he finally gives up. His eyes lock on my face, "You must be special." He smiles, but it's not friendly, more like an ironic baring of his teeth.

Rose and Maggie rush us along, obviously uncomfortable by my new trick. They put us into combat with each other, no weapons, no glows and no burning skin allowed. They want to test our strength. A category I would not have been able to even compete in a few weeks ago. Now I know I'll at least put up a decent fight.

Kheelan and Declan go first. Kheelan rushes at his big brother, clearly looking forward to letting out some of his pent-up aggression. He tackles him to the ground. They roll around for a bit, then Kheelan throws a punch. Declan sees it coming and is able to move his head just in time. Kheelan's fist whizzes past his face, slamming into the earth next to his face. "What the hell man?" Declan says bringing his hips up, knocking his brother off him. He moves quick, it takes less than an instant for him to get on top of Kheelan, pinning his younger brother's arms to his sides, fight over. "What was that about?" Declan growls as he pushes himself off the ground and off Kheelan.

A stunned silence falls over the group. Rose and Maggie don't say anything about Kheelan throwing a punch, but they don't look happy. Maybe as a precaution, they have me go up against Declan next.

I grin at my opponent. "Go easy on me, I'm just a *girl*."

Declan winks, "You got it sweetheart."

I lunge forward wrapping my arms around his legs sending him to the ground. I pounce on top of him before he can register what's happening. I grin down at his shocked expression. "You have to at least *try*."

He smiles up at me, "Who says we're done?"

His body twists under me, throwing me off guard. I find myself pressed against the hard ground before I can even begin to process he's moved at all. Declan's face now looms over me, a twinkle in his eye. "*You have to at least try.*" He mocks.

304

I laugh pulling my arms off the ground with his still clasped around my wrists. I wrap my arms around his torso, so his hands are behind his back. "Who say's we're done?" I do one last body twist to reverse our positions. Pulling my hands up at the last second to pin his shoulders with his arms stuck behind his back.

He struggles, but this time I hold him in place. My grin broadens as he goes still. "Okay, okay, you win. Let me up!"

"Kheelan?" I say, "Wanna give it your best shot?" I wiggle my eyebrows, taunting him. But he doesn't take the bait. He just shakes his head and says he's good.

The ladies keep us busy all day. Next, they have us call the glow. Then they start calling out body parts, forcing us to practice isolating the light in different regions. I'm pleased to find I'm now able to do this with ease. When they call out "Nose", I start singing Kheelan's song, but it barely gets a chuckle out of him.

When the sun begins to dip low, Jen finds us. Rose decides we should see what she's capable of in her new…State.

We race to the creek. She holds my pace with ease, her face relaxing into a smile as the wind whips our hair back. We get into fighting stance, when Rose says *go*, I don't have time to react, my sister is on top of me and holding me down. I can't move at all. Again, Kheelan refuses to wrestle but Declan volunteers. Jen pins him in seconds.

It's nearly dark when we retire inside. Making our way up the steps Jen whispers. "Have you tried concentrating your glow to your eyes? Do you think it'd help you see in the dark?"

I come to a stop, staring at my sister in disbelief.

"What?" She says stopping at the top of the deck steps looking down at me. "I was just wondering."

"You're a genius," I say. "I can't believe that never occurred to me." I call the glow and force it to my eyes.

Jen giggles. "You look like ironman."

I smile and turn my eyes back out towards the darkening lawn. I can see everything like it's the middle of the day. I turn back to my sister, "Seriously, a genius."

* * *

I lean forward stretching my icy fingers above the flickering flames of our campfire. I'm trying to enjoy myself, Emily came over with s'more supplies to celebrate Jen waking up. But after she was filled in about the prophecy and the eclipse, it feels more like a going away party than a celebration. A permanent going away party for one of us.

I stare into the fire, the chatter around me fading into my surroundings as my eyes glaze over. Tomorrow is August 20th the eclipse is happening mid-morning on the 21st. Tomorrow could be my last day alive. Tomorrow *is* going to be my last day alive, I've already decided. I can't let either of the Lane brothers die, they need each other. They're the only family they have left. Not to mention Maggie having to go through that kind of loss again, I don't think she could handle it. People will miss me, sure. But no one really *needs* me. I'm confident I'm the one who is meant to be the sacrifice. The point of the Fairies healing me was to prolong the inevitable.

"Whatcha thinking about?" Declan settles onto the log bench close to me, nudging my shoulder with his.

I break my gaze away from the flames and try to smile, but it catches.

"It's all I've been thinking about too," he says nodding his head with understanding. "Can you promise me something?"

"Probably not," I say honestly.

Declan chuckles, "Humour me."

I nod, returning my stare to the fire in front of us.

"You need to promise you're going to try your hardest to get out of there alive."

I snap my head up to look at him.

"I know you, and I heard you yesterday. You're going to try to make sure me and Kheelan get out alive. But listen to me. I've made up my mind. We're all going to get out alive."

"You heard the prophecy. You know that's not true."

"Well, what if I refuse to believe it?" The reflection of the flames flicker in his eyes as they bore into mine. "Your fate has been changed since the prophecy was created. *Please*, promise me."

Tiny wings of hope flutter in my chest, maybe he's right. *No*, I push the excitement away, we don't know that. I can't let myself get my hopes up. I nod my head anyway, and say, "I promise."

"LIA!" Emily's giggling voice shouts from the other side of the fire. "You have to show me these ironman eyes your sister is talking about!"

I can't help it, a smile covers my face at the sight of Jen and Emily cosied up on the opposite bench giggling like the past few months never happened. Like we're just a bunch of post high school graduates hanging out on a summer's night. I mean besides them asking me to do my glow in the dark eye trick, of course.

I get to my feet, but a searing burn in my forearm causes me to stagger. I fall back onto the bench. I expect to see a hot ember from the fire burning into my skin. Instead, I find a crown with a rose intertwined through it, it's thorns thick, seared into my skin which is still burning white. I gasp.

"What's wr—" Declan starts, stopping when he sees, "The royal mark." His voice just above a whisper. "What time is it?" He asks the group.

"Midnight," Kheelan says from just beyond the circle of light. He enters the glow of the fire holding a bag of marshmallows. "Why?" He asks taking in our worried expressions.

"The mark," I say, holding up my arm.

"Well, I guess we better have fun tonight then…" He says passing the marshmallows to Emily.

"Wanna see the eye thing?" I ask Emily, trying force the heavy silence and dread that has draped over our group aside.

She nods her head eagerly, but her brown eyes can't hide her sadness. I stand up and let my light loose. I concentrate on sending it all to my eyes, I look at Emily, I can see her clear as day. Her nose is red from the cool air, a lone tear leaves a trail down her cheek. She doesn't bother to brush it away, thinking she's hidden by the darkness. I turn to look at Kheelan and Declan. "I can see like it's daytime." I tell them, "You should try."

Kheelan, leaps to his feet happy for a challenge he can probably accomplish. He calls the glow, but only manages to get his forehead concentrated.

I laugh, "You look like a headache guy from a pain commercial." I situate myself so I'm in front of him. "Maybe try concentrating on my eyes, and that'll help you move it to yours."

Kheelan doesn't give up. He concentrates for a long while, until finally the only thing glowing on him are his eyes. He sucks in a deep breath. "Wow. This is amazing." He whips his head around, drinking in the forest around us. "This could be really useful in the NetherWorld…Dec, you gotta try."

Declan stands up, but his glow barely flickers before extinguishing. "I don't think I'm in the right mindset right now." I meet his eyes, he isn't able to dismiss the mark on my arm as easily as his brother.

I offer him a weak smile. "Let me help." I say, stepping close to him and grasping onto his hands. "Look at me," I instruct.

He does.

I call the glow with ease, never breaking our eye contact. Declan's glow follows suit, "Now," I whisper so only he can hear, "push all your warmth to your eyes."

The instant his eyes light up a bolt of lightning flashes, shaking the ground as it crackles loudly a few yards away from our fire. I drop Declan's hands, a surprised scream bursting out of me, sending us into darkness as both our glows snuff out.

"What was that?" Declan asks, his voice matching the panic pumping through my body. "Did I do that?"

"No," Jen's shaking voice carries from the other side of the fire. "I'm so sorry," she whispers, "I don't know what happened. I just got a burst of anger out of nowhere and then *that*," she motions to the lawn to her right, "shot out of my hand."

I bring the glow back to my eyes and scan the lawn. Sure enough, there's a sizable crater marking where her lightning struck, smoke still rising from the new hole.

"Are you okay?" I ask my sister, whipping my focus around to her.

Her eyes are huge. She's obviously freaking out, but she nods her head. "I think so. I don't know what happened..." She says again, turning to look at Emily. "We were just talking about college and how I'm supposed to go to orientation next week, but with all that's going on I'm not sure what will happen..." Her voice trails off, "I was happy and then the anger came out of nowhere...I'm so sorry." She buries her face in her hands and begins to sob.

I rush to her side. "I think we better call it a night." I say, helping Jen to her feet. "Emily," I say my friend's name, but I don't know what else to say so I trail off. Where do I begin? This might be the last time I ever see her. I pull her into a hug. "Thank you for everything this summer. Promise me if—"

"NO," she cuts me off, squeezing me tighter. "Do NOT say goodbye. I'll see you the day after tomorrow. We'll go into town and get some ice cream after the eclipse."

I pull out of our embrace and swipe at a tear that's found its way to my cheek. I nod my head in agreement. "That sounds good." I smile and pull her back into a hug. "I love you though, I just want you to know that."

"I love you too." She says into my hair.

* * *

Jen comes out of the bathroom in her pink polka dot pj's and slips into the bed beside me. "I'm sorry I ruined the night." Her voice shakes.

"You didn't," I say. "The mark did." I force a light laugh.

309

"Lightening shot out of my hand," she says, a nervous giggle shaking her body. "What is happening to me?"

I begin to laugh too. "Can you believe our lives right now?" I roll over so I'm facing my sister. "Seriously. If we told ourselves from June what was going on, we would not have believed us!"

Jen giggles more. "I eat raw meat, shoot lightening out of my hands when someone near me is jealous—"

"—Wait, what?"

"Oh, right. I didn't want to embarrass him. But right when the lightening happened, I could see you and Declan standing all close and glowy." She pauses to wiggle her eyebrows at me. "Except I was looking at Emily. It's like I was seeing and feeling what Kheelan was." She takes a deep breath, "This is hard to explain. So, I saw you through Kheelan, and he was jealous...and then boom." She throws her hands up to pantomime the lightening. "Emily does likes Kheelan, by the way." she adds softly, "She told me tonight."

"Oh," Is all I manage to say, my voice threatening to crack.

"Two things," Jen says. "One, I told you Emily liked Kheelan. Remember? Way back at the start of summer, so thank you, I'm a psychic. And two, you can't choose who you love. But you shouldn't stop loving someone because of how a third party feels." Her eyes lock on mine, the blue parts reflecting the moonlight, casting shadows down her face.

"What happened to your whole destiny theory and that Declan is a big no-no?" I ask.

"Well," Jen says, "I do think Kheelan is your soulmate." She holds up a hand to stop me from interrupting. "But Declan is too. Clearly the three of you are tied together. Maybe you're meant to be with one of them in a lovey way, but maybe you're just destined to save the world together. Who knows?"

"So, Declan isn't a bad distraction?" I ask, holding back my smile.

"He was!" She insists, "But I also didn't know that he was a part of all of this. Even if I had, I'd still classify him as a distraction. You and

Kheelan worked out and practiced things that would ultimately help you fulfil the prophecy. You and Declan slacked off."

"I'm glad we did." I whisper, "Especially if I'm dying tomorrow night. It's been the best summer of my life. Declan made me feel so *normal*, and that's all I want. I don't want the fate of the three realms on my shoulders. I don't want to be the one to retrieve The Lost Stave. I want to walk in the woods, find waterfalls, go fishing, lay in the sun."

Jen props herself up on her elbow, her face solemn, "When will you realise trying so hard to be *normal* only shows you lack courage?"

Her brutal honesty leaves me speechless. I study my sister's face, which suddenly looks years older. Is she right? Am I a coward?

"Lia," she whispers, "you were born to be extraordinary because the world doesn't need another *normal* person. It needs *you*."

I roll onto my back and stare up at the ceiling, her words weighing on me. I don't feel special. I know I have all these powers and I'm named in a prophecy, but it still doesn't make me *feel* different. "I'm scared," I whisper into the dark.

"I'd be worried if you weren't." She says, "But, you *can* do this. Because it's what you were born to do."

Chapter Twenty-Four

"Rosalia…" warm breath tickles my neck.

I groan and roll over, slitting my eyes open. Declan is perched on the side of my bed grinning down at me. "Do we really need to train today?" I grumble turning to smoosh my face back into my pillow.

He laughs.

I pull the blanket over my head.

"I promise we're not training, but I need you to come with me," he whispers.

"You're awfully chipper for someone who has to go to the NetherWorld tonight." I glare out from under my pillow.

"If it's my last day on Earth, I don't want to waste it." He pats my back, "And I'm not going to let you either. So come on, up and at 'em!" I glance at Jen's still body. Declan notices, "I promise you'll be back before she wakes up. You'll have plenty of time to spend with your sister."

I sigh. He's not going to let me go back to sleep. I roll out of bed and pad into the bathroom. "Is Kheelan coming wherever we're going?" I call through the closed door.

"No, he apparently *does* want to spend what could possibly be his last day alive training… I did try to convince him to come with us though."

Of course he wants to spend it training. Guilt pools in my stomach, we should all be training today. But I can't even bring myself to *think* about what lies ahead of us. I don't think a few hours of not preparing is going to make a huge difference. I let out a deep breath and comb through the tangles of my hair, pulling it into a braid down my back.

"I feel bad." I say as I emerge from the bathroom, ready to go wherever he's planning on taking me. "He shouldn't be alone today."

"He's not," Declan says from the armchair in the corner, "Emily's with him."

I raise my eyebrows, "Oh really?"

Declan laughs getting to his feet, "Don't worry. It's not like that, at least not for Kheelan."

My eyebrows drop into a furrow. "Why would I be worried?"

He gives me a pointed look, but ignores my question. "Come on, we're burning daylight."

* * *

It takes my eyes a moment to adjust after Declan's Light goes out. He gently places Kodi on the ground and begins walking through the thick forest. I scan the foliage looking for something to help me get my bearings but find no familiar landmarks. "Where are we?" I finally ask.

"The Darby canyon trail head is this way." Declan points in the direction he's already headed, "I didn't want to just appear in front of other hikers, figured middle of the woods was a bit safer."

"Why not just travel us straight to the waterfall?" I grumble as I trudge through the greenery.

"The journey is half the fun. If you don't work for it, it's not as rewarding." Declan winks and quickens his step.

I laugh and follow him to the path.

The wildflowers are gone with fire season upon us. The once lush hillside now dry and crisp, making the green of the sagebrush stand out.

We don't talk much as we wind our way up the path. I don't mind. I focus all my energy on memorising the shape of every tree and fern. I want to remember every single detail later tonight when we're surrounded by the grey, cold dampness of the NetherWorld. I commit the songs of the magpies and crows to memory, and the rushing sound of the water from the river below. I'm desperate to remember it all. I breathe in lungsful of

313

pine, the smell I now associate with home and pray I'll never forget the scent.

Kodi drops a stick at my feet, her sharp blue eyes penetrate my soul as she stares up at me. I throw the stick back down the path behind us, trying not to think about what will happen to her if I don't come back tomorrow morning. I know she'll be cared for, but the thought still brings a tightness to my throat.

I steal a glance at Declan. Studying his profile. Something else I don't want to forget. I know he'll be with me in the NetherWorld, but if I can take memories to the afterlife, his face is one I'll want for all of eternity. I drink in his chiselled jaw, his broad shoulders and long black eyelashes. His full lips that turn so easily from a teasing smirk into a wicked grin. I lean forward and breath him in, savouring the fresh laundry smell mixed with cedar and something else, something that's all him. His lips pull into his teasing smirk, "Stop staring at me. You're being weird."

I flush and cast my eyes down to the dirt path. "I wasn't staring," I mumble.

He just laughs and bends down to scoop up the stick Kodi brought back to us.

* * *

The waterfall is gone, dried-up. Where the pool had been at the beginning of summer is just a pile of dry rocks now.

"Dang," Declan says going to where the pool's edge would be. He plops down on a giant boulder, "I was hoping there'd still be some water to throw you in." His teasing blue eyes sparkle up at me.

I can't help but smile at the memory. It feels like a lifetime ago. I join him on the boulder. We sit in silence, gazing out at the valley below. Kodi wanders around where the water had been, sniffing every rock.

After a few minutes, Declan breaks the silence. "Promise me again you won't do anything stupid when we're down there."

314

"Why would I intentionally do something stupid?" I ask, not taking my eyes off the trees in the distance.

"I mean the prophecy. I don't want you to think someone *has* to sacrifice themselves, and just volunteer at the first opportunity," he says.

I feel his eyes burning into my face, but I keep my own locked on the horizon. "I don't want anything to happen to you or to Khee—"

"—Promise me Rosalia. Promise me you won't willingly walk into a sacrifice." He pauses to let out an exasperated sigh, "I'm just as scared as you are, just please, promise me."

I tear my eyes from the trees to meet his, a sea of worry. "Okay, I promise, *again.*"

"I meant what I said the other day. I'm not going to let anything happen to you." His voice is firm, determined, sending goosebumps up the lengths of my arms. "I wasn't expecting someone like you to come into my life so early." He says, his voice husky, "And I definitely wasn't expecting to fall in love so fast and hard."

I open my mouth to say something, but he stops me.

"Let me get this all out. I love you, and it's one hundred percent me feeling this way. It's not some prophecy or a silly dream making me feel this. I love *you*, not the *idea* of you."

My insides are mush, "I love you too," the words come out a whisper, but I realise I mean them. Kheelan's face flashes to my mind sending a fresh wave of guilt through me.

He must see something on my face because he asks, "Anyone else?" His eyes search my face for the answer he doesn't want.

I swallow but avoid answering his question. Instead, I say, "I'm guessing Kheelan told you he had the same dream as I did, before we knew each other?" Declan nods, and I continue, "I worry by acknowledging I'm having strong feelings for you, I'm breaking my destiny and something bad will happen to one of you because of it."

Declan smiles, "It was a manipulation, not destiny. Why would the Fairies care who you date?"

I crinkle my brow as his words sink in.

315

"Think about it." He goes on, his voice gentle. "Yes, the OtherWorld Fairies are the good guys in this situation, but no side is one hundred percent right. Not everything they do is *good*. Herne's speech at that feast wasn't completely fabricated. They were manipulating the two of you. The two from the prophecy they were sure were alive or untouched by The Hunt. They wanted you to find each other, so they could get to you before Herne." He stops for a moment, his eyes scanning the trees below us. "They're using all of us as much as Herne would. I love my brother, but sometimes I wish he wasn't so blinded by the Light." A smile tugs at his lips. "He can't stand the idea of breaking any rules, and he's convinced himself the dream was destiny leading him to his fate. He's latched onto that idea, refusing to stray. He thinks I'm trying to talk him out of it because of my feelings for you. He still doesn't fully trust me."

I let out a deep breath as I process his words. He's right. It wasn't fate or destiny, it was a tactic the Fairies and the Fates used. Playing on our emotions was just another move on their giant chessboard. "I never told you," I whisper, "but, I had a vision in the NetherWorld, when they stopped me from dying. You were in it. We were here." I look up my eyes landing on the cliff above, where the water usually pours down. "You said I needed to trust you. At the time I thought you had tricked us all, that you were an Underling. But in the vision, I still trusted you." I meet his eyes. "I trusted you that night you gave me a ride, even though I thought you were working with The Hunt. I trusted you when Jen told me not to. And I trusted you the night we escaped from the NetherWorld. I've always felt safe around you. Trusting you comes easy, even when everyone tells me not to." I let out a relieved sigh as my feelings finally begin to make sense to me. "I was so caught up in the idea of destiny and what I thought I was *supposed to do,* that I didn't see it at first." I meet his eyes, "You helped me find the best version of myself and I just want you to know, whatever happens tonight, the time we spent together this summer has been my favourite part of my life so far. I trust you. I trust Kheelan. There's no one else I'd rather have by my side in the NetherWorld."

316

∗ ∗ ∗

"Do you feel prepared?" Rose asks, the last bits of sunlight glinting off her silver hair as she settles into the oversized chair facing me, nestled on the couch.

"Physically? Yes. Mentally? Not at all." My gaze is drawn to the large windows, the mountains are glowing their brilliant gold as the last bit of sun dips below them. Golden hour. Tears spring to my eyes. This could be my last sunset.

"You're stronger than you know," my aunt says, her voice gentle as she stands up and shuffles across the room. She settles next to me, pulling me into her side. I let her, soaking up the warmth and comfort, she smells like freshly baked cookies.

"You keep saying that." But I smile anyway, wanting to believe her.

"That's because it's true. And I don't mean physically, which you are strong in that aspect as well, but what I'm referring to is your mind and your heart. These are the strengths Herne and his men lack. If you must only remember one thing, make sure it's to breath in courage and exhale fear. If you can remember this, the Light will always find you."

"You two better not be talking about the NetherWorld."

I snap my head in the direction of my sister's voice. She's standing in the shadows of the doorway. Ever since I fed her the berries, she has had a knack for moving around in an unearthly and soundless manner.

"Let's enjoy these few hours before she has to leave us." Jen says walking across the room, Kodi close at her heals.

"You're right," Rose says. "Have Maggie and the boys gone?"

"Yes," Jen says to Rose, but her eyes are on me. "Declan and Kheelan will come back around eleven o'clock…" She trails off, not wanting to finish her own sentence.

I smile. "There's no avoiding it. They're coming back so I can transport us all to hell."

Jen surprises me by returning my grin. "I'm glad you've lightened your mood about the situation."

I roll my eyes. "Nothing I can do now. I was born for this, after all." I turn my arm so the light glints off the mark on my skin.

"Where did you and Declan go today?" Jen asks settling on the ground next to Kodi who has rolled over waiting for a belly rub.

"Darby Canyon," I say. "It's the hike he took me on for my birthday." I can't stop the smile that spreads across my face at the memory of this afternoon. A perfect last day.

Ever observant Jen, "You've been awfully smiley since you've gotten back. Especially for someone who has to go to hell in a few hours."

My smile only broadens, even though I wish it wouldn't, "It was a really good day, considering." I meet my sister's eyes, "Save the lecture, a few extra hours of training wouldn't make a big difference in the grand scheme of things."

"No lecture coming from me," Jen mumbles.

"What was that?" I say, my smile widening.

My sister giggles.

"Change of heart on the whole team Kheelan front? Better not tell Emily," I laugh.

"I've noticed the way Declan looks at you. Like you're the only thing worth looking at in the room. And he makes you laugh like no one else." She shrugs, "You aren't nervous around him, you're *you*."

My heart swells. She's right. She's just listed the things I love most about him. She was able to perceive all that in the few days she's been awake and seen us together?

Rose reaches out and puts a knobby fingered hand on my knee. "Declan is a wonderful young man," she says. "Don't worry about Kheelan, I think all the interfering the Fairies have done this summer has his heart jumbled and his mind confused, but after the dust settles, he'll be able to see his true feelings again."

"His true feelings?" I take in my aunt's worn face, it's easy to forget the lifetime of experience and wisdom older people have to offer, hidden beneath their wrinkles and fragile exterior. "That he doesn't love me?"

She nods. My eyes must give something away. "You can't take it personally, you don't love him that way either. And for the record he does love you. I said earlier this summer he would go to hell for you, and he's proving that to be true tonight. But I believe he only thinks he's *in love* with you. Before you showed up, his heart belonged to someone else."

"Allie," I say.

Rose purses her lips and shakes her head. "Even before her."

"Emily," Jen says from the floor, her hand has gone still on Kodi's side.

Rose nods and winks in her direction. "I think she has finally realised it, but it's taking him a little longer to figure it out. A pretty blonde girl showed up out of nowhere and distracted him." She lets out a chuckle as she pats my knee and gets to her feet. "It's almost nine thirty. You should try to get a nap in before you have to go." She looks down at me, her eyes sad but somehow, she manages a smile. "I'm not going to say goodbye, only good night. I'll see you in the morning." She says it with too much force, as though she can make it be true if she believes it hard enough.

I smile and get to my feet, pulling her into my arms. "Maybe a little tighter good night hug, for luck." I whisper into her ear. She squeezes back.

"I'll make pancakes after the eclipse." She promises, before shuffling off in the direction of her bedroom.

I fight the tears threatening to spill, it isn't goodbye, I tell myself as I watch her tiny form disappear around the corner. I've been to the NetherWorld and back before, who's to say I won't manage it again?

"Do you love him?" Jen's hollow voice snaps me back.

I sink back into the couch, pulling my legs beside me. The corners of my mouth tug upwards, "I do."

"That's good, I'm glad." Her eyes flicker, like lightening flashing across the sky. "It's taking over," she whispers.

I feel a tear slide down my cheek. "I'm so sorry," I choke out. A fresh wave of determination surges through me. "I promise I'll fix this when I get back tomorrow."

"I don't blame you, Lia. I want you to know that." Jen gets to her feet, her hands are shaking. "There's something I've learned in my new condition," she takes a deep breath like she's trying to stay in control of her body, "although light can cast away shadows and illuminate the truth, it can also be blinding." Her hands are shaking uncontrollably, and her face takes on a strained look. "It's only in the dark that our sky opens us up to more. The dark gives us the ability to see beyond our own world." She's trying to stay with me but she's losing. "It's not always black and white. Try to remember that tonight." She says backing towards the door that leads to the deck. "I'm sorry," she mumbles, "I need to go for a run."

"I'm sorry," I whisper back, my voice cracking but the door has already clicked shut behind her.

Chapter Twenty-Five

Kodi jumps off the bed landing with a loud thud on the floor, her nails clacking the hard wood, startling me awake. I squint at the glowing alarm clock on my bedside table, my eyes are bleary but there's no mistaking that it reads 11:15. She must have heard the boys.

I gulp down my nerves, it's time. A shiver passes through me, I'm not ready for this.

"Ready?" Kheelan asks from the shadows of the doorway.

"Yes," I scramble out of bed. My pounding heart is reverberating through my chest so loudly, I'm afraid it's going to give away my lie.

"Do you need to do anything to get ready?" He asks, his eyes sweeping over my body.

I glance down at my black running tights and hoodie. I shrug, "We're going to hell. I think I'll be okay, just need shoes." I plop into the big yellow armchair and lace up my running shoes. I have a feeling I'll be putting them to good use, if all goes according to plan. I ignore the tremor that shoots through my body at the thought of our flimsy plan of action.

I leap to my feet. My buzzing nerves giving me too much energy. "Let's go."

"Don't forget those." He points to the pile of throwing knives on the windowsill.

I grab them and start attaching them to my body as I follow him out of the dandelion room, the last burst of colour I may ever see. Kodi keeps close to my heels, reminding me that I still haven't decided if I'm going to bring her along with us.

"She's not in the prophecy." Kheelan says, as though reading my thoughts. "I think you should leave her. One less thing to worry about."

I nod, knowing he's right. But that doesn't stop the tightness in my throat.

I don't ask where he's leading me, I just follow him through the dark halls of Rose's house in silence. The starlight through the windowpanes casting ghostly looking shadows across the walls. It feels like a set for a horror film. I shake the thought from my head. Where we're about to go is much worse. I pull my shoulders back, straightening my spine. I have to go in with a positive attitude.

Kheelan walks through the living room towards the back deck. I see Declan through the window leaning against the railing, a sword handle visible over his shoulder, his mouth set in a grim line.

I get down on my knees and pull Kodi into a tight hug. "I'll see you tomorrow," I promise her. Determination joins the anxious energy that's already pumping through my veins. I stand up quick, like a Band-Aid I think as I slip through a crack in the door and close it softly behind me. We'll get in, grab the fancy stick, and get out. Easy-peasy, right?

Declan's face lights up when his eyes meet mine, I'm only able to offer a shadow of a smile as I walk across the deck. My legs like noodles, my stomach full of butterflies. We go over the plan one last time, it doesn't calm my anxiety in the slightest.

I pull my hair into a ponytail and yank my hood up to cover the blonde, it'll stand out too much down there. The boys flank me, each grasping my outstretched hands. I cast my eyes around the yard, looking for any sign of Jen. She's nowhere to be seen. Together we call the glow, a beacon of blinding light. I focus on the dark, bleak world I have been trying so desperately to forget. The image Robin showed me sharp in my mind, as the familiar lurch in my stomach pulls us towards it.

* * *

The heaviness of dread fills the air. I know our Light Travel was successful before I open my eyes. Someone lets out a breath of relief.

"I think it's daytime here, hopefully that means everyone's sleeping," Declan says.

I open my eyes. I'm greeted by the darkness of night, "What do you mean its daytime? There's no sun."

He smirks and extends his hand pointing towards the horizon. "See that red glow? That wasn't here last time." He shrugs, "I'm just guessing it's their version of a sun." I follow his finger with my eyes to the spindly rock formations in the far distance, they're bathed in a crimson gleam, making them look like someone has dumped blood all over them. An involuntary shiver passes through me. I don't like it here.

"Creepy," Kheelan whispers. His eyes igniting as he takes in the barren landscape around us. Black mountains that look like they're made of pure onyx shoot towards the starless sky on either side of us. The valley we're standing in is bleak. Sparse patches of dead grass and foliage, but mostly it's just dusty, colourless ground. The only sound the distant chirp of cicadas.

I concentrate on calling my glow back and send it to my eyes. I scan our surroundings, trying to get my bearings. "That must be the woods Robin mentioned," I point a little to our right to where a large expanse of trees is situated. It looks like it's been burned recently, leaving no leaves or vegetation behind. A forest of charred trunks and few thick branches. The blackened limbs beckoning us like the fingers of a skeleton.

"So the Hunt's castle is just beyond it?" Declan asks, his own eyes flashing to life.

I nod and take a deep breath as I begin walking towards the tree line. I'm not sure what to expect. Are there living things here? Beasts we should be worried about? My hand instinctively goes to one of the many throwing knives secured around my waist as I lead us through the open expanse towards the ominous wood.

We don't see any animals within the trees. We do see the occasional Fairy, if they can even be considered that anymore. Their gaunt faces and hollowed eyes have them more closely resembling a corpse than that of a fae or sprite. What I'm sure were once beautiful iridescent wings, over time and circumstance are now a leathery and an oily black, like a bat's. We keep our heads low, our hoods pulled close, shielding our faces. The creatures don't seem to pay us any attention as we trudge through the scant trees.

Their bony frames suggest they're starving. My mind flashes back to the speech Herne gave at the feast. Could it be true? Did the Queen create this world? Is she responsible for the monsters they've become? What does it say about her character if she was able to send almost half of her people to this desolate place? Forcing them to live like vermin, all because they didn't agree with her politically? A heavy knot drags in my stomach, will The Stave really be better off in her possession?

Kheelan's warm hand grabs a hold of my free one. "We're doing the right thing." He says, keeping his voice soft.

I whip my face towards him. Can he read my mind?

He laughs, "I know you." He says in response to my startled expression. "I know what's probably going through your mind at seeing this," he motions around, "Herne, and his followers are the bad guys. Look at this place, it's literal *hell*. Whatever he said to you while you were here last, they were lies. Trust me." His blue eyes gleam, the light coming out of them making them an impossible shade of blue. "The OtherWorld Fairies, they're the good guys. We need to get The Stave for them."

A snort comes from Declan at his brother's words, but he doesn't say anything. I rip my eyes away from Kheelan's face. He's right, I know he is, Declan knows he is. But this knowledge doesn't stop my heart from clenching when we pass by a family. My head swivels as we go by, needing to get a better look. The baby clutched in the dark fairy's arms looks malnourished and sickly, her own cheeks hollowed and eyes shattered. The father's gaze locks on mine as his face contorts in anger. *Shit*, so much for staying incognito. I quickly dip my head back down, making sure my hood is close to my face, focusing on the dirt beneath my feet. But I know it's too late. He noticed us.

"We need to hurry." I murmur, picking up my pace.

"HALT." A booming voice bellows.

We still.

"Why have you entered the Wood of the Fallen Fae?" The voice demands.

We turn to face the speaker.

It's the father of the frail baby. Suddenly he doesn't look so weak. What I thought were bony limbs from lack of nourishment are lean ropy muscles, his face may be sunken, but upon closer examination I can tell he's not incapable.

"Just passing through," Declan says with a deep nod, going to turn back in the direction we were heading.

"You do not have permission to be here." The dark fae says.

"Look man, we don't want to be here. Just let us pass through and we promise we won't come back," Declan tries again.

The fairy shakes his head. "My people are hungry." His sunken eyes like puddles of black oil gleam as he drinks us in. Saliva drips from his fangs as his lips spread into a grimace, "I cannot deny them a meal that has walked into their home."

Kheelan and Declan draw their swords without a word. I pluck a knife from my belt as every hair on the back of my neck rises. My eyes scan the trees around us, at least a dozen bat-winged fairies have stepped out from behind the scorched trunks. I swallow, I guess it's time to put our training to use.

We form a circle, our backs to one another and we spin as one, taking in our situation. We're severely outnumbered, but not one of our opponents holds a weapon.

They move in unison. Crouching low to the ground, becoming more beast-like as their black eyes widen. Horror rattles my bones. They aren't going to fight our way. They're going to fight like wild animals. As if on cue one launches forward. I don't have time to think, I release the knife in my hand, sending it straight into the creature's eye. Black liquid squirts out as its body drops to the ground, its weight sending a puff of dust up around it. Agitated roars erupt around us.

I grab a second knife and am able to drop another creature before it can attack. But a third darts forward, so quick it's nearly a blur, tackling me to the ground. Declan is there in a flash, with one mighty swipe of his sword the beasts head is disconnected from its body. The warm blackened blood spatters my face as the dull thud of the decapitated skull reverberates around the space. For a moment, the wood falls into an eerie silence. So quiet you could hear a pin drop. Then like a switch being flipped, chaos erupts. I barely have time to scramble to my feet as the remaining creatures rush towards us, like a pack of hungry dogs.

They're upon us in a matter of milliseconds. Their black fingers clawing at our clothing, seeking flesh. I use a knife like a dagger, slashing at the taloned hands swiping at me. There are too many to keep track of. The sheer number of opponents so overwhelming my fire comes without me calling for it. The creatures screech in pain as the flames lick off my body.

"Get back!" I scream over the howls to Declan and Kheelan. The dark fairies are engrossed by the flames now covering my exposed flesh. The boys use the distraction and listen to my command, backing away from the swarm.

My power is pulsing through my veins, begging to be released. The dark fairies, whether it be animal instinct or brains capable of rationalising, are starting to back away. Sensing the danger they're in. I don't hesitate. I *want* to use the power. I *want* to destroy these *things*. The thought doesn't even make me flinch in the slightest as I release it. The blaze surges from my body in waves of heat and flames. Like a ripple in a pond. The roars that rip out of their throats are raw and mangled as they drop to the ground, the hot flames eating their flesh at a remarkable speed.

I let my fire fade, keeping only my hands burning, just in case more is needed. But not a single one gets back up. I watch without a flicker of emotion. I'm like a statue carved from marble, as the creatures around me writher and die.

Declan and Kheelan step out from behind the trees they'd taken shelter behind. Their faces ashen as they look at the charred corpses. "Whoa," Declan whispers, "how'd you know you could do that?" He asks.

"I didn't," my voice cracks along with my facade as the enormity of what I've done hits me. I just took so many lives without a second thought. Were they once good? Before they were sent here, forced into transforming into the things they are now? *They were going to kill you* the small voice reminds me.

"Here," Kheelan says, shrugging off his hoodie and handing it to me, his face pink with embarrassment.

I look down at my own, or what's remaining of it. It's charred and burnt, my bare stomach exposed. Heat rises to my own cheeks as I tear off the scraps of mine and replace it with the one in Kheelan's outstretched hand. I hastily collect my knives from the bodies on the ground. I try to ignore the smell of burnt flesh and the sucking noise of suction as I pull them loose. My stomach turns in disgust and I dart behind a trunk hoping to shield myself as I heave up the remnants of my dinner.

We walk on in silence, taking care not to make any noise, not wanting to draw more of the fairies to us. But we don't see any other living things. When we emerge from the trees, the castle enters our line of sight. My heart rate picks up. What we just faced in the woods is nothing compared to what we're about to walk into.

A million questions buzz through my mind as we continue out into the wide open. Will our plan work? Will we be able to enter the grounds unseen? Slip in, steal The Stave, and slip back out? Or are there guards posted around the wall? Can they see us now, walking across the barren desert? Have they already warned Herne that we're coming?

My pulse is drumming in my ears as the castle looms nearer. It's dark stonework, demon like gargoyles, and menacing turrets with deadly looking spires at the top scream 'this is the home of darkness'. Nothing about it is welcoming. It takes all my will power to keep walking. I concentrate on placing one foot in front of the others as we approach the massive, windowless structure.

I stare up at the castle's wall. It looks bigger now that it's directly in front of us. I glance up and down the long expanse. There doesn't seem to be anyone posted upon it. Maybe they have video surveillance?

"Do we just climb it or look for a gate?" I ask, unsure how we should tackle what might as well be a mountain before us.

"Climb it, I guess," Declan says.

"How did you get in, when you came the first time?" I ask him.

"Through the gate," he says simply, "but I was pretending to be on their side then, I don't think we'd be able to pull that off a second time.".

I nod, sending one last nervous glance around us, but we seem to be alone. "Give me a boost," I say, my voice grim. The reality finally beginning to fully settle in. *We're breaking into the Hunt's castle.* This is a suicide mission.

* * *

Somehow, we manage to get to the other side, after a lot of boosting and pulling. We can only hope we managed this without being noticed.

We creep through the gardens, I let out a sigh of relief when the door Declan and I exited out of on our stroll only a couple of weeks ago comes into view, and we see that it's unguarded. We creep into the castle. Excitement bubbles inside me. That was easy.

The halls are empty too. We tip toe, but still the taps of our light footfalls bounce off the walls, echoing down the passageway behind us. Sweat breaks out on my palms and forehead as we push forward.

"It seems odd," Kheelan says, his voice barely a breath. "Was it this deserted last time?"

My eyes glue onto his, mirroring his worried expression. My voice catches in my throat, all I can do is shake my head as dread continues to bubble in my stomach.

"Feels like a—" Declan starts but Kheelan holds up a hand, silencing him.

We come to a stop, collectively sucking in a breath. The flames from the torches along the walls dance around us causing odd shadows to flicker on the uneven stones. We listen for whatever Kheelan has heard. His eyes are wide. Sweat dripping off the curled hairs along his collar. He points down a passage to our left mouthing. 'I hear voices.'

Declan and I nod in understanding and follow him as silently as we can towards the sound.

My heart is hammering in my ears. I have no idea if my footsteps are silent or elephant clambers, giving us away. Kheelan's hoodie clings uncomfortably to my sweat drenched back.

Kheelan comes to a stop and points to his ear. I stop to listen. The voices drifting down the hall have become clearer.

"We will have just over two and half earth minutes to complete the task." Herne's voice is like fingernails on a chalk board as it makes its way down the corridor to us. We're close to him. *Too* close. My heart beats faster.

"My Lord," a second voice says. "Forgive me, but how can we be certain The Stave will be strong enough to cloak all the realms in darkness long enough for us to invade?"

"THE STAVE ALONE IS *NOT* STRONG ENOUGH. THE STAVE WITH *ME* IS STRONG ENOUGH," Herne's voice is thunderous as it reverberates through the stone passages. "How dare you question me, Forrest? Especially after what your son has just done. You're lucky I allowed you to keep your head, even if it is a bit…Altered now." Snickers pass around the chamber.

I glance at Declan, guilt flashes across his face. What did our actions cost his father? I shake the thought, he's a Hunter. He feeds off human souls, even if he wasn't the worst father to Declan, he's still an evil person. Not a person, a *creature*.

"Forgive me my Lord." Forrest's voice reduced to a whimper.

"Anyone else here want to doubt their leader?" Herne's voice echoes out of the otherwise silent room. "Good. As I was saying…" He allows a beat of silence to pass. I imagine he's throwing his intimidating stare around to each of his Hunters. "The total solar eclipse is when the natural energies of Earth are the strongest. It's the window we need. With the power of the moon over the sun, The Stave, and myself we will be able to use Earth. Or more specifically, the hot spot of Yellowstone on Earth as the steppingstone into the OtherWorld. We will finally be able to finish what we started so many centuries ago."

The room breaks into a deafening applause and my heart plummets. They've figured out how to use The Stave. That means Herne isn't going to let it out of his sight. Both Kheelan and Declan's faces reflect what I'm feeling as they connect all the dots. Our plan has just gone down the drain.

"The army is prepared, my Lord?" A voice asks.

"Of course. However, they won't be required until we've reached the OtherWorld. Only The Table will be present for Earth's eclipse, I don't see us facing many obstacles in that realm."

"What of the prophecy my lord?" Jesse's familiar voice turns the sweat on my back to ice.

"How dare you speak to our master boy?" Someone hisses.

Herne's laugh is piercing. "Ah the Underling who let them escape. You now worry your lack of action may have consequences?"

"I worry they might try to stop you, my Lord." Jesse whispers.

"Well, fear not young Underling. They are no match against me. Anyway, for all we know about the prophecy, it could merely state that three meddlesome Fairlings keep *barely* getting away from the fearsome Hunt." His loyal Hunters snicker, "That's all they've proven so far. They're good at running away." The titters grow into laughter.

After the chortling fades out, we're draped in a heavy silence. Sweat drips from my brow into my eyes, I swipe it away and exchange a worried glance with Declan. 'We need to get away from here.' I mouth. He nods in agreement, nudging Kheelan to follow. But Herne's voice causes my feet to grow roots.

"Perhaps you need a little reminder like Forrest here?" The room collectively draws in a breath. "Something to help you remember not to disobey my wishes ever again?"

There's a clash of metal with an oozing sound of flesh being cut, followed by Jesse's tortured wails.

The strangled sound escapes my throat before I even know it's forming. My eyes bulge, my heart goes into overdrive. I pray that Jesse's screams have drown out my moment of weakness.

"SILENCE!" Herne demands.

My heart drops to my feet. Kheelan grasps my arm and pulls me back in the direction we came from. We run as quickly and silently as we can. But it's too late.

"Seems we've underestimated the Fairlings after all." Herne's voice bellows after us. "BRING THEM TO ME AT ONCE."

"We're going to have to fight them." Declan says as the footfalls of our pursuers draw nearer. "We can't leave without it."

We stop running, he's right. I take a deep breath. This is it, the moment I was born for. With a shaky hand, I reach for a knife that's strapped to my ankle as both boys draw their swords from the sheathes on their backs. We turn as one to face the three Hunters barrelling towards us.

I can't help but smirk. They think we're weak and yet they're still afraid to be outnumbered. This gives me the confidence I need, my knife sails through the air hitting its mark with a sickening splat. The long-haired Hunter with the slimy voice drops to his knees, crying out in agony. His grey hand grasping the knife lodged in his right eyeball. Blood gushes down his cheek as he yanks it out, my stomach churns.

The two hunters behind my target hesitate at the sight of their fallen brother. Declan and Kheelan don't waste the opportunity as they charge forward, blades gleaming.

I reach down and grab a second knife. When I look back up, a fire ball is rushing towards my head. I duck out of the way, somersaulting to the edge of the passage. I squat and set my second knife free. I close my eyes right before it sinks into the Hunter's left eye, his yelps of pain alone, are still enough to make my stomach turn. At least, he can't see now. I take off after Declan and Kheelan. I don't look down as I leap over the motionless Hunters they've incapacitated but the smell of coppery blood still reaches my nose stirring up a fresh wave of nausea.

"They're not dead," Kheelan warns, "although I do wish it were that easy to kill them." He mutters as we near the chamber where more of them are waiting for us. "We need to get The Stave and Light Travel out of here. It's our only hope." His eyes meet mine briefly, they're full of regret. He opens his mouth to say more.

"Don't." I cut him off. "Don't say any more, we'll discuss it back in Wyoming." I turn my eyes to Declan, "We got this." But my voice catches, we all know one of us isn't going back to Wyoming, don't we?

Declan reaches out and brushes his fingertips over mine, his sad eyes locked on my face. He gulps back the words he's about to say and leads us into the enemy's chambers.

There are less creatures than I expect. Three Hunters, Herne being one of them, Jesse and just one other Underling.

I grab a knife and send it flying in the direction of the Hunter closest to me. As it lodges deep in his throat, I realise it's Declan and Kheelan's father. His face nearly unrecognisable with his nose missing. I shake the image and dodge a fire ball sent from one of the other Hunters. I grab another knife from my belt and throw it at Flint's pointy black smile, he dodges it. Running at me with unnatural speed, his skin blurring as he passes through the room in a fraction of a second. I don't have time to react before he has me in an embrace. I can't move.

Kheelan's eyes land on me as he pulls his sword out of Jesse's motionless body, it crumples to the ground. I force my eyes away. My heart unsure how to feel. The boy I thought was my best friend for so many years, *dead*.

"Drop the swords, or she dies," Flint's voice rings out. Declan freezes mid swing, the second Underling who he's battling takes the opportunity to lunge forward. He knocks Declan's sword out of his hand and kicks it away. In a quick sweeping motion, he's behind Declan, his black dagger tight to his neck.

It feels as though all the blood has left my body. It can't be *him*.

My eyes dart around the room. Forrest is beginning to stir, the wound on his neck nearly healed already. That probably means the three in the hall are healing as well. Herne is perched in a golden throne at the far end of the space. His devilish horns casting long shadows on the stone wall behind him, they almost seem to be dancing in the torch light. My eyes find The Stave. It's leaning against the wall behind him. He's not holding it. My eyes jump to Kheelan, I look back at The Stave, hoping he'll notice.

His eyes bulge slightly, but he quickly collects his features, careful to keep them neutral.

"To what do we owe the pleasure?" Herne asks, his voice full of fake pleasantries.

I jut out my chin and stare back, unblinking.

"Ah yes, how could I forget," he clucks his tongue, "stubborn." He turns his horned head to take in his fallen soldiers. "Looks like you've been hiding some tricks from me, young Rosalia." His burning red eyes bore into mine, "Flint, will you do the honours?"

"With pleasure." Flint's voice drips with excitement as he spins me around, forcing me to stare into his ugly face. Disappointment settles in my gut, all my handy work from Jesse's basement has healed.

His red eyes bore into mine. The sadness is heavy in the air, I can't feel my light. I take a deep breath and focus all my energy on everything I memorised earlier. I picture the trees, the different shades of green, the way Declan's hand in mine makes my heart sing, I remember the songs of the birds on the wind, the way the water babbles over the rocks in the river, the smell of pine filling my lungs. I imagine myself standing in the forest with Rose's parting advice ringing in my ears; *if you must only remember one thing, make sure it's to breath in courage and exhale fear. The Light will always find you.* My light sparks to life like a match inside me, I focus all my energy on sending that tiny flame to my brain, then I concentrate on all the people who will be hurt if I don't succeed today. My Glow expands. I know it's working. I'm keeping him out. Flint doesn't know what's happening. My glow hidden inside my skull. He shakes his head as though to clear his thoughts and begins again.

I hold my focus. My light burns brighter. I know the light is leaking from my eyes now, but I don't care. I want him to know I'm not weak anymore, I've Awakened. I smile. "Is something the matter?" I ask, putting as much innocence in my voice as I can.

His hand crashes across my face and I fly backwards.

Then everything happens at once.

Herne leaps to his feet, taking a few steps towards his loyal Hunter. "What's the matter with you? Can't you do a simple mind crack?" He asks, his voice huffing in annoyance as he walks towards my crumpled form.

Declan drives his elbow into the Underling's gut, twisting free from his embrace. The Tenebris dagger drops to the floor, the metal blade clattering on the stone. Declan doesn't waste a second, he sprints straight at Herne.

I watch wide-eyed from the ground where I've landed. My heart shattering, he's going to sacrifice himself so Kheelan and I can get away.

But Kheelan is running towards Herne too. *No. They can't both sacrifice themselves.* I can't lose both of them.

Time slows as I realise what they're doing. They're not running at Herne. They're running *beyond* him. They're running towards The Stave.

Herne realises it at the same time I do. I see the fire forming on his fingertips.

I'm on my feet before I can fully form a plan. As I dive through the air, I call my light. It comes in full force. Brighter than I've ever burned before. I don't think. I throw myself in front of fire ball, shielding the brothers.

I watch as Declan's fingers curl around the shaft of The Stave, just as the full impact of the fire hits me.

There's an explosion of light. Declan's face, The Stave, the entire chamber disappears. All I see is burning white. There's a low hum reverberating through my skull, a deafening ringing in my ears.

Chapter Twenty-Six

I can't see anything but the extreme amount of light coming out of me. The low hum grows louder in my ears. It's like I'm moving in slow motion as my body continues to fly backwards from the force of Herne's fire ball. Why haven't I hit anything yet? I concentrate all my energy to holding onto my Light. I'm certain I've positioned myself in the right spot. I'll block Declan and Kheelan from the fire. I hope I'm enough to absorb the full impact. I hope they take the opportunity to get out of here. I hope they can get home.

Time catches up. My body barrels into the boys, sending us into a tangle of limbs. My head smacks against the stone wall, or maybe it's the floor. I still can't see, my glow too bright. *Or maybe it's flames and I'm on fire.* The thought is dim as the throbbing from the back of my head starts to dull out my other senses. I feel my light begin to slip away. Darkness weaves its way through, cutting it to shreds. Before I die, my memory rewards me with one last glimpse of the Tetons. The view from the meadow where I was created. The mountains in their full glory, glowing gold beyond the trees.

* * *

"Because of her we were able to get out." A voice says in the distance.

Someone's sobbing. It sounds far away, but I feel wetness drip onto my face. "In an act of sacrifice," my sister chokes out between gasps for air. "I really believed she'd come back alive."

"Rosalia," Declan's voice pleads, "wake up."

My heart flutters. Their words sinking in. They think I'm dead. But I'm not. Does that mean we all managed to get out? I open my eyes to Declan's face, his head almost directly above my own. A grin quickly breaks across his tear-streaked cheeks. Jen lets out a sob of relief and I catch a glimpse of Emily swiping away tears over my sister's shoulder.

"Is the girl dead? Hurry. The prophecy is almost complete." The familiar voice of the Fairy Queen jolts me up right.

I'm sprawled in the meadow where I was created, where we met the antlered man. Quite the crowd is gathered. Declan and Kheelan, of course. Then there's Jen, Emily, Aunt Rose, and Maggie. They're not the unusual ones. It's off putting seeing the Queen and her two Hands, Quill and Robin in this world.

Then I notice everything else. The familiar trees, and mountains in the distance. They're all cloaked in an ominous darkness. The forest around us has gone completely still. Not a single sound emitting from any animals. Even Robin's three small birds have stilled. I look up at the sun, it's almost completely covered. Only three diamonds of light remain along its top edge.

The Queen sees me sitting up, her face pales. "All three are not meant to survive." Her eyes flick to the stave still clutched in Declan's hand, "One was meant to die in sacrifice." She glares at me, angry for being alive, "What have you done?" She glances around the clearing, as though expecting something bad to happen instantly, "Give me The Stave boy." Her voice oozing with hunger, eyes unblinking. "Quickly!"

Declan takes a step towards the Fairy, just as the remaining sparks of light disappear from the sky, the Queen lunges forward snatching the stave from his hands.

I leap to my feet as lightening cracks through the sky. I instinctively position myself so Jen is behind me. Declan takes a step towards his brother, freezing when the lightening fades.

Herne, and his six Hunters have us surrounded.

"Lucille," Herne says, his high-pitched voice a forced calm. "You look," he pauses to grin, exposing every one of his pointy teeth, "really *old*." He finishes with a sneer.

The Queen isn't fazed by her enemy's sudden appearance. Greed fills her eyes as she thrusts the Lost Stave high above her head. A wave reverberates from it, rippling through our gathered circle. As soon as it passes through my chest, I realise I'm paralysed. I can only move my eyes. Panic pulses in my chest. My eyes find Declan, his frantic blues tell me he can't move either. I flick around the circle. Everyone I can see has been affected, including Herne and his Hunters.

The Queen keeps The Stave raised high. A purple mist circles around the invisible globe she's created. She begins to speak. "The Lost Stave has been recovered, and my true power finally restored." Her voice is thunderous, filling the space around us, bouncing off the unseen walls of the circle. "I hereby renew the banishment of The Dark one named Herne, and all those who reside within the NetherWorld."

I whip my line of sight to Herne's ugly face. He can't move but both rage and hate are seething in his burning eyes.

The Queen's voice grows louder. I dart my attention back to the power crazed woman. "Any who are not aligned with me, The Light, are destined to live out their days in the shadows of the NetherWorld. They will never see daylight again. They shall continue to roam Earth only in darkness, and not one will enter the OtherWorld again!" She brings The Stave crashing to the ground. A quake ripples from it, knocking everyone to the ground.

High pitched screams echo through the forest around us as the Hunters burst into flames. As quickly as they appeared, they're gone. Tiny puffs of smoke, and singed grass in the shape of their footprints the only evidence they were ever here.

I let relief wash over me. We did it. No one died! Able to move again, I rush forward into Declan's waiting arms. My heart swells as I melt into him. It's all over. We get to be normal now. Long summer days filled with hiking, and kissing, and fishing, and kissing.

I open my eyes and smile at my sister, but she doesn't smile. Her brow is furrowed in concentration. I follow her gaze as it darts from the Queen, back to me. Her blue streaks gleam as she mutters something under her breath.

I pull away from Declan, taking a step towards my sister. Somethings wrong. I need to go to her. Before I can take another step, she brushes past me. Determination set on her face. "Light can be blinding." She mutters, "Stop tyranny…Sacrifice."

A gargled noise of unformed words rips from my throat. But they don't reach her. She darts forward at her new inhuman speed straight at the Fairy Queen. Before anyone can register what's happening, my sister is holding The Stave in her hand. Her marbled eyes find me.

"Don't," my plea drops from my lips in the form of a sob.

"This has been our destiny all along," Jen says. Without any kind of warning her body emits a strike of lightening so powerful thunder crackles across the land. The boom reverberates in my chest as it echoes against the mountains in the distance. The Stave in her hand dissolves to ash. It lingers in the air for a split second before falling to the ground like snowflakes, with Jen's limp body.

I can't move. Anguished screams erupt around me, but no noise comes from me. There's a ringing in my ear. I'm very aware of my blood pumping through my body. But other than that, it feels like time has frozen. I'm not sure when my legs give out, but I know it's Declan keeping me upright. I don't move. I can't blink. I can't tear my eyes away from my sister's motionless form. I stare, willing her to move. Praying for her to get up. But she doesn't.

The Queen's rage brings me back. Time pushing forward. I whip my head in her direction. She's marching toward what remains of our group. Her finger pointed at us. Murder in her eyes.

I don't think. I leap in front of them and call my light. Declan follows suit, grabbing my hand. Kheelan grabs my other. I can feel both Aunt Rose and Maggie as their weaker lights glow to life behind us. A united front.

"Stop." My heart is racing as I shout the command at the Queen, "If you kill us for someone else's actions, you're only proving my sister was right." I look the Fairy dead in the eyes, "You'd be proving you're just as evil as Herne. That all you're after is power."

The Queen's eyes flare up in rage at being compared to her sworn enemy, "How dare you accuse me of such things!"

"Only saying it as I see it," I say, my voice stronger than I feel. I refuse to let Jen die in vain. Her pure goodness came through and triumphed over the monster I had turned her into. She knew the monster had to die, and with it herself. She also saw the danger The Stave held. Too much power, even for those who start with the best intentions is never good. Determination to finish what she started pumps through me, the only thing keeping me from crumpling to the ground and crying.

"The Stave and it's unlimited power have been destroyed." Kheelan points out, "There's no chance of it finding its way into the wrong hands again."

The Queen's expression doesn't soften. Her loyal servants are watching their ruler closely, waiting for her to speak. Robin's birds perched neatly in her hair looking down at their Queen expectantly.

After the silence has stretched on for too long, Quill steps forward. "Your Majesty," he says, his voice soft, "if I may remind you that there is a *due process* for matters of this sort. We must uphold our law."

The Queen turns her glare to the antlered man, her lips tight. She nods curtly. Without sparing us another glance, they vanish. No light, no lingering smoke, no trace they were ever here.

I let my light flicker out. The sun is emerging from behind the moon now, painting the landscape in an other-worldly orange. I don't feel it's warmth on my skin. All I feel is cold. The creatures of the world around us have gone back to their normal lives. Their woodland song replacing the heavy silence that had draped the earth.

I'll never get my normal back I think as I drop to my knees at my sister's side. I reach my shaky hand out and cover her eyes, closing her lids.

I collapse over her. She's still hot from the lightening. Sobs rock my body. I know unnatural sounds are ripping from my throat, but I don't care. I let the grief roll through me. It wasn't supposed to be Jen. It should have been me. I was the one doomed for this fate the day the prophecy was first spoken. It wasn't supposed to be Jennifer. She was supposed to have a normal life, a happy life. She was going to go to college. Meet someone and fall in love. She would have been such a wonderful mother. She was already becoming a fantastic nurse. This is wrong. This isn't fair.

"I can't do this without you." I whisper through my sobs into her still chest. "I can't live in a world where you don't exist. Please don't make me."

I don't know how much time passes. I can hear everyone around me crying and murmuring softly to one another. But they keep their distance, giving me the space I need. After some time, I feel Aunt Rose's gentle arms come around me as she peels me away from Jen's body. New sobs rip through me as I try to push the old woman off me.

"Dear, the paramedics are here." Her voice is raspy from her own grief, "It's time to let her go."

"I don't want to let her go. I don't want this to be real. Please don't take her away from me." I collapse into the old woman, my tear-soaked cheeks wetting her blouse. But she doesn't seem bothered as she strokes my hair.

"They're asking to talk with you." Declan says, his voice unsure. He doesn't know how to act in a situation like this. No one does. No one should.

"Me?" I ask.

"No, Rose," he says nodding his head in the direction of two people in blue uniforms. They have a stretcher, with a black bag on top of it, waiting for my sister.

Rose nods solemnly, breaking away from me as she walks in their direction.

A chill runs through my body and my chest tightens. "I can't watch," the words come out choked.

Declan nods. He drapes his arm around my shoulders and steers me in the direction of the house. I steel one last glance back at my sister's lifeless body lying in the middle of the small meadow. She looks so small surrounded by the giant trees. My fingers find my necklace at the nape of my neck. The habit that would normally calm me doesn't bring me any comfort now. *I never got her a birthday present.* The thought sends a new wave of grief though me, shaking my core. Declan tightens his grip around my shoulders, pulling me into him.

Kheelan and Emily are already on the deck when Rose's big house comes into view. Emily's eyes are puffy and her nose red. A sombre-looking Kodi by her feet, like she knows to be mourning too. When she sees me, she gets up to greet me. Her tail doesn't wag. She knows something isn't right.

Our Jen is dead, I want to say to her. Never again will we get to hear her walk through the back door, announcing in her contagiously cheerful voice that she brought home ice cream. Never again will we get to curl up together in one of our beds, giggling late into the night about nothing in particular. We'll never have a movie night where we eat so much popcorn and candy that we make ourselves sick. We'll never see her smile or hear her laugh again. We'll never get to know what kind of an old woman she'd have made. Because she's gone. She's dead. But I don't say any of this. I drop to my knees and pull my dog into a tight hug. I bury my face into her soft black fur. She rests her head on my shoulder as an endless stream of tears pours out of me.

CPSIA information can be obtained
at www.ICGtesting.com
Printed in the USA
BVHW032210061222
653632BV00002B/7